Praise for *The Rose Garden*

'A warm, original and upbeat novel. Tracy Rees is a natural storyteller and I couldn't stop turning the pages. I loved the setting of Victorian Hampstead and its vivid range of characters. What a treat it is!'
Rachel Hore

'Tracy Rees has a rare gift for creating characters you are rooting for from the first page. The writing is fresh and engaging, with a gentle humour . . . The research is meticulous, and the women's stories are told with immense compassion. This is a novel that immerses you in its world as if by magic, and keeps you enthralled till the very end'
Gill Paul

'Beautifully written and vividly imagined, *The Rose Garden* strikes the perfect balance between period drama to savour and compelling escapism to devour. Tracy Rees has such a talent for writing engaging characters who stay with you. I loved it!'
Hazel Gaynor

'A rich, compelling and intricate tapestry of women's lives . . . Their wants, needs and dreams through the characters' diverse lives. I couldn't put it down'
Liz Fenwick

'A rich historical drama that is b
treatment o'

'Such a treat . . . I loved Tracy's elegant writing and the vivid and relatable characters, and historically rich story . . . wonderful and uplifting'
Nicola Cornick

'A truly captivating tale of female friendship, courage and empowerment, all wrapped up in the wonderful escapism of an exquisite period drama'
Samantha King

'*The Rose Garden* is an absolute delight to read and holds you spellbound from cover to cover. Full of wonderful characters woven into a story that tugs at your heartstrings, this is a truly beautiful novel that confirms Tracy Rees is at the height of her game'
Rebecca Griffiths

'Gorgeously written, deeply atmospheric, tense and vivid and a total page-turner'
Jenny Ashcroft

'In this engrossing novel Tracy Rees takes the reader directly into the drama and action, her writing bringing every scene to sparkling vivid life . . . Totally unputdownable'
Dinah Jefferies

The
ROSE
GARDEN

Tracy Rees was the first winner of the Richard & Judy Search for a Bestseller competition. She has also won the Love Stories Best Historical Read award and been shortlisted for the RNA Epic Romantic Novel of the Year. A Cambridge graduate, Tracy had a successful career in non-fiction publishing before retraining for a second career practising and teaching humanistic counselling. She has also been a waitress, bartender, shop assistant, estate agent, classroom assistant and workshop leader. Tracy divides her time between London and the Gower Peninsula of south Wales.

Also by Tracy Rees

The House at Silvermoor

Florence Grace

The Love Note

The Hourglass

Amy Snow

The ROSE GARDEN

TRACY REES

PAN BOOKS

First published 2021 by Pan Books
an imprint of Pan Macmillan
The Smithson, 6 Briset Street, London EC1M 5NR
EU representative: Macmillan Publishers Ireland Ltd, 1st Floor,
The Liffey Trust Centre, 117–126 Sheriff Street Upper, Dublin 1, D01 YC43
Associated companies throughout the world
www.panmacmillan.com

ISBN 978-1-5290-4637-3

Copyright © Tracy Rees 2021

The right of Tracy Rees to be identified as the
author of this work has been asserted by her in accordance
with the Copyright, Designs and Patents Act 1988.

Pan M   r,
ar

A CIP   ry.

Ty
P

Visit **www.panmacmillan.com** to read more about all our books
and to buy them. You will also find features, author interviews and
news of any author events, and you can sign up for e-newsletters
so that you're always first to hear about our new releases.

For Marjorie, Beverley and Gill
and all my other roses

Mabs

The metal ladder pinned to the wall of the ice well rattled as Mabs climbed down, her heart sinking further with every rung. Forty feet below ground, she jumped off to land knee-deep in shadows. The cold was thin and green and razor-sharp, merciless through the layers of shirt and jacket in which she'd wrapped herself, even through the woolly scarf one of the wharf boys had lent her. She'd wound it round and round her neck and the lower part of her face but still the cold cut through.

She was swiftly joined by three other labourers, all boys of course, who threw brief nods at Mabs and each other. It was a strange, twilight world. The shouts and bangs of the canal wharf high above them were muffled and remote. The stacks of ice stood tall and silent, and Mabs couldn't shake the feeling that they were watching her. It was like a scene from a nightmare, she thought. By rights, she would wake with a gasp, and a flood of relief that it wasn't real. But it was real.

When she'd arrived at work that morning, it was a hateful surprise to learn that she would be working in the ice wells – shades, they called them. To add insult to injury, it wasn't even ice season. Winter was when the ice arrived from Norway, in glistening mountains roped to the barges, and had to be lowered into the shades. Summer was when it was all brought up again, loaded onto carts and taken to the homes of the rich. Usually, in October, you were safe from it. But this week was hot and sunny, with bright blue skies. The late burst of summer meant that the grand homes wanted to serve ices at their dinner parties again and the ice-cream vendors decided to keep their stalls open a little longer. So down went Mabs and the others, to bring up the last of the ice.

They looked around, assessing where to start. Their job was to shift the great, greenish blocks of ice to within reach of the giant tongs that dangled on a massive chain from forty feet above. They set to, Mabs and two of the boys pushing the recalcitrant bulk of the ice with all their might, while the last boy, a tall fellow with a shock of hair the colour of hay, directed them and pulled the chain as far as it would reach. When the block was positioned just so, they fastened the tongs – or ice dogs – securely around it before shouting for Swiss Louis to haul it up. As one block lifted away, they immediately turned their attention to the next.

Most of the regular ice workers had returned to their native lands – Switzerland, Italy, France. A few, who didn't have much to go back to, worked at the canals year-round. They got called all sorts – Frenchie, Garlic Head, Wop – with little care for their actual nationality. Apart from that, they fitted in all right. It was Mabs who wouldn't, if they knew.

She wasn't a likely labourer; she was small at the best of times and there'd been precious little food of late. But Pa had fallen apart with grief when Ma died nearly a year ago and Mabs had six little brothers and sisters. Somebody had to earn something, so Mabs dressed as a boy, tucked her hair under a cap and went by the name of Mark.

She kept herself to herself at work; it meant she missed out on the lively banter that was a consolation for working there, but she was afraid of being found out for a girl. So she kept her head down, worked the ice, and stayed quiet while the boys broke the monotony with jokes and laughter. The two working alongside her were called Big and Mikey, she gathered, and the other one was Kipper, a nickname, she hoped, for his sake. In any case, there wasn't much point making friends. Labourers were rotated from cargo to cargo as they were needed. You were never part of the same team for long.

All sorts of cargoes travelled along the Regent's Canal – timber, grain, arsenic, manure – but ice was the one Mabs hated most of all. It was slippery when you needed it to be stable, and sticky when you needed it to slide, and altogether spiteful, Mabs always thought.

Hours later, her arms and legs were shaking; her feet, inside her worn boots, were completely numb. She wasn't certain her negligible strength was even helping any more. Exhaustion, cold and the murky light blunted her senses. As yet another block of ice swung up and away from them, Mabs groaned and leaned back against the remaining stack, her face tilted up towards the distant sky. She closed her eyes, unbearably weary.

A sudden, resonant clang and a horrified yell from above startled Mabs out of her soporific state and she opened her eyes to see a three-hundredweight block of ice dropping like a boulder. The boys sprang away, sharper than she was, but Mabs couldn't move. The shock of seeing that huge, heavy deadweight hurtling towards her was too great. The next instant she was knocked sideways and found herself face down, cold ice beneath her, a warm body above. She felt that body flinch with every crash as the ice smashed to the ground, sending daggers of ice flying everywhere. And then it stopped. The shade was eerily quiet once more and the weight above her lifted. Mabs rolled onto her back. Then she climbed to her feet. Her legs were as weak as water but she couldn't stay lying there; she'd freeze.

One of the boys – Kipper – had saved her, knocked her clean off her feet. He stood in front of her now, a disbelieving expression on his face, hay-coloured hair sticking up in alarm.

'You wasn't movin'!' he said in a disbelieving tone.

'I couldn't,' she said.

Swiss Louis came scrambling down the ladder, babbling apologies, terrified in case someone had been killed. They showed themselves to him, all intact except for Big. One of the flying ice daggers had buried itself in his leg and Swiss Louis helped him to climb out of the ice well. Mabs watched him disappear over the top, stared at the trail of blood that was left dripping down the ladder. She felt sick.

'*Oi!*' An incensed bellow came from above: the foreman, come to glower and see what was going on. 'May as well employ a bunch o' bleedin' monkeys!' he shouted, and spat into the well. 'Clear it up, get it sorted. We ain't wasting it. Stick it in buckets and get it up here. *Now!*'

'Right then,' said Kipper. 'Back to it.'

'Wait!' cried Mabs. 'You saved me! Thank you.'

'No need for thanks, there's little enough we can do for each other round 'ere,' he called back as he jumped down a level and started gathering ice shards. Mabs was shivering hard, the shock setting in. But what could she do other than follow suit?

❖

Much later, Mabs dragged herself home, feet scuffing the hard canal towpath, then the cobblestones of Clerkenwell and finally the filthy streets of Saffron Hill. A light rain had come in, and the purplish night closed around her as she went. Dark shapes in doorways suddenly writhed and resolved into human beings, stretching out hands for coins or calling out unseemly remarks. Mabs kept her head down and her coat drawn tight about her, glad of her boys' clothes. She'd lived in this area all her life and apparently it wasn't as bad as it used to be; still, it elicited no sentimental attachment in Mabs.

The men of the Daley family had been working the London canals for more than a hundred years. Her great-great-grandfather Jack Daley and his sons had been part of the crew that had built them, and all the male descendants thereafter had laboured at the wharfs, loading and unloading the barges. When Mabs was small, she used to think the canals were exciting. Pa would come home with his man's tales of life at the hub of the universe, and he made the waterways sound like roads of high adventure. He thought it a fine heritage that the Daleys had. But now, Mabs imagined she knew what hell looked like: not all fiery red and roasting, but green-grey, blank and shadowy, with huge barges groaning under the weight of unnatural cargo and mighty horses straining their muscles to pull them; even the occasional corpse floating palely in the thick, indifferent water.

It had been a close shave today, that was for sure. They'd learned afterwards that the ice dogs had simply broken, jerking open before they reached the top. On such fragile instances lives depended. If the hay-coloured boy hadn't knocked Mabs off her feet, she would have been crushed to death, simple as that. She wished she'd been able to thank him properly. The accident had left her so dazed that she was the last one to climb the blood-spattered ladder when the work was done. By the time she'd reached the top, there was no sign of her rescuer.

It was all too easy to imagine this evening proceeding along a very different course – her brothers and sisters at home, a knock at the door, the news that Mabs was dead. A beloved sister gone, no one to take care of them any more. She'd always known it was a precarious life but today had driven it home in a whole new way. Problem was, there was no alternative. Not for the likes of Mabs.

Mabs turned off Shirley Street down a covered passageway that had led to stables once, a long time ago. The Daleys lived in one of the old courts beyond it. Around here they called it Mushroom Court. Mabs had no idea if that was its official name or if it even had one. It was dark and cramped, crowded round by decaying houses. Mabs let herself into one of these and climbed some splintered stairs to the second floor. She hated Saffron Hill. She hated Mushroom Court. She hated the canal. But when she opened the door to the Daleys' room, she forgot all the things she hated and saw only the faces she loved.

'Mabs!' cried Jenny, her first sister, looking up with pleasure. Mabs frowned. Jen was straining her eyes again, mending for a couple of pennies in the faint light of a flickering lamp. She was only fifteen and already she peered when she looked about her. But they needed those pennies.

Peg, twelve, was setting out supper, such as it was: some bread and cheese and a few apples. She grinned at Mabs, showing the wide gap in her front teeth.

After three girls, Pa had been determined to create a son. Named after their father, eleven-year-old Nicky had followed close on Peg's heels. After Nicky came Jem, nine, then Matthew, seven. Nicholas and Maureen had decided that six children were plenty. But three years later along came another, a girl. Maureen had called her Angeline.

Angie came to Mabs now, reaching up for a hug. Mabs lifted her in aching arms and went to open the window; the room smelled too strongly of their sweat and hair grease. But the window only let in the odours of night soil and cabbages so she shut it again. Better their own smells than those of others.

She turned back to the room and looked at them all. Oh, but she wanted more for them than this. She didn't even know what more there was, but they were precious and she ached to make good things happen for them. *Just give me one chance*, she thought fiercely. *Anything. And I will take it*.

'Pa?' she asked, but Nicky shook his head.

'Ain't seen 'im all day.'

Mabs's heart sank but she just nodded. She put Angie down with a smacking kiss to the top of her head and took off her jacket and cap. Her hair fell about her face and she felt a little more like herself at once.

It could be worse, she told herself as she looked around. True, one room wasn't much space for eight people, but she knew families the same size and larger who shared a room with two or three other families. At least this room was private to them. At least they were all together. At least they slept in the same place every night. The court wasn't a nice place, but behind it, even meaner buildings were tucked away. Before Ma died, they'd lived in two rooms in a nearby court where the light was a little better, but there were levels more they could drop and Mabs was determined not to let that happen. Even so, if Ma could see them now, it would break her heart clean in two, that was a fact.

'Yer doin' wonderful, Mabs,' said Jenny softly, reading her mind. 'We're all right 'ere, ain't we, kids?'

The children nodded eagerly, as if life in Mushroom Court was one long entertainment.

'I won a conker fight today!' said freckle-faced Matt.

'Did you, Matt?' Mabs's voice was soft. 'Goodness, conkers already!'

'They wasn't very good,' he frowned. 'Bit small. But there'll be some grand ones in a few weeks, I should think.'

'I should think so too.'

Bless them all: at such tender ages they understood their situation well enough to try to lift her spirits and make out there wasn't a thing wrong in their world. She loved them with all her heart and that's why she kept going and kept going at the wharf, even when she was fit to drop. The survival of eight people was a heavy load to carry on her thin, eighteen-year-old shoulders, and there was she in a job she wasn't legally allowed to do. If Pa could only overcome his grief enough to go back to work regularly, that would help. But for now, her wage from the canal was the only thing stopping everything from getting much, much worse.

Olive

All evening there has been an atmosphere in our happy little household. Of course, when I say 'little', I refer to the family – my parents and myself – not to the size of our house, which is rather embarrassingly large. We sit together after dinner as always and the tension in the air is so thick we might spread it on toast.

'I do wish you would reconsider, Olive,' says Papa, sounding melancholy. You would think I was planning to sacrifice myself on a spit.

'You don't *have* to do it, simply because you *said* you would,' murmurs Mama in her best persuasive tone. 'You might wait another year perhaps, dear.'

But my mind is quite made up. Tomorrow, I shall adopt a daughter.

I am a spinster. Many women shy away from the word but not so Olive Westallen! I am the only child of Captain Westallen, former hero of the merchant navy, whose exploits were for many years the toast of London. I am privileged, educated and, not to put too fine a point on it, rich. I do not need a husband. And, despite my fortune, I'm not considered a catch. I am plain; not startling in any way – if you saw me on the street, you would not take fright – just plain. Also, I am too independent, too scholarly. Even in the very death throes of this nineteenth century, I'm an unlikely bride.

And yes, there were years – two or three – when I shed tears over this. But I came through. So I would remain in my parents' home in Hampstead all my life. Well then, it is a beautiful, comfortable, enviable home, so am I to weep over that? Hardly. The truth is that managing a household – employing servants and holding dinners, checking the quality of the linens twice a year – holds no interest for me whatsoever. If I *had* to do it, I believe it very likely that my brain should fry.

As for marriage, well, I am not opposed to it. My parents' example is inspiring. But not *all* unions are similarly harmonious. I would do well as the wife of someone kind and sensible who would recognise me as his equal and not seek to impose upon me the nonsense of men. But where would I find such a one? Certainly not in Hampstead! For I have lived here a very long time and take a spinster's interest in the affairs of my neighbours. If there were a man within a ten-mile radius who could make Olive Westallen happy, I would know him – and I do not.

I have, however, surprisingly determined dreams of motherhood: of romping on the nursery carpet enjoying riotous adventures of the imagination; of splashing through puddles in January; of gathering fallen, flame-coloured leaves in October. Our house, as I mentioned, is large. But we are just three Westallens to fill the upstairs rooms. It seems a waste to me.

I couldn't see a way around it at first. I would hardly traipse to the docks and offer myself to a sailor; I'm progressive, not depraved. Then three years ago, as part of my charitable endeavours, I began visiting the girls' home in Belsize Park.

There, material needs are taken care of, to a basic level at least. But what about love? What about knowing that you always have a place, the sort of knowing that can only grow in a home where you are wanted and valued? I could provide that, I realised. I decided that if I remained unmarried at the age of eight-and-twenty, I would adopt. Tomorrow, I shall be eight-and-twenty.

My parents were opposed from the first. They think that I will ruin my marital prospects conclusively if I proceed through life as an unmarried woman with a daughter.

'But I will simply explain that she's adopted!' I argued, aggrieved that they could not immediately embrace my scheme.

'That's what we would say if she weren't,' pointed out Mama.

Papa got us back to the point. 'It's not that people will think the child is *yours*, Olive. The orphanage is nearby, it will be public knowledge where she came from. It's the fact that many people will find it hard to receive a little girl such as that. They won't know her people, her blood. *We* wouldn't care about that but many would. And we worry for *you*, my dear. An unmarried woman weighed down by a child? I know you maintain that you'll never marry but you're a woman of impeccable breeding and fortune. Men may yet be interested in you, Olive, but not, I shouldn't think, with an acquired daughter in tow. What man would want a woman who has encumbered herself thus? It's too unconventional.'

'Not to mention the unsavoury associations,' shivered Mama. 'With all your eccentricities, Olive, you're a good and moral person. I couldn't bear for our neighbours to think you would do anything . . . unappetising. The Brixton scandal was before you were born, dear, but our generation remembers it well.'

It's true that adoption is not a favourably viewed practice.

Some decades ago, it came to light that unscrupulous types were taking money to care for orphaned babes, then leaving them to die! Now, people who wish to adopt are often tarred with the same brush. Of course, I don't *like* the fact that adoption has no legal status and that everyone wrinkles their nose at the word. I like order, and honour. But am I to deny myself and a child a chance at happiness because of what other people might think? I am not so feeble.

Besides, one thing I have never told my parents is how much I fear my existence after they are gone. I am very content in my unmarried life, but that contentment is possible because of *them*. We have always laughed together and we have always stood together through any hardship. The very fact of them ensures that although I am not wed, I never feel alone. I know it is the natural order of things that we should lose our parents at some point and I trust that day is a long way off for me. Even so, sometimes at night I have devastating nightmares that they are gone. When that becomes my reality, I must have a reason to go on and love to fill my life.

I've said nothing of this to them because I do not wish to distress them. All they ever want is for me to be happy. That's why Mama begs me to wait another year; they still hope some Victorian version of a knight on a white horse might come along and save me from myself. They still hope, I learn now, for a grandchild of their own.

'It's not that we would not care for an adopted grand-daughter,' Mama says and to my great discomfort I see tears in her eyes. 'But it would be *wonderful* to have a new little Westallen. You brought me such joy, Olive. Don't you long for a child of your own? To look down at that sweet little bundle in your arms and see your father's nose, or my eyes?'

'I certainly hope it wouldn't have Papa's nose,' I joke,

because I feel badly for disappointing her. 'I'm sorry, Mama, I know that is not the point. But honestly, no, I don't consider all that. I simply want a child to love. When she comes here, you will love her too.'

I have already picked out the child. She is ten years old and her name is Gert. Her parents are definitely dead and that is important for adoptive parents have no rights. I could not bear for a mother to turn up years from now and take my daughter away. I have learned that older children are harder to place since most people prefer babies first, and adorable moppets of two or three after that.

Mrs Jacey, who runs the girls' home, has explained that older children can be very difficult in all sorts of ways. They already have a character of their own, formed through familial hardship, then glazed by rejection at the home as they are overlooked again and again in favour of younger children. It breaks my heart to think of those silent children waiting for their chance at a family, knowing that they are the ones who will always be on the sidelines, watching. I had imagined that this would make them more grateful than anyone if their turn did finally come but Mrs Jacey assures me that this is not the case.

'They gets cracks in 'em, see,' she said. 'Between four and seven is the age for cracks, I seen it a hundred times. I runs into them families sometimes and I asks how it goes and hear stories of tantrums and torments, of pinchin' other children and even of runaways. You'd think bein' 'ere would make them glad to be in a proper 'ome but it ain't so easy for 'em, see, not once the cracks come.'

Cracks, Mrs Jacey said. Her phraseology may be crude but I have come to respect her wisdom, borne of experience as it is. Cracks there may be, but I feel sure that enough love, enough luxury, can smooth them over until they disappear. Gert has been at the home six years and apparently no one has ever shown the slightest interest in her. She is unprepossessing, it's true, both in looks and demeanour, but I am not one to value the qualities of a doll in a human girl. I wonder, though, if she would be willing to change her name . . . I do not mind a plain face, but a plain name! Foolish the foibles we have, but I cannot imagine a Gert Westallen.

'I *cannot* wait, Mama,' I assure her, heartfelt and passionate. 'I have set my heart on bringing home a child tomorrow and I cannot wait another year in the hope that a man will happen along and allow the rest of my life to begin. I should proceed even if a handsome stranger appeared and proposed to me this very night.'

We are sitting in the drawing room with the oil lamps turned down low. Candles supply the extra light needed; we all prefer their gentle, reverent glow. Just as I finish speaking my piece, a thunderous knocking is heard upon our front door! The candle flames jump upon the wick and my parents and I look at each other, startled. We are sensible people, yet it does seem for a moment as though I have conjured a suitor with my words.

But when our maid Agatha shows the visitor in, it's only Mr Miles, an elder in the Quaker church. He visits us often. Since he is seven-and-forty, and married to Faith (both in the sense that his religion is everything to him and that Faith is his wife's name), it's safe to assume that *he* will not deliver me from romantic desolation. My parents' faces actually fall when they see him! I'm sure he never had such a reception at our hearth.

Mr Miles is always in a haste and an uproar over a wrong that needs righting. Tonight, his indignation is all for the women who are caught up in the 'old profession', working at the docks making the sailors happy. I applaud him for caring but tomorrow is a big day for me so I excuse myself early and go upstairs.

I sit on my bed, looking around the familiar, dear room of my girlhood, which somewhere along the way became the familiar, dear room of my womanhood. I feel unsettled, and why? Because when I heard that knocking at the door, my heart leapt! What strange vagary of femininity is this? I have set aside old hopes of romance; I am forging my own way. Yet just in that moment, when I invoked the idea of a man coming into my life after all, and Mr Miles hammered at our door, there was a part of me that hoped, still. *Oh Olive.*

Are my parents right? If I waited a little longer, *would* I meet a husband, have children of my own? But I do not think it good practice to shy away from a significant step when the moment is upon one. Surely that can only lead to a life that is timid and uncertain. Bold steps, forward steps, are the way to conduct the solitary life, to combat the sense of isolation at the core, to create meaning and purpose. I am sure of it.

I go to the chest of drawers and reach beneath layers of silk and muslin undergarments to withdraw a velvet bag. I return to my bed. Inside the bag are my divination cards, the deck tied with an emerald-green ribbon. Mama disapproves of them; she says the Bible is the only source of guidance we should need. And yet I use them when I am alone, in moments of duress. The Bible has wisdom, but these cards speak to me.

I pull at the ribbon and the cards slither; I catch them in my hands. They are large and silky from use. A few have blunted corners and one, the Turtledove, has a little crease. That's why I close my eyes when I use them, so I can't see any of the clues, for these cards are as familiar to me now as my own face. I shuffle with expert hands and the smell of the cards rises up to me, a little musty, a little spicy with the warm, sweet aroma of print. Sometimes I bury my face in those cards. Sometimes their scent is the most comforting thing I know.

I need not form a question; the cards know what I am thinking. I shuffle and cut, shuffle and cut, shuffle and cut, until I have three cards before me, face down. The backs have a faded pattern of red lines criss-crossing in diamond shapes, with a border of curlicues. This on an ivory background, darkened to primrose with age.

I lay the deck aside and regard the cards before me. I don't know what I expect to see; I'm not even sure what I *hope* to see. If something were to divert me now, it would be very inconvenient. I turn the cards over to see the spread I have dealt.

The Rose. The Star. The Woman. Representing, respectively, the vagaries of fate, good fortune in a general sense and, well, a woman!

I nod. I suppose I thought as much. No sign of an affair of the heart. No indication of marriage. No stranger on the horizon, or letter, or ring, or anything that suggests, however tenuously, that romance and marriage are to be part of my life. I am reaffirmed and comforted. I put the cards away and make ready for bed. Tomorrow I shall go and see Gert, and ask her if she would like a new mother.

Mabs

Sometimes, guiding angels appear in unlikely forms. For Mabs, salvation arrived in the guise of her old friend Lou, coming to find her on the wharf. It was Lou's evening off and Mabs had just finished work. She was so tired that she didn't see Lou until she was three feet in front of her, waving her arms and shouting, 'Mabs! Mabs! I got news!'

Immediately Mabs looked around to check that no one had heard.

'Oh, sorry, MARK!' cried Lou, remembering. Mabs rolled her eyes. 'I've heard of a job you should try for,' said Lou, clutching her hand and talking in a normal voice at last. '*In service!*'

Service? For a brief, sparkling instant Mabs let herself imagine it, then shook her head. 'I wouldn't get it. And if I did, I'd only mess it up somehow.'

But Lou wasn't having it. 'You oughter let them see you,' she insisted. 'This one sounds a bit different.'

Lou had been in service for two years. She worked for Mr Blythe the banker, in his grand house up in Highgate. She would have loved Mabs to go and work there with her but the Blythes insisted on attributes in their servants that Mabs did not possess: cleanliness, a basic level of education and a minimum height of five foot six for the maids (six foot one for the manservants).

Mabs heard plenty of tales from Lou about the hard bloody work it was, up every morning at five to clean out the grates and set the fires before the family arose, pounding the door-step with a donkey stone every day to keep it buffed and shining. But Mabs reckoned *she* was no stranger to hard work and since she was knackered all the time anyway, she'd far rather be knackered wearing a clean dress, in a lovely house, on a decent wage.

Lou rattled on. 'Cook read us out the notice last night. Over in 'Ampstead they are. They want a "useful maid of good conscience". They don't even want no employment record or nothing, just a letter from someone who knows you, sayin' yer a good girl, like. A character reference, they call it. You could get one of them, Mabs.'

'A useful maid? What's that?' asked Mabs. She'd heard of parlour maids and kitchen maids and lady's' maids. Weren't they all useful? Wasn't that the point of them?

'It's an in-between sort of a thing. Halfway between a house-maid and a companion. A bit of both.'

'But that's a proper nice job, Lou. All sorts will be after it. They won't want me. I never done that kind of work.' She *had* vowed to take any chance that came her way, she remembered. Only she was scared to get her hopes up.

Mabs sank to the ground, landing at Lou's feet on the towpath, narrowly missing a steaming pile of horse dung. The wharfside clamour was beginning to subside as dusk fell and the workers started for home, but the thick, textured air still reeked of pondweed and sweat. The last barge of the day was just pulling off.

'Oh, come on, Mabs!' scolded Lou, perching gingerly on a

boundary marker embossed with the Prince of Wales's feathers. 'What's to lose? It may be a funny job and who knows, they may not pay very well, but anything's better than this.'

She was right, of course. Earlier that day, Mabs had passed out. Fainted clean away like a lady! She'd been dragging sacks of manure to the water's edge, ready for loading onto the barges. It wasn't the smell or even the thought of it that had got to her; it was pure exhaustion. She'd got away with it this time; she was working alone so no one had noticed. She'd scrambled to her feet and carried on as best she could. But it was a warning.

'Gawd, Mabs, love, you look awful,' Lou said, leaning forward and looking into her face. 'I'm sorry, running on at you like that. I didn't see.'

Mabs smiled weakly. 'I'm all right,' she said. 'Thanks, Lou. I'll go and see about the job, I will. I can't keep this up much longer.'

'You don't look like you'll last another day, if I'm honest,' said Lou, handing her a parcel. 'It's me spare dress, Mabs. For Gawd's sake, look after it. They're mad on us being clean and smart. If I get something on this one and I can't change, I could lose me job. But you can't go about a position dressed like that.'

'Thank you,' Mabs whispered.

'And here . . .'

She handed Mabs a shilling and Mabs pushed it straight back at her. You didn't take money from a friend.

'Keep yer hair on,' Lou growled, pushing it back again. 'It's only a loan. Pay me back when you get the job. You 'ave to, Mabs, look at yourself. You can't stand up. If you don't eat, you won't be able to have a proper talk with them. You need to buy food and *don't* give any to the littl'uns or your pa.

Think, girl, you gotta help yourself first, so you can help them.'
Lou got up and rubbed her backside ruefully. Boundary
markers did not make comfortable seats.

Mabs buried her face in her arms. Her cap fell off and her
fair hair fell out. She rammed it back on quickly, shoving the
long hair up and out of sight. She felt utterly overwhelmed,
but Lou was right: she would have to do as her friend said if
she was going to try for this impossible chance.

After Lou had hauled Mabs to her feet, she marched her
to the market on Gray's Inn Road, where she watched Mabs
scoffing down sausages and roast potatoes. Then they went to
Mushroom Court to tidy Mabs up a bit. Lou had grown up
in this very court but she'd been able to stay in school longer
than Mabs and had an impressive inability to take no for an
answer, which was how she'd got the job with the Blythes.
Mabs washed and brushed her hair then clambered into Lou's
spare dress while the children watched in surprise.

'Don't ask,' said Mabs briefly. She didn't want to get their
hopes up either.

Once they'd left the narrow streets of Saffron Hill, Lou
summoned a cab. Mabs felt awful that Lou was spending her
hard-earned cash on her but Lou insisted. She reckoned that
if Mabs had to walk the full four miles after a day on the
canals, she wouldn't actually get to Hampstead. And so, before
she could believe she was doing this, Mabs found herself
standing in front of the house of this new-in-town family who
needed a useful maid.

'Right across the heath from the Blythes they are,' said Lou
gleefully. 'We'd almost be neighbours again! Promise you'll
tell me soon as there's news. And give me dress back as soon
as yer done with it. Right, gotta go.'

Mabs watched with a sinking heart as her friend hurried

away. Without Lou egging her on, it seemed ridiculous that she was here at all. They would laugh at her, chase her off like a stray cat. The house wasn't huge, white and gleaming like the Blythes', but it was smart. Brown brick, with a pale blue door, white columns on either side and a shining white doorstep. Leaves and stems climbed a wrought-iron archway above a small, neat gate. A short garden path cut between glossy shrubs and trees. Mabs sighed. It was so lovely.

Get on with it then, Mabs, girl, she told herself. *Yer eighteen years old, not five.*

The call, once she mustered her courage, was over in a trice. A business-like housekeeper explained on the doorstep that it was a live-in position as companion to the lady of the house, with a little light housework and general duties as required. Mr Finch, the master, would be seeing girls about the post on Wednesday and Thursday. If it was of interest, Mabs could present herself at eleven o'clock on Thursday with a suitable letter of recommendation.

'I'll gladly come then, ma'am,' said Mabs meekly. *Interest? I'd cut off me arm for it!* she thought.

Mabs let herself out through the little gate and stood for a moment in the elegant hush of the Hampstead street. Mabs lived in a world of noise: at work, machinery groaned, horses clopped and whinnied and men shouted all day long; at home, doors slammed, babies wailed, and swear words, wild laughter and shouted threats all filled the air like rain. Quiet, Mabs thought, was a certain sign of wealth. She sighed, and set off walking.

Olive

When I awake on my birthday, October rain lashes against the window and the wind surges through the trees, making a great uproar. Unwelcoming weather – and after our recent Indian summer! I pray that a little sunshine returns by the time Gert reaches her new home.

I sit up in bed to read. Is there anything cosier or more delicious, when the wind and rain sing their storm song and you are warm and snug indoors? But I'm too excited to concentrate and my thoughts drift to my divination cards. I fetch them again, not to conduct another reading but to ponder last night's: the Rose, the Star and the Woman.

The motto on the Rose card reads: *You sport with fortune, but whatever the cards refuse, Your good sense, Your skill and learning will amply compensate.* I take this as confirmation that although I'm taking a bold action, I am a person of sense and education and my judgement can be trusted. That for whatever I lack – romance, passion, marriage – other things will compensate – family, friends, purpose. It exactly echoes my own appraisal of the situation.

The legend on the Star card reads: *Do Your part and You will soon experience the good effects of it.* Precisely my feeling. I have so much and Gert so little. I shall do my part and give her a home and all will be well. The star as a symbol has always had special significance for me; I am a keen astronomer. How could I not be? My father was a seafaring man and the stars always guided him home. Whenever I draw the star, I feel it is a particularly affirming message.

As for the Woman, well, the wording is clearly intended for a male user: *Gratify Your partiality to the Fair Sex, but never offend decency.* But although the message is irrelevant, the image alone tells me everything I need to know. A lady wearing a dress and bonnet of ancient fashion stands, clutching some wildflowers, against a bare horizon. There is no male counterpart, no lover, she has picked her own flowers. She could be me.

I dress and ring for a pot of tea. 'Happy birthday, Miss Westallen,' says Anne when she brings it and hands me a small parcel.

'Why, bless you, dear, you shouldn't have taken the trouble!' I exclaim, knowing full well there is nothing more irritating to the ears of those who *have* taken the trouble. Good manners *will* dictate!

'It's from all of us below stairs,' she explains. 'We hope you have a very happy day, miss. We know it's an important one.'

With the gift there is a small square card bearing the motif of a chubby blue tit. Inside is written:

Wishing a happy birthday to Miss Olive Westallen. May you shine.

Each servant has signed their name, in painstaking or poor handwriting: Anne; Agatha; Mrs Prowse, the housekeeper; Mrs Brody, the cook; Johnson, the footman; Brown, the gardener; and even Nell, the girl who comes to do the rough work twice a week.

'Why, bless you all!' I say. 'What a lovely start to the day.

Please convey my thanks to everyone.' I kiss her cheek, an impulse, and she looks pleased and awkward as she leaves.

I marvel, not for the first time, at the lunacy of living in the same house as someone, of seeing them every single day, yet etiquette dictating there should be no warmth or affection. Just as I wonder at the fact of seven people to take care of three. But there are many things I do not understand in this world and my birthday is not the day to solve them. Instead, I sip my tea and rip into my gift. It is a small enamel locket with a little red rose painted against a cream background. It hangs on a gold-coloured chain which I suspect will tarnish swiftly. Inexpensive, but thoughtfully chosen and pretty to the uncritical eye. I fasten it around my neck at once, and it shows to fine advantage against the dark green fabric of my costume. It is my autumn best and, of course, I have chosen it to honour the occasion.

I dare a glance in the glass. *May you shine*. A lovely wish. I have never been one of those shining girls, like Rowena Blythe or Verity Crawford. Whenever our paths cross, I show up poorly next to their smiling, scintillating beauty. Still, I fancy today that impending motherhood has warmed my complexion and brightened my eyes. Anne has dressed my nut-brown hair very neatly indeed. I look rich, well put together. I wonder how I will appear to Gert as prospective mother material.

I finish my tea and hurry to the breakfast room where I receive gifts and kisses from my parents and scrambled eggs aplenty. And thence to the orphanage!

It is but a fifteen-minute walk to the girls' home but it feels like an hour. I am impatient, and the morning is cold and wet. When I arrive, Mrs Jacey shows me in, her smile one of relief that I am coming to lighten the load by one small child.

Her office is a pleasant room where we have conducted all our serious discussions; I had expected that Gert would be brought to me there. So often I've practised my little speech to her, and imagined her response. The scenario is so long-cherished, so *real* to me, that I am completely thrown when we walk straight past Mrs Jacey's office. Its door stands ajar; a maid is inside, scrubbing. A child vomited copiously not ten minutes before, Mrs Jacey explains. A mistimed breath on my part confirms it.

Instead, I am shown into the playroom, where above twenty girls of varying heights and degrees of dishevelment play with broken dolls or scratched building blocks. Black-haired Gert is alone, as always. Today she sits on the floor with her hands clasped around her knees, scowling.

'Gert, dearie, you've got a visitor,' says Mrs Jacey in weary tones. 'Miss Westallen is 'ere to see you about summink important. Ain't that nice?' Gert refrains from looking up or answering. 'Oi! Madam! Be polite to the nice lady now or she may change 'er mind and then you'll never 'ear what she 'as to say!'

'It's quite all right, Mrs Jacey,' I say, sounding more confident than I feel. 'If Gert's not feeling chatty, I perfectly understand. I like a bit of peace and quiet in the mornings myself.'

Mrs Jacey sniffs. She's tried a dozen times to talk me out of Gert. 'I'll leave you to it, then, miss. Let me know what transpires.'

I promise, but really, what *can* transpire, other than Gert coming home with me? Mrs Jacey does her best but this is hardly an uplifting place. I glance around at the dull, scuffed walls and old, broken toys. I am afire to get her out of here, to show her love and grace and beauty and let her new life begin.

'Gert, my dear,' I begin in a soft voice, trying to engender
a feeling of intimacy in a room full of children chanting
nonsense, banging drums and scolding dolls. 'I know you have
no reason to feel excited to see me. You don't really know me
after all. But . . . I have an idea and I wish to talk to you about
it. I think . . . you might be very happy when you hear it. You
see, I wish to change everything for you. For the better,' I
add hastily, considering that on its own, everything changing
might seem a daunting prospect.

Gert continues to frown at the floorboards. Bending over
as I am, with my hands on my knees, I feel my back protest
at the strain. I straighten up and look around. Most of the
children are caught up in their games but a few stare openly,
longing expressions on their faces. It's because of my fine
costume, I assume, my rings and fur-collared pelisse. Or
perhaps it's because of the symbol I represent, a woman of
motherly age, and a world most of them will never get to see.
It crosses my mind that any one of those children might be
more responsive than Gert but I push the unworthy thought
from my mind. I'm not doing this for gratitude.

There are twins of about six who gaze at me with a kind of
hunger; they are little more than skin and bones, with hollows
beneath their dark eyes. How I long to feed them up. There
is an extraordinarily pretty child of around three, with a tangle
of golden hair, who pretends not to watch, though I see her
peeking more than once, before looking shyly away again. My
heart catches for a moment before resuming its steady rhythm.
I will not be one of those who take the easy route, captivated
by an adorable moppet. I positively *scorn* adorable moppets!
All these children are younger, more appealing, they stand
every chance of finding a home. But Gert . . . glaring, glower-
ing Gert . . . this is the child who needs me.

I sit on the floor beside her. It takes quite some effort getting there, between the length of my skirt and the tightness of my bodice and the fact that a dignified lady is not used to sitting on the floor. But I cannot keep bending over her like the shadow of Fate.

'Gert,' I resume, when I get there at last. 'Would you like to live with me? You see, I have no children of my own. I would love you, dear, and we should have a jolly time. Walks on the heath and books and toys and parties at Christmas and . . . well, anything you like, my dear.'

Gert springs to her feet as though stuck with a pin and dashes away. I would *like* to believe that she is overwhelmed with emotion but I catch a look in her flashing dark eyes that suggests she has waited until I am all the way down on the floor before doing so. I am left sitting alone in the middle of the floor with my legs stuck out in front of me. Let Mrs Jacey not come in and see me now!

Gert darts over to the window and climbs onto the sill. She doesn't look out, just perches, sullenly, gazing at the wall. I feel a flash of annoyance. But I quell it and scramble back to my feet, an even less elegant process in reverse, my bustle sticking up into the air. My heeled boot slides a little on the wooden floor. I take a deep breath and cross the room.

'Gert,' I say, still kindly but firmer now. 'Perhaps I haven't been clear. And I understand that this is a lot to take in. If you need time to consider it, I certainly shan't hurry you. I wish to adopt a child. I wish to make her my daughter. And I wish that daughter to be you.'

I am aware, at the periphery of my vision, of several small heads watching us, several small mouths hanging open.

Gert looks at me at last. Hope flares in my chest. Here, finally, is the moment I have dreamed of. Instead, she fixes me with a look of such withering scorn that I feel quite ashamed.

'Clear orf an' leave me alone,' she demands, not quietly, and angles herself to face the window. Something tells me she is not admiring the autumn colours.

'Gert!' I cry, shocked. 'I do not wish to bother you if you don't want me, indeed I do not. But I'm not sure you understand what's at stake! I live with my mother and father and we are all ready to love you. We would educate you, dress you, give you a beautiful, happy life. We are . . . well, we have plenty of money, Gert. You surely would not rather stay *here*, where you have no one?'

The thin shoulders remain hunched and square in their rejection of me. All my plans drain out of me into the ground. If Gert will not come with me . . . what then? True, there are plenty of others in need, but I had set my heart on Gert! I have made her a bedroom and thought of a new name for her and one does not simply swap one child for another at a moment's notice! And for Gert, when will another chance come?

Again, I'm aware of the watching faces. Of the many children who would give anything for a chance like this. I rue the loss of Mrs Jacey's office and the privacy it would have afforded. I lower my voice, not wanting to make them any sadder.

'Dear Gert. I know this must be very hard for you. I cannot imagine what your life has been. But I know this. You deserve better. I cannot force you to come with me. I would not wish to. But please let yourself take this chance, my dear. It's yours to seize and we will be very kind to you, I promise. Tell me now, Gert, wouldn't you like a beautiful home and a new mama?'

It would be possible to hear a ghost moving through this

place. The silence is absolute. Then Gert jumps from the sill at last. 'No!' she shouts. 'I don't *want* you. *Go away!*' She shoves me hard, her expression savage; I stagger several steps backwards. Then she runs, banging the playroom door behind her as she vanishes.

I stand motionless, oddly embarrassed, hurt and uncertain. *No?*

I cannot accept that I must leave her here. But she has not been equivocal. And you cannot force a child to want you. You cannot force someone to be happy. But then . . . what shall I do?

Amidst my confusion I feel a tugging at my skirt. I whirl around; there are pickpockets aplenty here. I expect to see an older girl turn aside hastily, with an innocent air, but no. It is the beautiful child I noticed earlier. Her expression is wistful and her hand is not buried in my pocket, it quite deliberately clutches the material of my skirt. She looks up at me with plaintive, dark hazel eyes. She is the very definition of an adorable moppet. The *most* adorable of moppets, in truth.

'I wish you would be *my* mama,' she whispers.

Mabs

On Thursday, Mabs woke with her stomach in knots and waves of something sharp and fiery rising up her throat. Was she *ill*? But it was fear. Just fear. All she'd been able to think about for the last three days was how much she wanted this job! She'd never get another chance like it. The hope of it had somehow kept her going. She'd eaten her fair share of food at every meal to keep her strength up, and while she worked, she'd daydreamed about what it might be like, living somewhere like that.

Peg went to the wharf to tell the foreman that her brother Mark was ill but would be back at work tomorrow. She returned with the couple of coins Mabs was owed and a message not to bother, the job had gone to someone else.

'You *are* joking?' Mabs exclaimed in horror but, of course, Peg wasn't.

Her hands were shaking so much she had to call on Jenny for help. Jenny was solemn and silent as she checked Lou's dress for smuts and stains, brushed Mabs's hair, tied it back. That was why Mabs *had* to go, scared as she was – for Jenny and the others.

She arrived at the brown house with the pretty blue door on Willoughby Walk in plenty of time. As the town clock chimed eleven, she knocked, despite the sweat pooling in her armpits and crawling on her palms. What on earth would she say to a gentleman who lived in a house like this? She'd never spoken to one before, couldn't imagine what he would make of her.

The housekeeper let her into a square-shaped hallway with a black and white tiled floor from which a staircase rose to the upper, unimaginable regions of the house. The walls were painted the colour of a robin's egg. An enormous jug of some orb-like, rich blue flowers stood on a small table and there was a painting of a beautiful, dark-haired woman in a lilac dress on one wall. On the opposite wall hung a gilt-framed glass and Mabs caught sight of her reflection. She winced. Lou's dress was tidier than anything she owned, but it drowned her. There were dark hollows under her light brown eyes and her fair hair was escaping its plait. She looked . . . desperate.

'Mr Finch is in the parlour,' the housekeeper said. 'Follow me.' There was no mention of Mrs Finch, or any sign of her.

The parlour was another lovely prospect, quiet and ordered. Mabs gazed at the lamps and rugs and china, not a speck of dust anywhere, caught between delight and terror. Mr Finch was quite tall, with receding chestnut hair and a well-covered, high-coloured look about him. He greeted her kindly: 'Miss Mabel Daley, I presume.'

Mabs wiped her palms on her dress. If he noticed, or minded, her damp handshake, he didn't let it show. 'Please, take a seat. I see you've brought your reference. May I?'

On Monday evening, while there was still food inside her and strength in her legs, Mabs had gone to see Mr Miles. He was important in the Quaker church, but before he became a Friend, he'd been a minister at the church that Mabs's mother went to on Sundays. Mabs hadn't seen him for months but she'd felt certain that if she explained everything, he would give her a letter. And he had.

She handed it over, tongue-tied. Mr Finch set to reading it and Mabs was glad of those few minutes to gather herself. He looked up and smiled. 'This is a glowing recommendation, Miss Daley. I feel as though I know you already. I suggest we start with a few basic questions.'

'Yes, sir,' Mabs managed, dizzy with relief that she'd somehow got off to a good start.

'Can you read, Miss Daley?' he asked.

A short-lived good start. Mabs shook her head. 'I know me letters, I learned 'em all, but I weren't in school long, sir, so I never come to join 'em together.'

'And I presume you cannot write?'

She shook her head again, mortified. What had she been *thinking*? Why had she come? Any minute now he would ask her about hairdressing or fancy stitchery and what did Mabs know about any of that? Any minute now it would be over and she'd lost her job because of this.

Instead, he asked about her family. Mabs attempted to answer him truthfully without sounding as though she was trying for the sympathy vote. Then he asked about her values and beliefs. Mabs was wrong-footed; in her life, there wasn't much time to sit around discussing right and wrong. Mr Finch had to draw her out, asking her questions about things like discretion, confidentiality and integrity, but they weren't words Mabs knew.

Oh, how stupid she felt. Some people, like Mr Finch, were polished and clever, while others, like her, couldn't even answer a simple question. Stupid, stupid Mabs. This was what happened when you reached for something that was too high. You fell flat on your blimmin' face!

But then she felt a wash of indignation. How was it *her* fault? If she'd stayed in school, she might have learned to read but she had to stay home to watch the babies while Ma went out to work in the laundry in King's Cross. And the babies kept coming. But in their world, they didn't need big words or book learning. With two wages coming in they were just about clothed and fed, and there was joy, in small, snatched flashes, just because they were together. Except now they weren't. Ma was gone and Pa might as well be and Mabs had to try to make her way in a world she knew nothing about. Her anger prompted her to speak up.

'I'm awful sorry, sir, but I don't rightly understand those words. Can you tell me what they mean so I can answer you, please?'

And he did! It turned out that discretion meant not meddling where you weren't wanted, confidentiality meant not gossiping, and integrity meant doing the right thing. Once Mabs understood, she had no trouble answering! They may have been as poor as fleas on a rat but they'd been brought up right. Ma and Pa had taught them good from bad, and put the fear of God into the children if they ever misbehaved. Mr Finch seemed pleased to hear all that. Mabs started to relax. Somehow, she was holding her own.

'Let me tell you more about the job,' said Mr Finch, and Mabs sat up a little straighter.

'My wife is a dear woman, a lovely woman,' said Mr Finch. 'Sadly, over the past years she has suffered some trouble with her nerves. She has better days and worse days. Her moods, you know, bother her terribly.'

Mabs nodded. None of the women *she* knew had time for moods or nerves. But then she thought of her father. They were all grieving Maureen, but it had gone far beyond that

with him. Something seemed to have broken in his mind so
that he could forget that he had responsibilities, that life went
on, even without a beloved person. So perhaps she did know
something about it after all.

'Has Mrs Finch suffered a loss, sir?' she asked softly.

'A *loss*? Oh, you mean a bereavement. No, Miss Daley,
nothing of that sort. Her troubles are intrinsic and, on the
surface, quite inexplicable. But I would not want you to think
badly of her.'

'Life can be very hard in all sorts of ways, sir. I wouldn't
think badly of her.'

'I suspected you would not. Also, occasionally, she becomes
ever so slightly confused. Please don't be alarmed, Miss Daley;
she is not a lunatic, I wish to make that very clear. She's
simply . . . delicate. Someone who finds life a little more
difficult than most people.'

'Yes, sir.'

'So you see, you would not be readying her for parties
and balls. I hope that doesn't disappoint. Gentle companionship and a little light care, that's what she'll need. I'd
also expect you to accompany her on the rare occasions
when she can be persuaded to take some air, and to keep
her quarters tidy; I think it best she have just one trusted
servant around her, rather than one to dress her, another to
light the fires and so on. Does it sound very onerous to you?
Very demanding?' he added when he saw that she didn't
understand.

'Not at all, sir,' Mabs cried. 'Not one bit. I understand.
When Ma was unwell she always said it hurt her head to have
all the kids around her, much as she loved us, so she'd pack
'em off to a neighbour. She kept just me at home because I'm
quiet and I could guess what she needed.'

'Of course, you have experience of caring for someone in a delicate condition.'

'Yes, sir. If Mrs Finch is poorly, it sounds like a good way of doing things to me.'

'I thought so too, Miss Daley. Now, do you have any questions?'

Mabs could scarcely think beyond the voice in her head screaming, *Please, please, please give me the job!*

She felt her face grow warm. 'I don't think so, sir. You've been so kind as to tell me a great deal about it. At least, there's one thing. Will Mrs Finch want to meet the girl before she's appointed, sir? Seeing as how it's for her own companion, like.'

'No. I'm an excellent judge of character. And it's very wearing for my wife to meet new people. I spare her that when I can.'

'I see, sir. Well . . .' Mabs paused. She knew what she wanted to say, but did she dare? She didn't know the etiquette. She took a deep breath. 'I should like the position very much, sir, if you don't mind me sayin'.'

'I'm delighted to hear it! I had only one more girl to see but I shall ask Mrs Webb to tell her the position is taken. You're just what we were hoping for, Miss Daley.'

'Really, sir? *Me?* Yer givin' it to *me?*'

He smiled. 'You needn't look so astonished, Miss Daley. Given the case, personal qualities are far more important than training or professional experience. We need someone who can care for my wife sensitively, with the discretion not to discuss her condition with anyone but myself. And your character reference is second to none – from a man of the cloth, no less! I'm more than satisfied. Oh, foolish me! We haven't discussed the salary.'

And then he named a figure that made Mabs's head spin.

It was more than Lou earned! Even after two years, even working for a banker. Take what Mabs had imagined in her wildest dreams and double it. She felt truly dizzy and struggled to bring herself back to earth. It wouldn't do to pass out now and make him think she wasn't up to the job.

'Thank you, sir,' she said in a very small voice. 'When would you like me to start?'

'Why don't you arrive on Sunday afternoon? At five? That way Mrs Webb, the housekeeper, you know, can show you around the house and you can settle into your room. On Monday you can meet my wife and start work. Would that suit?'

'Perfectly, sir.'

'Marvellous. I'll have Mrs Webb look out a uniform for you; we had a maid about your size in Durham.'

Increasingly, Mabs felt that she was dreaming. She knew from Lou that maids often had to buy their own uniforms out of their earnings. That's how it was in the Blythe household, and Lou moaned about it plenty. But even *that* would be taken care of! This was a *perfect* job, better than she could ever have hoped or imagined. Oh, what this would mean for her family! She couldn't wait to tell Pa and the others that they'd be able to *eat* from now on!

Mabs shook hands with Mr Finch and left, floating on air, hope glowing all around her like a halo. How things could change in less than a week, she reflected as she left a stranger's house, in a borrowed dress, on a Thursday morning. Thank God for Lou. Sometimes guiding angels appear in unlikely forms. But they always appear at the perfect moment.

Olive

Just like that, I fall in love. Her hair is a tangle, exactly halfway between blonde and brunette – the colour of meadow honey, in fact. Her little cheeks are as smooth as silk and not as plump as they should be. Her mouth is pink and pursed; it makes her look extremely winsome.

'Oh!' I exclaim. 'My dear!'

I feel a pull in my heart as if there is a line planted deep inside it that hooks, at its other end, firmly inside hers. Her eyes are swimming in tears. Yes, there will be others – plenty – who will want to adopt such a pretty, pleasing creature. But will they be good enough for her? Will they love her the way I already do? Will they be able to give her what I can? And what about Gert? Already I feel disloyal, as if by considering it for even half a minute I am dealing her another blow. My head swims; it has been quite a morning.

I struggle to take a calming breath. It will not do to make a hasty decision, off-centre as I am. I crouch down to be nearer the little girl.

'You wish to come with me?' I check. She nods.

'What's your name, dear?' She shrugs.

I raise a brow. 'You don't know your name?'

She shakes her head, curls waving. Good heavens!

'Are . . . are you sure about this, dearest? We have not seen each other before. I'm certain we shall be the greatest of friends but wouldn't you like a little time to get to know me? I could come again, tomorrow and the next day.'

Again, she shakes her head and a mass of tangles drops over her eyes. I ache, and softly brush them clear of her face.

'Want you to be my mama,' she whispers again. 'Want to live in your house.'

Very well. A child who, in her own sweet way, clearly knows her mind. What is the right thing, the sensible thing, to do? It's all I can manage not to gather her into my arms and smother her with kisses.

I stand up again, squeezing her small hand. 'My dear, I must just speak to Mrs Jacey for a moment. I shall come back in a trice, I promise. You won't go anywhere, will you?' Another shake of the golden head.

I hasten from the room, not trusting myself to stay. Gert is nowhere to be seen. I lean against the wall and pray: *Dear God, guide me*. My intentions towards Gert have been so pure, so sincere. And yet, she wants none of me and this nameless cherub has swept into my heart like a high tide. I should go home and let it all sink in; I should think it through rationally before we proceed. And yet I know that I will not leave without her. It's like that sometimes: a decision arrives in one's heart ready-made. Pointless thinking it through for thinking can make no difference.

I venture to Mrs Jacey's office. The stench remains. I go in search and soon come across her.

'What's 'appened?' she asks at once.

'Oh Mrs Jacey, I hardly know where to start.' I lay my hand over my heart and she ushers me into an empty schoolroom where we sit in small child-sized chairs which do little to contain my green skirts or my companion's considerable haunches. There I recount word for word my conversation with Gert.

'Did I say something wrong?' I wonder. 'Was it all too much for her? I do not know how I could have been gentler but . . .'

The good manager of the home shakes her head decisively. 'No. It's not you. It's 'er. Cracked right down the middle, she is, broke beyond repair.'

'Oh Mrs Jacey, don't say that. I can't bear it. Perhaps I'm just not the right person for her. Perhaps a different sort of person might have a different response. I want her to be happy.'

'Don't think that'll 'appen, miss. Sorry not to talk on the bright side. Only I seen it before and I knows it when I sees it. That one's too broke for happiness. No one else'll want 'er and she'll be stuck here till she's fourteen, then she'll go out there and get 'erself in trouble and then get 'erself killed, most as like. I'll keep her safe and fed 'ere, long as I can, in the 'opes it'll change, but it'll be a bright green moon before it does, that's my view.

'It ain't you, Miss Westallen. You're a kind lady. If she can't see it, well then, that's it! But there now, yer poor face is fallin' and fallin'. I'll stop talking. You did yer best. I 'ope you'll keep visitin' us and you'll soon see another child as'll catch yer fancy.'

She takes a deep breath after her lengthy monologue and reaches over to take my hands in her meaty red ones. I can only imagine what a picture of woe I must appear. I look at her, guilt-ridden.

'But that's just it, Mrs Jacey. I already have! After Gert ran off, I was approached by a younger child. She'd heard everything and she said . . . that she wants to come with me. She wants me to be her *mother*! Oh Mrs Jacey! She's . . . well, she's irresistible. I haven't seen her before. A golden-haired child, around three years old.'

'Oh yes, I know the one. Only been 'ere a few days. You know what? She'd be just the girl for you. I can't say as I'm sorry about this. That Gert would've made your life a living hell and that's a fact. This one, sweet nature, nice and young. Four she is, miss, but small for 'er age, like lots of 'em. Take 'er, Miss Westallen, before she's here too long. She cries her eyes out every night. I does me best as you know, but it's no place for a child, not if there's another way. The other girls've been slappin' 'er about a bit. Take 'er now, before this place sticks in her memory and makes cracks in 'er.'

That decides me. She won't stay here one hour longer. 'Mrs Jacey, what's her story? I will take her, indeed I will, but prepare me – is there an errant mother likely to turn up and claim her? I couldn't bear to make her mine only to lose her.'

'No, nothin' o' that sort. Brought in by a neighbour she was. Her mother hanged 'erself. Had ten children, couldn't afford to keep 'em, worked 'erself to the bone. No father, or ten different ones to put it plain, none of 'em around. The older kids've scattered to the wind, the neighbour said. She's seen 'em scavenging around the neighbourhood, one of 'em's already wearin' the broad arrow over at Pentonville. She found the little'un sitting on the doorstep one day, 'alf starved and sobbing, and brung 'er 'ere. So there's no parents to worry about. Just a poor mite who needs some love.'

Tragic though the tale is, it's reassuringly conclusive. 'I'll take her. But Mrs Jacey, I must ask Gert once more. If she'd only change her mind, I would take them both!'

Her face darkens. 'I wouldn't, Miss Westallen. I really, really wouldn't!'

'I know. I understand. But I so wished to help an older child, one who won't have other opportunities.'

'And admirable it was, but leave it go, miss, and take the little'un.'

'Please, Mrs Jacey. Please ask her for me. Tell her I'm taking one of her comrades. It may reassure her.'

Mrs Jacey snorted. 'Who do you think was slappin' the little'un the most?' she retorts, spreading her hands on her thighs and levering herself off the schoolroom chair. She returns five minutes later to report that Gert has graciously declined my offer. I detect a note of sarcasm.

Then she fetches the child who has no name that anyone knows, and no possessions. She and I walk out of the home, hand in hand, and sure enough, the sun has come out to greet her. It is exactly the picture I have conjured again and again since I first conceived my plan to adopt – except that the child beside me is some four-and-twenty inches shorter than I had imagined.

Otty

I can't for the life of me fathom why everyone must be such a *grump*! This should be a *happy* time. Papa has secured a wonderful new opportunity to make money, and he likes doing that more than anything. He's bought shares in the Regent's Canal and secured a very impressive position with the company. So of course, we *had* to move to London – how could it be otherwise? Yet my entire family is sighing and brooding as though we all await the noose.

It's understandable that Mama would be morose; she's had her troubles for a long time and struggles with life a great deal. It makes me so sad. She seems much worsened since we arrived, but Papa says the move has exhausted her delicate system and she will improve very soon. He is certain that the change will benefit the whole family in time.

'I shall become truly wealthy,' he told me with the twinkle in his eye that I have always adored. 'I shall be able to give your mother the life she deserves, without counting the cost. You children will have every opportunity.'

But we children, myself excepted, are proving singularly ungrateful! My brother, Charlie, misses his sweetheart in Durham. He shuts himself away and writes long letters to her on a daily basis. My sisters, Elfrida and Averil, flounce around the house, sulking, when a whole new world sits outside our pretty blue door! They miss Durham. Well, it was our home, yes, and we left it very suddenly. But *I* think they're just scared. In Durham they were quite something: popular and busy. Here we know no one, and they worry they will not measure up so finely in the capital.

So, since Papa is occupied with setting up the household and making his mark at the office, and Mama is languishing, and my siblings are no fun at all, I have to explore by myself! Not the done thing at all, but everyone is too distracted to realise how far I have gone and all I have seen. In Durham I used to tell them everything. I still wish to but . . . I shall be starting school after Christmas; I do not want my freedom curtailed in the meantime! At dinner I am careful about what I say. I have permission to take short walks around Hampstead, which Papa knows to be safe and respectable, so I report that it is a delightful village-within-the-city, full of beautiful houses that Elfrida would delight to see, and wonderful shops in which Averil could spend a fortune. I tell them that the heath is just splendid, a rolling wilderness full of birds and animals, flowers and trees, hills and ponds. Once everyone bucks up, I know they will all love the heath. Personally, I'm enchanted with our new neighbourhood.

What I do *not* tell them is that I have been farther afield too. But how could I resist? London Zoo is only two miles away. I should have *liked* to go with my sisters, but how long will they remain disinclined? How long could I be expected to wait? I had never seen a lion. So I went this morning. Papa would be furious, but really, I'm perfectly capable of looking after myself! My sisters would be outraged if they knew, but then they should pay me more attention, shouldn't they? Oh, I could speak raptures about the zoo, the lion! But then, something even more exciting happened. From the zoo it was logical that I should explore Regent's Park and *then* somehow, I found my way to the canal – Papa's kingdom!

It seemed marvellous to me at first – roads made of water, ingenious machinery, barges as flat and wide as dance floors. Enormous horses with hair covering their feet and falling in their eyes and swishing the many, many flies away. And men and boys by the hundred, shouting orders, shouting warnings, shouting jokes, endlessly shouting to keep the world turning. *Canals can go where there are no rivers!* Papa has told me often. They are the connection between London and the wide world out there, and to think, this is the endeavour in which Papa is now involved! I am so proud of him.

I walked in a trance, drinking it all in. I was barely aware that some of the shouts were being directed at me and that they weren't all nice. I suppose a twelve-year-old girl with ringlets is not a common sight there. I was startled out of my wonder by a hand taking my arm and pulling me away from the waterside. I looked down; the hand was brown. I looked up to see a dirt-streaked face, eyes full of concern, a flat cap: a brown-skinned boy. I had never seen a brown person before.

'Are you lost, me deah?' he asked in a soft voice. 'Or you just crazy?'

It was then that I became aware of a number of men close by, watching me, of unpleasant grins, a shift in the air. My parents would not want me to be there.

'Can I 'elp you, love?' asked one man. 'That darkie botherin' you? Come over 'ere, pretty lady.'

I felt very afraid, and very stupid. I glanced back at the boy beside me and I knew whom it was that I trusted. 'No thank you,' I said, wishing my little girl's voice didn't sound so refined and squeaking. 'He's my friend.'

A ripple of laughter ran through the men. 'Darkies ain't no one's friend,' said one. The boy tugged at my arm and I followed. We threaded our way through the onlookers and away from the canal. When we reached a busy road, a safe distance away and out of sight of the water, we stopped. I heaved a big, relieved sigh; it was good to be somewhere that felt safe and ordinary again.

'Thank you,' I said to the boy, who pulled his cap off. Out sprang a mass of curly black hair, soft as clouds, which tumbled about a face which I now saw was pretty and smooth beneath the dirt. 'Oh!' I said. 'You're a *girl*!'

'Guilty as charged,' she grinned. 'Me name is Jill. And who are you, little crazy girl?'

I held out my hand. 'Ottilie Finch. But please call me Otty, all my friends do. Pleased to meet you, Jill.'

She shook my hand. 'Ottilie,' she said. 'A nice name. Why you at the canal, Otty? You need something? Were you lost?'

I shook my head. 'No, I was just exploring.'

Jill looked incredulous. 'On your own? A nice-dressed child like you? Don't you know, me heart, that the canals are no place for you?'

'I didn't. But now I do. Do you work there?'

'Yes. I have to pretend to be a boy so I tell them I am Jim. Not that they care *what* me name is. They just call me Boy, or Darkie, if they speak to me at all. Well, I'm not there to be friends with those men. I'm there because I need to keep a roof over me head.'

I bit my lip. I wanted to empty my purse on the spot and give her all my money but somehow I knew she would hate that. 'How *old* are you?'

'Fifteen. I best go back or I'll lose me day's pay. Are you all right now? You know the way home?'

I didn't, but I wouldn't have her losing money because of me. 'Yes,' I assured her. 'Thank you again.'

'You're welcome. No more wandering like a lost sheep around the canals, you promise? It's not safe.'

'I promise. Only, Jill, I should like to see *you* again. Could I come back if we arrange to meet? My family's new to London and I should very much like a friend.'

Suddenly she looked far older than fifteen. In her eyes I could see that she had seen all sorts of things that I couldn't imagine. 'You want to be friends with *me*?' she said at last. 'I'd like a friend too, but I don't think your family would be very happy, do you?'

I thought about it. I couldn't imagine *why* they would not, yet somehow I suspected it was true. I supposed she meant because she was brown. No one *I* knew ever spoke about dark-skinned people. Perhaps there aren't many of them in England, but wouldn't that mean they needed a warm welcome? I badly wanted to invite her to Hampstead for tea but I knew I couldn't.

'They don't need to know,' I said.

'I suppose they don't. Well . . .' She thought it through. I crossed my fingers. 'We could meet here sometime when I'm not at work? Maybe a Sunday. Can you remember the place?'

I nodded eagerly. 'I can! Not this Sunday, I'm promised to Papa, but the next, if you're free. I could come at three.'

She grinned again, and nodded. 'See you then, Otty Finch.'

I turned and waved over my shoulder. 'Bye, Jill!'

So now I have a secret even bigger than going to the zoo by myself. I can't say for *certain* that my family would disapprove. I don't honestly understand what's wrong with having a friend who looks different. And she *saved* me – so you'd think they'd be grateful. Even so, I know I must keep quiet.

It makes me feel sad and uncomfortable deep down, different from how I felt when I set off this morning, *but* . . . I have a friend!

If I were to tell anyone, ever, it would be Mama, but she must not be troubled with anything and concentrate wholly on getting well. So far, she hasn't left her room and I miss her very much. But Papa is interviewing young ladies to find a companion for her. I hope he finds someone wonderful and that she can start very soon for I'm certain that, once she is with us, *everything* will get better.

Mabs

On Sunday, Mabs took a last look around the room in Mushroom Court. The room, the court, she would miss not at all. Her family, she felt she could scarcely live without. Their dear, tear-streaked faces crowded round her as they wished her luck, told her they would miss her. Even Pa was there. When she'd told him about her near miss with the falling ice, it seemed to rouse him a bit; he went back to work, hauling grain for a foreman who'd known him a long time and was sympathetic to his troubles. But after a week he'd lapsed again, spending a whole day brooding in the Mucky Duck . . . But when he heard about Mabs's job, he actually smiled.

'Per'aps our luck is turnin' at last, Mabs, girl,' he'd said. 'I'm proud of you. I'll follow yer example, have a word with Dennis. I'm sure he'll give me another chance.' Mabs wasn't so sure, or that Pa would stick with it if he did. But at least he was admitting now that he *should* be working. She had to see it as an improvement. And how could she blame him after all? Losing Maureen had been the bitterest blow. She wished her mother could see her now.

At last she untangled herself from her brothers and sisters, promising to visit on her very first day off before giving Pa a final kiss. Mabs was scared stiff. She'd never spent a night away from her family before, never lived anywhere but Saffron Hill. Hampstead might as well have been the moon, it was so unlike home. And yet, she was eighteen years old. She was leaving home to pursue a golden opportunity that she'd seized for herself, and there was a great excitement in that.

Her only option was to walk, but her bag was light. All she had in the world were the dress, coat, shawl and boots she wore, and her spare undies which were in her bag. She'd packed her boys' clothes too because they were the only others she had. She'd returned Lou's dress to Highgate the day she got the job, entrusting it to a grim-looking housekeeper.

Fabric to make a dress, that was the first thing she'd have to buy when she had some wages, she mused as she walked. The look on that housekeeper's face had told Mabs what she looked like more surely than any mirror. She hoped she didn't look so disgraceful that Mr Finch would change his mind if he saw her before she could put on her uniform.

The day was iron-grey and she walked beneath a frowning sky but the rain held off. She was cold, but that was nothing new. She arrived at number six exactly on time and Mrs Webb appeared to take her in at a glance.

'Miss Daley, you're freezing,' she said, leading her to the back of the house and drawing her into her own small domain near the kitchen. The housekeeper's parlour was tiny, no more than five feet squared. Yet a fire danced in the grate and there were two chairs, a clock, a lamp and a painting of some country hills. Mabs thought it was a wonderful little room.

Please let me pass muster, she prayed, tongue-tied. *Please don't let her pass on a bad report to Mr Finch.*

They sat by the fire and Mrs Webb looked at her appraisingly. 'The master apologises for not being here to welcome you,' she said. 'He's at the office all hours. You look tired and hungry, Miss Daley. Would you like to take some supper before I show you around? Then you can get an early night. The mistress will see you at eight in the morning.'

Mabs nodded. Thank goodness Mrs Webb seemed more sympathetic than the Blythes' housekeeper! 'Thank you very much. And Mr Finch was so good as to say something about a uniform . . .'

'Yes indeed. I've laid one out on your bed and a spare is hanging in your wardrobe.' Mabs felt herself wilt with relief. She couldn't have borne meeting the mistress looking like this. 'There's a pair of black shoes too. I don't know if they'll fit you, they belonged to the Durham maid. Apparently, she was small, like you.'

'Wasn't you with the family in Durham, Mrs Webb?' Mabs had assumed the whole household would have transported itself here, but now she came to think of it, Mrs Webb had a London-sounding voice.

'No, indeed. I was formerly employed by Mrs Zenobia Lake of Belsize Park – do you know of her?' Mabs didn't. 'Her house used to be one of the busiest and grandest in all of north London. But her fortune dwindled and she had to let one servant after another go. Now there's just one maid left, poor thing. Me, I don't like to be solitary. Mr Finch came along at the perfect moment for me.'

'For me too,' said Mabs with feeling.

'I'm sure,' said Mrs Webb. Her shrewd gaze rested a moment on Mabs's miniscule luggage. 'Do you have a nightgown?'

Mabs felt her face flood with colour. 'Ah, no, I . . . don't.' At home she just slept in her chemise.

'I'll look out a spare from the linen cupboard on our way up. There are all sorts in there. Now, some food, Miss Daley. Stay here and warm yourself, why don't you?'

Mrs Webb was back a moment later with a bowl of beef stew and a hunk of bread. Mabs could have cried from the unexpectedness of it. She tore into it; it was the most delicious thing she'd ever tasted, the bread soft and fresh and buttered, the stew flavoured with herbs and onions. This job was worthwhile for the food alone!

Next, they undertook the tour of the house. Mabs had never seen such care and attention lavished on surroundings before. The way the dining room curtains picked out the red colours in the rug. The way the drawing room drapes were held back in graceful lines by silky ropes. Mrs Webb tutted when she saw them. 'Betsy's forgotten again,' she muttered, unhooking them so the drapes fell into place against the encroaching night.

Mabs gazed in wonder at the carefully placed bowls of flowers, the paintings on the walls, the whimsical china ornaments. Mrs Webb ran a finger over one to check for dust and seemed satisfied. Mabs was shown Mr Finch's study, and of course, she was already acquainted with the parlour. How things had changed for her during that short interview.

They climbed gleaming stairs that sported a central band of patterned carpet to a carpeted landing. The bannisters were smooth and polished. The stairs in Mushroom Court were scuffed and splintered, with spindles missing where people had bashed them out for firewood. Mabs had never trodden on carpet before.

'Bathroom, Master's room, Mr Charlie's, Miss Elfrida's, Miss Averil's,' Mrs Webb told her, gesturing at the five closed doors. So many Finches! Mabs had had no idea.

They climbed another set of stairs. 'That's Miss Ottilie's room, she's the youngster. That's the mistress's suite, where you'll be spending your time. There's the lavatory – you can

use that. Miss Otty and Mrs Finch have their own. And here's
the linen cupboard.' Good as her word, Mrs Webb looked out
a nightgown for Mabs, before leading her up a final flight of
stairs to a small room alone in the eaves. 'All yours, Miss Daley.
I hope you'll be comfortable.'

Mabs hesitated. 'Where do the other servants sleep?'

'Why, not a one of us lives in. We all live at home, Miss
Daley, and report for work at six sharp in the mornings. You'll
meet the others tomorrow. There's just Mrs Derring, the cook,
and two maids.'

'Oh!' Mabs knew that it was luxury indeed for a servant to
have a room to herself. At the Blythes', Lou had to share with
Plump Patricia, whose snoring kept her awake at all hours.
Mabs had dared hope for her own room, but she'd imagined
other servants' rooms nearby. It was unnerving to think she
would be all alone at night.

She stepped inside the room that was to be her home now.
It had a sloping roof and a woven yellow rug the colour of
sunlight on a scrubbed wooden floor. There was a proper bed
on legs, with white linen and a yellow blanket. The window
was small, with a simple white curtain. In addition to these
niceties Mabs saw a cupboard, a small shelf and an oil lamp.
She boggled.

'Washroom's through there,' said Mrs Webb, laying the
nightgown on the bed. A small door stood ajar and Mabs
peered into a dark space in which she could make out a tin
bath and a china ewer on a wooden stand. When she spotted
a bar of soap and some towels, she wanted to cry. It would
be ever so easy to keep herself clean here. Mushroom Court
certainly did feel a long way away.

Olive

I'm sitting up in bed wide awake, as has become my custom these last few nights. I am a mother! And it differs from my imaginings in every particular. My daughter is asleep, not in the beautiful room that I spent weeks carefully readying, but on a makeshift bed at the foot of my own – the sorrel-coloured chaise which usually lives beside my window. Agatha and Anne moved it when it became apparent that the room next door would not do.

I swing my feet to the floor and go silently to watch over my girl. I can scarcely breathe for fear of waking her. I can't make out her features in the dark but I see the unmistakeable mass of another living form, defenceless, in my care. Satisfied that she hasn't mysteriously perished, I return to my bed to relive the momentous day when I brought her home. It may take me some time to digest the changes I have made in my life!

For a while, when we left the children's home, there was no conversation between us. I merely walked, slowing my stride to match her little steps, clinging to her small hand as if she were the lifeline, not I.

I took my usual route, which cuts across a small corner of the heath. Her eyes widened when she saw the expanse of wild

land, the autumn colours. Probably she had never seen countryside before. I can only imagine the surroundings she is used
to. I shall ask Mrs Jacey if she knows what area she hails from
and I'll go there one day. I should have some idea of her
beginnings.

I wiped the raindrops from a bench with my sleeve so that
we might sit. My wits started to return and I noticed how
ill-clad she was for the weather. Hastily I wrapped her in my
pelisse. I began to realise that the clothes I had bought for
Gert would not fit. The toys would not entertain her. The
activities I had planned would not suit. I had to adjust, and
swiftly. I was her mother now.

'Do you really not know your name, dearest?' I asked her.
She shook her head. I was beginning to think I had dreamed
her initial, very definite, remarks to me.

'Well, my dear, what would you like to be called? Is there
a name you've always wished for? *I* always wished I was called
Francesca.' But she shook her head again.

I suppose, if you are four years old and you have no food,
no father, and then no mother, there are many other things
you would wish for before a pretty name. All the same, she
deserved the perfect one.

'Then . . . shall I pick one for you?' An emphatic nod.

'Are you sure? If you like, we can wait a while for you to
think of one and I can call you dearest until then?' A frown.
Another head shake.

'Very well, then let me have a moment to think.' I gazed
at her sitting beside me, cheeks pink from the cold, her hair
a mess, but glorious. Hair like honey, eyes like treacle and lips
like petals . . . She looks like a meadow creature, like a fairy
or a flower . . . And then I had it. A meadow flower. One I
had always loved. A pretty name just *made* for her.

I beamed. 'Dear daughter, how should you like to be called Clover? Miss Clover Westallen?'

And my little sprite beamed too. 'Yes, Mama.'

We arrived home just minutes after Clover received her new name. I looked at Polaris House, trying to see it through the eyes of an orphaned four-year-old whisked not fifteen minutes since from a children's home. It stands at the very top of Hampstead, hidden from view by a high stone wall that we pass through via a tall black gate that stands on the cobbled street. It is vast, an orange-red mansion with oriels and a pointed turret and countless sparkling windows. We have lawns and an orchard and a tennis court. Clover gazed open-mouthed, but she held my hand and there were no tears; it seems she made up her mind to trust me from the first. For this alone I love her.

'Here we are, my darling,' I told her. 'This is our home. This is where you live now.'

We went inside and there were my parents in the hall, Anne and Agatha hovering behind them like the chorus in a Greek play. My parents wore nervous, determined faces; what I had told them of Gert was designed to manage expectations. When they saw Clover, they looked confused, relieved, delighted.

'Hello, Mama, Papa. I'd like you to meet my daughter, Miss Clover Westallen.' I feel I shall never grow tired of saying those words. *My daughter. Miss Clover Westallen.* How lovely it sounds. 'Clover, dear, these are your grandparents. This is my father, Captain James Westallen. And my mother, Margaret.'

Clover shrank behind my skirts, overwhelmed finally. I placed a reassuring hand on her curls. Mama crouched down to Clover's height and smiled warmly. 'That's right, but you must call us Grandmama and Grandpapa. Welcome to Polaris House, Clover. We shall make sure that you're very happy here.'

My father did not try to crowd the newcomer, nor shake her hand; he gave a jolly naval bow and saluted. 'Yes indeed. As your grandfather, dear, *my* job is to give you everything you ask for, and earn a scolding from your mother and grand-mother, for the sensible parenting always falls to the women, don't you know?'

Doubtless Clover didn't understand his meaning but I think she sensed his intention and detached herself a little from my leg. Mama remembered our audience. 'These are Agatha and Anne, Clover. They're our maids, and will help to look after you too. Would you like a glass of milk? If you do, they will fetch you some.'

Clover looked up at me, awestruck.

'Well, I should think so!' cried Papa. 'With a little nutmeg sprinkled on top and a slice of plum cake. Isn't that the ticket, Clover?'

Clover nodded. She's extremely good at conveying her meaning without words.

'I'll see to it right away,' said Agatha. 'Where would you like it, Miss Olive?'

'Perhaps the parlour,' I murmured. It didn't feel right to take her to the room I had prepared for another girl. And indeed, when I did show Clover that room later on, explaining that we would soon fit it out to suit her, we had tears for the first time. She didn't have the words to explain what was wrong, but I thought of the rough neighbourhood she came from, the cramped quarters, the many brothers and sisters, and I guessed that she was afraid to sleep alone.

'Would you like to sleep with me, in my room?' I asked gently and at once the tears dried. That is how she comes to be here, on the sorrel-coloured chaise at the foot of my bed.

I want to go shopping! I want to furnish a room for Clover

just as lovingly as I did for Gert. Clothes too will need to be organised but so far, I haven't liked to leave her – it has only been three days. Anne hunted out some childhood clothes of mine, just for now; praise the skies that Mama is sentimental and throws nothing away. But they are woefully outdated and worn, not the way I wish to dress my little girl at all. One of the maids would happily shop for her, of course, as would Mama, but *I* put together a wardrobe, carefully chosen, for Gert and I wish to do the same for Clover.

What to do with Gert's things? Already I can see Clover at ten years old. They will not suit her. More importantly, they will not *delight* her. I could donate them to a needy child, or children. Heavens, I could donate them to *Gert*! But a little voice in my head, surprisingly like Mrs Jacey's, mutters that Gert will scorn them. *Set fire to them, most as like*, judges my imaginary Mrs Jacey. Heavens, what will become of Gert now?

I'm assailed by guilt, as deep and strong as an ocean current. That poor child, too damaged to recognise a life-changing moment, or else too angry and afraid to embrace it. Should I have *made* her come? No. No spirit responds well to force. I had no choice but to leave her there. *Did I?*

The question whispers doubt into my heart until I'm driven from my bed again and tiptoe to fetch my cards. I'm so afraid that I took Clover instead of Gert for the wrong reasons. Did I take the easy road, instead of the right one? I'm a great believer that each right step leads to the next. If my motivation was flawed, will that affect Clover? Yet she *seems* happy, so far as I can judge given her economy with words.

I return to bed once again and shuffle and cut until three

cards, face down, lie before me in the moonlight. I turn them over with the greatest trepidation.

The Moon. The picture shows a crescent moon shining over a placid water – the image suggests no note of discord or caution. I read the legend carefully. *The liberality of Your mind will always rather increase than lessen Your prosperity; it will also daily endear you more to your friends.* Well, that is comforting. It was indeed a liberal impulse that moved me to sweep Clover away to our lovely life. I hope the second and third cards will be as auspicious. Sometimes they can be very contradictory. I turn over the next.

The Letter. *You may flatter Yourself with good hopes in your enterprise but act prudently and speak not always as you feel.* I swallow. *Did* I act prudently? I cannot tell, still. The picture is of a sealed envelope face down upon a table covered by a cloth. It seems to me enigmatic. You cannot see to whom the letter is addressed, or its contents, or even the table itself. Just as I cannot quite see the truth of this. Could I have done more for Gert? Am I *allowed* to embrace this happiness while she is stuck in the home?

I turn over the third card and laugh out loud, then clamp a hand over my mouth. I feel my eyes prickle with joyful tears as I regard it, for it has told me everything I need to know. In all my years of using the cards I have found that there are several that come to me over and over again – they that are now dog-eared and creased – and one or two I never draw. This is a card I have never once pulled before. The Clover. I smile with relief and hug myself. I am free to enjoy this glorious blessing of a daughter.

You may be very fortunate indeed, if you always discharge Your duty with honour and integrity. Well, quite. I shall do just that. I shall be the very best mother that Clover could possibly want. In the picture, a clover grows somewhere that looks very much like Hampstead Heath! I tie the cards together with the ribbon and place the deck on my bedstand. I settle back onto my pillows, waiting with a smile on my lips to drift into sleep. *The Clover*. Today of all days!

Mabs

On Monday morning, Mabs was awake before dawn. It was a strange experience spending the night in someone else's house. She imagined this must be what it was like to be on holiday, a feeling enhanced by the luxury of her surroundings. But this was where she *lived* now. This was where she *worked*. She lay staring into the dark with a beating heart and listening to the scratch and stamp of pigeons on the roof as the pieces of her new reality dropped into place.

She dressed in her new uniform, which fitted her perfectly, and took great care over her hair, brushing it smooth and coiling it tightly. She wanted to make a good first impression. She spent twenty minutes shining her shoes with spit and the corner of her old dress. By the time Mrs Webb came to collect her, she was as ready as she'd ever be.

Mrs Webb knocked on the mistress's door and turned the handle. Mabs swallowed. If Mrs Finch was half as nice as her husband, she'd be a treat to work for. *My wife is a dear woman, a lovely woman*. Still, there was no telling with folk and if Mrs Finch didn't like her, she could be back in Saffron Hill before you could say 'knife'.

They stepped inside. Mabs had been astonished by her own accommodation. But *this* . . . Mabs had always known there was something better than the life she'd been living but, not being blessed with a vivid imagination, she hadn't been able to picture it. Now she drank it in, disbelieving. Enormously long ivory velvet curtains swept down to swirl like pools of cream on the dark blue carpet. The walls were pale blue. The bed was a vast white island set with four wooden posts and nestled beneath a gauzy canopy of white. She saw a mahogany bureau, chairs of several shapes and sizes and a great deal of gold on mirrors and lamps . . .

Over all this presided Mrs Finch. She sat in a chair by the window, gazing into the dark morning, but when they entered, she rose. If the room was a palace, then Mrs Finch was a queen. She had long, dark hair, loose in waves over her shoulders, and wore a primrose robe, full at the bottom like a royal cloak. She was, Mabs saw at once, the beautiful woman in the portrait in the hall, at once more and less beautiful than her likeness. The painted Mrs Finch had been young and smiling, with roses in her cheeks and lights in her eyes. This Mrs Finch was thinner and paler; her eyes held nothing but shadows. Her face was unsmiling and no trouble had been taken with her appearance, yet there was a pulsing power about her that demanded attention.

'Good morning, ma'am, I hope you slept well,' said the housekeeper.

'Tolerably, Mrs Webb.'

'This is your new companion, ma'am, arrived last night. Miss Daley.'

Mabs didn't know how to greet her. She had a majesty that made Mabs want to curtsey, yet she was an ordinary woman, not even rich by the standards of some, and Mabs was to spend every day beside her. She couldn't do reverence every time they met. Would a handshake do? But Mrs Finch made no move towards her and Mabs was too shy to move.

At last, Mrs Finch inclined her head. 'I see. Thank you, Mrs Webb.'

'Well then, I'll leave you to it. If you need anything, ma'am, ring for me, Miss Daley being new and all.' Mrs Webb departed.

They looked at each other a long time. Mrs Finch regarded her from head to toe and back again; she might have been seeking the answers to the puzzles of the universe in Mabs's face and person.

'I'm ever so 'appy to meet you, ma'am,' Mabs said at last. 'This position, for me . . . well, I'm delighted to be here, that's all.'

Mrs Finch's lovely curved brows drew together a little, creating a small crease in her forehead, but she said nothing.

'You must tell me anything you want me to do for you, ma'am, and I'll gladly do it. I wish to be an 'elp, I wish to ease your days. If you have a . . . a routine you like to keep to, tell me and I'll see it done. Would you like me to dress you?'

A spasm of something that might have been laughter or pain crossed Mrs Finch's face. 'I'm two-and-forty years of age, child. I'm perfectly capable of dressing myself.'

'Oh, of course you are! I didn't mean that. I just thought . . . seein' as how I'm your maid, as well as companion . . . I'm sorry if that's wrong. I never done this kind of work before, see. So if you did want me to dress you, you'd have to tell me how anyway!' Mabs smiled nervously.

Mrs Finch regarded her steadily. 'You've never been in service before?'

'No, ma'am.'

'What manner of work were you doing previously?'

Mabs fidgeted. Why hadn't Mr Finch told his wife all this? Saying it aloud only served to emphasise how wildly unsuited she was to the job. 'I was workin' at the canals. Loadin' the barges and such. Labouring, ma'am.'

The lovely brows rose higher. 'They employ women to do that?'

'No, ma'am. I had to pretend to be a boy.'

'Accomplished at subterfuge then.'

'Sub . . .? Pardon, Mrs Finch?'

'Dishonesty. Lying.'

'What? Oh no, ma'am. I never lie normally. Only, you see, my ma died nearly a year ago and my pa . . . he sort of . . . well, he can't do his job no more. And I've three little sisters and three little brothers. The youngest, she's only four. The work was all I could get. I hate lying, ma'am, but it was that or watch me brothers and sisters starve.'

Mrs Finch laughed, a long, hollow laugh. 'So you've no education and you're desperate. Oh, he has chosen well. He has chosen well indeed.'

'I beg pardon, ma'am?' Mabs was becoming frantic. She didn't understand what was happening.

Mrs Finch was silent a long while and Mabs fretted. Perhaps when his wife reported to him, Mr Finch would dismiss her. She would have to leave this lovely house after only one night. What would become of them all then? Her new mistress held all their fates in her snow-white hand.

After a long while she spoke again. 'A companion was my husband's idea, Daley, not mine.'

'I see, ma'am.'

'So don't expect a long list of tasks and duties from me. I didn't want you here in the first place.'

Mabs bit her lip. 'I'm sorry, ma'am. Only then . . . what am I to *do*?'

'Well –' the dark eyes travelled smoothly over her again – 'there's no timber to stack here. What do you suggest?'

No timber to stack? Was she taking the mick? What could Mabs suggest? She knew nothing of being a companion, nothing of this household. She wracked her brains.

'Would you like to take a walk, Mrs Finch? I'm new to this area and I understand you are too. Perhaps you'd like some privacy to dress, then we might take a gentle stroll and get our bearings together.'

Mrs Finch sighed, and turned back to the window. The darkness was lifting and shapes were starting to appear. Mabs dared to step closer and peer outside. The room looked over a garden – there were no flowers but Mabs could make out the shape of the branches and bushes. And thorns. Rose bushes, perhaps. Despite the sorry circumstances, something in Mabs was delighted at the thought of a rose garden. She'd heard of such a thing, but never seen one. Beyond it were the backs of other houses.

'It's early yet, of course, but it might be nice to go out just as the sky's gettin' light, and the day's all new. Oh! Would you like some breakfast first? Should I go and order some for you? Or ring for Mrs Webb?'

Mrs Finch fixed her with a withering stare. 'Do you know *anything* about how things work here, Daley?'

'Not really, ma'am, if I'm honest. I only arrived last night. Why don't we start there, then? Why don't we take a seat and you talk me through it all? I'm quick at rememberin'.'

But the mistress turned away again as if she could only bear to look at Mabs for so long. She began to pace around the room, the train of her pale-yellow robe dragging behind. The silence lengthened and prickled. Mabs had suffered plenty in the past, in ways both physical and emotional. But she'd never felt so *uncomfortable* in her entire life.

She'd had two or three pretty good ideas, she thought, and

wasn't sure she could come up with any more, so far from familiarity as she was. When her discomfort outweighed her shyness, she burst out, 'So what's it to be then, ma'am? A walk? Some breakfast? Talk me through the 'ouse? 'Ow about all of 'em, why not?'

Mrs Finch stopped pacing and glared at her. 'I shall *not* be taking a walk today, Daley. *Nor* do I have the heart to explain the workings of this sorry household to a dockworker. And neither do I have an appetite for breakfast. But since you are here, you may as well fetch me a pot of tea. Weak. Black. No sugar. India, not China. Go on.'

❖

Outside on the empty landing, Mabs leaned against the wall. *Oh!* She hadn't known what to expect, but she hadn't been expecting *that*! She suddenly missed her mother so much it was as though she'd only lost her yesterday.

Mrs Finch was . . . well, Mabs didn't like her much and that was a fact. It wasn't her imagination, was it? Mrs Finch had been . . . *rude*. Yes, it was awkward: two people who'd never met before brought together for the purpose of spending their days together. It wasn't easy, finding a starting point. But she, Mabs, had *tried*. Whereas Mrs Finch . . . well! A *dockworker*!

Outraged, confused and worried, yet relieved to be out of that beautiful, terrible room, Mabs went to the kitchen. There she found Mrs Webb as well as the cook and the maids.

'Ah, Miss Daley,' said Mrs Webb. 'Everything all right?'

'Yes, Mrs Webb. That is . . . yes. Mrs Finch has asked for a pot of tea. Black, she said, and weak, with no sugar, and something about India. Or wait, was it China? Oh dear.'

It was true that Mabs had a good memory but she was

flustered and she didn't know there were different types of tea. Tea was just tea where she came from. You took it as it was given and gulped it down.

'India tea she likes,' said the cook, going to a tall larder. 'I'll fetch it. Good morning, Miss Daley. I'm Mrs Derring. Have you met Lydia and Betsy?'

'How do you do?' Mabs greeted the maids who were busy peeling spuds. 'I'm Mabel Daley. Mabs.' They waved potato knives in her direction.

'How are you getting on with the mistress?' asked Mrs Webb while Mrs Derring set the kettle on the range and spooned tea leaves into a pot.

'Um. She's very fine,' said Mabs tactfully. 'I'm worried she don't like me much, though. I couldn't seem to start a conversation.'

'Don't take it personally if she's a little . . . difficult. The move's been very hard on her by all accounts. I'm sure she'll take to you once she gets used to you.'

'Did *you* come from Durham with the family?' Mabs asked the others. She hoped they could give her a tip about how to win the mistress over. She'd left the canals but she was still breaking ice.

'Not us,' said Betsy. 'Started this whole household from scratch he did. We never set eyes on Mrs, nor the youngsters, till they arrived three weeks ago. You'll have to come out with us one evening, Mabs, to the Flask, and tell us your story.'

Mabs smiled and nodded. It was a relief not to be the new girl, trying to fit in with an established set of colleagues. But wasn't that strange? Not a single servant had come from Durham with the family? Perhaps they hadn't wanted to move so far from home, but this was London. Odds were *one* of them would have wanted to try it. Perhaps Mrs Finch was the reason they'd all preferred to stay put and look for other jobs.

'Here you are, Miss Daley,' said Mrs Derring, bringing her a red lacquer tray with gilt handles, on which sat a china teapot and a cup and saucer painted with red roses. 'Weak black India, just as she likes it.'

'Thank you, Mrs Derring. Well, I'd best be off. Pleased to meet you all. Oh, and Mrs Webb, might you talk me through the household sometime, the way things is done, like?'

'Of course. We might find some time this afternoon. Failing that, I'm usually down here around eight in the evening.'

Mabs carried the tray back upstairs. What a shame Mrs Finch was so hard to like when everyone else was so helpful and easy. It wormed away at her. The rest of them only had to please *Mr* Finch. But Mabs was here for the mistress, and she had to make this work.

She'll take to you once she gets used to you, Mrs Webb had said. 'I 'ope so,' muttered Mabs as she set the tray carefully on the floor. 'I blimmin' well 'ope so.'

But when Mabs turned the handle, the door was locked. Her heart sank; this was worse than she'd thought. *How's she supposed to get used to me if she won't even let me in?* she wondered.

Olive

It's little wonder that I have always gazed at the stars. As a small girl, knowing that my sea-captain father charted his course by them, I watched them too. Then, I understood nothing of longitude and latitude or the points of the compass. To me, the stars were sentient beings, silver and lofty, in whose care I could place my father's safety – and I did, with a child's infinite trust. My mother humoured me; perhaps she needed to believe it too. That is why our house is called Polaris House: Polaris, the pole star, our guiding light.

As I grew older, I wanted to learn. I became fascinated by the heavens and my room was covered in maps and star charts. For my eighth birthday I asked for and received a telescope. I have it still, a beautiful thing, made in Sicily. I studied the science of astronomy, along with mathematics, economics and other subjects not usually taught to girls. But my parents encouraged me to pursue my interests in any direction I pleased.

I had a governess when I was young but soon she could not keep pace with the things I wished to learn. My father interviewed many young women all highly accomplished in French, art and poetry, but eventually had to employ a tutor to facilitate my voracious learning in other subjects. *That* provoked my interest in the matter of the differences between men and women in our society . . . All learning leads to more questions, I have come to see.

These reminiscences have arisen because I'm sitting in Gert's room, which is not Gert's room any more. It must be overhauled to suit Clover perfectly. I'm fondly looking at my very first star chart, which I had pinned up for Gert. It's dog-eared and somewhat worn in the folds, but as beguiling and exciting as ever, at least to me. Clover is too young to enjoy it yet, but I shan't wish the time away; I'm blessed to have a few extra years of my daughter. Yet there is a vast difference between a ten-year-old daughter and one of four. I understand it more clearly every day.

I begin to dismantle all my hard work. How presumptuous of me, in hindsight, to go to so much effort and expense before ever consulting the person in question! Well, Agatha will pack up the clothes and send them to Mrs Jacey's. As for the toys, I keep two or three I think Clover will like when she's older. The rest can go to the home too. Christmas is coming. I'll wrap and beribbon them so that each child has a Christmas gift; Mrs Jacey won't have the resources to do it.

The books I shall keep. I chose my favourite childhood stories to share with Gert, and I'll share them with Clover equally gladly. There are also illustrated books about the planets and stars. I'll have to wait some years before I can discuss those with her, or explain the constellations, or sit out at night, stargazing. Those daydreams I must fold away carefully for a year, or six.

I've only been away from Clover half an hour yet I miss her already. I abandon my task and find her in the parlour with Mama. Clover looks quaint and old-fashioned in an old blue dress of mine while Mama regales her with stories of my childhood. Mama, who is tall and dark-haired like me but far more beautiful, greets me with a sentimental look in her eye and I know that, already, Clover is as much a Westallen as Mama could ever wish for her to be.

We take Clover to explore; it will be some time before she learns all the corners of Polaris House, its many quirks and memories. It's an old house, built during the time when Hampstead was an isolated village on the edge of a windswept heath plagued by highwaymen. They used to hang them from a gallows between two elms on the high part of the heath and one of the Gibbet Elms still stands. It gives me a delighted shiver whenever I pass it. It's funny how we never want to *live* somewhere full of scoundrels, but we like to have a few lurking in the past.

Over the years, Mama has decorated the house in a modern style – we have cosy corners and a large white overmantel in the parlour and a stunning geometric mosaic floor in the hall – but the house still feels old. It has corridors that go up a few steps and then down again, for no reason that anyone can discern. It has odd little rooms in addition to the large and gracious ones that we use in the Victorian way. We cannot guess their original purpose and now, rather mundanely, we use them for storage. And it has the turret, where the telescopes are set up, Papa's fine naval one and my cherished childhood gift.

Mama lifts Clover to look out of a window and points at the weeping willow in the garden. 'Grandpapa brought me that tree from Japan. It was only a sapling then, a little tree. But we planted it here and you can see how it flourishes.'

'This ruby ring of mine comes from Peru,' I add when Clover is on her feet again. 'That's in South America and it's very far away.' The light of our stories dances in her hazel eyes. I have so many treasures I want to show her: an enormous umbrella of yellow-ochre silk from Paris; a giant blossom-pink seashell from the Caribbean; a mirror from India (my reflection is not much to celebrate but the carved, silver frame of elephants, tigers and snakes is something to behold!).

'Shall we go and disturb Grandpapa in his study?' suggests Mama. 'And he can tell you some of his adventures himself!' Clover nods enthusiastically.

We troop off to Papa's study and he humphs a great deal about how we are a terrible disturbance but his eyes are twinkling the while. He lifts Clover onto his lap and turns his globe, patiently showing her all the places he has been. Clover mostly seems to want to watch it spin.

When I was a girl, Papa went away on voyages for months on end. Perhaps that's why being a mother without a husband seems quite natural to me: for large parts of my childhood, my mother was in that very situation. When he was gone, we wrote him long letters together. We didn't post them, since we could not know where he might be. Instead, we saved them for him to read on his return, so he might know how much we missed him.

While he was away, we did not mope; Mama taught me to be useful – visiting the poor, aiding charitable endeavour – and she taught me to savour life. Walks, rides, food, music, literature . . . she let me take none of them for granted. If I adored my father, well, my mother is imprinted on me.

Then Papa would come home! He always returned laden with exotic treasures and stories and I knew I was the luckiest girl in the world, deeply rooted in my happy Hampstead home, yet able to travel and explore vicariously through Papa. Since he retired from sailing thirteen years ago, my father has been a steady and welcome presence at Polaris House. He bought a ship and then another and now he owns a fleet of trading vessels and is richer than ever. Heaven knows we don't need the money but it keeps his mind active and maintains his link to the sea. Besides which, he is a great philanthropist.

Rightly speaking, he should be *Mr* Westallen now, with his sailing days so far behind him. Yet such were his deeds, and so great is the respect in which everyone holds him, that he is still called Captain now, even though his shock of hair and beard are white. It suits him as no other title could. I was surprised he left the sea so young, for he was, and still is, hale and active. And he loves the ocean. But he said that seeing so much of the world and its wonders taught him best to value home, his wife and daughter.

'I've seen plenty of obstinate old sea dogs cling to life on the ocean until they were no more than gristle and bone and bad temper,' he said. 'I wanted to come back to you while I was still able to enjoy life on land.'

I'm glad Papa chose as he did. I only hope *he* feels he made the right decision. For sometimes I catch him staring into the fire with a look on his face that I simply cannot read, close as we are. Once in a while, he suffers a fit of melancholy, shutting himself away for days at a time, speaking to no one, saturnine. It troubles me, but then I reflect that I am like the devil incarnate for two days every month. Perhaps men, like women, have rhythms and tides. Perhaps people are not meant to be always even, but to crest and plunge like the patterns of nature.

When Mama deems that we have interrupted Papa long enough, we head next to the kitchen. Mrs Brody asks if Clover would like to bake biscuits. Delightful suggestion! Clover and I take the lesson together. We are each as unpractised as the other when it comes to tackling a stove and soon we are both covered in flour.

Mabs

'**M**rs Finch,' called Mabs. 'I've got your tea. Won't you let me in before it gets cold?' But Mrs Finch did not care about tea, she realised. That had only been a ruse to get rid of her. Mabs felt a right idiot.

She spent a while knocking on the door and talking through it. 'I know it's a big change, 'avin' someone new around. I know I'm very different to what yer used to. Only please, ma'am, give me a chance. Let me in. Please, ma'am, I'm just tryin' to do my job . . .'

After twenty minutes of intermittent knocking and pleading, Mabs became worried. What if Mrs Finch had done something terrible? What if she wasn't answering because she couldn't? Were her moods worse than her husband had ever thought, or admitted? Her first instinct was to go to the kitchen; there was a warm atmosphere down there and she felt sure they would help. But then she remembered what Mr Finch had said during her interview, that she should discuss his wife's condition with no one but him. Her heart sank. She didn't want to admit to the man who had employed her that it was all, already, going horribly wrong. But what choice did she have?

She hurried downstairs, trying to accept that she might be seeing her last of this lovely house. Even if he didn't blame her, Mr Finch was unlikely to keep on someone to whom his wife had taken such an obvious and thorough dislike; where would be the sense in that? Every step felt like a sigh. She admired the polished bannisters, the decorative coving, the lovely oil paintings on the robin's-egg walls. Heart sinking, she knocked on the parlour door.

A man's voice answered; Mabs squared her thin shoulders and went in. To her embarrassment, it wasn't Mr Finch at all, it was a gentleman who would look very like him in thirty years' time. He was talking with a beautiful young woman who, disconcertingly, was the absolute spit of Mrs Finch.

'Oh, I'm sorry!' exclaimed Mabs. She was putting her foot in it left, right and centre. 'I was lookin' for yer father. But he's at work, I suppose. Silly me. I'm so sorry to disturb.'

But the young Finches waved away her concerns. 'Please don't worry yourself,' said the son, rising to greet her. 'You must be Daley, am I right?'

'Yes, sir, thank you, sir.'

He shook her hand. 'I'm Charlie Finch and this is my sister, Elfrida.'

Mabs bobbed a curtsey. 'Good morning, sir, miss.'

'Hello, Daley. Welcome to number six,' said Elfrida. 'You arrived yesterday, didn't you?'

'Yes, miss, thank you. I feel very lucky to be here. Beg pardon, *is* your father at home?'

'As a matter of fact, he is,' said Charlie. 'I'll take you. Back in a mo, Freds.'

Mabs curtseyed again and scurried after Charlie Finch.

Mr Finch was in his study. Charlie announced her, then bid them cheerio. Her employer looked up mildly. 'Miss Daley. How are you settling in?'

'Very well, sir, thank you. Everyone's been so kind. My room is very comfortable.'

'Good, good. Then let me guess. You seek me out because of some difficulty with my wife.'

Mabs became aware that she was fidgeting and tried to stop. 'I'm so sorry, sir. I 'ate to tell tales, only it is a little hard, and you said not to discuss it with anyone else . . .'

'I did indeed. I'm pleased you remembered. There's a world of difference between telling tales and having a constructive conversation in a difficult situation. Tell me so I can help.' He smiled reassuringly.

Mabs was mortified, but there was no good way of putting it. 'She's locked me out, sir.'

'Pardon me?'

'She sent me to fetch tea, sir, and when I got back, the door was locked. I've been knocking and calling to her, for ever such a long time. Only, she wouldn't answer and I didn't know what else to do. I started worrying, in case, in case . . .'

'You're quite right, Miss Daley. With a delicate nature such as my wife's it's always best to err on the side of caution. I'm sorry you've had such a poor welcome. But please don't worry, it won't always be like this. I'll go and have a word now. It hasn't given you second thoughts about the role, has it?'

'Oh *no*, sir, of course not, only I was worried *you* might wish to find someone she could take to more easily.'

'She would be this way with *anyone*, I assure you. She's so unhappy about the whole situation, you see – the move, the very fact of her illness. It's hard for all of us to accept her decline. But I believe you'll do wonders for her, in time, Miss Daley. We must all be patient, compassionate, even in the face of some very upsetting behaviour. Can you do that?'

'Oh, I can, sir, yes. So long as I know I'm still wanted here, sir, then I can be as patient as you like!'

He smiled that lovely warm smile and stood up. 'Let's go and see her together.'

They climbed the stairs. 'You've met Charlie,' said Mr Finch. 'What about the rest of my brood?'

'I've met Miss Elfrida, sir.'

'Not Otty? Or Averil?'

'No, sir.'

'Why don't you come back to my study later? Just before seven. You can let me know if your day improves and I'll have the girls pop in and say hello. Then you'll know the whole roost!'

'Yes, sir, that's very kind.'

'Good. Well, here we are then.' They were standing outside the mistress's door. Mr Finch tried the door but it was still locked.

'Abigail, my dear, it's me. Let me in, please.'

An almighty crash made them jump as something was hurled at the door. The mistress wasn't dead, then!

'Abigail, dearest. You know how sorry I am about all this. Let me in now and let us talk reason. Miss Daley is here with me and she wishes to care for you. Things *will* get better, I promise.'

Mabs marvelled at his even tone, his loving words, his optimism. The man was a saint! To her astonishment, the key turned in the lock. Mrs Finch stood in the doorway, lips quivering, a quite unreadable look in her fine dark eyes. Shards of cream china littered the dark blue carpet.

'Ah, your washbasin,' sighed Mr Finch. 'A shame. Miss Daley, you'll find a dustpan and brush in that cupboard. Please clear up the mess and take great care not to cut yourself. It can be dashed hard to get all the fine fragments and they're painful if they get under the skin.'

'Yes, sir.' Mabs dared a glance at Mrs Finch who was looking at her with such contempt that Mabs thought she might wilt from it. She was glad to set to the task, which had her looking minutely at the carpet and not at her mistress.

Was it a regular occurrence then, this hurling of objects? It must be, for items like a dustpan and brush to be kept in a lady's bedroom, for Mr Finch to be so conversant with the qualities of broken china. Of course, it was better than the canals, better than labouring by the fetid green water, soaked in blood, sweat and blisters, wearing her brother's trousers. All the same, there was something unsettling about the atmosphere in this room. The woman's pain sat heavy on the air, unexplained and dangerous.

As Mabs worked, she kept her back to the Finches but, of course, she could still hear their every word.

'My dear, I did tell you that Daley was coming.' Mr Finch spoke in soothing tones. 'I hope you'll give her a chance. She's a compassionate young woman who wishes to do her best. I know you feel you've lost a great deal but the house is well appointed, the new staff are excellent people and my job at the canal is all that I had hoped.'

The canal! thought Mabs. *Fancy that.*

'We can have a wonderful life here, Abigail. We only have to get you well first.'

She spoke through gritted teeth, in a voice that was quiet and forceful. 'I have told you before, Lucius. I am not *unwell*. There is nothing wrong with me.'

'Abigail, darling, you locked your companion out of your room on her very first day. You smashed a brand-new china basin in a fit of pique. In front of a stranger!'

'I did not know that she was with you.'

'Your temper is not even. You were once so proud, so dignified. You will be yourself again, my dear, I am certain of it. I trust you will let Miss Daley attend you in future? No more locked doors?'

'If you insist.'

'So if I send her now to fetch you a new wash bowl, you'll admit her when she returns?'

'Yes.'

'Splendid. All done, Miss Daley? Then take the detritus down to the kitchen and ask Mrs Webb to find a replacement.'

Mabs got to her feet, the dustpan brimming. 'Would you like me to bring more tea, ma'am?' Mrs Finch shook her head, not looking at Mabs.

'Have you eaten breakfast, my dear? Has she eaten breakfast?' Mr Finch asked Mabs when his wife didn't answer.

'No, sir.'

'Then order something light while you're down there. Don't wait for it, one of the girls will bring it up. It's important that she eats, to keep her strength up, to keep her on an even keel.'

'Yes, sir.'

As Mabs left the room, she heard him give a heavy sigh. How difficult it must be to deal with her kindly day after day, Mabs thought. She was his *wife*! A sudden flash of how her mother and father had been together popped into her head. Her mother working as a laundress, while her father laboured on the wharves, the two of them meeting at home, exhausted. Maureen Daley had never had a red lacquer tray or a soft blue carpet yet Mabs never once saw her mother sigh or pout. Her parents held hands, and hugged, and Pa used to say that Ma was his homefire. Mabs had to stop for a moment, dizzy with homesickness for her family, the way it used to be.

Olive

Motherhood is strange and intense. I attend to Clover with a clarity that makes me feel as if I've been sleep-walking my whole life before. We eat together, bathe together, drink tea with my parents together and I spend hours reading to her. I can't let her out of my sight. Her well-being is my raison d'etre and yet, *beyond* motherhood, I feel . . . aimless. I have the feeling there is something else I need to attend to in life – I'm just not sure what it *is*, consumed as I am with motherly love. I find myself longing for Parliament Hill.

It has long been a favourite place of mine, somewhere I go regularly for inspiration, or to lift my spirits when they dip low. They are not low now and yet . . . I've undergone a big change in my life – the very *biggest*, in truth. The unease that has tickled me each time I've realised how unprepared I am for Clover – the wrong clothes, the wrong toys, the wrong bedroom – escalates into a liberal terror and suddenly I feel a great need to contemplate my actions beneath a canopy of stars.

Usually Papa accompanies me on these expeditions, lest I run into any or all of the dangers awaiting a woman alone on the heath at night. If Papa will not, one of the servants often indulges me. The skies are clear, after days of rain; I could go tonight! I know Mama will sit with Clover so that if she wakes, she won't be alone.

Mama agrees readily. Papa is not so helpful; he has a cold brewing and does not wish to sit out on a chilly night. It is reasonable, I suppose. I wander to the kitchen to plead with our staff and eventually persuade Anne to be my escort. At first, she is reluctant. She has a new sweetheart – the seventh, at least, since we've known her – and he's taking her to dine in the Bird in Hand tonight. I pointed out that if she were to escort me, *he* really should escort us both, and then she could spend longer with him. A solution for all!

At half past ten they return from dinner and I join them, happily unembarrassed to be a gooseberry. When I was eighteen I would have hated such a situation. Being unmarried at eight-and-twenty has inured me. I wish to see the stars.

I have a tarpaulin sheet folded under my arm so that we may sit without getting damp and muddy bottoms. I also carry a large flask of hot cocoa and a small one of brandy, hoping these will reconcile Anne and Colin to their involvement in my odd whims. I walk at a brisk pace, allowing them to follow behind and continue their private conversation.

We breast Parliament Hill where the bowl of the heavens is poised above, tipping out stars, tipping out wonder. I spread the tarp and fling myself down at one end of it, setting the flasks behind me so the others can help themselves, and immerse myself in the contemplation of infinity. I'm dimly aware of the sweethearts seating themselves at the other end, of murmured endearments and the unscrewing of flasks. I feel a twinge for the romance that has never come my way, or at least, not for more than two or three weeks at a time on rare occasions. This has been the sorry sum of my sentimental life.

Well, I have not come out to moon (witticism intended)

over suitors lost. I have come to think about Clover and all the adventures we shall have together. I stretch my legs out and rest back on my elbows, turn my face up to the starlight the way people do to the sun. Idly I trace the pattern of Orion with my eyes, and follow it towards my favourite constellation, Gemini: the twins, the Dioscuri, the patrons of sailors. *Thank you, Castor. Thank you, Polydeuces*, I murmur in the privacy of my own head. I shall not alarm Anne and Colin by talking to stars in front of them.

Seeing the twins makes me think of another inseparable pair. My father once had a best friend, as close as a brother, called Malvern Blythe. Their fathers were both financiers who wanted their sons to follow in their footsteps. Malvern obliged, while Papa ran off to sea. The wide world called to him and he was always headstrong; he wonders where I get it from! Malvern followed soon after and the two shared many adventures. I remember our families dining together when I was young.

Then it was all over. They had a great, great falling-out and, though it's unlike Papa to hold a grudge, they have never spoken since. A state of feud reigns. He has never told me or Mama the reason. All I know is that we are the richest family in Hampstead and the Blythes are our counterpart in Highgate. Both families are supremely thankful for the wide expanse of heath between us and if we were ever to be cordial again, it would be an ice-cold day in hell.

The sight of a trillion scintillating stars eases my mind. The feuds of men, the fact that I have a small daughter, the fact that I could not save Gert, all acquire a different aspect out here. The sun and moon rise and set every day. The stars wheel, holding in place patterns and symbols that have guided us for thousands of years. Impossible that the power that achieves this made a mistake when it sent Clover to me instead of Gert. It can certainly guide me through motherhood.

I blow out a gusty sigh. The world is so *big*. Within it, my life is as privileged as is possible. Not only the wealth and luxury, but the freedoms granted me by my parents. They are bastions of society, and yet, in this oh-so-conventional world of ours, they allow me to be Olive. I'm aware that all the things I have done that make my life worthwhile – schooling, philanthropy, my daughter – would not have been possible with different parents. What would my life have been then?

I lie back flat, feeling dizzy for a moment. The heavens are vast and unfathomable. The affairs of men are as multitudinous and microscopic as ants. And somewhere in between, there is a middle level, neither personal nor divine. It is the law. Society. The bigger structure within which we mortals toil. And it is very, vastly flawed. I think of our divorced neighbour, Julia Morrow, shunned and lonely, all because she decided to end a marriage in which she was the victim of heartbreaking brutality. I think of the limited opportunities available to women who want or need to work. I think of the fact that a woman cannot have a bank account, or vote for government. I think of Mr Miles, haring off to rescue the ladies of the night at the docks.

I've long known that I am protected from the harsher realities of life because I'm rich. I am protected, too, from the harsher realities of being a woman because I have a father who would never, ever abuse his legal rights over me or my mother. But what of those women who don't have a Captain James Westallen to champion them? Clover is a little girl now but she will grow up. I have to consider what kind of world I want her to live in and what sort of mother I wish to be. What do I want to teach her about being a woman?

I want to leave her a legacy, I realise. I don't mean the material sort – that is assured – but something else . . . Something that will also give me purpose and self-expression. The stars float in silver inscrutability, watching over a world in which we cannot, ultimately, control what happens, and yet are beholden to try our best and do what we can. Being a mother makes me feel as if my coat has been removed and I feel the chill to my bones. My parents, myself, Clover, we all exist in the great transit of past to future. I know now that I must play my part in making a better world for her to live in – though precisely *how* I might do that remains shady.

Mabs

Mabs couldn't sleep. She lay in her pleasant attic room, but her mind still haunted that other apartment on the floor below. Its stifling atmosphere clung to Mabs like January fog. It had been an extraordinary first day. From Mrs Finch's unbearable manners, to the locked door and the smashed basin. The hours had dragged, broken only by Lydia bringing up boiled eggs and toast for breakfast and, later, mushroom soup with soft bread for lunch. The mistress ignored both meals. Mabs tried to encourage her to eat, remembering Mr Finch's concern that she should do so. In response, Mrs Finch lobbed a hard-boiled egg directly at Mabs. Mabs was taken by surprise; it caught her on the chin. Mabs had known far worse hurts but this was so unexpected and humiliating that her eyes smarted and she didn't know where to look or what to say. Throughout the afternoon, she made valiant attempts to converse with Mrs Finch but all were rebuffed.

What will I do if I can't win her over? How long a chance will he give me? What will I do if I have to go home and they won't take me back at the canal? The questions kept her tossing and turning well beyond midnight.

Eventually she jumped from her bed and looked out of the window onto a clear, star-strewn night. Through the darkness, she could discern the street and the houses opposite, jagged scraps of gardens. The sharp bark of a fox rang out. *It was only the first day*, she told herself. *It has to get better.*

She'd seen Mr Finch at seven as planned, and had to admit to him that she and her mistress had sat inside the same four walls, in their separate worlds, from the start to the finish of the day. He reassured her once more. It wasn't personal. Things would improve. He didn't seem disappointed in her at all. But surely, fretted Mabs, padding back to bed, it was only a matter of time.

The two youngest Finches had stopped in to say hello. Miss Averil was a young lady of nineteen. In looks she took after her father, although on her, his chestnut hair was taken to an extreme shade – a bright, carroty orange. She had wide grey eyes and a round face that wasn't beautiful and yet somehow *was*. She had an ease about her, an open gaze and sparkling eyes.

The youngest, Ottilie, was another cast in the dark-haired, creamy-complexioned mould of their mother and sister, but she hadn't quite grown into her looks yet. Only twelve years old, she was awkward and kept bumping into things. Her eager eyes seemed too big in her face. She had a determined brow and showered Mabs with a dozen questions, prompting her father to exclaim an apology. She was a dear, thought Mabs.

Next, she had found Mrs Webb, who had made good on her promise to talk Mabs through the household. Mabs's working day was to be from eight until seven. A long day, but not as long as some. She would have no formal breaks during the day, but as well as having every Sunday off she would have a half day on Wednesdays too. Many servants would envy her.

Mabs would never have thought her job at the wharf had anything to recommend it but she learned now that there was one thing: she could always, always sleep after a day at work. She used to get home so physically exhausted she could hardly undress. Now she lay in a clean cotton nightgown in a comfortable bed and she was tired all right, but in such a different way.

When she went down the following morning, Mrs Finch was already dressed, in a lustrous navy-blue gown. Her dark hair was piled up and a pearl brooch sat at her throat. Mabs wanted to compliment her but didn't dare.

'Good morning, ma'am,' she said brightly.

Mrs Finch flew across the room and gripped her by both arms, her fingers digging in painfully and her face gazing into Mabs's with startling intensity. 'I understand you gave my husband a full report of our hours together last night. Let us see what entertainment we can provide for him today.' Mabs pulled away as far as she could but Mrs Finch held her fast. 'Yes,' she hissed, giving Mabs a little shake. 'He came to see me first thing this morning, to tell me how vexed I make him. It must be quite the highlight of your day, running to him with the tales of my misbehaviour.'

'Mrs Finch, I'm sorry, I'm not sure what I done wrong. Mr Finch is my employer. He asked how we got on yesterday. I told 'im the truth is all.' Mabs was too deprived of sleep to tread carefully. Her eyes felt gummy and sore. To her relief, her mistress let go of her at last.

Mrs Finch gave her a considering look. 'You're entirely my husband's creature then. No dash of loyalty to your mistress in your conscience.' She said it flatly.

Mabs sighed. It seemed today was to be hard in a different way. Today Mrs Finch was ready to talk but Mabs couldn't understand her.

'But 'ow could there be? Beg pardon, ma'am, but you've

said not two words to me since we met. You locked me out yesterday! I 'ad to tell someone, didn't I? I was worried you'd hurt yerself! And last night he asked about me day. I didn't want to lie and make it seem like I was getting on better than I am. I'm sorry to speak so plain, ma'am, only if you was me, what would *you* have done?'

There was a long pause. Then she turned her back on Mabs and returned to her place at the window.

After that, the day was just like the first. Mabs tried to chatter, Mrs Finch ignored her. Lydia brought them their meals; Mrs Finch ate little. Mabs tried to coax her and Mrs Finch flung a glass of port at the wall. 'God in heaven, you really are as stupid as you look and sound,' she cried in a voice of anguished frustration. Mabs cleared up the broken glass but spent longer trying to soak the dark stains out of the cream carpet. Eventually she ate her own lunch, now cold, sitting on a chair in the corner of the room, struggling to balance the dish and cutlery. She could only imagine the picture she looked; probably her table manners were horrible at the best of times. For once she was glad her mistress wouldn't look at her.

By mid-afternoon, Mabs felt chilly. She offered to light a fire. No reply. She asked if Mrs Finch wanted a shawl. No reply. The autumn wind picked up and shook the windowpane. Elegant as the room was, it was draughty. Mabs noticed that her mistress was shivering. This was stupid! It would help neither one of them to catch cold.

She opened the wardrobe door, aware of those dark eyes following her as she did so. A rainbow seemed to burst out and Mabs hastily closed it; it felt too intimate, somehow, to see the gowns this woman had worn in a life she was now mourning. She tried a drawer. Worse! Undergarments! She slammed it shut. At last she found a pile of folded shawls, and selected one in shades of yellow and orange, hoping to bring a little sunshine into the gloomy room.

Mrs Finch looked at Mabs as if she were offering her a slop bucket. So Mabs wrapped it around her mistress's shoulders, arranging the ends to cover the cold white hands that lay in her lap. Then she set a fire. She was freezing, and she certainly wasn't going to borrow a shawl. When she'd got the fire going good and strong, she pulled her chair up close to it.

'Well,' said Mrs Finch at last. It was the first word she'd said in seven hours and Mabs jumped. Lord, she'd never been so nervy at the canal. 'Now that we're nice and cosy, and seeing as we are stuck with each other, I suppose it would be as well to pass the time a little more quickly.'

'Yes, Mrs Finch, yes indeed!' said Mabs, delighted.

'Why don't you read to me? I'm in the mood for something rich and tragic. *Tess of the D'Urbervilles*, perhaps, or maybe some Eliot. Fetch something from the shelf.'

'Oh ma'am.' There was no quantifying the dread Mabs felt at the answer she would have to give. The first concession from her mistress, the *very first*, and she was going to disappoint. 'I'm so sorry, ma'am, but I can't read.' She wanted to sink through the floor when she saw the contempt on the other woman's face.

'Oh, for heaven's sake! A companion who can't *read*! *Truly?*'

'I'm sorry, ma'am, I didn't fib to get the position. I did tell Mr Finch.'

'I'm sure. And yet he chose you still. How then are we to pass the hours, my companion and I? *In conversation?*' Her tone was full of derision.

'Well, yes, ma'am, if you like. I mean, why not?'

She gave a brittle laugh. 'What do you foresee, Daley? The

two of us with our heads together exchanging confidences of the heart? I don't think so.'

Mabs fumed. Of all the arrogant, superior *bitches*! So, Mabs wasn't good enough to talk to? So, the very thought that a gentlewoman like Mrs Finch might take any pleasure in the company of someone like Mabs was laughable? Mabs could think of a thing or two to say to *her*! But she swallowed them all down. It wasn't personal. Mabs was to be patient. It was her job to find a way to exist beside this dreadful woman. Silence fell over the room once more.

Otty

My day to visit Jill has come around at last. And I am relieved to be out of the house! Every Sunday we have a family lunch at one on the dot; Papa insists upon it. And every Sunday it is torture.

Mama always appears, fully dressed and beautiful, and it's wonderful to have her among us again. But she's always very quiet. Elfrida sulks and flounces as though she's angry with Mama. I know she wanted to stay in Durham but surely if she must blame anyone, it should be Papa, for it is his job that brought us here. Averil is sensitive to such undercurrents and toys with her food. Charlie laments how he misses Felicia and stares at his fork as if he would like to stab himself with it.

Only Papa and I make the effort to be cheerful. He speaks of his job managing investments at the canals and of the notable people of the area whom he would like to meet; Papa is always very keen to meet people who can advance him. I chatter on about my explorations and how lucky we are to be here, until one of my siblings, usually my sister Elfrida, snaps at me to, 'Stop! Just stop!'

Released, I make my way to the corner of Helpman Street where I promised to meet Jill. She's not dressed in her boys' clothes today. She's wearing a dress and a bonnet. I can tell at once that they are very cheap. I wonder if I appear very grand to her. It's a funny thought, when Papa aspires so desperately to *be* grand.

'Hello, Jill!' I beam. 'You look very pretty today.'

She smiles. 'Thanks, Otty. You too. You came!'

'Of course!' I had wondered if *she* would! I worry that I might seem young and silly to her. For a minute we stand looking at each other with pleased expressions. It's funny how sometimes you know someone before you know them. 'Would you like to go to a tea room?' I ask.

'No indeed,' she says. 'I come with an invitation to take tea at my place.'

'Why, Jill! I'd be delighted.'

'It's not much, mind you. Don't you be disappointed now.'

'Impossible!' I claim rashly. Provided it's somewhere I can ask her a million questions, I shall be perfectly happy.

As we walk, we talk of simple things and I try not to notice the odd looks we attract. Jill, I learn, is an only child, an orphan. She never knew her father and her mother died two years ago. She comes from a small town called Layou, which is on an island called St Vincent, which floats in the Caribbean Sea. My schoolgirl geography fails me. I cannot imagine a place so far away.

'Why did you come to London?' I wonder.

'To look for work,' she says. I'm confused. If I needed to work, I'm sure I wouldn't travel halfway across the world alone only to labour somewhere where I had to pretend to be a boy. But Elfrida says I'm nosy, so I don't question her.

Jill leads me along streets that grow narrower and narrower. I see several faces – not many, but a few – that are dark like hers. Even more people are looking at us now. In fact, though

I have worn only a very ordinary brown skirt and bodice, they are looking at me. I stay close to Jill.

'Never come alone to visit me,' she says over her shoulder. 'Always meet me somewhere respectable.'

I nod. It's like the canals: not safe for me. Is it safe for *her*, then? I'm not sure it can be, but she seems very sure of herself as she hurries along.

'This is me,' she says at last, stopping at a wooden door that is scratched and faded. The bricks of the house are blackened and unwelcoming. There's a nasty smell in the air – I'm not sure what it is. I search for something nice to say.

'Gosh, what a large house you have.'

'I don't have it. I have a room in it.'

'Oh,' I say as she ushers me in. We climb some stairs, then more and more. We're puffing as we reach the top of the house.

'In fact,' she says, pausing, 'I don't have the whole room, I share it.'

'Oh!' I say again. 'It must be fun to live with a friend.'

Jill pulls a face. 'She no friend of mine. I'm just tellin' you, in case she home.'

We go inside and immediately see a skinny brown girl with an angry face and a fuzz of hair scraped up into a very tall knot on top of her head. I can see at once that she would look prettier if she wore it loose, like Jill, but I'm also fairly certain that she's the sort of girl who doesn't care about pretty. When she sees me she rounds on Jill with an outraged look.

'What the matter with you, Jill Joseph? Why you bring a white girl here? Don't we have enough o' them everywhere else?'

'Hush your talk, Maggie Dupont, this here is my friend, and if you object 'cause o' the colour of her skin, you're as bad as *them*.' Jill cocks her head sideways, to indicate the general population of London.

'It not the same,' snarls Maggie. 'It not the same thing at all.'

'It's *exactly* the same thing,' says Jill calmly. 'Otty is staying for tea. You welcome to join us if you can keep a civil tongue in your head.'

Maggie seems speechless, taking little shallow breaths as if there are so many things she'd like to say she can't decide where to start. Then she growls, flounces out and slams the door behind her. We hear her feet thudding down the stairs.

Jill shrugs. 'Don't you mind her, Otty, she sour as a grapefruit. Now, let me welcome you to me humble home.' She giggles. 'And it is *very* humble.'

I can't contradict her. The room has bare floorboards with two piles of blankets, one at either end. I think they must be where Jill and Maggie sleep. I see a table and two chairs. There's a wash tub with some grey water in it in a corner and a line is strung across the ceiling of another corner with some garments hanging from it: a dress; a chemise; some bloomers.

'Oh!' Jill sees where my eyes are drifting and snatches them down, throws them onto one of the piles of blankets. 'Not the sort of thing at all to have when company coming. That blasted Maggie.'

'She didn't know I was coming,' I say. 'Don't worry, Jill, I don't mind. We all wear them.'

'You're sweet. But do *you* greet your guests with wet undergarments hanging in your house? I don't think so.'

I go to the small window and cry out in genuine pleasure. 'Oh Jill! We're so high up. Look, it's *London*!' The views from our house are pretty, this one is *fascinating*. I gaze over crooked rooftops and winding alleys like tricksy lengths of string; I see cracked, cloudy windows, ancient eaves and tiny glimpses of a hundred lives. 'If I lived here, I would look out of the window all the time and make up stories . . .'

I expect Jill to scoff at me, as my sisters do, but she looks at me eagerly. 'You like stories? Have you read *Jane Eyre*?'

I feel my eyes widen. 'Have *you*?'

She glares at me. 'You think because of the colour of my skin I can't read?'

'No. I thought because you work on the canals maybe you couldn't. My mother's companion, Miss Daley, used to work there because she can't read. She said if she could, she would have gone somewhere else.'

Jill's eyes soften. 'Sorry. I'm touchy as that damn Maggie. I can read and write. I know my numbers. Only the reason *I* can't get better work is because of this.' She touches her face. 'Anyway, this is not teatime talk. So. *Jane Eyre*?'

'Yes, of course. I adore it. Only I think Mr Rochester is too grumpy. I prefer a man to be cheerful and smiling, like my father.'

Jill grins and wraps her arms around herself, fluttering her eyelashes. 'Me, I'd like a fine gentleman like that, all stormy and passionate. But you, you too young to be thinking about men.'

I laugh. 'Thank goodness! What's for tea, Jill? If I'd known I was visiting, I would have brought something.' I wish I *had* known. I would have brought flowers to cheer up this dismal place, or a box of chocolates the two of them could share. Maybe they'd sweeten Maggie up a bit!

A kettle sits on the floor. There is no stove, or fire, or tap. Jill picks it up and lays her hand on the side. 'Ah,' she sighs with a blissful expression. 'Still warm.' She places it on the table and fetches two cups. They don't match. 'You take the pink one, Otty, it's my favourite. And look! A treat!' She opens a paper bag containing what turns out to be two sticky buns. 'I hope you like them.'

'I love them!' I beam. 'Thank you, Jill. Um . . . how do you make the tea?'

'I don't. We can't. I do miss a nice steaming pot in the afternoon. But our neighbour at the end of the street, she has a stove. I ran down there and begged a hot kettle just before I came to meet you and it's still warm. I'm afraid I can't offer you milk and sugar as I have neither. I hope you can drink it black.'

I blink. 'Goodness, Jill. You went to so much trouble.' I think of her toiling up all those stairs an extra time to bring home hot tea. I take a big bite of one of the buns. It's very stale. 'Mmmm! Lovely. And I prefer my tea black.' That, at least, is true.

She lays her hand on the table and I try not to stare at how rough it is, with broken nails and a nasty blister. 'I miss a nice table too,' she says. 'I would have liked a white cloth for our tea, Otty, linens for our laps, perhaps some flowers. Ah well, another place, another time.'

We munch our way through stale buns and sip at lukewarm tea, in Jill's strange, sad home, and we might be two children playing at tea parties. There's an air of pretending a different world about us. When we finish we stay, elbows on table, chins propped on hands, and talk.

'I bet your house not much like this,' says Jill with that grin that means I just can't help smiling too.

'Not much,' I admit.

'I bet it has a wide hallway and many rooms. I bet it has a garden and fine furniture and paintings on the walls.'

I nod that it has all those things.

'And a wide veranda all around, with a door you can leave open to hear the swish of the palms and the sound of the sea, and ceiling fans to keep you cool . . .'

I laugh. 'Now you're thinking of *your* old home, aren't you? If *we* leave the windows open, we hear the swish of rain . . .'

'I am, yes.' She tells me about it. White beaches and blue waves, coconuts and mangoes growing on trees. I have never tasted either but their names alone promise heavenly flavour. She tells me about the boys who scramble up the trees and shake the fruits down and the old men who row into the waves every morning in small, pointed fishing boats, half filled with clouds of net, and the women who wrap their heads against the heat of the day and sing low, sweet harmonies while they work. I sit entranced, as though hearing a story.

When it's my turn I complain about lovelorn Charlie, haughty Elfrida and weepy Averil. She hoots at their foibles, on my side just because she is my friend. I need that. I tell her about Mama's mysterious illness and she says kind things, even though she's lost her own mother. I tell her that my explorations will come to an end after Christmas because I'll have to start school and she clucks her tongue sympathetically. When it's time for me to leave, she walks me back to Helpman Street to see me safe.

'You wouldn't be able to go to a tea room, would you?' I ask when we're about to say goodbye. I'm young but I'm not stupid. I've never seen a person who looks like Jill in a tea room.

'I could go in,' she says, 'but they might not let me stay. Most likely not. And if they did, I would not feel comfortable. Do you know what it's like, Otty, to be somewhere where every head turns to look at you as if you're a curiosity, or worse?'

I don't, of course, and I don't imagine I'd like it one bit.

'Then where shall we go next time?' I wonder. 'You've already treated me once, it'll be my turn.'

'I'm happy for you to take tea with me any Sunday you like. I like you, Otty Finch, you a smart girl. And if nothing else, it'll make Maggie roundly mad. I always enjoy that.'

Mabs

Mabs had had high hopes for her time off, imagining rushing home in her uniform, full of tales, her family flabbergasted by this new, smart Mabs. But on Wednesday afternoon the gulf between her daydreams and reality stopped her. They weren't expecting her and she had no good news to impart.

So she explored Hampstead instead, enraptured but wistful. It was only a few miles from Saffron Hill, where Mabs had lived all her life, and from the wharf where she used to work – no great distance at all – and yet, it was a different world. Mabs was fascinated by the front doors: the gleaming paint-work, the whimsical knockers, the spotless steps. *What's behind that green basement door?* she wondered. *Who lives in that pretty little terrace with the dipping roofs? Who's in the grand house with the stained-glass windows?* It was easy to imagine nothing could ever go wrong behind such charming facades, but she already knew from the Finches' home that *that* wasn't true.

On Sunday she *had* to go home, because she'd promised. She wore her old dress because she felt like old Mabs – useless and close to disaster at all times. The rain kept coming in stops and starts and it was a thoroughly bedraggled Mabs that turned up in Mushroom Court that morning. She climbed the rickety stairs with mixed feelings, longing to see her family but dreading having to put on a cheerful face.

She paused at the door, resting her head against the wooden frame for a minute, then she went in. Nicky sprang to his feet, belligerent, until he recognised his sister. 'Mabs!' He flew across the room, transforming from protector of the family to little brother in an instant. His bear hug sent the pair of them staggering across the wooden floor.

'Nicky, you idiot,' laughed Mabs. 'I'm pleased to see you too, but give a girl a chance to get through the door, would you?'

She looked around, unbuttoning her coat, as one sibling after another launched themselves at her. 'Where's Pa?' It was always a fearful question since Ma died.

'It's all right, Mabs,' Jenny reassured her. 'He's just popped out for something for our lunch. He's been working all week and he wanted to get something special.'

'All week? Really?'

'Yes, if you can believe it. He's on the grain, over at Camden. Long hours but he's been coming straight home and bringing the money.'

'Well! That's proper good news to come 'ome to. I can't tell you how pleased I am,' said Mabs, untangling Angie's arms from around her knees and lifting her to look at her properly. After the Finches, the first thing she saw was how thin and dirty they all were. It wasn't news, but the contrast! However, they were no worse than the last time she'd seen them and there were smiles on their faces.

'Mabs, why ain't you wearing a pretty dress?' asked Peg, disappointed. 'I thought you'd be all smart now as you're a lady.'

Suddenly Mabs felt ashamed of her decision to come in sackcloth and ashes. She wanted to cheer them up after all. 'I'm not a lady, you daft 'apeth, I'm just a servant, but I do have a smart uniform. I didn't want to spoil it by wearing it on me day off but it's silly really. I'll wear it next week.'

'What colour is it?' Peg asked avidly.

Ah, she's gettin' to that age, thought Mabs. 'It's black,' she said and laughed at Peg's crestfallen face. 'I know, love, not the most romantic of colours. But remember, I'm just workin' over in Hampstead, not goin' to balls and livin' the high life. It's very smart, with white trimming and shiny buttons. I'll wear it next time, I promise.'

'What's in there, Mabsy?' asked Jem, poking the bag she carried, with a boy's unerring instinct for edible goods. Mrs Derring had given her a beautiful yellow pound cake and a small caddy of Mrs Finch's special India tea. Mabs hadn't the heart to tell her they had no way to brew it.

'Oh, some lovely tea,' Mabs teased him, holding out the tin. 'All the way from India it is.'

Six faces fell. '*Tea?*' Jem scoffed. 'Unless it's made of solid gold, I don't see what's so special about that!'

'But what about *this*?' said Mabs, setting the fragrant cake on the table. 'Mrs Derring – she's the cook – baked it special for us.' She smiled at the excited exclamations and looked around. The room was shadowy, overcrowded and as shabby as her dress. Same as ever.

'Oi!' she cried when she saw Matt stuff a chunk of cake into his mouth with his bare hands. 'Stop that! We're savin' this for after lunch. We'll cut it nice and have it together, Matt Daley!'

But Matt was busy chewing, a blissful expression on his face, while the others picked the crumbs off the table like pigeons in Trafalgar Square. Mabs couldn't blame them. She remembered how hungry she used to be all the time. A week of three meals a day was already changing her, making her stronger. She fetched a knife and cut off a small piece for each of them. 'To keep you going till lunch,' she said. It was too much to expect them to wait.

Peg fetched plates and set out half a spud each from the stall along the way, then Pa came home with a cabbage, a small ham and a bottle of elderflower wine.

'Mabs, girl!' he cried. 'How are yer, lass? Let me look at you.'

Mabs hugged him, overjoyed. He sounded just like himself again. 'I'm well, Pa. And you? The children say yer workin'.'

'I'm all right, love. Back to it this week. Bloody knackered, if I'm honest. But it's good to 'ave the wage. It's you, love, getting that job, that's had the effect on me. It's made me want to do me bit again. Having one less mouth to feed, knowing you'll help out with a coin or two when you can . . . well, it's made a difference, if you know what I mean.'

'I'm glad, Pa. That's good!'

Tomorrow, she was going to try harder than ever. They were all depending on her. Incentive for Pa, cake for the boys, the promise of seeing a new dress for Peg . . . and that was merely the start of what she wanted to give them.

❖

But her second week was just as excruciating as the first. Mabs tried everything she could think of to endear herself to her new mistress. When she discussed things with Mr Finch, she didn't lie, but didn't emphasise how difficult it was either, in the hope that somehow Mrs Finch would sense that Mabs was being loyal to her too. During her working hours, she alternated between sympathetic appeals, cheery chatter and supportive silence. Sometimes she sat quietly and patiently; sometimes she bustled round with a duster and some polish. But far from appearing to take any pleasure in Mabs's presence, Mrs Finch gave no sign that she was even resigned to it. She spent most of her time staring out over the garden, which was still nothing more than a stark tangle of bloomless branches. Mabs asked if it was a rose garden, and received a scornful glance and a dismissive nod in response. She'd always imagined a rose garden would be a thing of rich colour and loveliness but this one, so far, was as barren and cheerless as her relationship with Mrs Finch. The days passed very slowly.

On Thursday morning, Mabs arrived at her mistress's room to find Mr Finch there. He held up a warning hand as she opened the door. There had obviously been another outburst of temper for there was broken glass everywhere.

'Careful, Daley, watch your step. I'm afraid you have more sweeping and shard-picking to do this morning. Sadly, our Renaissance mirror, a family heirloom, is no longer with us.' He sounded weary.

He was referring to a mirror she had often admired, its frame an exuberance of gilded leaves and cherubs. It used to hang beside the wardrobe and Mabs would have looked at it more except it was hard to look *at* a mirror without looking *in* it and she disliked to see herself, all scrawny and inadequate as she was. Now the frame rested on the floor, an empty oval.

'Oh!' she said, then pressed her lips together. It wasn't her place to comment, but to destroy something so beautiful seemed shocking to her. Something so valuable too, when so many people were starving. She looked over at her mistress, disliking her more than ever.

Mrs Finch didn't acknowledge Mabs but that was nothing

new. Even so, there was something different about her today. She sat, as ever, in her chair by the window but her posture was lifeless. For a moment Mabs had the horrible feeling that she was dead but then she saw the slow rise and fall of her shoulders. Frowning, Mabs picked her way around the edge of the room. Her mistress's head was lolling, her eyes were half closed and very dark.

'Good morning, ma'am,' said Mabs softly, not expecting an answer. 'I'll have things cleaned up in a jiff, don't you worry yerself about that.' There was no reaction. It wasn't her usual haughty indifference; it was as if Mrs Finch wasn't really there at all. Mabs gave Mr Finch a questioning glance.

'Regrettably, I had to sedate her,' he said soberly. 'Only a negligible dose. Even so, it's a measure I always try to avoid. It's hard to do so without feeling like a . . . well, a brute.'

'Oh sir, you're anything but that!' cried Mabs, quite riven with sympathy for both of them. 'What an 'orrible, 'orrible thing. I'm sorry, sir.'

'Quite horrible, you're right. A last resort if ever there was one. We had a very sympathetic doctor in Durham, Doctor Broome. He had vast experience of cases like these and when we left, he gave me a small supply, to be kept for extreme moments. Just a drop or two in her tea and safety and sanity are restored for a while. But I deplore it, truly.'

'I'm sure, sir. It's ever so sad.'

'Well then, I'd best get to the office. Investments to make!' He attempted a shaky smile but there was little cheer to be found in a room scattered with glass and a lolling, inanimate wife.

'You leave it to me, sir. I'll clear up in 'ere, 'ave it as good as new before you can say Bob.'

'Very good, Daley. And afterwards . . . There's no point you sitting with her – she'll be like this for hours. Take a walk if you like. Don't make this job more oppressive for yourself than it needs to be.'

It made sense and Mabs did long to be out in the open air. But something about Mrs Finch's slumped form pulled at her heartstrings. *I'd almost rather see her fierce and proud than reduced to this, however vile she is to me*, she thought. There and then she knew she wouldn't leave her, not like this.

Olive

At last, Clover is dressed as a little Westallen should be, in a grey coat over a frock of pale pink, peach and grey plaid, her outfit completed by a straw boater circled with a peach ribbon. She looks so sweet I could squeal! After nearly a month with us, she's entirely at home with Mama, Papa and the servants – so I went shopping! Now, my daughter is furnished with pretty dresses and coats, adorable bonnets and sensible boots of a small size which melts my heart. Today, longing to show her off, I took her visiting. It was not a success.

First, we called upon Mrs Zenobia Lake who lives in the grandest house in Belsize Park. She hailed from Cornwall some fifty years ago and married a banker. They were tremendously rich and quite the couple, by all accounts. But her husband died fifteen years ago and she determinedly tarries in that large house while her fortune dwindles and her household with it. Now only one servant remains. I enjoy Zenobia's wit and faded grandeur but soon realised that Lake Hall is not a wholesome place for Clover, with its empty rooms and silent corridors, its ancient owner gaunt and greyed.

Next, we visited Julia Morrow, the divorcee who lives alone in the whimsically named Vale of Health on the edge of the heath. Personally, I have always thought divorce an eminently sensible idea but, evidently, I'm the exception to the rule. The rest of Hampstead is *scandalised* by Julia, so she lives a retiring life. She's near my own age, but was surprisingly awkward with Clover. She has no children of her own, and the scandal, of course, has been very hard on her.

It appals me how many people dwell within our busy community, yet alone and looking on from the fringes. Even so, I must find some younger, livelier friends for Clover else she will have a very dull time of it. Of course, it will be better once she starts school, but I have not yet thought where or when *that* should be. Goodness, there are more important things to organise than clothes!

When we left Julia's house, I asked Clover what *she* wanted to do. 'Can we see the big grey bird?' she asked. And so we are tramping across the heath in search of the heron.

It's muddy going, but this southern stretch of the heath usually is. It doesn't matter; we both wear sturdy boots. I tell her it's the particles in the London clay underfoot that hold the water but she is more interested in the effects of stamping her feet in the puddles. I can't imagine Gert much relishing a geology lesson either!

It's a beautiful day. The last leaves have dropped, paring back the branches to blackness. They are stark and glossy against a satiny blue sky. It's the kind of weather that invites you to stretch your legs and open your lungs. I do just that, and Clover's legs twinkle valiantly at my side until she tugs my hand.

'Mama!' she cries. 'Slower!'

I apologise and adopt a more leisurely pace. It is so very new to me, still. We're rosy-cheeked and laughing when we reach the ponds. Clover squints all around the perimeter then points. Sure enough, away along the waterline stands the heron, grey and austere among the rushes. His ragged head feathers put me in mind of the lank-haired clerk at Papa's bank. He – the bird, not the clerk – is perfectly still and almost invisible.

Clover lets go of my hand. 'Careful, darling,' I warn. 'Don't fall in the water.' She gives me a reproving look.

I can see she's being sensible so I look around at the joyful prospect of Hampstead Heath on a Saturday. Nannies with small children point out nature's wonders to their charges. Courting couples linger beneath the trees. I see poor people from the city, their faces pinched and pale. The heath is a popular weekend destination; trippers come in droves on the train. And the fine folk are out too, carrying extravagant parasols which they use only to gesture and point since the sun is not strong.

And then, I see two familiar faces, too close for me to pretend I haven't seen them. I cannot turn away without appearing horribly rude, though there is no one I wish to speak to less than Rowena Blythe and Verity Crawford.

'Miss Westallen! Olive Westallen! Heavens, it's been an *age* since I saw you!'

So exclaims Miss Blythe, only daughter of my father's former-best-friend-turned-mortal-enemy. Had things turned out differently, we might now be friends, but I cannot imagine it. The fact of our fathers' enmity is not the sole reason that the sight of Rowena always sets my teeth on edge. The other is that she is so beautiful it would take a wiser woman than I not to resent it. I mean, there are countless pretty girls in the world and I do not upset myself over all of them but Rowena has had beauty heaped upon her – *dolloped* – in quite unnecessary quantities. I manage to greet her with civility, if not cheer.

'Miss Blythe. Rowena. Yes, it's been some time, I think. How do you do?'

It has been exactly three and a half years. In March of 1892, Rowena Blythe turned eighteen. There was a grand ball which I had precisely no wish to attend, but due to a series of social connections I found myself obliged to go. The memory of her that night, lovelier than a rose in a pale pink gown, has stayed with me.

The one thing that had reconciled me to going to that ball was the prospect of Whitford Sedley, a gentleman who had called upon me once or twice. A gentleman I had briefly imagined I could come to respect, perhaps even love. But Whitford, like every other male at that ball, had eyes only for Rowena. He even proposed. When I greeted him, he floundered; he had momentarily forgotten my name.

I do not resent Rowena because of Whitford Sedley. She cannot help being as captivating as a mermaid. And all Whitford did was succumb to inevitability. But Rowena has been my counterpart from the moment she was born and though she is younger than I, I have failed to measure up to her in every conventional measure of a woman. I assume that I'm more gifted academically, not because I don't believe a woman can be both pretty and bright, but because it would be unfair if there was *nothing* at which I could outshine her.

As for marriage proposals! Well, I have had one, and that does not even count. Rowena, rumour has it, has received *eight*! So far, she has turned them all down. I believe she will marry a king.

And here she is, standing before me, a vision in tangerine and white stripes. 'I do very well, I thank you, Miss Westallen. You remember my friend, Miss Crawford?' Miss Crawford and I incline our heads at one another with some *froideur*. 'I have been in Europe this summer,' continues Rowena. 'Heavens, it was splendid. Paris is a delight I cannot describe. Have you been to Paris, Miss Westallen?'

'I have not had that pleasure.'

'Then you *must*! You could not fail to adore Paris. And was your summer enjoyable?'

'As a matter of fact,' I say, 'I've had a rather interesting time.' My Clover chooses that very moment to dart back and grab my skirts.

'Mama!' she cries. Miss Blythe's and Miss Crawford's eyes widen. 'It's flown away!' She points at the heron, which now roosts on a drooping branch in a nearby tree.

'That's a shame, darling. Clover, dearest, this is Miss Blythe and Miss Crawford. They are distant neighbours of ours. Ladies, I should like to introduce my daughter, Miss Clover Westallen.'

They cannot move or say a word. I know they have noted Clover's age and compared it with the length of time since they saw me and their ringlets and ribbons are whirring away.

'Heavens,' says Rowena at last. 'You *have* been busy.'

Clover beams. 'Mama!' she cries, pointing at Rowena. '*Pretty!*'

Rowena's face bursts into an angelic smile. 'Oh, what a darling!' she exclaims, crouching down so that all her pretty stripes rest on the ground. 'What a very darling child!'

'Her father must have been *very* handsome,' says Verity.

'Heavens, and I have been calling you Miss Westallen still,' says Rowena, standing up again. 'I beg your pardon, I had not heard that you were married.'

'I'm not,' I say cheerfully, enjoying the horror on their faces more than I should at my age. 'And I don't know who her father is.' I believe Verity is about to choke.

'Bird!' shouts Clover with determination and runs off to resume her quest.

I relent. 'She is adopted. I've been visiting the girls' home in Belsize Park for some time now. I have a large home and fortune to share and there are so many children who have nothing. This way I have the pleasure of a daughter without the encumbrance of a husband.'

'Well,' says Verity. 'How very unconventional.'

'And . . . worthy!' says Rowena. 'Worthy indeed. Such a delightful, sweet, pretty little girl. Just the sort I would have chosen.'

I resist the urge to grind my teeth.

'But how do you know where she came from?' asked Verity. 'Aren't you afraid that bad blood will come out? What if she proves to be . . . depraved?'

I laugh at the thought of Clover engaged in any depravity. 'Miss Crawford, Clover has the sweetest nature imaginable.'

'Of course she does,' says Rowena. 'Well, Olive. We've detained you long enough, I'm sure. How very . . . interesting it always is to see you.'

'A pleasure. I wish you both good day.'

We curtsey, then they depart in the direction of Highgate. As they leave, a light wind picks up and blows back to me a little of their conversation. 'What a *strange* woman,' I hear Miss Crawford say. 'And what an *unfortunate* jaw! No wonder she never married. What man would fit on a pillow next to that?'

'Hush, Verity,' Rowena reproves. 'She cannot help her jaw and she truly *is* very interesting.'

I stand and watch them go. I wonder how many moons it will be before I see either of them again. Then I hear a horrible, sickening snap behind me and a single piercing scream.

Otty

I can't help kicking at stones. I should be happy. I'm out on the heath, the sun is shining . . . but my solitary walks are losing their charm now. I'm tired of tossing my head and ignoring the strange looks I attract. *I know*, I want to say. *It's odd, isn't it?*

Daley has been with us for more than three weeks now and Mama has not improved at all. My brother and sisters are beginning to show some enthusiasm for Hampstead life, but none whatsoever for discovering it with *me*. I suppose that to them, I am a baby. But really, if my siblings won't spend time with me and my mother remains indisposed and my father is at work . . . what is to become of me?

I start school in January, but I scarcely hope *that* will be any better. I've met the headmistress, who seems very stern, and I'm sure the girls will be prissy. The only bright spots in my week will be Sundays, when I can go and meet Jill, the one true friend I have, but she must be kept a secret for reasons I don't understand.

I've tramped across the Northern Heights where the soil is sandy. I can imagine how the gorse will blaze come spring. Now I've circled round to the lower reaches and I come to a pond, aflutter with birds and very pretty. I dawdle, contemplating cocoa when I get home, and perhaps I'll re-read *Little Women*. How I envy the March girls their lusty enjoyments and companionship.

I hear a sudden snap, and a shriek. I whip round to see a very finely dressed lady standing under a tree at the water's edge, peering up into the branches. Her posture is rigid and her hand is flat over her heart as if to keep it within her chest. A small, very pretty child clings like a monkey to a broken branch. A heron flaps off.

The mother composes herself admirably, I think. 'Don't worry, darling. I won't let you fall,' she calls out, standing beneath her daughter, arms outstretched, but it's a risky venture, *I* think. I run over and set my foot to the trunk of the tree. I didn't grow up in the beautiful north without learning a thing or two about climbing trees.

'Oh! Be careful, child!' exclaims the grand lady, seeing what I am about.

I reassure her that I'll have the little girl down in a minute. I climb about halfway and from there I can clearly see her route down. I climb a little higher and talk her through it. 'Hang on tight and stretch your right leg down. That's it. Now bring your other foot to join it. Hold on to that forked branch. Don't worry, I shan't let you fall.'

I climb a bit more until we are within touching distance and she leans back against me. I can *feel* her trust. I wrap an arm tightly around her, she wraps her legs around my waist, and I make my way down, one-handed.

'There!' I exclaim, planting her on solid ground. 'Safe and sound and back with your mama.'

The mother grabs her and covers her with kisses. 'Clover! Oh Clover!' she says, half rapturous, half scolding. I watch them and smile. That's what a family *should* be like. Out and about, getting into scrapes, getting out of them again – *together*. Then the lady looks at me.

'Child, how can I ever thank you?' She clutches Clover with one hand and holds out her other to me. I shake it and bob a little curtsey.

'It's my pleasure, ma'am.'

'She wanted to see the heron,' the lady continues. 'She's fascinated by them. I was distracted by some acquaintances and had no idea she'd begun to climb after it! Heavens, how dreadful.'

'Well, that was very brave!' I say, bending to Clover's height. 'But you must be careful with trees. It's always easier going up than coming back down, you see.'

'When I heard that branch snap . . .' The lady shudders. 'I thought it would be her neck, any minute. I truly can't thank you enough. What is your name, please?'

I straighten up and beam at her. She's not beautiful. I see that at once, accustomed as I am to the lavish beauty of my mother and sisters (poor old Charlie didn't do so well on that score). Even so, I like her face. It is open and confident and she's obviously very clever. I like people who are clever.

'I'm Ottilie Finch,' I tell her, 'but please call me Otty. All my friends do. Not that I have many here . . .' I kick myself for sounding pathetic.

'You're new to the area?'

'Yes. Nearly two months. I love Hampstead, but I wish my family would come out and about with me.'

'They're busy settling in perhaps?'

'Yes. That is, Papa is at work all day and Mama is unwell . . .'

'Oh, I'm sorry. I wish her a speedy recovery. Well, Otty, you have made two devoted friends today, though one is a little old for you perhaps and the other a little young. My name is Olive Westallen; this is my daughter, Clover.'

Westallen! This is a name I know since my father has mentioned it several times. He would love to be friends with people so rich and influential, I know. I badly want to be friends with them too, but for different reasons.

I bob another curtsey to Clover and she smiles. She doesn't say much but the adventure with the heron tells me much about her. I like girls who strike out for what they want.

'It's lovely to meet you both.' I'm reluctant to go but I can't presume to detain them. 'Good day, Mrs Westallen.'

'Oh, it's Miss,' says Olive Westallen, to my confusion. 'I'm not married, you see. Clover is my adopted daughter.'

'Oh, how wonderful!' And it *is* wonderful to see them so close, so happy. I've never met anyone adopted before. It seems a fine arrangement to me.

She beams. 'I think so. But please, call me Olive. Westallen is such a mouthful. Would you care to continue your walk with us? I would offer to buy you a penny lick but we're a little late in the year for ice cream.'

I light up. Company! Who cares about ice cream?

'Will no one be worried about you?' she asks as we set off.

'Oh, no one at all,' I reassure her, though it's not a particularly reassuring thing, really. I can tell by the swoop of her brows that she doesn't think much of it either. 'I like exploring alone. I can go wherever I please and I've seen so many interesting places. But I do get bored sometimes.'

'Where do you live, dear?' I tell her and she knows it well. She tells me she has lived in Hampstead most of her life, that her father is a sea captain and ship owner, very wealthy and respected. I know that from Papa but I don't say so. It must be awful to have people interested in you for those kinds of reasons. It is Papa's one fault, his eagerness to mingle with the rich and accomplished.

'We're very near neighbours,' she adds. 'If you'd like, Otty, and if your parents are willing, you'd be most welcome to visit us. Wouldn't she, Clover?' Clover gives a decisive nod. 'I realise we're not friends of your own age, but if you're at a loose end, we would be better than nothing perhaps.'

'Oh, I would *love* to!' I speak loudly, wanting there to be no misunderstanding my feelings about it. 'I would. Thank you, Miss . . . Olive.'

Mabs

After a month at number six, Mabs was starting to think that *anything* – wharf labour, starvation, the workhouse – would be better than this. It was a strange set-up altogether. Averil visited her mother occasionally and the pair seemed to be on good terms, and likewise Otty. Elfrida and Charlie never visited their mother, at least not that Mabs had ever seen. Mrs Finch seemed to live an almost entirely separate existence from the rest of her family which was just . . . well, it was strange, wasn't it? Her hostility towards Mabs continued unabated. Only yesterday, when Mr Finch came to see them towards the end of the day, his wife had referred to Mabs – in front of her – as 'gutter filth'. He had winced and given Mabs a look of such deep apology that she swallowed down her own choice words, feeling herself turning purple with the effort. Oh, if her family didn't need her wage so badly . . . Even so, how long could she go on like this?

Late one wet Tuesday afternoon, realising that Mrs Finch hadn't spoken a single word all day – again – Mabs was wondering if she should just admit defeat and resign when the door burst open and Otty Finch flew in. A very dishevelled Otty Finch, hair in disarray, bonnet bashed in and dangling askew from its ribbons. Her dress was covered in mud down one side.

'Mama, Mama!' she cried and hurled herself into her mother's arms.

Mabs looked up in alarm from an embroidered sampler she was working on. Lydia had started it as a gift for her mother's birthday but she hated needlework and complained so much that Mabs had offered to finish it for her, just for something to do in the long, silent hours.

Based on Mabs's knowledge of Mrs Finch so far, several thoughts occurred to her. One: the woman hated to be disturbed. Two: Otty's muddy frock was pressed against her mother's immaculate pale blue silk. And three: how could a woman as cold as an ice well be relied upon for comfort?

But to Mabs's astonishment, Mrs Finch transformed before her very eyes; she became alert, capable, maternal. Her arms held fast around her daughter, mud and all. She rested her cheek on Otty's head and murmured to her.

'There, there, darling, don't cry. Mama's here. Mama's here. I've got you.'

'Mamaaaa,' grizzled Otty, sounding much younger than her twelve years. She'd obviously had the fright of her life, thought Mabs, a lump in her throat. After a long while, Mrs Finch gripped her daughter's arms and gently unglued them from her waist. She inspected Otty carefully, her own dress quite gloriously dirtied.

'Darling, it's time for you to sit down and tell me all about it. Daley, bring up a chair for Miss Ottilie if you please.'

Mabs startled but didn't hesitate. She set a comfortable chair next to Mrs Finch's favourite chair, drawing the two of them close as befitted a mother–daughter chat.

'Thank you, Daley. Now sit, Otty. Good girl. Daley, would

you ring for one of the maids, please, and order a pot of cocoa, the brandy bottle and Otty's favourite cup. They'll know which it is. Actually, two cups. No, three. Now, Otty, tell me.'

Mabs rang the bell and returned to her seat in wonder. *Three* cups?

'Oh Mama,' wailed Otty, a little calmer now. 'I was out walking and . . . I was attacked by thieves! There were three of them. They've taken my purse and my locket . . . They pulled off my coat and took that. And then they pushed me to the ground and ran off! I'm sorry, Mama, I know those things were expensive. I didn't mean to lose them. I came straight to you, Mama. I'm sorry, I know you like to be alone and quiet.'

'What? *No!* At least, not when it comes to my children, Otty! If you need me, you can always come to me, *always*! Ah, the door.'

Mabs was already opening the door to Betsy, giving their order. Betsy looked mighty curious as she disappeared. Otty was shivering, so Mabs stoked the fire and offered to fetch a shawl.

Mrs Finch nodded. 'The cream one with fringes. It's my warmest.'

Mabs brought it, and Mrs Finch wrapped it around her daughter and held her little hands. 'Did this happen in Hampstead?' she demanded. 'Were you out on the heath again?'

'No, not Hampstead,' said Otty cautiously.

Mabs looked at her sharply. Having six younger siblings, she knew at a glance that Otty had been somewhere she shouldn't.

'Um . . .' Otty glanced around for inspiration, catching Mabs's eye then looking away. 'I was at the canal, Mama.'

'*What? Why?* Why would you ever go there, Ottilie Finch?'

'I . . . wanted to see Papa.'

'And did you?'

'No, it happened just before I got there, and then I only wanted to come home.'

'I should think so too! What on earth did you need to say to your father that couldn't have waited until tonight?'

'Nothing, Mama. Nothing at all. I just wanted to go somewhere different. I was *bored*. Charlie and the girls won't come with me.'

'But Averil told me they're getting used to being here now, going out and meeting people.'

'They are, but not with *me*! All they do is take tea with people their own age. They say if I want to be with them, I have to go too. But it's *boring*, Mama. I want to have adventures. Only, not *this* kind of adventure.'

'I see.'

Mabs could see the hole in Otty's story. Surely if Otty had been robbed when she was close to her father's office, she would have gone there, instead of walking back to Hampstead alone in a state of fright. Mr Finch would have dropped everything to escort her back, or at the very least put her in a carriage. Mabs doubted that Otty had been going to see her father at all.

Betsy brought the cocoa and Mrs Finch poured for the three of them. She tipped a little brandy into Otty's. 'Warming, and good for shock, my dear.'

Mabs had never drunk cocoa before. She gazed in awe at the silver pot with its curved spout and curly handle. She could hardly believe the smell that rose from her cup. She just wanted to cradle the precious drink between her two hands and savour the prospect of it.

'Drink, Daley, before it gets cold!' Mrs Finch instructed. It had been worth every slight, insult and difficulty, Mabs thought, sipping her chocolate, just to be here now, drinking this hot, sweet richness and to see that her mistress did, after all, have a heart.

When the drinks were finished, Mrs Finch took Otty to her room to help her change. 'I'll get you comfortable and then I think I'd better change myself! Daley, would you look out a clean dress for me? The dusky pink, I think.'

'Yes, ma'am. And take care of yourself, miss. I'm glad all's well that ends well.'

Otty ran to Mabs and squeezed her hands. 'Thank you, Daley. I hope I see you soon.'

Mabs strangely missed them when they left. She found the pink gown and laid it on the bed. She took the tray to the kitchen, and when she returned, Mrs Finch was wearing the clean dress and back in her usual position by the window. Mabs resumed work on Lydia's sampler, completing the D in the legend *Beloved Mother* before beginning the M.

Twenty minutes passed, the shadows deepening, the clock ticking softly. Then Mrs Finch turned to her.

'Daley, I've been thinking,' she said.

'Yes, ma'am?' The surprises just kept coming. Mabs laid down her needle so she didn't stab herself.

'How old are you?'

'Eighteen, ma'am.'

'And you have young brothers and sisters, you said?'

'Yes, ma'am. Six.' Mabs hadn't thought Mrs Finch ever listened to one word she said.

'That's right. Otty, as you'll have gathered, is a restless soul. She doesn't start school until January and her explorations are the joy of her life. I don't wish to forbid them. But clearly, she's not always the best judge of her surroundings. We have been very remiss with her. I want you to accompany my daughter for two or three hours every afternoon.'

Lydia's sampler slid to the floor. 'I . . . I'd love to, ma'am!' Wasn't *that* the truth! But . . . 'But I'm meant to be looking after *you*, ma'am. I don't know if Mr Finch—'

'I'll settle it with my husband. He won't want Otty to come to harm. You'll be with me all the rest of the day to attend to my needs. You must go with Otty, Daley. Please start tomorrow.'

Mabs reached down to pick up the needlework. 'Very well, ma'am. It would be my pleasure . . .'

'But?' Abigail Finch's dark eyes were shrewd.

'But wouldn't you like to accompany her yourself sometimes, ma'am? I'm *happy* to take her – I like Miss Otty very much and I'm keen as mustard to know the area better – only wouldn't it be fun for *you*, exploring with your daughter?'

Her words appeared to give her mistress a little jolt. 'Ah, but Daley, you've heard my husband: I'm very sick!'

'But . . . *are* you, Mrs Finch? I understand you have . . .' – she couldn't say moods, she just couldn't! – 'melancholy, ma'am, I believe that's the word. But surely fresh air, an interest in your surroundings, time with your children . . . would *help*? I beg pardon if I speak out of turn but I don't feel I'm much use to you so I may as well give me tuppence worth . . .' Mabs hoped she hadn't overstepped the mark just when things had taken a positive turn.

'Perhaps in time,' said Mrs Finch at last. 'But at present you will do me a great service – an *invaluable* service – by accompanying my daughter. You're a Londoner. You are . . . excuse me . . . you know the streets. You're the best person to ensure she doesn't stray where she shouldn't.'

Gutter filth, thought Mabs, still smarting. 'Well, that's true, ma'am. I do know exactly where she *shouldn't* go.'

'Precisely. And when you return, if you wish, you may tell me of your wanderings and so we shall have a little conversation after all.'

Otty

I'm overjoyed to have Mabs as my walking companion. I should call her Daley, of course, and we did try at first to be Miss Ottilie and Daley, but really, it felt from the outset that we were friends and one simply does not address their friends that way.

Papa was quite cross with me for going somewhere dangerous. But he's such a dear that he couldn't maintain it very long. From the moment he agreed that Mama might spare Mabs for a while each day to explore with me, I've had one thought in my head: Jill! It will be easier to see Jill if Mabs is with me. I understand now about good and bad parts of the city.

But it's too soon to tell Mabs about Jill. I need to know her better, to guess how she might feel about my secret friend. After yesterday, I understand more than ever that some people find her intolerable. When they don't even *know* her!

I think Mabs knows that I didn't tell Mama the truth yesterday. I could see it from the way she was watching me. Of course, I was with Jill. We had taken tea in her room a second time and I had brought flowers – acacia, carnations and winter jasmine – to brighten the table and a huge box of chocolates that caused Jill's eyes to grow almost as large. I only wished there was a way I might take her tea – hot tea. It is too harsh that someone as lovely as Jill cannot have so simple a pleasure.

Jill had to work the following Sunday but was free Tuesday afternoon. We didn't even make it to her room before a gang of ruffians encircled us, taunting her and challenging me. Why didn't she go back to where she came from? Why didn't she stick with her own kind? Why didn't I stick with mine? What was wrong with me? Why didn't they teach me a lesson? If they wanted to convince me that I was better off with people the same colour as me, they picked a funny way to go about it!

I've recovered, because I came through safely and I'll never go there alone again. But I was terrified. At first I followed Jill's lead; she stayed quiet, kept walking. But the taunts continued and then they blocked our way. I grew angry. What they said didn't make any sense! We weren't interrupting *them*, telling them how *they* should spend their time! And they said horrible – *really* horrible – things to Jill. So I yelled at them to mind their own business and then they attacked me.

Jill tried to stop them but there weren't really three of them, as I told Mama, there were five. There was nothing she could do. So she ran off and they jeered, calling her a coward and they held me down and took my coat and the rest.

'If you was older,' they said, 'we'd give you a good beating. But as yer only a little girl, we'll keep it mild.' Well, how magnanimous. Pillars of society!

Jill came back, of course, with a policeman. He blew his whistle a lot and our attackers ran off. He set me on my feet; I was shaking. His face creased into confusion. 'This darkie 'ere called me,' he said. 'Said 'er friend was in danger. But . . . you're a nice white girl!'

'She *is* my friend,' I cried in fear and frustration.

'*Really?*' he asked, disbelieving. And then he said, 'Well then, you was askin' for it. Go 'ome to yer family and stay away from darkies. They're nothin' but trouble.'

I was so furious I wanted to cry. *Jill* was trouble? It wasn't Jill pushing me around and robbing me, was it? But I said nothing. The shock was setting in, I suppose, or I'm not as brave as I always thought I was.

The policeman escorted me to the edge of Regent's Park. He talked about taking me home and telling my parents, but when I told him I lived in Hampstead his enthusiasm dwindled. He was quite fat so he probably didn't fancy the walk. Instead, he made me promise not to see Jill again. It was no business of *his* and what would he do if I didn't promise? Arrest me? But he had me fast by the arm and wouldn't let me go till I said it. I felt so unhappy and confused and I just wanted Mama. So I said it, even though I didn't mean it, and he was so stupid he seemed satisfied with that. But I felt horrible.

The business with the policeman upset me every bit as much as the business with the ruffians. Both wicked people *and* those who keep order seem to know an obvious reason why brown and white people can't be friends. What *is* it? Why don't I see it, if it is there? And if it's *not* there . . . what's *wrong* with all of them? That's why I'm afraid to talk to Mama or Mabs about it. What if they see it too?

When he was well and truly gone, I saw Jill. She'd followed us at a distance and I was so pleased. But she'd come to say goodbye.

'Otty, I'm sorry. None o' this would have happened if it wasn't for me. You shouldn't be coming to my place. We shouldn't be friends.' Her eyes brimmed with tears and she couldn't look at me.

'Jill, don't say that!' I exclaimed.

She shushed me, looking around nervously. Sure enough, people were stopping to look at us. There was no other pair of companions in view of whom one was white and one was brown. I pulled her behind a chestnut tree.

'We can't just stop being friends!' I whined. 'I hate this, Jill. Why is it like this?'

'Now's not the time for history lessons,' she said sadly. 'You've had a nasty shock. You need to get home. I don't mean stop being *friends*. We just can't see each other any more.'

'That's the same thing!' I wailed.

'No. No it's not. Being friends means caring about each other and thinking about each other and liking each other in our hearts. We can still do that. It's *because* I'm your friend that I have to say this. Being around me, it puts you in danger, Otty. I'd like to say today was a one-time thing, but it will happen again and again. I didn't mean to be thoughtless, I was just so excited to have a friend. It can get so lonely here for me.'

'I'm lonely too.'

'I know. But that will change. You have the pick of the white girls in London. You can go to tea rooms with them, all the things you deserve to do, and no one will want to *teach you a lesson* for it.'

'It should be *different*,' I scowled.

'Yes. Now, go home, think kindly of me, and enjoy your life. You have so much ahead of you.'

'But *you* don't!' I burst out. The loss of my friend would cut me deeply but I still had a comfortable home and books and treats . . . Whereas Jill would go back to a horrible room at the top of a horrible house and her horrible job . . . and she couldn't even have hot *tea*! I started crying. I was beginning to understand why Maggie was so angry.

She gave me a quick hug. 'Otty Finch, pull yourself together now, girl. I need to know you'll get home all right. I can't come with you, I can't be seen over that side of London. But I can't leave you like this.'

I wiped fiercely at my trickling eyes and took a deep breath. I didn't like what Jill was saying, but she was being unselfish, I could see that. She needed to get back to the forgotten streets where she could go about her business without attracting notice, without *me* drawing attention to her. I wanted to be unselfish too.

'I'm fine,' I sniffed, wiping my nose on the back of my hand. 'Go, Jill. I'll be fine, I promise.'

She nodded. 'I never would forgive myself if something worse happened to you. We're young and we're girls. We'll never change anything.'

I didn't like that either. I gulped back another wave of tears. 'I understand, Jill, thank you. Goodbye.'

'Bye, Otty Finch.'

Mabs

From the moment Otty Finch burst in on her mother, distraught, dishevelled and lying through her teeth, Mabs's life began to improve at last. She didn't expect that her new assignment would transform her relationship with Mrs Finch overnight and she was right. But things were better, there was no denying that.

Mabs had seen with her own eyes how Mrs Finch cherished her daughter. She would never have entrusted Otty to Mabs if she didn't think well of her, somewhere deep down. She might have chosen one of the maids, or insisted her older children spend some time with their sister. But it was Mabs she asked.

Knowing that Mrs Finch didn't completely hate her changed everything for Mabs. Her spirits rose and life in Hampstead became more like she had hoped it would be. The working days were bearable at worst, pleasurable at best. Accompanying Otty on her daily rambles was a joy. Otty was lively company and reminded her a little of her sister Peg: they were both brown-haired and bright. Mabs wondered what Otty had really been doing the day she was set upon, but it was too soon to ask. Meanwhile, Mabs enjoyed getting to know Otty and exploring Hampstead properly. Otty conducted their outings like a tour guide; it seemed there wasn't a corner of their neighbourhood she didn't know and delight in.

Otty showed Mabs the tomb of the artist John Constable in the yew-fringed churchyard of St John-at-Hampstead, and the house where the poet John Keats had once lived near the southern end of the heath. From top to bottom this place was full of worthies, alive and dead. Could Mabs from Mushroom Court ever expect to find a place here in this land of poets and painters? But sometimes there was a crack, a sliver of light between worlds, and somehow she had stepped through it. Now, all Mabs wanted in the world was to bring her brothers and sisters through it too.

Sometimes, in the evenings, Mabs had a drink in the Flask with Lydia and Betsy. And some Wednesdays she visited her family to leave her free on the Sunday to meet Lou. Lou would walk over the heath and meet Mabs at the Hampstead Tea Rooms where they shared a sandwich and a pot of coffee for lunch. It was unspeakable luxury to Mabs.

'Oh Lou!' Mabs was rapturous the first time they did this. 'I'm in *love*!'

Lou's eyes widened and her mouth grew as round as a cherry. 'With Mr Finch?' she whispered.

Mabs laughed out loud. 'Yes!' she declared, though it wasn't what Lou thought. 'With Mr Finch and Mrs Finch and Miss Ottilie and *all* o' them. With Hampstead. With me life!'

Lou rolled her eyes. ''Appiness has unhinged you, Mabs, that's what. All the same, I'm glad it's worked out for you.'

After lunch, they would walk on the heath if it was fine then Lou would return to Highgate. A footman at the Blythe house had a sister in Hampstead, and on the afternoons that he visited her, he would walk Lou back and she could stay longer. When darkness drew in and it was time to be cosy,

Mabs and Lou would retire to the Holly Bush and prolong their time together in the cosy, bustling pub.

John Hobbs was a lovely young man and handsome too, Mabs thought. She hoped at first that he and Lou . . . But Lou assured her that was never going to happen.

'He's nice enough, mind you,' she acknowledged. 'I can see he's a catch an' all . . . but it's never, ever going to 'appen.' She shrugged.

'He's not . . . the other way, is he?' asked Mabs. Since the playwright Oscar Wilde had been tried and imprisoned for gross indecency earlier that year, his liking for the same sex had set everyone talking.

'The opposite. He's in love, Mabs. But that ain't gonna 'appen either. He's 'ead over 'eels for Miss Rowena Blythe, if you please.'

'No!' Mabs loved hearing all Lou's tales about the mighty Blythes. They were rich, properly rich, and therefore quite fascinating.

'And she's turned down eight proposals. Think of it, Mabs, eight! We should be so lucky to get one! She's aiming high, that one, and I don't think an 'umble footman like our John is going to catch her eye. Added to which, her pa would kill them both.'

With such pleasant conversations and outings, the time flew and it was soon almost Christmas. Mabs was to have two whole days off! The week before Christmas, when she received her fortnightly pay, Mr Finch gave her a Christmas bonus besides, a wholly unexpected three shillings. Mabs nearly cried. She had plans, did Mabs. She treated herself occasionally with Lou and whenever she went home, she took some coins to help the others or an edible treat. But that was all she spent. She kept the rest in a small box under her bed, determined that one day she would help her family in some more substantial way.

The day before Christmas Eve, to her astonishment, Mabs received gifts. Otty gave her a small blue beaded bag. Mabs was certain she'd never go anywhere to need such a thing, but she hung it from a nail in her bedroom, where it shone and scintillated. Mr Finch gave her a box of chocolates flavoured with things Mabs never knew could go into chocolate. Lime, violet, geranium . . . with little crystallised petals glittering on top. They were so pretty that she could hardly bring herself to eat them – until she tried the first. The whole box disappeared pretty quickly after that! Mrs Webb gave her a lilac shawl that she had knitted herself.

'I thought it would look very well with your fair hair and hazel eyes,' Mrs Webb said when Mabs wrapped herself in it. 'I must say, I was right. Merry Christmas, Miss Daley.'

Mabs had never considered whether she was pretty. Her reflection had always shown her someone thin, pale and untidy. Really, she'd had bigger worries. But now that she'd enjoyed a month of proper meals, of keeping clean and had a smart uniform to wear, she dared a glance in the mirror a little more often.

For Mabs, her best gift came from, of all people, Mrs Finch! It was Mabs's last day before going home for two nights. She had mixed feelings about that. It would be lovely to wake up with her brothers and sisters, to see their faces on Christmas morning and feel herself back in the fold. On the other hand, she'd grown used to privacy, her soft bed, the ease with which she could wash. Being back there would bring back bad memories and good.

'I haven't bought you a Christmas gift, Daley,' said Mrs Finch as dusk fell.

'That's all right, ma'am, I weren't expecting nothing.'

Mrs Finch's lips twitched. 'I'm quite sure you weren't. And yet, I should like to give you something, Daley, to apologise for my earlier behaviour towards you and to thank you for being . . . not as bad as you might be.'

Mabs laughed. Things were such between them now that she could. 'Not as bad as I might be? My, that's 'igh praise, ma'am.'

Mrs Finch smiled gracefully. 'You know that I was against the idea of a companion from the start. I did not agree with my husband's reasons for employing you. But you have been . . . more than patient. And I appreciate the interest you take in Otty.'

'Thank you, ma'am. Even so, you don't need to give me nothing.'

'But I've had an idea, Daley. I've been considering it for a while, only I don't wish to put you in a difficult position.'

'Oh?'

Mrs Finch sighed. 'Daley, would you be prepared to promise not to tell my husband? I don't wish to make things awkward for you, but if you accepted my gift, I wouldn't want him to know.'

Mabs was intrigued. 'Why don't you tell me the idea, ma'am? Then if I don't feel right to keep it from him, we'll leave the matter there.'

'Very well. I wondered if you wished to learn to read. If so, I should be happy to teach you.'

Mabs was struck dumb. Learn to *read*? Oh, but she would *love* to. For Mrs Finch's sake, so Mabs could be a better companion to her. And for her own, to have that knowledge, that power in the world . . .

'Ma'am,' she breathed at last, 'I'd like nothin' better. I'm so *very* grateful. Only may I ask . . . why don't you want Mr Finch to know? Do you think he'd object?'

'I do.'

'But *why*?'

Mrs Finch stood and went to the window. She stared out over the rose garden, more lifeless now than ever, and Mabs feared that she'd spoiled the moment. But Mrs Finch turned back to her.

'The honest answer, Daley, is that I don't *know* why he should mind, yet after all these years of knowing him, my instinct is that he would. So, there it is. I can't give you a solid reason for secrecy and I know that he's very good to you. That's why I've hesitated to ask. To learn to read would be a good thing for you, Daley. But I leave it to your conscience.'

Mabs was flabbergasted. She thought carefully. She didn't want to lie to Mr Finch, but this could harm no one and would make Mabs a better companion. Most of all, as Mrs Finch had said, it would be a very good thing for Mabs.

'I don't see the harm in it, ma'am,' Mabs said slowly. 'I don't tell Mr Finch every single thing we do.' She gave a little laugh. 'It ain't that interesting! I don't see as I'd feel wrong learning to read and not mentioning it, ma'am. It would be my business and yours, wouldn't it, and we wouldn't be doing anything bad.'

Mrs Finch's eyes sparkled in a way that Mabs had never seen. 'Is that a yes?'

Mabs grinned. 'It is, Mrs Finch. And thank you, from the bottom of my heart.'

Olive

Of all times in the year I love Christmas the best! And now I have a child to share it with – what greater felicity could there be? Clover and I have spent December in a frenzy of artistry. We have cut out paper snowflakes in, I believe, their thousands. We have strung ornaments and rolled peppermint creams and covered wreaths with holly and fir, gold ribbon and berries. I have had the sheer joy of teaching Clover her first carols.

I told her the story of the birth of Baby Jesus and she listened very solemnly. I took her to church and showed her the nativity and the star. We light our advent candle every night with great ceremony; Clover watches it narrowly, puffing it out the minute the evening's portion is spent.

We make up baskets for our own church and for Mr Miles to take to the needy neighbourhoods. I explained to her the importance of helping those less fortunate than ourselves and I wonder if she remembers that, just weeks ago, she was one of them. She has never spoken about anything before Polaris House.

And, of course, there has been Christmas shopping! I have shopped *with* Clover, for other people, and *for* Clover. I don't know which I enjoyed more. The former brought the joy of seeing her absorb, wide-eyed, the luxurious displays, growing serious as she considered our choices. The latter gave me the thrill of choosing things I know she will love, and commissioning lavish gift wrap and ridiculous bows, imagining her face on Christmas morning.

I shall wake her with a kiss and a large white box tied with a wide blue ribbon. Inside will be the dress I have bought for her to wear on Christmas Day; it's bright blue velvet with an enormous organza bow at the back. Then we'll go downstairs and she will find a bulging stocking hanging from the mantelpiece in the dining room. We shall unpack it before breakfast, *of course*. It will be full of little oddments – a locket to match mine, fruits and candies, ribbons and small toys. After Christmas Day breakfast, beneath the tall, twinkling Christmas tree in the drawing room, we shall open dozens of presents. My heart has been full the entire month. My moments have been gilded. Motherhood is a dream.

Only two concerns tarnish my delight. Throughout December, Otty Finch has visited several times. Well, *that* is not the concern – the child is delightful: she's precocious, intelligent and interesting, yet she also plays with Clover with all the enthusiasm and freedom of a younger child. I welcome her visits for both our sakes. It's just that I know I should call on her parents, and I do not wish to. The mother, of course, is unwell – some mysterious malady, the nature of which Otty cannot precisely describe. The father, I've ascertained from discreet enquiries, is terribly ambitious. I've learned that it's well to steer clear of people like that. I fear that, once I introduce myself to Mr Finch, he will be all over me with a view to meeting Papa.

Perhaps I do the fellow a disservice. Even so, I do not wish any note of discord to colour my first Christmas with Clover.

If Otty's parents send word, or come calling, I shall be civil, of course. But if *they* are not curious about where their daughter spends her time, I shall not pre-empt. And Otty rarely mentions them. Instead, she talks about someone named Mabs, whom I understand to be a servant who takes an interest in young Ottilie. Well, thank heavens she has *someone*.

As for the second concern . . . well, it is Gert, of course. With Christmas drawing near, a shining, perfect apparition, I couldn't help but think of those who will not have a Christmas like ours. It almost drove me to the orphanage to ask Gert again to come home with me. But I could not impose a second granddaughter upon poor Mama and Papa, this one a recalcitrant ball of spite, and I must put Clover's interests first now. But Gert haunts me.

As the day draws on, I feel restless and I decide to pay a call on Mr Miles, our Quaker friend. I leave Clover with Mrs Brody in the kitchen, making cranberry buns. I carry a hamper for Mr and Mrs Miles over the crook of my arm and dusk draws about me as I hasten to Gospel Oak. It always makes me smile that his wife is Faith and his home is in Gospel Oak.

I find him at home. Faith Miles shows me into his study and withdraws; I assume she is used to sharing her husband with half the spiritual crises in north London.

'Olive Westallen, as I live and breathe!' he declares, jovial. I realise I haven't seen him since the eve of Clover's arrival, when he appeared so dramatically and I was so short with my attentions. We shake hands and pour sherry.

'You're just the person I wanted to see. I'm raising funds, Olive, for a new home for convicts who have served their time and struggle to get back on their feet. I'm two hundred pounds short and we hoped to open in January. I don't suppose . . .?'

'Of course, Mr Miles. As much as you need. Goodness, convicts! How brave you are!'

It's true. Every time I open a newspaper to an account of some dramatic incident involving the desolate folk of London, Mr Miles can be glimpsed in the background of the photograph. He has championed, at one time or another, every group you can possibly think of. There is no individual and no class of person that he fears, believing as he does that we are all equal in the sight of God. I agree in principle, of course, but still I take precautions in certain situations. Mr Miles takes no such care. He strides among the violent and the desperate, leonine in looks and bearing, and they fall into line about him. I admire him very much.

'Thank you, Olive. But how are you? I hear there is a new addition at Polaris House since I saw you last! I've been meaning to visit and meet her but God has not yet blessed me with that opportunity.'

'I'm well, Mr Miles, and happy, and yes, Clover lives with us now and she is a great blessing. Very great. In truth, I . . . I love her more than I thought it would be possible to love a child I have known less than two months!'

'I hear a "but" in your voice.'

'Yes. And that is why I came to see you, of course. The "but" does not pertain to Clover, it pertains to another girl.'

I quickly explain the ill-starred business of Gert. 'What do you make of it, Mr Miles? Having Clover for my daughter is all I could wish for and more. Yet I cannot forget this rotten, ungrateful wretch and I feel guilty all the time that I have failed her.'

'You value your own will more than God's,' said Mr Miles.

'No! Or perhaps . . . Do I?'

'Of course. We all do. You were born with a fire in your

heart to help. So far, so good. But, like all human beings, you wish to decide whom you should help, where, when and what it should achieve. Those aren't your parameters to decide, my dear. They are God's. If Gert was meant to come to you now, she would have.'

'So I have told myself! But the fact remains that Clover and I are now sublimely happy, while Gert still languishes in the home. She has no prospects and even Mrs Jacey paints a very dim view of her future.'

'Sadly, Mrs Jacey is probably right. But Olive, there are girls, children, people, all over London, all over the *world*, who are suffering, unloved, who have clouded futures. Will you take them all to live in your parents' house? You cannot. Then what is the difference between Gert and those others? Only that you have taken a personal interest in her. Only that you had set your heart on her. It is time to let those interests go now. Include her in your prayers, but not in your plans. And the next time you feel the urge to reach for her again, go instead and help *three* others. Anyone at all. For every thought of Gert, do three good turns to people more willing to accept them. Gert will be no worse off and they will be better.'

His advice is beyond helpful. It is practical, godly and redemptive all at once. 'You are a wise man, Mr Miles. I'll do as you say. And meanwhile . . . I can . . . enjoy Clover? With Gert – and the others – so much less fortunate . . . I'm allowed to be happy?'

'My dear,' he smiles, 'it is your Christian duty.'

Mabs

Christmas was bittersweet for Mabs. It was the first since Ma had died and any one of them would have given anything to have her back. Ma had succumbed to a long, wasting illness one week into January, hanging on through sheer determination to have one last Christmas with them. Mabs had started labouring at the beginning of February and the whole family had been like sleepwalkers all spring. By summer, when it became apparent that Pa wasn't going to come back to himself anytime soon, Mabs had forced herself to buck up a bit, for the children's sake; she didn't want them growing up thinking life was all bleak and fearful, even though she privately felt that it was.

Yet despite everything they had been through, the Daleys enjoyed some Christmas cheer after all. There was a sense of hope that they hadn't felt that whole year. Obsessed though Mabs was with saving her money, she had bought a present for everyone. Tobacco for Pa, a shawl for Jenny, caramels for Nicky, and so on. No one could remember a time when there had been presents to open.

Best of all, Pa didn't have to worry about Christmas dinner. Mrs Derring had promised Mabs a turkey – she was buying one for her household, one for her daughter's and one for the

Finches, she said; one more wouldn't make a difference. She roasted it the day before Mabs went home so she could carry it to Saffron Hill on Christmas Eve, along with a jar of cranberries, a Christmas pudding and a bottle of wine. Mabs's arms were nearly stretched to the ground by the time she arrived but it was the first real, proper Christmas dinner any of them could remember.

Mabs returned to work on Boxing Day morning. She had her second reading lesson and was pleased with how quickly the letters she had learned at school were coming back to her. She couldn't make them into words yet, but she remembered the shapes and sounds. Mrs Finch filled in the gaps and was proving a surprisingly patient tutor. In the afternoon, there was to be a household party for family and servants alike.

At three o'clock Miss Averil put her head around the door. 'Hello, Mama.'

'Averil, *dear*!' Her mother looked delighted. 'How wonderful to see you. To what do I owe the pleasure?'

'It's three o'clock. The party's about to start. Are you looking forward to it?'

'Oh, yes, dear, very much,' said Mrs Finch, with a notable lack of conviction.

Averil seemed to notice. 'Good-oh,' she said uncertainly. 'Hello, Daley. Aren't you going to change?'

'Change, miss? No, I got nothing else to wear. But that's all right, I feel perfectly comfortable in me uniform.'

'Oh!' said Averil, with great surprise. 'But it's a party! I mean, *we* don't mind, of course, but . . . Daley, would you be very offended if I offered you one of my costumes? To keep, I mean. One I don't wear any more?'

Mabs looked at Mrs Finch, wondering what the etiquette was in such cases. The one thing she'd promised herself on her way here was fabric to make a decent dress. But she'd been so busy saving, she hadn't done it. And Miss Averil's cast-off was likely to be finer than anything she could make herself.

'That's very kind of you, Averil,' said Mrs Finch. 'And your room certainly does need a clear-out.'

'I'd be ever so grateful, miss,' said Mabs at once. 'Only if you're certain, mind.'

'Why, bless you, Daley, quite certain. Come on, come with me. Mama, shall we call back for you?'

'No, I'll see you downstairs,' sighed her mother, as if she were planning to board a convict ship. Averil frowned as they hurried off.

'We're all very grateful you're here with Mama, you know,' said Averil as they entered a room decorated in white and silver, with a glass chandelier. 'My sisters call it the Snow Kingdom,' she added. 'They say it needs colour but I like it. Anyway, we love poor Mama very much and we're glad she has someone to care for her.'

'Thank you, miss.' Mabs felt uncomfortable. She wasn't sure how much caring she did, really. She was just *there*, most of the time. It was strange, she reflected, how everyone spoke of Mrs Finch as though she were fevered and delicate, whereas to Mabs she seemed perfectly strong – bloody-minded if anything!

'I miss her, you know,' sighed Averil. 'We used to be splendid chums. But Papa says that she put me first for many years and now that I'm grown-up it's my turn to put her first and give her peace to get better. So I do, though it's hard not to rush in and tell her every little thing the way I used to. Anyway, the clothes!' she exclaimed, giving herself a little shake. 'I shall look out several I've grown out of, then you can choose which you prefer.' She opened her wardrobe and leafed through the gowns. 'This,' she murmured under her breath. 'This, and this. No, I can't part with that one yet . . .'

At last she dumped a pile of colourful fabric on the bed. 'Cream, green, cobalt, orange sherbet or peony?'

Mabs's mouth dropped open. They were beautiful! Far too grand for the likes of her. Most appeared to be in three parts: skirt, bodice and a matching jacket. Mabs wasn't even sure how you'd put them on; she was used to sticking a frock over her head and off she went!

'Miss!' she breathed. 'They're just heaven, that's what! But ain't you got anything more ordinary you want to be rid of?'

Averil frowned. 'They're mostly just day costumes, Daley, nothing special.'

Mabs continued to stare. They *were* special, each and every one. She'd never even heard some of the words Averil had used. Cobalt, it seemed, meant bright blue. The orange sherbet was what Mabs would have called 'light orange' and the peony was what she would have called 'pinky-purple'. She approached them nervously, as if they were wild creatures, trying to imagine a reality in which Mabs Daley wore any of these.

'Perhaps the cream, since you are to start by going to a party,' said Averil eagerly. 'It's the most elegant, I think, and look! There are tiny crystals sewn into the neckline so it sparkles under the lights. It will look very well on you with your fair hair.'

'Oh, not the cream, miss,' sighed Mabs. 'It's a princess dress all right, only I need something for walking in, you see, and meeting my friend for sandwiches. Ordinary things. I need something that won't get dirty in a trice.'

'What do you wear for sandwiches with your friend now?' asked Averil. 'Not your uniform?'

'Why, yes, miss, and very glad to 'ave it I've been.'

'Well then, for heaven's sake, have *two*!' said Averil in a rush. 'Take the cream for parties, to indulge me. And take the peony for everyday – it's certainly the most practical. Hurry, Daley, they're waiting for us.' She thrust them into Mabs's arms, cutting short all her protests, and bundled her out of the room.

Mabs ran up to the attic in something of a daze. She laid aside the peony costume with its many hooks and eyes and layers – Lord, wait till Lou saw her! – and wriggled into the cream dress. She brushed her hair and tied it back in a simple loop, which was the fanciest thing she could manage. To please Otty, she hooked her beaded bag over her wrist, even though she didn't have anything to put in it. Then, before she lost her nerve, she ran to the drawing room.

Catching sight of herself in the hall mirror, she quailed. She looked like a child playing at dressing up. *Too big for yer boots. Gettin' above yerself*, said the voices of Saffron Hill in her head. But then Averil appeared and pulled her in.

'Look!' she cried. 'Doesn't Daley look wonderful? It's my old dress, remember, Papa? You gave it to me for my sweet sixteen but it doesn't quite fit any more.'

'Small wonder with all those candies you eat,' observed Elfrida, with the licence of an older sister.

'Hush, darling, Averil has a lovely figure. She's growing up, that's all,' said her mother.

'And out,' muttered Elfrida.

Mabs was embarrassed to be the centre of so much attention; she'd hate for the other servants to think she was putting on airs. But Lydia and Betsy were both wearing very pretty dresses and Mrs Derring and Mrs Webb glittered with large brooches and fine ear-bobs. A party with the family was clearly an occasion.

At first the servants stuck together, marvelling at the finery of the Finch women and growing pink-cheeked from wine. But then the younger Finches came to talk to them. Mr and Mrs Finch stood by the fireplace, talking quietly. After a few glasses of wine, Mr Charlie proposed a game and Lydia suggested Blind Man's Buff.

They quickly grew rosier; hair escaping restraints, top buttons loosened, smiles broad. Amid the whirl and flurry, Mabs felt compelled to keep an eye on Mrs Finch. She wasn't sulking or throwing things, she was altogether civilised, but it was still there, her look of complicated unhappiness.

After Blind Man's Buff, they played charades, a game entirely new to Mabs. She couldn't make any sense of Mr Charlie's elaborate pantomime so she drifted to the edge of the group, seeking the cool air drifting in through the open door. She found herself beside Elfrida Finch.

'Miss Daley,' said Elfrida, rousing herself from what appeared to be a deep reverie. 'Are you enjoying yourself?'

'Very much, miss. Ain't it a lovely party?'

Elfrida gave a small, sad smile very like her mother's. 'Splendid.' She was watching her parents, Mabs noticed.

'She'll come right, miss, don't worry,' said Mabs. 'I'm sure with time and sympathy everything will come right.'

'I beg your pardon, Daley,' said Elfrida in a tight voice. 'I know you mean well but the truth of this household is not something that can be healed so easily.'

'Oh, I'm sorry, miss.' Mabs was mortified. Of course she didn't know everything about this family. She was a servant; it didn't fall to her to make things right. A change of subject, that was the way to go. 'I'm all at sea with them charades, miss,' she said cheerfully. 'Not me natural gift, I don't think!'

But when she looked at Elfrida, she saw tears glistening in

her dark eyes; her face was turning burgundy-red with the effort of holding them in.

'Miss!' whispered Mabs. 'Can I 'elp?'

Elfrida shook her head and slipped from the room. Mabs barely hesitated before following. In the hall, she found her leaning against the wall, heaving with sobs.

'Miss Elfrida,' said Mabs firmly. 'Don't stay out here where anyone can see you.' She knew instinctively that Elfrida would hate that; she was such a dignified young woman. Mabs ushered her into the parlour then turned to leave.

'Don't go, Daley,' croaked Elfrida, sinking into a chair. 'I apologise . . . Stay a moment, won't you?'

'Of course, miss. And there's nothing to apologise for. Can I get you a brandy or anything?'

'You're kind,' said Elfrida, wiping her eyes and nose with a handkerchief. 'I can see why Papa employed you. He wants the best for Mama, you see, still. I needn't ask you to keep this to yourself, I suppose?'

'Of course not, miss. Rest easy on that.'

'I feel . . . a little discomforted to have been caught out like this.' She sat up tall and took a shuddering breath.

'You're used to worrying about your ma in silence,' Mabs guessed.

'Used to keeping her secret, more like,' spat Elfrida, shocking Mabs. 'Protecting her. I'm sick of it, Daley. I dislike secrets. I like honesty, and honour and . . . *good behaviour*!'

'Yes, miss. Those are good things,' said Mabs, wishing she could leave.

'Papa has always adored Mama, you know. Worshipped her. Oh, she was the *exquisite Miss Farrah*, and he never thought he stood a chance. He's never felt good enough for her.'

Mabs remembered something Betsy had said one day. *Married above 'imself, did Mr Finch.* Way *above.*

'We were so happy, Daley. In Durham we knew *everyone.* Yes, some people thought Papa was . . . not quite the thing, but they soon decided that if he was good enough for Mama, he could be good enough for them. Oh, how we all miss Durham. But we can never go back.'

Elfrida sighed. 'Daley, promise me you won't tell anyone what I'm about to tell you. But I feel I owe you some explanation after you've seen me like this. And I'm *tired* of protecting her. All we ever do is protect her and she doesn't *deserve* it.'

And, observed Mabs, whatever her resentment was, she wanted to spite her mother by telling it to *someone.* 'Please don't feel you need to tell me anything, miss. Perhaps I'll leave you to it now.'

'The others don't know,' Elfrida went on, as if Mabs hadn't spoken. '*They* all believe the story that a perfect new position for Papa opened up at the canal company, *an opportunity so great there could be simply no delay!*' She parroted the legend scornfully. 'They have absolutely no idea that the reason we left everything and everyone overnight was because she had an *affair,* Daley. *That's* why we left Durham so abruptly.'

Mabs heard a rushing in her ears. An *affair*?

'Papa dragged us here to protect us from scandal. We couldn't be the respectable Finches in Durham any more. Felicia's parents – Charlie's intended, you know – wouldn't want her embroiled with him any more. Marriage prospects for me and Averil – gone! She didn't think of *that*, did she? Papa didn't want us disillusioned about Mama – that's why he puts it about that she's delicate and suffers moods and all that – but I found out anyway. She's not delicate at all! She's *selfish*!'

Mabs was tongue-tied. She couldn't deny that she'd often thought the same thing. Delicate wasn't the first word that sprang to mind in connection with Mrs Finch. There were so many thoughts and questions jostling in her brain that they'd ground each other to a halt. 'I'm so sorry for your family's troubles, miss,' she said at last, helplessly.

Elfrida gave a noisy, inelegant sniff. 'Thank you. Perhaps it was unfair to tell you, only you saw me crying . . . Oh gracious! Will it be very hard to work with Mama now?'

'No, miss. I'll put it from my mind when we leave this room.' Mabs only hoped it would be as easy as that. 'Only, are you *sure*, miss? Yer ma . . . I mean, she loves you all very much.'

'There's no mistake, Daley. I heard them fighting about it – Mama and Papa, I mean. She didn't even deny it. That's why I don't go and see her. I've always loved her so much. I look just like her. We were such a *pair*! But now I don't want to be anything like her!'

'And you never told the others? Mr Charlie doesn't talk much to her either, does he?'

'No, but that's just because he's a boy and all caught up in himself. He misses Felicia so much he can't think about anything else. The others were all out when the argument happened and no, I haven't told them. Why make them as miserable as I am?'

Otty

I have one more week of freedom before I commence my career at the Hampstead Academy for Young Ladies. I used to enjoy school in Durham, but now I'm used to walking for hours in every weather, doing as I please. I suppose I have a strange life for a twelve-year-old but at least I'm the mistress of it. School will constrain me like an old-fashioned corset.

I asked Papa if we might think of an alternative solution to my schooling. A governess, perhaps, or even Mama? She's at home all day and she's very clever. But Papa, though I love him dearly, is the most conventional of men. *Unconventional* is not in his nature. School it must be, he maintains, just for a few years, until I marry. *Marry!* Why not just strangle me now?

So all I can do is make the most of these last days. Mabs and I have been to London Zoo (it *is* more fun with a companion!), to Trafalgar Square (though it is *cold* to be outside!) and to the National Gallery to feast our eyes. The best part of *that*, for me, was watching Mabs, who had never been to a gallery before. She says that being with me made her more comfortable there.

I still haven't told Mabs about Jill. I want to beg her to take me to visit, but I just don't know. I don't *think* Mabs would mind about things like the colour of a person's skin, but what if she felt duty-bound to tell Papa? I'm sure Papa wouldn't like it. He'd worry about my reputation, how it would reflect on *him*, how it would affect his prospects of getting in with the best families around here . . .

Speaking of which, I do feel guilty that I haven't told him about Olive when I know he'd give his left arm for an introduction. When did I start keeping so many secrets? I love to make Papa happy, only Olive is my friend and Papa wouldn't see her for herself, only for her name and her father. Goodness, that's rather a dismal thing to think about one's papa! But in all other ways he's such a darling and everyone has their faults. His ambition is only so strong because he wants the best for Mama and for us; it's actually a sign that he's very loving. Only it can come across all wrong sometimes.

It might be very selfish, but I want to keep Olive to myself. Mabs is a splendid pal, but she's only just beginning to find her way in the world and she's so *grateful* all the time. Olive challenges me. She's confident and unusual and doesn't worry all the time what people think of her. I want to be just like her when I grow up.

On the Wednesday of my last week of liberty, the weather is a perfect match for my mood. The sky is a thick, woolly grey. The rain pelts ceaselessly, a drone on the pavements, and the wind buffets and plunges like an ill-humoured nag. It's Mabs's afternoon off, so off to Polaris House I go! I pull on my hardiest coat and bonnet *and* I grab an umbrella. Then I dash the short distance to see my friends. Not ten minutes away, yet when Agatha lets me in, my hem is soaked to ten inches, my hat's bashed in and my coat channels the rain into rivulets. Golly, I'm giving the beautiful mosaic floor a good sprinkling. Agatha takes my outer garments gingerly while

Anne shows me into the parlour. Olive and Clover are playing Snakes and Ladders on the carpet in front of the fire.

'Goodness!' cries Olive when she sees me. 'Come and sit by the fire at once!' She clambers up and looks around. 'The piano stool, I think,' she adds. 'You can spread your skirts out and they'll dry more quickly.' She drags it over to the fire. Once I'm ensconced on the tapestry-seated stool with the flames roasting me nicely, they finish their game and ring for cocoa. 'You look glum, Otty. The weather?'

'I *wish* that were my only problem.' I sigh. 'It's school. I won't be able to come and visit you any more – though you may be glad of that, I've been here rather a lot lately. I hope I haven't worn out my welcome.'

'Nonsense, Clover and I will always be pleased to see you. Why, Otty, you talk as if your life will be over once you start at the academy.'

'That's how it feels. I'm sure the other girls will be intolerable. I'll miss you and Clover, and Mabs.'

'True friends can't be lost. I must say, Otty, I'm surprised you feel this way. I know the last two months must have felt like a long holiday for you but you're such a bright girl, I'm sure you're *very* good at your lessons. I would have thought learning would be important to you.'

'It was! I was top of my class in Durham. But . . .'

'But me no buts!' Olive quotes. 'Education for women is vital, Otty. Use your intelligence, hone it. I would have thought a good school the very *best* place for you. What are your ambitions? Whatever they are, they begin with a sound education.'

'Ambitions?' I echo. No one's ever asked me that before. It's an expansive, blustery, open horizon of a word when Olive uses it. When people use it about Papa it sounds like a mean-spirited, tasteless sort of a thing. What is the difference? I wonder. The thought that I might have any is exciting. 'I've never thought about it,' I admit. 'But I'll come up with some pretty soon, I expect.'

'What about university?' suggests Olive. 'Cambridge, perhaps, or Oxford? I'm sure you could do it, Otty. Not enough women go.'

I feel tipsy, as I did once when I drank some of Papa's champagne. Cambridge? Me?

'Did *you* go?' I ask.

'I didn't. But I could have. I'm very clever, you know. I consider myself a lifelong scholar still – there's a never-ending supply of things to learn. But I did not wish to leave my parents, or Hampstead.'

I look at her with surprise.

'I know, it sounds strange when you see me all grown-up. But truly, Otty, I have everything I need in this life of mine. I can learn, I can love, I can help others, right here in Hampstead. I believe some people are born in their right corner of the world and their greatest happiness lies in knowing it, and staying there. I am one such. I don't believe you are, though, Otty.'

'What happens to the other sort?'

'Well, they have to go out into the world to *find* their right corner. But for *them*, the explorations are part of the joy.'

Yes, that's me, I decide. I love my parents. I love Hampstead. But I can't see myself following Olive's course. She's right. I need to explore a *lot* more, and not just the streets of London.

'So . . . women are allowed to go to university?' I muse.

Olive scowls. 'Yes, though we are not *allowed* to earn a degree. Which is a subject you should not start me off upon, Otty, if you do not enjoy resentment and wrath. But I still think education, even without its outward awards, is essential. It enriches, it challenges, it changes one. Men don't want any of those things for women but we have to start somewhere. How else can our lunatic world ever change?'

I feel a little shiver, remembering what Jill said when we made our final farewells. *We're young and we're girls. We'll never change anything.* Was this a way to start addressing that? 'University,' I murmur. 'I wonder what *that* would be like.'

'Well, you won't find out if you don't go to school,' says Olive tartly and, her point well made, we talk of other things.

'Bring Mabs to see us,' she says when I finally decide to go home. 'I've been meaning to say so for a while but with all the busyness of Christmas I never found the moment. Bring her before you start school, why don't you?'

Olive

The day after Otty Finch turned up looking like a drowned rat, she appears again with her mother's companion in tow, Mabel Daley. Mabs. I asked to see her for two reasons. One: I know from Otty that she comes from an impoverished background and has an assortment of a hundred or so small siblings she is trying to keep afloat more or less single-handedly. I have not forgotten Mr Miles's advice to help people more willing to be helped whenever I think of Gert, which I still do, often.

Two: on New Year's Day, the cards gave me pause for thought. It has been my custom for years now to conduct a reading on the first of January. It's a neat date for planning and I like to receive a little advice from the powers that be at the start of each year. Oddly, this entire reading made me think of Otty Finch.

The first card I drew was the Dog. One or two of the cards in my deck appear to have challenged the abilities of the artist, and this is one of them; the dog in the picture is not of a breed that *I* have ever seen. However, with its lustrous eyes, drooping ears reminiscent of bunches of ringlets and eager, loyal expression, the resemblance to Otty was notable. With her on my mind, I read the legend: *You will easily find better*

Friends among Strangers than among Your own Relations.
Well, that has certainly been the case for my young friend.
And if the cards are pointing it out to *me*, presumably I'm
supposed to do something about it.

Next, I drew the Moon. *The liberality of Your mind will
always rather increase than lessen Your prosperity; it will also
daily endear you more to your friends*.

Yes, yes, I thought. I know it well for it's a card I draw
often. On this occasion it only served to deepen my guilt. As
an older person, I have a duty of care towards Otty. I *should*
broach her parents. I cannot explain my aversion but I have
a deep reluctance to getting embroiled with that family – the
socially voracious father and the vapid, vaporous mother. Or,
I reflected, I could meet Mabs in the first instance. I felt sure
I would find her amiable and it's clear she means the world
to Otty. That would be a constructive compromise.

The cards are uncanny at times. No sooner had my mind
framed the thought than the third card responded. The House.
*From the visit which You and Your house will receive, great
Advantages must ensue, but let prudence guide Your conduct*.

Well then. Mabs it would be. And reprieve for a little longer
from the Finches and their problems. For problems there
must be if they are comfortable to allow their young daughter
to float about the world like a dandelion seed.

So, on a January day barely more clement than the previous,
here is Otty with Mabs. I answer the door myself. Otty hugs
me and Mabs hovers on the doorstep, plainly nervous. She
wears her sober companion's uniform and an old shawl as thin
as gauze. Her uninspiring attire does nothing to disguise how
pretty she is, though I doubt she is aware of it. I draw them
in at once and shake her hand.

Fortunately Otty, never the most formal of girls, bounds

ahead, defusing the awkwardness. Then Mama comes along, with Clover in tow. She too greets Mabs kindly before disappearing on her own business and leaving Clover with us. My daughter is a wonderful distraction for Mabs who coos over her gratifyingly. Then Anne brings us tea and cake and by the time we are settled and peaceful, it's too late for Mabs to be shy or awkward. She's already enjoying herself. I know too much about her from Otty – and doubtless the reverse is also true – for her to stand on ceremony.

'Tell me about your family,' I invite. 'Otty says you have several brothers and sisters. I envy you. I'm an only child, you see, and dear Clover looks likely to follow the same fate.'

Eyes shining, her pale face flushed petal pink, Mabs lists a great number of Jens and Jems and so forth, extolling their virtues at some length. I laugh, because to see someone express affection so freely is a lovely thing – catching, like the flu, only desirable. As she talks, I glean a picture of a close family negotiating a chasm of heartbreak. From the gaps between the lines I also realise that they are shockingly poor. Dangerously poor. Really, where is the improvement from Dickensian times?

I have so many questions for Mabs but I cannot go rushing in as the great saviour so early in our acquaintance. *Let prudence guide Your conduct*, I remind myself. She's proud, especially of the fact that she's earning a good wage and taking money home *and* saving up to give them a better future. It's a lot for a young person, I think, then berate myself for being patronising. She's smart, strong and healthy and there's no reason she can't do whatever she decides. Although . . . her speech is very rough and Otty's mentioned that she can't read or write and these are decided disadvantages, *I* think, if one wishes to earn enough money to support half a dozen children.

When I ask about her job with the Finches, her aspect immediately changes. It's quite remarkable. 'I'm so grateful for it, miss,' she says fervently. 'I fell on me feet the day Mr Finch give me that job an' that's a fact. He's ever such a kind gentleman. I get to spend time with Miss Otty here, as you know, an' I 'ave a bedroom all to meself. The family are that polite with me, miss, I couldn't ask for a better position, not in me wildest dreams!'

Her words don't surprise me but her mannerisms do. We've been chatting so easily but now she might be at a formal interview. Her shoulders are high and hard, her smile disappears and she looks as if she's reciting a lesson at school. She's squeezing her hands tightly together as if there's something she doesn't want to let out.

'I mean,' she goes on, 'companion to the lady of the 'ouse. 'Ow lucky am I? You've seen me, miss, I ain't exactly the genteel sort. I don't talk nice, I never done that kind o' work before. When I went to see about it I felt sure I'd fall flat on me face, only Mr Finch, he don't care about that sort of thing. So there I am, living with the family and counting me lucky stars every day.'

'I'm sure they feel equally lucky to have you,' I say when I can get a word in. 'You talk the way people talk where you come from, Mabs, and Mr Finch is quite right not to care about that. Never be ashamed of where you come from. It's who you are and where you're going that matter. I know Otty thinks the world of you.'

'Oh, thank you, miss. Of you she does an' all. I don't know what I'll do with me afternoons when she goes to school next week. It's not like I'll be able to 'elp her with 'er 'omework, is it?'

'We shall go a-wandering on Saturday afternoons, Mabs,'

says Otty, her gleam tempered by the prospect of homework. 'And when spring comes there'll be daylight after school too. It'll be all right.' I think I have inspired her with my talk of university. It was none of my business, of course, but I am single and I am clever so I must always know what's best for everyone.

'Perhaps before too long, Mama might join us,' Otty adds, brightening again. 'Do you think, Mabs? Wouldn't that be splendid, the three of us exploring in the spring twilight?'

'Yes indeed, Otty,' says Mabs.

Well, *I* am not convinced. Is it that she thinks Mrs Finch will *not* be ready for spring strolls and doesn't want to disappoint Otty by saying so? Or is the prospect of strolling with her mistress one that she deplores? In either case, why? What's wrong with the woman? I'm coming to adore Otty and Mabs is a dear. Therefore I must, after all, go and meet these blasted Finches, because my sense persists that all is not quite as it should be in that house.

Mabs

As January crept on, Mabs became increasingly disenchanted. Her brief, bright optimism seemed to have washed away down Hampstead high street along with the winter rains. No matter how many times she told herself it was none of *her* business what Mrs Finch had done in Durham, she couldn't help feeling uncomfortable. With all those children, with darling Otty, and such a loving husband . . . how *could* she have? It was the elephant in the room, the conversation she could never, ever broach with her mistress. And why should she? It wasn't *her* place to question or judge.

It even tarnished their reading lessons. If Mrs Finch was capable of dashing her husband's heart through the mud like that, then perhaps she was planning further mischief, though what Mabs might have to do with it, she couldn't fathom. Was she just a piece in a puzzle she couldn't understand? The worst of it was that she had actually started to like Mrs Finch, and feel proud that she had won her over a little. Now she was questioning whether she had ever done any such thing. Mabs remained determinedly cheerful in front of Otty and if Mrs Finch noticed a change in her, she said nothing. Lou, however, was one person who would not let things go so easily.

'What's wrong?' she asked more than once when Mabs was distracted and slow to laugh for the whole of one Sunday.

'Nothing!' protested Mabs. 'It's just the weather, ain't it?'

'It's rained every January that *I* can remember,' pointed out Lou, 'and I never seen you like this before. Mrs F up to her old tricks again?'

'No, she's civil. It's all fine, Lou, honest.'

If she could confide in anyone, thought Mabs, it would be Miss Olive Westallen. She was clever, Miss Westallen. Mabs might be more worldly, if it was worldly to know what it was like to be poor and scared and fierce from lack of options. But now that she lived at number six, she realised what a big, complicated place the world was. She thought having a friend like Miss Westallen, who knew how to negotiate it, must be a very great boon indeed. But although she had been kind, Mabs could not consider that the two of them might ever be friends. It took the innocence and the cheek of someone like Otty to discount social differences so entirely. Even so, her memory of that visit was warm.

She told her brothers and sisters about it when she next visited and they could hardly believe that someone so rich and genteel, the very cherry of society, could be so natural and friendly to *one of them*. 'Not hoity-toity *at all*?' asked Nicky, his world view visibly shifting inside his head.

'Not one bit!' Mabs assured him.

Pa took little interest. He was slumped at the table, his chin in his hands. The atmosphere in the Daley home was subdued.

'What's wrong, Pa?' Mabs asked.

'Pa's off the grain,' Jenny said softly. 'Tomorrow he's on the ice.'

Mabs's heart sank. Of course, it was always a possibility this time of year. 'Oh Pa,' she said, sitting down beside him.

'Can't be 'elped,' he sighed, 'but I can't say I'm lookin' forward to it. I'm gladder than ever you got yerself out,' Pa added, grabbing Mabs clumsily around the wrist. 'I'm proud of yer, Mabs, and don't you forget it.'

'Pa,' laughed Mabs. 'Don't talk as though we ain't goin' to see you again. You're tough! And look on the bright side: January's half over, February's a short month . . . Before you know it you'll be back on the grain, or the timber.'

'But oh, ain't it a terrible thing? All these children to support and no wife to 'elp me through it.'

Mabs patted his hand. She hated it when he talked like that, as if the children were to blame. As if, without them, he'd be free to idle his days away instead of forced to work.

'It's an 'ard life I'm in,' Nicholas went on. 'But Jen's coming up to the age you were when you started on the wharf. Maybe—'

'*No*, Pa!' Mabs's voice was forceful from shock. 'You can't mean that! You *surely* couldn't want Jen working there.'

Pa looked uncomfortable. 'Well, I'm just sayin' that even with what you bring, it's still a lot on my shoulders. If Jen had a go and all, then we'd be seein' a difference. She don't mind, she's a good girl, like you.'

Mabs glanced at Jenny, whose face told a different story. 'No,' said Mabs again. 'That's not the direction this family's headed. I'm not havin' Jenny or any of the others go through what I did. Now, Pa, you hang on for just one more winter and who knows where we'll be by next year. Next Sunday I'll bring an extra pound. And . . . Gawd help me I'll think of something for you lot, see if I don't.'

'Mabs, you're already doing so much,' said Jenny, coming over and stroking her hair. 'You should keep some of your wages for you.'

'Yes, love, thank you,' said Nicholas, recovering himself somewhat. 'Now then, Peg, what's for lunch?'

Mabs walked back to Hampstead that evening in a daze, barely noticing the cold. Jenny labouring indeed! She was furious with her father even for thinking it! She'd never told them how hard it was when she first arrived at the Finches'. She hadn't gone through all that just so her sister could end up where she, Mabs, had started! Over her dead body. It was a new year, a new chapter. She had to stop looking into things so deeply at Willoughby Walk. Taken at face value, they were fine. Mr Finch was kind. Mrs Finch was thawing towards her. And she was saving money . . .

If she could just afford tidy clothes for them, make them presentable so at least one of them could get a job in service . . . surely, then, Pa would feel the family's fortunes tilt in another direction. Surely then he would feel the burden lift. When he talked so despairingly of his lot, it was all Mabs could do not to promise him her entire savings then and there. But Mabs knew how it went with money. When you were poor, you somehow just kept getting poorer. A family their size could eat Mabs's money in a couple of weeks. But if Mabs kept it safe, and if it kept growing, there would come a time when it could really make a difference . . . help them to make significant changes, maybe even get them out of that horrible room . . .

She imagined her sisters in clean dresses in comfortable homes, Pa cheerful and unburdened, the boys full of life and learning . . . Mabs dawdled and dreamed as the dusk fell and the road led her away from Mushroom Court, back to peaceful Hampstead, where the lights of houses glimmered like fairy lamps and it seemed as though nothing bad could ever happen.

✣

When Mabs arrived she lingered in the hall. Blue hydrangeas no longer filled the vases; instead, they brimmed with dull bronze branches and spikes of holly, the bright red berries now starting to wrinkle. Mabs looked up at the portrait of Mrs Finch, marvelling as she always did that a woman that vibrant and lustrous could become so insular and confined. A door flew open, making her jump.

'Miss Daley, I thought I heard you.' Mr Finch was peering out from his study. 'I hope you had a good day with your family?'

Mabs dragged her eyes from the painting to her employer's tired, good-humoured countenance. 'Yes, sir, thank you.'

'Miss Daley, I hate to trouble you on your evening off, but might I beg five minutes?'

'Of course!'

He came to join her. 'I shan't keep you, Miss Daley, only I've heard a report about my daughter and I thought it couldn't possibly be true. I wondered if you could shed any light.'

'If I can, sir. Which daughter?' Mabs feared that he'd somehow heard that Elfrida had told Mabs the family secret. She hoped not! That would make for a very awkward conversation.

'Why, Otty, of course!' Mr Finch looked surprised at the question. 'It's nothing bad, only a little . . . perplexing. I've heard a rumour that Otty has somehow forged a friendship with Miss Olive Westallen. Have you heard of her?'

Mabs wanted to sink through the floor. Even *she* knew that Mr Finch had been longing to meet a Westallen. Otty wanted to keep Olive to herself and Mabs hadn't thought it her place to say otherwise. Only now *she* had been and gone and met her too! How could she tell him that *she* had met a Westallen before he had?

'Ummm . . . she's that grand lady from up the hill, ain't she?'

'Precisely. I've been wanting to make that family's acquaintance ever since we arrived. Her father would be an *excellent* connection. And Otty *knows* this. I can't believe she would conduct a friendship with this lady without telling me . . . Does it seem likely to you?'

Mabs thought the world of this man. But how could she be truthful without dropping Otty in it?

'Let me ask her, sir,' said Mabs. 'You know what gossip's like. Probably they run into each other once or something and it's turned into something bigger than what it is. I'll find out.'

'Very good. Enjoy your evening, Miss Daley, and thank you for your time.'

He was always so courteous, thought Mabs, going upstairs. She hoped she'd handled it pretty well. She would pop her head round Otty's door now; it would be awful if Mr Finch spoke to her first and realised Mabs had been less than transparent. She frowned. Considering Mr Finch was the person she owed the most to in the world, there were an awful lot of things she felt she couldn't tell him. And she wasn't at all sure how that had come about.

Olive

I'm not much enthused about the day ahead. For one thing, I'm very tired. After three happy, untroubled months, Clover has started to have nightmares and I have not had an unbroken sleep for the last two nights. She cannot tell me what the dreams are about, but climbs into bed with me, crying, and I cuddle her until she drops off again. But after that, I cannot. What memories or fears torment my little one? I cannot bear for her to suffer. Also, I dislike this diminished version of me. My head is foggy, my eyes are as gummed as envelopes. I feel like half the Olive I used to be.

As if sleep deprivation is not enough to contend with, I am to call on the Finches at last. Otty pelted straight from school to see me yesterday; her father, it transpires, has learned about our friendship. Was he angry? I asked, kicking myself for not acting sooner. Not at all, she said glumly, quite the opposite.

There followed a long tangle of an explanation about how he had said this and Mabs had said that and then she and Mabs between them had settled on a party line which I was to adopt immediately . . . I gather Mr Finch has long been desirous to meet a Westallen. Though Otty adores her father, she seems uncommonly perceptive about his faults and wanted to save me from his vaunting ambition. So Otty told him, and

I am to corroborate, that I met her once, on the heath when she rescued Clover from the tree.

I promised I would go along with the story; I don't wish to make things difficult for dear Otty. I sent my card there and then, saying that I would call on Mr *and* Mrs Finch today. I want to meet them both in one fell swoop and get them over and done with. The Finches annoy me without our ever having met, especially her. I realise that there are many different unhappinesses, but a well-off lady who keeps to her room and, essentially, refrains from partaking in the great obstacle course we call life is not someone I can imagine understanding.

And now the hour is upon me. Otty's home is a dear little house. Built of light brown stone, it occupies the end of a small terrace. The front door is painted a pretty light blue. Inside is a hall of black and white flags, with a portrait that makes me stop and stare. Surely not Mrs Finch? The painted lady is vivacious and passionate-looking, with dark eyes full of a quick intelligence. The Finches' housekeeper, to my surprise, is Mrs Webb, who worked for my friend Mrs Lake until the money for a housekeeper ran out. We greet each other with pleasure and remark upon the great sadness of Mrs Lake's diminished fortunes, then she shows me into a small, neat parlour.

I hardly notice the father at first, so fascinated am I by the mother, who is at once entirely different from her portrait and exactly the same. She cannot be much more than forty; her hair is still dark and lustrous, her skin unlined. She wears a beautiful dress of rose silk and is quite lovely. But she is no glittering girl, she is a grown woman, carrying herself with dignity, sadness and strength.

She is like a pool of secrets – the thought flashes through my mind as we shake hands. I find myself immediately wanting to become her friend, but how do you befriend someone who does not leave the house?

Mr Finch is red-faced with delight, though I do not flatter myself that his interest is in *me* – his thrill is to have a *Westallen* in his home. I have seen it often enough and recognise the syndrome at once. He has thinning chestnut hair and a round, open face. His eyes sparkle and he can hardly contain himself as he pumps my hand up and down.

'Miss Westallen, you are welcome, most welcome. Very welcome!' I deduce, then, that I am welcome! 'Welcome to our humble home. It is modest but, in truth, newly arrived from the north as we are, we are struck by the, er . . . higher living expenses of the capital. And we still have Otty to put through school. And we have two other daughters we hope to see married in due course. One cannot underestimate the expense of a wedding! Our house in Durham was far larger. But London is a splendid city, so bracing! We feel most fortunate. And I've always maintained it's better to have the smallest house in the best neighbourhood than the biggest house in a poor one. It suits us very well. We need only a modest staff and we find that what it lacks in size it more than makes up for in charm. This, for example, is a lovely apartment. Will you take a seat by the fire, Miss Westallen? Can you credit that February is nearly upon us already? How the time passes.'

His wife looks faintly uncomfortable, as well she might. I have never before met a man who greeted a new acquaintance by launching into explanations about the size of their house and their financial considerations. They really are the oddest match!

'Yes, please do sit, Miss Westallen,' she says, as if remembering long-neglected social skills and dusting them off. 'It is a cold winter. Will you take some tea?'

Mr Finch rings a bell and I note that the maid who answers looks completely nonplussed to see the mistress of the house sitting at his side. She soon returns with tea and cake and a second maid to help her carry them, though she could certainly manage alone. They both gaze at Mrs Finch as though she is a comet, rarely sighted and extraordinary.

We talk of Otty, of course. I recount the story of Otty's rescue of Clover in full, since I have been given permission to do so. 'My gratitude was, and remains, immense. I beg your pardon for my manners. I have been meaning and meaning to call, but then it was Christmas, and suddenly finding myself the mother of a four-year-old is somewhat all-consuming. As you said, Mr Finch, how time passes.'

'It does, Miss Westallen, it *does!*' he agrees, overjoyed that we share an opinion. 'Think nothing of it, we understand. Heavens, with all the calls you must have on your time, we think it wonderfully civil of you to come at all.'

I feel uncomfortable with his vastly deferential manner; I always do when people efface themselves before me, as though I'm some sort of higher being. I don't doubt that many people of my class insist on being treated that way, but to me it seems absurd. The sooner we all, rich and less advantaged alike, stop thinking that way, the better. We are all people. If I am someone of worth, I hope it is because of my personal qualities and the efforts I make in life, not because of my surname and the amount of money I carry in my purse.

'Miss Westallen.' Mrs Finch interrupts his flow of gratitude in her pleasing, low voice. 'Otty has told us that your daughter is adopted. I find that fascinating and admirable. How do you find it, suddenly becoming the mother of a four-year-old, as you put it?'

'Abigail, my *dear!*' Mr Finch looks appalled. 'Miss Westallen will not wish to discuss such matters with *us*! Her visit is a courtesy we must not abuse.'

'I beg your pardon,' says Mrs Finch at once.

'No, please,' I say hastily. 'It is no abuse. I delight in talking about Clover and I'm grateful for your interest, Mrs Finch. You know how it is, sir, women love nothing more than talking about their daughters. How do I find it? Well, I find it terrifying, baffling, exhilarating and joyous. Sometimes all at once. I feel ill-prepared, and it seems incredible to me still that I am the person solely responsible for Clover. But you, Mrs Finch, are mother to four, are you not? I am in awe of you, ma'am.'

I notice Mrs Finch make a tiny sideways glance at her husband and, out of the corner of my eye, observe a minute nod from him. How strange. I would not have thought her the naturally deferential type. Mrs Finch and I talk for a short while about our families, our different experiences of motherhood. If Mr Finch is at all put out that his prize, a nice, juicy Westallen, is caught up with his wife instead of him, he hides it well. But after a time I feel I should draw him back into the conversation.

'Of course, it must make all the difference having a husband. Someone to share the endless worries of childhood, not having to make every decision alone. My parents did warn me against adoption for this and many other reasons, but I'm shockingly headstrong, you see.'

Mr Finch looks puffed and proud and I smile at him before turning to Mrs Finch for her answer. I am struck by the look of echoing blankness in her eyes. 'My husband is present in everything I think and do,' she says. 'I cannot imagine life without him.'

We make small talk for another twenty minutes or so, then

I make to leave. I have done my duty and found Otty's parents, on the whole, more palatable than I had imagined. I ask if Otty might call at my house and permission is granted – gushingly by Mr Finch, and also by Mrs Finch, who says she should be glad for Otty to further her acquaintance with Clover and myself. It feels a thousand times more of a compliment than her husband's showering joy.

'And you too, Mrs Finch,' I add on impulse. 'If you wish to accompany Otty one afternoon when your husband is at work, please consider yourself welcome. I know it can be lonely being the new lady in town. I have friends who have gone through it.' A little bold of me perhaps, given what I know of her, but there has been no mention of her mysterious malady today and they are not to know how much Otty has confided in me.

This time there is no glance at her husband. She drops her eyes. 'You're most kind,' she murmurs, non-committal. I will not press her. I shake hands with both Finches and a maid brings me my things.

'Stay in the warm, my dear,' Mr Finch says to his wife. 'You know how draughty the hall can be.' And he shows me out himself.

'A pleasure to meet you,' I say on the doorstep and almost mean it.

'An honour,' he replies. 'I wonder, Miss Westallen, if I might mention one more thing? I didn't wish to say in front of my wife, because business matters vex her . . .'

Ah, here it comes, I think.

'I wondered if your father might be willing to meet with me to discuss the canals? My investments are successful but I see so much untapped potential. Even ten minutes with a man of your father's reputation and intelligence would be an immense boon.'

By 'reputation and intelligence', of course, you mean fortune.

'I would *greatly* value the chance to discuss my ideas with him briefly. But I would not wish to impose, Miss Westallen, no indeed. Captain Westallen is far, far above me in the firmament, I realise that.'

I smile tightly. 'Mr Finch, my father does not consider himself to be far, far above anyone. The impediment is likely to be not his position in the, er, *firmament*, but considerations of time. If he gave ten minutes to everyone who wishes to benefit from his . . . *advice*, he would have no minutes left. But I shall ask, you may be assured.'

'Thank you, Miss Westallen,' he blusters, shaking my hand all over again. 'I am *most* grateful. Thank you again!'

Otty

I admit, school is not as bad as I thought it would be. Very well then, I *love* it! I think Papa would be very disappointed if he knew the reality of my days. The academy *does* intend to fit girls out with manners and social graces, that is true, and those lessons are an excellent opportunity for dozing. They are taught by Miss Lemon, a woman so vertical I'm convinced she has never slouched in her life! But we have other lessons, too.

Mathematics, literature, geography, history – even politics! – are all taught by a man, Mr Ferris. I've never *met* a man who thinks as he does! He believes that girls are equal in intelligence to boys. He says that many of the differences between men and women, were we educated equally, would disappear! He was at a boys' school in Chelsea before, and says he will treat us just as he treated his pupils there, and foster the same standards and competitive spirit between us. There will be tests designed to stretch us. I shan't mind any number of tests if I can have the opportunity to learn and discuss and be treated like an intelligent human being!

I've made a friend, too: Edina. As the new girl I had a certain curiosity value in those first few days. But already my gloss is fading; many of the girls in my class prefer Miss Lemon to Mr Ferris and that says everything. They turn up their noses when they hear my slight northern accent. They raise pretty eyebrows when I tell them where I live. Apparently, Willoughby Walk is not the most fashionable street in Hampstead! As if *I* care.

Edina Hammond is quite different. She lives with her father, a widowed English professor. They have a house filled with books and she plans to go to university. She has an aunt who is active in the women's movement! I hadn't known there was one – that is not the sort of news to penetrate into the Finch home. We have many an enthusiastic discussion during our breaks. And she's kind. She remained welcoming to me when the others fell away and gives sweet treats to Beatrice, the scholarship girl, whom the others mostly ignore.

In class, Mr Ferris invites our opinions and questions. We've discussed the women's movement, current affairs and the class system. It tends to be only myself, Edina and Beatrice who put our hands up while the other girls listen with alarm in their eyes. But I think what Mr Ferris is doing is wonderful. *This* is how you change the world!

I'm so emboldened by these adventures that on Saturday afternoon I finally tell Mabs about Jill. We've had a bracing march on the heath – the rain was good enough to hold off for a whole hour – and when the first, fat droplets fell, I begged to conclude our outing with a visit to the tea rooms on the high street. My treat, I promised. I could tell Mabs doesn't think much of a child paying for her, but if we went home, we'd be sure to be joined by *someone*.

When we're seated in a corner table, cocoa for me, strong tea for Mabs, macaroons for us both, I take a deep breath. 'Mabs,' I begin. 'I want you to know that I've come to think of you as a trusted friend.'

She beams. 'Thanks, Otty. That means a lot to me, it does.'

'Good. Well. I want to tell you something. I have a secret. I don't know enough about things and I want to talk to someone and I don't want to worry Mama . . . Can I talk to *you*, please?'

'Of course! What is it?'

'Well, do you remember that day I burst in on you and Mama, when I had been attacked at the canals?'

"Ow could I forget that?'

'Well, I *wasn't* at the canals. Not that day, anyway. But I *had* been at the canals several weeks earlier . . .'

I explain the story of how I met Jill, how she rescued me and how we agreed to meet up. 'What do you think?' I ask Mabs.

Mabs frowns. 'I can see why you wouldn't tell your parents you'd been to the canals. Honestly, Otty, it ain't safe for you. But why haven't you told them about Jill? I suppose yer worried they won't approve because she's poor and uneducated? But I should think they'd be glad to meet her after the service she done you. And you'd be far safer meeting around here than going to those places.'

I shake my head. 'She *can't* come here. And she isn't uneducated. Quite the opposite.'

Mabs looks incredulous. 'What's she doin' workin' there then?'

'Well, she doesn't have a choice. She's . . . well, she's not a *white* girl, Mabs.' I pat my cheeks to show what I mean. I don't think the word 'white' is a very good description for most of us anyway. I myself am a sallow sort of beige. Papa, Charlie and Averil are decidedly pink. Mama and Elfrida are an enviable magnolia. 'She comes from a place in the Caribbean and she has dark brown skin and she's very pretty and lovely and funny but . . .' I stop in frustration. I don't know how to express the conundrum. But Mabs understands immediately.

'Folk like her ain't too welcome here.' She nods. 'White people look on them suspicious, I know. There was one or two in Saffron Hill from Africa. Oh, the trouble they had from rich folk and our folk alike. They find a little corner and they stick to their own – it's the only way they get by. Oh Otty, that's an awful big secret.'

'Well, it's all academic now.' Quickly I tell Mabs about the attackers and the policeman and Jill. 'She told me I wasn't to visit her any more. She said we'd be friends in our hearts but it wasn't safe for me to visit her.'

Mabs sniffs. 'She's got more sense than you then! And you 'aven't seen her since?' I shake my head. 'And you don't intend to, I hope? Because, Otty, if you did and yer parents found out I knew about this, I'd lose me job. No question.'

'I know. I won't meet her. Only Mabs, I don't *understand*. *Why* wouldn't they want me to have a friend like that? I mean, I *know* it's because of how she looks and where she's from. But why does that *matter*? That's the bit I wanted to ask you. I've heard Jill called such names! Everyone seems to think people who look like her are . . . wicked, or lazy, or stupid . . . But she's *not*! What am I missing, Mabs? Do *you* think I'm wrong for liking her? I just want to *know*.' I've been carrying these questions for so long now that I start to cry a little. It's such a shock learning that the world isn't the way I want it to be.

Mabs takes my hand and squeezes. 'There, there, love. Don't cry, Otty. It's an 'ard thing, ain't it? I don't know as I understand it any better than you. But I'll tell you what I think, if you like.'

I nod and sniff.

Mabs smiles sadly. 'The human race is full of cruelty, Otty. It's full of goodness too, mind you, so don't you despair. But people can be . . . really nasty, treat each other like dirt, sometimes. People don't like what's different, what they don't understand, that's what I've noticed. I'm like you, I don't really know why that should be. I think different is . . . interesting.

'The folk where I come from don't even like people like *you* – people with money and comfort and such. They think you're all stuck-up and uncaring. I never thought that. I always thought, probably some rich folk are like that and others ain't. Just like some poor folk are kind and honest, and others ain't. So when there's someone who *looks* so different, and *sounds* so different, someone from a foreign land . . . well, it's the same thing again only bigger, that's what I reckon. People say stupid things, Otty, just to make themselves feel better. It ain't fair. It ain't fair a bit. And it's sad. But it's the way it is.'

'So you don't think brown people are all those horrid things they say?'

'Oh *no*! It's not like all of our lot are so wonderful, is it? I told you, Otty, people are stupid. There's a lot of Italians in the courts, because of the ice cream, you know, and Frenchies in the winters to work the ice . . . and even *they* get grief because they come from somewhere else. Maybe one day it'll be different, who knows? You're sharp as a tack, Otty, no question of that, but you're twelve, and you're a girl. So *you* ain't the person who's going to change things. I'm sorry, Otty.'

Just what Jill had said. I feel a deep, sweeping sorrow. I understand a *little* more now. But I don't like it. Not at all.

Mabs

That evening Mabs went for a drink with Lydia and Betsy. She stayed out later than usual, enjoying their uncomplicated company, and feeling wistful when they said goodnight and set off home while Mabs returned to Willoughby Walk. Sometimes life with the Finches felt stifling. There were *four* things Mabs had to remember to keep from Mr Finch now: the reading lessons, her knowledge of Mrs Finch's affair, how long Otty had been friends with Olive and now Otty's friendship with Jill! She'd never known such a family for secrets!

She felt deeply sad for Otty. A true friend, one who always looked out for you, always cared, and who could make you laugh while they were at it, was a rare thing, Mabs knew that. Just look at her and Lou – where would Mabs be now without her? But the complications attached to Otty and Jill in this time and place, especially at their tender ages . . . well, it was lucky that Jill was smart enough to handle it the way she had, that's what Mabs reckoned. But it was a crying shame. She hated to think of that poor girl labouring at the canals with the double burden of her sex and colour to contend with. And she hated to see Otty's bright spirit dulled and her open heart bruised as she rubbed up against reality. *People*, she thought. *Do they really deserve this beautiful world when they fill it with such unkindness and so many stupid ideas?*

She let herself in and tiptoed upstairs, finding her way by the moonlight falling into the hall and landings, taking care not to wake anybody. She was about to start the final climb to the attic when she heard voices, low but tense. She turned. Mrs Finch's door stood ajar, outlined by a narrow edge of light. She couldn't make out any words but Mr Finch was talking in his usual measured, slightly pleading tone and his wife was replying with her customary short, scornful interjections. Mabs glanced anxiously at Otty's closed door. She knew she should go to bed at once but a force stronger than sense drew her nearer to the barely open door.

'I can't, my dear, I simply can't,' Mr Finch was murmuring. 'I would like nothing more than for you to have a normal, appropriate social life. But you know as well as I that you simply cannot be trusted. What you might say, what you might do, whom you might meet . . . I think you should wait until you are much, much better.'

'And when will that be, Lucius? When I am old and grey?'

'My darling, don't be foolish. I wish you better immediately! Yesterday, if possible. It rests with you, does it not?'

A distinct snort. 'Does it indeed? Well then, leave me, Lucius. I am tired. Perhaps I shall sleep tonight and wake miraculously cured.'

A slight creak of the door, as if a hand had come to rest on the handle. Mabs froze. What was she *thinking*, eavesdropping like this? 'But my dear, if you would only admit the damage you have caused to this family, if you would only take some responsibility . . .'

'Ha!' The exclamation was so explosively derisive that Mabs glanced again at Otty's door. 'I suppose you mean Jonathan.

Or perhaps you refer to one of my other indiscretions. I don't know, Lucius, I am such a difficulty in every way, am I not?'

'Yes, your actions in Durham caused me pain. Do you not care? You are my *wife*, Abigail. We have had four children together. And then to learn that all the while your old lover was calling on you . . .'

Mabs suddenly came to her senses and crept at speed to the stairs. She fled to her room, thanking the heavens that she hadn't been caught out. That was the most private sort of conversation imaginable and nothing that she should be hearing. Hastily she undressed and hopped into bed, where she lay staring wide-eyed into the dark. It was true then. Part of Mabs had been hoping that there had been some mistake after all, that Elfrida had fallen prey to a grievous confusion. But there *had* been an affair and Mrs Finch didn't sound repentant, not one bit. *Perhaps you refer to one of my other indiscretions*, she had said. Did she mean other lovers? Or other sorts of wrongdoing? Mabs couldn't imagine and didn't wish to. It was true what they said about eavesdropping – you never heard anything that made you glad.

'Not yer business, Mabs, not yer business,' she muttered into the dark. It was becoming a constant refrain.

✣

The following morning Mrs Finch was morose, as silent and brooding as London fog. When Mabs brought out the book they had been working through together, her mistress turned away. 'Not today, Daley,' she said without explanation.

'Very good, ma'am,' Mabs murmured, heart sinking. Things had started to feel so much better. Were they to go back to the old ways again? Why must Mrs Finch be so changeable? They sat without speaking throughout a wet morning. Mrs

Finch kept her gaze firmly upon the rose garden, dismal as ever in the rain. Mabs struggled alone with her reading, for something to do. She hoped this wasn't to be the end of the lessons. She was starting to make head and tail of the letters, but she still had a long way to go, and it was so much easier with a tutor.

At lunchtime the rain cleared. The sky faded to a washed-out blue and sunshine glimmered in the garden. Mabs was filled with a great longing to escape this stifling room. 'Look, it's cleared up lovely,' she said. 'Why don't we take a walk, ma'am? Just a short one'll do. Today's the day, don't you think?'

'No, Daley. Today is most certainly not the day.'

'Is anything the matter, ma'am? Can I help?'

Mrs Finch gave one of her expressive snorts for answer.

'Only it's turnin' into such a beautiful day,' Mabs pressed on. 'It might lift yer spirits to venture out in it.'

'It would take more than a sunshower, I assure you. Quiet, I beg you.' The tone was imperious, not supplicatory in the slightest, the words mere formality. Mabs subsided. Unable to concentrate, she gazed at the slim back, ramrod-straight before her, the glossy dark fall of hair. *That's what an enigma looks like*, she thought. It was a word she had recently learned from Otty. Was it last night's conversation with her husband that had set her off again? Was it the talk of her lover? Was she missing him? Was she angry at being thwarted?

Another hour crawled by and the sun grew bolder. A shimmering rainbow stole into the rose garden and Mabs cried out without thinking. 'Oh, look! A rainbow! Ain't it beautiful? It's a sign of good luck, that is. Let's go out there, ma'am. Not a walk if you don't feel up to it but just into the garden. We could sit and feel the air and—'

She was cut off by a mighty roar. Not a scream, the way

women in stories were always screaming, but a deep belly cry, like a warrior going into battle. Mrs Finch flew to her feet and was halfway across the room so swiftly that Mabs thought she was going to strike her. But she stopped six feet away from Mabs, facing her down, her eyes boring into Mabs's so fiercely that Mabs shrank back.

'Get out!' hissed Mrs Finch, her voice scraped and raw. 'Get out of my room and don't come back for the rest of the day.'

Mabs hesitated. Mrs Finch advanced on her, brandishing a crystal vase she had snatched from an occasional table nearby. She was a woman who could make a household ornament look like a lethal weapon. 'Get out!' she hissed. 'I don't want to see you. I don't want to hear you. Go and chase your rainbows, your signs of hope. And tell my husband about all of this if you like, I *dare* you!'

Mabs fled.

Olive

At the time, my visit to Willoughby Walk was less excruciating than I had anticipated. But it has left me with an odd feeling ever since. I can't put my finger on why.

Mrs Finch – not at all as I expected. I ponder her obvious strength of will, my unexpected wish to befriend her. She was nothing like the invalid lady of my imaginings. Mr Finch – not as bad as I expected. I think of all I know of him from Otty and Mabs. A doting father. A kind and fair employer, willing to take a chance on a girl from the wrong part of the city. I have dreaded the Finches for nothing, it seems. And yet this feeling that I am missing something persists.

After weeks of mulling it over, I can pinpoint nothing and grow bored from thinking about this odd little family. Otty is straightforward and lovely and that is all that matters. I decide to concentrate on my own family instead. Clover is still waking up at night screaming; last night was the worst yet. I should have known it was all too easy. Ever since she arrived, she has seemed happy, a healthy, well-adjusted little girl. I was subjected to so many warnings against adoption yet for so long there wasn't a cloud on the horizon. It felt as though Clover had been with me forever. Pursuing life's course together as mother and daughter felt – and still feels

– so natural that it's hard to imagine she ever had any other life.

But she did. Four years of a very different life indeed, one which I cannot imagine and she cannot describe. Does she see it when she sleeps? What do I know of children's memories? It is time to seek out her origins. I must go and see for myself.

So I go to the children's home. I haven't been there since Christmas. I take three large rose and lemon cakes baked by Agatha, a small luxury for the children to enjoy at tea one day. I take a bouquet of early spring flowers for Mrs Jacey and a small bottle of port wine. I think I can hazard a guess as to which will please her more. And I take a cheque for the home, to encourage continued improvements, to ensure that when those poor children slip through the cracks, they don't fall farther than they need to.

I'm somewhat bleary-eyed from lack of sleep but nevertheless Mrs Jacey is glad to see me and my offerings. 'Cake,' she says with satisfaction. 'Yer good to think of it, miss. Nothin' puts 'em in spirits like the promise of cake. There's one or two is playing me up at the moment. Cake puts me in a strong position. Gives me something to blackmail them with, in short. Good thinking, miss.'

Blackmail hadn't exactly been my intention but I'm glad to have helped. 'I suppose Gert is one of those with whom battle is waged?' I say lightly. It's a good way of asking about her without seeming to, *I* think. But Mrs Jacey isn't fooled.

'Still thinkin' about her, are you? I wouldn't waste my brain. No, she ain't one of them I mentioned. But that's only because *everything's* a battle with her, every single day, so it wouldn't be news. Cake won't get me nowhere with madam. Nothing will.'

I'm sad to hear it, but remember my promise to Mr Miles and get to the point. Mrs Jacey looks up Clover's arrival – October 1895 – and finds the meagre notes from the day. My daughter was brought in by a Mrs Lily Duckworth, from Harlowe Place in Saffron Hill. It all sounds rather rural and lovely. I know it will not be.

'Yer not thinking of going there?' Mrs Jacey chastises, with the same drawn brows with which she warned me off Gert. 'You shouldn't go alone, that's what. Get someone to go with you. A man. And dress down a bit, if you get me drift.'

I promise to follow her advice, only to hasten outside and disregard all of it. It's not that I don't respect her judgement, it's only that she has a habit of thinking I'm some sort of precious ornament that needs to be kept in wads of cotton and a padded box. I have the bit between my teeth! I'm not about to postpone my plans now, just for the sake of a chaperone and a dowdy dress. I hail a cab.

'*Harlowe Place?*' echoes the driver in disbelieving tones. '*Saffron Hill?* Are you *sure*, ma'am?' It does not instil confidence. Nevertheless, I repeat my instruction.

We rattle along at a fair pace. As London flashes past, I see signs of spring everywhere – magnolia blossoms unfolding in luxurious, lustrous languor within gated gardens, crocuses flickering on the verges like tongues of flame. Egg-yolk yellow. *Saffron yellow*, I think, and tell myself it is a good omen. We cut past the north-east corner of Regent's Park and I remember Otty's tales of big yellow lions. I must take Clover very soon.

The view grows more congested as we proceed, the colour leaching, the open spaces shrinking, the impressive buildings jostling to centre stage. Then the less impressive buildings. And soon there is no loveliness at all, only cramped housing, massed together like a mob. The cab cuts down streets so

narrow I fear we will scrape the sides. There's an air of despond-
ency underlaid with a thick layer of menace. We draw to a
halt. In doorways, beggars sit, dirty, listless, some clutching
babies, some with crutches. They stare at the cab. I don't want
to get out.

'This is Harlowe Place?' I query, leaning out of the window.

'No, ma'am. I can't take the cab all the way, it won't fit. It's
down there.' He points at the shadowy entrance to an alley
on our left. I squint at the rough sign on the wall.

'That says Mellis Court,' I point out.

'That's it. Harlowe's just off Mellis.'

How appalling! The street we are on is mean and narrow.
Mellis Court is half its size. And Harlowe Place is *another*
afterthought? I realise I have made a sizeable mistake.

Now I understand why Mrs Jacey told me to change my
dress and come with a companion. I just hadn't realised it
would be *so* bad. It's like a scene from a Dickens novel but
we do not live in Mr Dickens's London now. We are but a
whisker away from the twentieth century; how can there still
be squalor of this magnitude? Then I think of Mabs Daley. I
should have known.

If I had the sense I was born with, as Mrs Jacey would say,
I would ask the driver to take me home and come another
day with Mr Miles. But no, it must be now. I cannot justify
my determination but I *need* to see it. Perhaps I would think
differently if I had had more sleep.

'Driver, what is your name, please?'

'My name?' He twists in his seat and looks at me. 'Dawkins,
they call me.'

'Mr Dawkins. If you would be so good, please wait here
for me. I shall be two or three minutes at most. Then I wish
you to drive me back to Hampstead. I understand that the

fare will be sizeable and I promise you there will also be a generous tip. Will you wait?'

'Aye, ma'am, all right. Only, I don't think you should go down there alone.'

'Are you offering to come with me, Mr Dawkins?'

'I can't leave the cab, ma'am. It'd be smashed to pieces by the time I got back and I'd never see me horse again.'

'Then I must go alone. But you *will* wait?'

Reassured by his glum nod, I step out of the cab. The air is thick and smells unhealthy. The beggars float etiolated hands towards me. Their listlessness is disturbing. 'In a minute, when I return,' I tell them and set off down Mellis Court.

'Court' is an amusing pretension. It's an alley, with sooty brick walls so close that my skirt brushes them as I walk. I try to hold my dress out of the dirt, then realise that a dirty hem is the least of my problems. I stride out more confidently than I feel, thinking of Mr Miles's crusading nature and his apparent ability to move invisibly through the city's underbelly. Here is a small turning. There is no other, so I take it. A tiny walkway opens into a small yard. Around it the houses are grey and sour; no sign here of the spring day I enjoyed on my journey. A few children are sitting on steps: girls cradling dolls, boys fighting with swords made from sticks.

A woman comes out and snatches the doll from one girl's hands. 'Bloody Alice!' she cries. 'I told you not to pinch the firewood. What d'yer think we are, made of money?' It's not a doll at all, just a few sticks tied together and dressed in a rag. I want to cry. This is how my Clover used to live.

The girl puts up no argument; she shrinks away and surrenders her plaything. Then the woman sees me. She goes stock-still, a cat spying a bird. ''Ere, who are you?' she shrieks. 'What you want? We don't want no strangers round 'ere.'

'I'm just leaving.' I step closer so we don't have to shout at one another. 'Can you tell me, please, is this Harlowe Place?'

'So what if it is?'

Goodness, how to explain? 'A promise to a friend,' I improvise. 'A long story.'

The child Alice tugs the woman's skirt. 'Ma,' she says. 'P'raps the lady come to give us something.'

The woman slaps the side of her head with casual ease so the child's head hits the wall. Alice's eyes fill with tears but she makes no protest. To see violence so small and ordinary, like blowing a nose, makes me flinch. I ache to speak out, but I know what Mrs Jacey would say to that.

'Stupid child,' sneers the woman. "*Course* she ain't come to give us nothing. The likes of them never give nothing to the likes of us. She's a fancy bitch, come to gawp. I'll fetch me 'usband if you don't clear orf.'

'No need, ma'am,' I say and I'm appalled to hear a slight tremble in my voice. 'I'm leaving, but first, I *have* come to give you something.'

Her face clouds over like a stormy sky. 'Oh yeah? And what's that?'

'Five pounds.' I pull it out of my purse. 'Here.' I hold it out. She does nothing but stare so I step forward and push it into her hand. Her fingers tighten on the note.

'What you trying to do?' she says. 'Get me in trouble with the law or something?'

'Certainly not, only to help. You're wrong, you see; sometimes people *do* want to help. Good day.'

Oh, the satisfaction of telling her she was wrong and in front of the child. I glance at Alice and see that she's listening.

'I'm fetching Terence,' says my nemesis, going inside.

I kneel down in front of the child. 'And this is for you,

darling,' I whisper, handing her a shining shilling. 'Keep it for yourself. You have very pretty hair.' Then I get up to go.

My way back to the alley is blocked. Five boys, hard-faced, ragged, bar my exit. Shoulder to shoulder they stand.

'Come on then, give us the rest,' says one of them. He sounds old, as old as the hills, but his face puts him at no more than fourteen. How can a mere boy be so frightening? I know immediately that this will go very badly wrong unless I am either very smart or very lucky. Suddenly I am very wide awake.

'Good day, gentlemen.' My voice belies the sinking dread within me. 'Perhaps you heard me tell your neighbour that I'm here to help. Please allow me to give you some money – no, don't argue, I have come for this very reason. Now, this for you, and this for you . . .' I hand over the entire contents of my purse and their rough hands grab at mine until they have everything. They know and I know that I have no choice in the matter but I'll be damned if I'll acknowledge the fact.

'It was a pleasure to see you all but now I must go.'

'Oh yes?' says one of them. He tilts his head to one side, revealing a grimy expanse of neck beneath a dirty kerchief. 'What if we want your ear-bobs, or your locket? *Or something else?*' That is what I had feared. He sounds so knowing, so adult, in all the worst ways. But it's that grimy neck that gives me the courage to speak.

'Children, stand aside. I'm afraid I can't give you my earrings, they're not mine but my mother's and she would be furious if I lost them. The locket is very cheap and worth nothing to you. But here, take my gloves. They are silk-lined and should fetch a price. Now I must go. Good day to you all.'

My brisk tone carries sufficient authority that the smallest boy steps aside, just enough for me to push through. I make it into Mellis Court and stride towards the cab. I hear footsteps behind me but I don't run; they could catch me up in a second. Counterfeit confidence is my only resource. My heart beats wildly. To my very great relief I see Mr Dawkins at the entrance to the alley, looking worried.

'Two or three minutes, you said!' he cries as I reach him. 'Oh,' he adds, seeing the crowd of boys behind me. 'You all right, ma'am?'

'Yes, thank you. Just barely. I'm very glad to see you, Mr Dawkins.' I glance behind me and the boys are gone.

The beggars are still on the steps. *They* will not harry and pursue me. But I promised. 'Mr Dawkins, I must ask you one more boon. Please lend me some money, just until we reach my home in Hampstead. I promised these people I would give them something but I have nothing left now.'

'Ma'am, due all respect, and it's very kind of you, et cetera, but it won't do no good. Opium and drink, that's what it'll go on. Even if there's one or two who ain't like that, what good's a shilling or a pound? It's too big for that, ma'am.'

'I understand perfectly and you're right. But I must honour my promise. It's my money.'

'Due all respect, ma'am, but it's mine.'

'Yes, but I will pay it back within the half hour.'

He sighs, reaches under his driver's seat and withdraws a handful of coins. 'I'll do it, ma'am.'

I can't deny that I'm glad to clamber into the cab and collapse. My legs are very weak and the full impact of my stupidity hits me. When we drive off, my relief is indescribable.

I feel stunned, all the way to Polaris House, where he jumps down to open the door for me. 'I hope I won't have any more fares like you today, ma'am.'

I smile. 'I hope so too, Mr Dawkins. You've been very forbearing. Thank you for everything, especially for waiting. I wouldn't have got out of there alive.'

'No, ma'am, you wouldn't. It's expectations, see. They sort of mass together until they become real. Those people expect nothing but bad – with good reason, I don't say – and then that's what they get. No amount of shillings can change that. It'll take something more.'

I'm very interested. 'What more, Mr Dawkins? Do you have an idea of what's needed?'

He considers the matter for a long time. 'I don't rightly know, ma'am. Schooling is important but it's more than that. It's education about the world, and the different sorts of people in it. When that's all you know, those places, that way of life, when all your family's grown there too and can't tell you about anything different, how can you imagine anything else? *Hope*, ma'am, is what they need, though that's nothing you or I could give. If you haven't got that, why *wouldn't* you steal or beg, or just give up? That's my tuppence worth anyhow.'

'A very valid tuppence worth,' I tell him as I clamber out and brush my skirts smooth. I feel I have lived a lifetime in this day.

I hasten indoors, find money, hasten back out again and pay Mr Dawkins for his fare, his wait, the money I insisted he lend me and his wisdom, all topped off with the promised tip. On a whim I ask for his card, though I'm sure he prays never to see me again. Something is brewing in my mind.

Mabs

When Mabs turned up for work the morning after Mrs Finch's latest outburst, she was full of trepidation. But to her astonishment, Mrs Finch apologised. It was nothing elaborate; she simply said, 'I apologise for my behaviour towards you yesterday.' It was, Mabs considered, something that would never have happened in the early days. Even so, being cooped up with her day after day was like being in a cage with a lion. By unspoken mutual consent, they didn't read together for a few days; their tentative accord was damaged. But the following week they started again and somehow Mabs muddled through to March. There were no further outbursts – towards her at any rate – but her mistress continued to be as unpredictable as the wind. Mabs tried hard to be the constant in their baffling equation.

One Sunday, Mabs made her way home in high spirits, not because of any improvement at work but because it was truly spring at last. Daffodils danced at the wayside and filled the morning air with their sweet, fresh scent. Ice season was over. The French and Swiss boys had gone home and her father had made it through without mishap.

But when she entered the room in Mushroom Court, her festive mood fizzled out. Pa was nowhere to be seen and the children looked glum. 'What's wrong?' she demanded. 'Where's Pa?'

'He's all right,' said Nicky gruffly. 'The girls are making a big fuss about nothing. They're being . . . *girls!*'

Jenny growled at him. 'And you're being a mule,' she said. She was sitting at the table and dropped her head into her arms.

'What?' pleaded Mabs.

'Nicky's going to work,' said Peg, coming to perch on the table edge nearest to Mabs. 'On the wharf.'

'*What?*' repeated Mabs in an entirely more menacing tone.

'I'm the man of the house after Pa!' Nicky declared. 'The only people bringing money into this place apart from Pa are you and Jenny. Girls. It ain't right. It's my turn.'

'Nicky, love, you're only a baby. And . . . the *canals*?'

'I'm twelve,' Nicky corrected her, suddenly sounding frighteningly adult. 'It was me birthday last month. *You* remember, Mabsy, you was there. I know you want us to get more schoolin' but it ain't for me. I don't enjoy it and I ain't good at it. I'm big for me age and I want to work. If it's good enough for Pa, it's good enough for me, Mabs, so don't start on!'

'All right,' said Mabs tightly, knowing well that look on Nicky's face. He had a stubborn streak as wide as the Thames. Let him start at the wharf then, see what it was really like. He might have ideas now about being a man and doing his bit, but once he'd had a few weeks hauling nightsoil and dredging silt, he'd think again.

'Besides,' he went on, as if Mabs hadn't given way, '*she's* left school too!'

Now Mabs was really amazed. 'Who? *Jenny?*' she asked. 'No, you ain't, Jen? You *do* like it. You always said so.'

'I do,' moaned Jenny, still with her head in her arms. Then she sat up and looked at Mabs. 'Leastways, I like the idea of

it. But honestly, Mabs, it ain't worth it. I'm fifteen. Everyone
leaves at fourteen. Mr Winkler don't mind me being there
because I missed so much when Ma was ill and . . . after. But
he don't teach me nothin' new either. It's the same old lessons
as last year, word for word. I'm just sittin' there, straining me
eyes. I might as well strain 'em sewing, *earning* more. We
need the money, Mabs.'

'Nothin' new there,' said Mabs. 'Why's it so urgent all of a
sudden? You're taking on more sewing and Nicky's off to work,
both in the space of a week. 'Ow come?'

The children looked at each other. Jem went to the door
and looked down the staircase. ''E ain't coming,' he said.

'Because Pa's on the coal tomorrow,' said Peg.

'Oh Gawd,' said Mabs, sinking into a chair beside Jenny.

Coal. With all her worries about ice, she'd managed to
forget all about coal, which was one of the canal's most important cargoes. It wasn't the coal itself that was the problem. The
work was the same old business, lugging it from the barges to
the wharf, onto the coal carts, sometimes with the aid of
hydraulic cranes, sometimes without. The problem was how
the men got paid.

Mostly, coal went in the first instance to agents or middlemen,
who were usually publicans. And while pub folk were often short
of cash they always had plenty of beer. So they part-paid the
porters with drinks, and beer wasn't a currency you could buy
food with or take home to your family. The sociability and luxury
of a few pints at the end of a hard day's labour made working on
the coal seem genuinely desirable at first. Until the men realised
their children hadn't had a square meal in weeks and they hadn't
seen their wives to talk to properly because they were in the
pub so much. Families with fathers more stable than Nicholas
Daley had been plunged into deprivation by this arrangement.

Pa hit the bottle hard when Maureen died, even when Mabs begged and begged him to stop. The last few months had been a good run, with Pa not quite back to his old self, but doing well enough. Now there was no doubt in anyone's mind that half their food money would vanish in the Bunch of Grapes in Limehouse. No wonder Jen and Nicky were planning ways to make up the shortfall.

'I'll kill him,' muttered Mabs, her stomach twisting into knots.

'Well, he ain't done nothin' yet,' Jenny reminded her fairly. 'And it ain't his fault; he didn't ask to go on the coal.'

'I know. It's just we all know what's coming, don't we?'

'It might be different this time,' suggested Jem, who had such kindness in him, and such a disposition to see possibility in the world, that it broke Mabs's heart to think that in just a couple of years he might be forced to work there too. She wouldn't let that happen; she *wouldn't*.

✲

By the time Mabs left that night, the sunny morning and dancing breezes had given way to a darkness as hard as nails and a high wind.

'Bleedin' 'ell,' she muttered, staggering a little as she walked. If she'd known, she'd have left earlier, but Mushroom Court was so tucked away you couldn't really see what the weather was doing and she'd been reluctant to go back to Willoughby Walk. Every step was a fight, and by the time she was walking up Heath Road, she was exhausted. By then a bright white moon was shining full and lovely above her. Mabs would have liked to draw comfort from it, but she couldn't convince herself that the moon cared whether or not Nicholas Daley overdid it on the booze.

Turning into Flask Walk, her head ducked against the wind, she collided with some figures emerging from Back Lane and apologised profusely. 'Our fault entirely,' cried a familiar voice. Mabs found herself looking at Olive Westallen.

'Oh!' she cried. Honestly, there was no one she would rather have run into just now. She often thought of Olive, and would have given almost anything to be able to confide her woes in her. But Miss Westallen was with companions, on her way somewhere; she wasn't going to stand about chatting. 'Miss Westallen!' said Mabs. 'It's good to see yer.'

'Why, good gracious! Mabs Daley! Good evening. How are you?'

'I'm well enough, miss. And you?'

'Oh, I'm wonderful! I'm off stargazing. This is my long-suffering maid, Anne, and her sweetheart, Colin, who have to accompany me in case I am robbed and plundered. Poor souls, how they are burdened with my eccentricity.'

Mabs smiled at the others, who did look as though they wished they were elsewhere. 'But where do you go to do that?' she asked curiously. 'It's a cold wind, miss!'

Miss Westallen laughed. 'It is. But it has blown the clouds away. Look, Mabs! No veil between us and the heavens. A rare glimpse of the Great Beyond. We go to Parliament Hill. Would you like to come?'

Mabs hesitated. A moment ago, she'd wanted nothing but to get inside, wrap herself in warm blankets and forget today and all its gloomy news. But Miss Westallen's company was a great inducement.

'I don't know nothin' about stars,' she said. 'I won't be a learned companion, miss. But I'd like to come, if you're really willing.'

'Oh, learned, fiddle,' decreed Miss Westallen. 'And I've told you before, call me Olive. Come on!' She strode off. It was no earlier than ten o'clock. Eccentric was about right, thought Mabs as she hurried after her.

With Olive at her side, Mabs didn't feel the cold so much, rather the exhilaration of battling over the heath, strands of hair plastered to her face, skirt snapping like a flag. When they reached Parliament Hill, Colin spread blankets on the ground – they all stood on the corners to stop them blowing away – while Anne produced flasks and sandwiches.

'Yer all prepared!' Mabs observed in delight.

'I've done this many times,' agreed Olive, shouting a little over the wind. 'My father taught me about how sailors follow the stars. I was convinced they were guiding angels. The night skies have always been a passion of mine.'

'How lovely,' sighed Mabs. Sailors might follow the stars, but was there an equivalent guardian for canal workers?

Olive sat down and gestured for Mabs to join her. Anne and Colin settled a little way off behind them. 'We always sit like this,' explained Olive. 'When I'm alone, you see, I do nothing but stare and think. No fun at all, so they leave me to it. But no such luck for you, I'm afraid. I shall subject you to a lesson about the stars!'

Mabs couldn't help smiling. 'I'd love one,' she said.

'I'm pleased to see you again, Mabs. It's Sunday – I suppose you were coming back from visiting your family when I kidnapped you. I hope they're well?'

Mabs couldn't help pouring it all out. 'Not so very well, no, miss . . . Olive. Me pa, they've put him on the coal, so he's going to drink it all away, and Nicky's going to work at the wharf and Jen's left school to do nothin' but sew and—'

'Wait, my dear, please,' said Olive, holding up a gloved hand. Mabs's own hands were bare and sunk deep in her coat pockets

for refuge from the wind. 'Please slow down, I don't understand. When you say they've put him on coal, what do you
mean? I have visions that he's being roasted slowly.'

Mabs gave a shaky laugh. 'Oh, yes, I forget it sounds odd
to people who don't know the work. Sorry, miss . . . Olive.'
She took a breath and explained more carefully.

'I see,' said Olive, when Mabs had outlined the problem.
'And what else? You said something about Nicky, and someone
else. Your brothers and sisters, I take it. Forgive me, I know
you've told me their names but they're so many and I can't
quite remember.'

'Of course you wouldn't remember, I only told you the once.
Well, Nicky – he's the eldest boy, just turned twelve – he's
decided to work on the wharf too. Pa does it, I did it, it's the
way we make money in our family. If I'm honest, he ain't much
of a one for school. He's bright, don't get me wrong, but there's
bright and there's book-bright and they ain't always the same.
Do you know what I mean?'

'I do indeed and you're quite right.'

'Even so, it breaks me heart that he's got no other choice.
He's *young* and it's dangerous there.'

'How dangerous?'

Mabs told Olive about the ice nearly crushing her, about
the shards that flew like daggers. She told her about the men
that drowned and collapsed and trapped their hands in
winches. 'That's where me little brother's going to work,' she
concluded bitterly. 'I promised I'd give them a better life, but
I'm taking too long and that life's swallowing them up one by
one.'

'How?' asked Olive. 'How do you plan to save them?'

Mabs explained about her savings. 'Say, if a job come up
that one of them could do, then I'd buy them a dress, or a

suit, so they could try for it and look respectable. When I went for the interview with the Finches, I'd nothing to wear so me friend Lou lent me hers.' She explained that she was learning to read and teaching the others on Sunday afternoons. 'Only please,' she added in sudden fright, 'don't say anything about the reading to Mr Finch. Mrs F don't think he'd like it and I promised I wouldn't tell.'

'I shan't say a word,' Olive promised calmly. 'And what else did you say earlier? Something about sewing?'

'Oh, Jen, me next sister. She's fifteen.' Mabs related Jen's sweet nature, her cleverness, her failing eyesight. Then Olive asked about the others and Mabs described them: gap-toothed Peg with her pigtails and her love of beautiful things. Gentle Jem with his gift for seeing the best in people. Little Matty with his freckles and his great love of conkers. And the baby. 'Angeline, Ma called her,' said Mabs. 'It was the name of the daughter of a lady she did sewing for – she often took on extra work outside the laundry. The lady told her it meant little angel, so Ma used it when Angie come along.'

'They sound very special,' said Olive quietly. 'I can quite see why you want to help them. Only Mabs, you do realise there are *six* of them?'

'I am aware, miss,' said Mabs wryly.

'And only one of you.'

'Yes.'

'You do realise it's an almost impossible task you've set yourself?'

Mabs nodded. 'But is that a reason not to try?'

'Certainly not! I'd never say any such thing. I just want you to be a little easier on yourself for not having achieved it yet. It's not for lack of trying, but it's a very large mountain to climb.'

Mabs sighed. 'Thank you, miss. Olive.'

Anne passed the flasks and the sandwiches over. 'Oh, you've left some for us, how kind,' teased Olive. 'Here, Mabs, help yourself. I don't know what the sandwiches are . . .'

'Chicken!' Anne called over her shoulder.

'Chicken. And this is cocoa laced with some of Papa's rather special Caribbean rum. We have a lifetime's supply of it from his travels so I feel no compunction whatsoever about stealing it from time to time.'

Mabs took a swig and felt fiery warmth and sweetness flood through her. 'Oh my,' she sighed. 'That's gorgeous.'

'Isn't it? Anyway. Your grand plan. Tell me, would you be averse to accepting a little help?'

'I won't take yer money, miss, if that's what you mean. It makes me proper proud that I'm earning. I know I keep calling you miss instead of Olive but I do think of you as a friend. And you don't take money from a friend, not where I come from.'

'Nor where I come from. I just wondered if you'd like me to ask around for any suitable vacancies. My rich acquaintances are always bemoaning how hard it is to get good staff. It may be that if I recommend some young people who are honest, conscientious and hardworking, their lack of experience might be overlooked.'

'*Would* you, miss? I mean, Olive. Would you *really*? Yes! Please! That's what I'm waiting for, you see. Opportunities for them. Since I started reading, I've been looking in the paper – the maids told me the situations vacant bit in the *Morning Post* was a good place to look – but I ain't seen nothing likely yet.'

'Winter's a quiet time.'

'And I'll keep looking. But I'd rather they work for someone *you* know. Someone you know to be kind. My friend Lou works in a very difficult place . . . *She's* all right because she's tough as hide, but I wouldn't like to think of my lot there; they've soft hearts.'

'Well, I have them straight in my head now, your sweet, clever Jenny, your strong, capable Nicky and the rest. If I hear of anything, Mabs, I'll let you know at once.'

'Thank you, Olive, with all me heart,' said Mabs, pulling her hands from her pockets to take Olive's. 'I know I'm partial, but they're such good children. You can't imagine what it means to have hope. Now then, tell me about these stars that looked after yer father.'

Olive

Clover is in bed and I'm sitting with my parents in the drawing room; a fire warms us against the spring chill. I'm drooping with exhaustion but fight to stay awake; I have things to discuss!

Clover's nightmares have eased again, God be thanked, but now it is the daytime which presents the difficulty. Lately, she is content to be with no one but me. It is the strangest thing. For months, she has loved her time with her grandparents, with the maids and Mrs Brody. I have gone out on errands and visits without any concerns and I've returned to hear her gurgling laughter, to see her carefree and content. But all that is at an end. She won't be left behind; she is not even very happy to be physically detached from me and I often walk around with her clinging to one of my legs until I consent to pick her up.

We are sleeping better at night, but I'm as tired as ever, drained from the sense that not one waking breath is my own. The last time I had any time for myself was when I went stargazing a week ago and bumped into Mabs Daley. Delightful creature. I promised her my aid but have been able to do nothing but care for Clover. After just a week I feel emptied out and desolate. Without my books, my projects, my visits to friends, who am I? If this goes on much longer, would I, after all, consider employing a nursery maid? I was so determined to be a full-time mother. But there is full-time and then there is impossible. These evening hours when she is asleep and I can be quiet are precious and so I fight to make the most of them, even when all I really want is to go to sleep too!

Apologetically I explain to my father about Mr Finch – I've been shockingly slow in fulfilling my promise to the man but I've been preoccupied and I feel bad for Papa. Sure enough, he sighs and throws up his hands, but he understands my predicament and promises to invite him round for a short call. 'You never know, he might have a worthwhile idea and I'll be glad of the introduction,' he says. Always, Papa has an open mind.

'He does seem intelligent at least,' I concede. 'You know the general opinion is that the canals have all but had their day. But Mr Finch is convinced they have a last hurrah ahead of them, because of the sudden growth in the building industry around London. So far, he's been proved right. He's made a lot of money for his company negotiating contracts for timber, coal and so forth.'

'Canny,' agrees Papa. 'Don't worry, Olive, I'll give him some time.'

'Why not invite his wife?' asks Mama. 'Make a social occasion of it, perhaps a lunch?'

Papa shrugs. 'The shorter, the better as far as I'm concerned. What do you say, Olive?'

'Actually . . .' I ponder, 'if you can bear it, Papa, I'd like that.'

'Really?' Mama is astonished. It isn't often that I agree with her on such matters.

'Yes, well, she's Otty's mother after all, and Otty is something of a fixture in our household.'

'I suppose it would be polite,' admits Papa lugubriously.

'But not only that, I rather liked Mrs Finch. I'd like to know what you both make of her; she's something of a mystery.'

'How so?' Mama puts down her embroidery. She's always fond of a little intrigue.

'Well, she's supposed to be an invalid. She keeps to her room, apparently subject to fits of melancholy and who knows what else. She has a full-time companion. To hear Otty tell it, she's a fragile, emotional creature and her husband speaks the same way. But that's not how she strikes me at all!'

'What's she like?' asks Papa. Now *he's* intrigued. Mama will certainly get her way.

'Beautiful,' I tell them. 'That's the first thing that strikes one. She's intelligent, well-bred – I'd guess he married up – and she seems to me to be not so much fragile as . . . tortured.'

'Tortured?' echoes Mama. 'Good heavens.'

'Perhaps I state it too strongly. At any rate, because she's famously unwell – though she didn't *look* unwell to me – I can't go and pay her a call at any old time. But if Mr Finch wants an introduction to Papa so badly and we issue an invitation to them both . . .'

'They'll feel she *has* to come!' exclaims Mama. 'And then we can meet her too! Olive, you *do* have something of me in you after all. What do you think, James?'

'Very well,' sighs Papa.

Soon afterwards, Mr Miles arrives to discuss my new project. I have never forgotten my night on Parliament Hill soon after Clover came to me, when I decided I must somehow make the world a better place for her. Since my investigations into her past, my intentions have solidified. And Clover's new, demanding demeanour, though it saps me of energy, renews my determination. Always I must remember what she has surely endured. Hearing both Mr Dawkins and Mabs, within days of each other, talk about the importance of hope gave me an idea. I wrote to Mr Miles at once. I'm going to start a charitable foundation to address the plight of those who have nothing.

Mr Miles is much more experienced in such matters than I and gives me first-class advice. We shall need a president, he says, a manager and a treasurer. I had assumed that I would shoulder all these roles. He tells me I shall regret it bitterly if I do.

'Trust me,' he entreats. 'I've been involved with charity enough to know that no matter how great your enthusiasm, it will all get swallowed up by the mundane minutiae of running the thing. From what you said in your note, Olive, you wish to be at the coalface, so to speak: helping people, talking to them. You won't be happy tucked away behind the scenes wrestling with paperwork.'

Thank heavens for lifelong friends who know one well!

'And you must have a remit,' he continues. 'A specific remit, identifying the areas that your project will address. There should be no more than three, four at the most. It's all very well saying "help the needy", but you cannot help all of them, entirely and forever. You need to know what you are trying to provide that other organisations do not. And you need to be able to explain that succinctly.'

I smile. This is precisely why I asked Mr Miles to come.

'Education,' I say at once. 'That has to be the first thing.'

'Then you wish to start a school?' asks Papa.

I wrinkle my nose. 'Perhaps not a school per se, or maybe, yes. I don't know. I think I was imagining a sort of . . . central something or other . . . where people could go to learn what was important to *them*, or at least be directed to where they might learn it. Reading, writing and numbers are bound to come up over and over again but those wishing to be a lady's maid might need to learn needlework and hairdressing, for example. Or perhaps someone has an affinity with animals or the outdoors, but has not the opportunity to learn about equine care or gardens . . .' I'm frustrated at my inability to explain my vision but as yet, it's very hazy.

'It's an excellent idea,' says Mama, sounding excited. 'You could arrange days where they might learn the ropes: a day in a kitchen watching the cook, say, or in a shop to learn how it works. Goodness, with all the people we know between us, I'm sure we could set up some wonderful opportunities.'

'That's wonderful, Mama! *Just* what I was imagining. Wouldn't it be *splendid*?'

'So, education, in whatever form,' interjects Mr Miles, reigning in my almost delirious enthusiasm. 'What else?'

'Practical help,' I say promptly. 'Clothes. Food. I don't know what term we will coin for it but there has to be a facility for immediate help where it is needed. People can't be expected to think of their future in any sort of productive way if they are starving, freezing, sleep-deprived. And hope, that's the third. Yes! Those are my three areas, Mr Miles.' I have my remit.

'Hope?' queries Mama. 'How exactly do you plan to provide that, dear?'

'I don't quite know yet. But it's a word I've heard a lot lately. Perhaps we have someone who can encourage people when they're feeling particularly low, point them in a wholesome direction. And we must give encouragement along the way. Rewards for effort, or even just little gifts to lift the spirits. I shall think it through.'

'You should hold a meeting,' suggests Mama. 'Invite people

from different walks of life, who will have different ideas from ourselves. And you should write down every single idea they suggest until you have a long list, then decide which are the most useful.'

'Mama!' I cry, deeply impressed. 'You're so clever! I love that idea. I'll invite Otty, because she's young, and not yet jaded. And Mabs, her mother's companion. Mr Miles, because he knows, well, everything, in short. And Mr Dawkins the cab driver for *he's* a philosopher if ever there was one . . .' All at once my fatigue is forgotten and I'm filled with enthusiasm and, yes, hope. Even if Clover continues to cling to me and me alone for the next months, I can do this. I know I can!

'Olive, darling, I'm delighted you like my idea, but you needn't draw up the guest list this minute. Mr Miles is here now after all, and I'm sure he has more guidance for you.'

'Of course. Mr Miles, forgive me. What else must I do?'

'Did you say Mabs? Do you by any chance mean Mabel Daley?'

'Why, yes! Do you know her?'

'I've known her family a long time. I gave her the character reference for the position she now holds. An excellent girl. I'm glad you've befriended her, Olive. She needs someone like you behind her. She's well, I take it?'

'Very well, and I'm delighted to know her. Shall I give her your regards, Mr Miles, when I see her?'

'Please do. Now, what else? Well, you must hold an event to raise money, for two reasons. The first is that you cannot pay for everything single-handedly. You're a wealthy woman but you are only one, and the needy are many. If this endeavour is to be a success, it needs to be sustainable.

'I understand. And the second reason?'

'We wish the cause to have a reputation. We wish it to

attract interest and patronage from the people who can help. You have to make people *want* to be involved, so that it reflects well on them when they *are* involved. Not everyone is philanthropic out of the goodness of their heart; many people are generous only when it is fashionable. You must make your cause fashionable.'

I nod. That makes sense. 'Certainly we should do that. I shall invite the great and the good. More to the point, the rich. It will be high society, so pockets will be deep. Thank you, Mr Miles. I shall hold . . . a dinner.'

Mama gives a kind of strangled groan, the sort that, as her daughter, I know very well.

'Mama?' I say with dignity. 'Is there an observation you wish to make?'

'A *dinner*?' she says, exasperated. 'Honestly, Olive, you're capable of producing such extraordinary ideas – yet when it comes to social occasions you have *no* imagination. You have approximately *one* evening gown and your idea of society is having a twelve-year-old neighbour come for tea.'

I frown. 'You like Otty!'

'That is not the point, dear. Mr Miles has just told us that you must make your foundation as attractive as you possibly can, whip our acquaintance into a positive frenzy to help, make it the cause *du jour*. And your best idea is a stuffy old *dinner*. Such as bankers and businessmen hold on a routine basis. No, Olive. We need something bigger than that. We need a night that everyone we know will be wild to attend, a night they will talk about for months afterwards. For *years*. We shall hold a *ball*!'

Mabs

'Daley,' said Mrs Finch one morning. 'I've been cooped up indoors far too long.'

Mabs was cleaning shoes for Mrs Webb, since Mrs Finch still generated little actual work. She was currently buffing Mr Charlie's town shoes, which he would keep wearing on the heath. She looked up distractedly from creating the perfect shine. Was she hearing things?

'Well, yes, ma'am,' she marvelled. 'I've often said it. Are you saying you'll take a walk with me?'

'Perhaps not a walk quite yet. I'm ashamed to say it, Daley, but I've become rather anxious about the outside world. It's been so long.'

'I was worried that might 'appen, ma'am. What was you thinking then?'

'What *were* you thinking, Daley. Pardon me, I know you haven't asked me to correct your speech and I'll stop if it offends, but I know you wish to improve yourself and at the moment your poor speech belies your fine character and intelligence.'

Mabs stared with an open mouth. Talk of going outdoors? Giving Mabs compliments? What was going on? 'I'm very grateful, in fact. What *were* you thinking, ma'am?'

'I wondered if we might step into the rose garden. It's such a fine day, Daley. I can't bear to spend it all indoors. It's been months . . . I can't quite think how that happened. Enough is enough. I cannot spend the rest of my life in one room.'

'I should say not, ma'am! Oh, I'm so pleased! Wait till Mr Finch hears. He'll be over the moon!'

Mrs Finch shot Mabs a javelin glance, her eyes cold and hard. 'You're quite sure about that?'

Mabs was confounded. From happy and hopeful to this, in less than a minute. Mrs Finch was shifting ground, that was for sure. 'Well . . . *yes*,' she said. 'He's been wanting nothing more than to have you back to health and strength, ever since I known you all.'

Mrs Finch's demeanour changed again; a look of such desolation washed over her that it was like watching someone pulled under by the ocean. Mabs wanted to wade in and rescue her.

'Of course,' said Mrs Finch. 'And it's since *I've* known you all, Daley. Shall I explain why?'

'Explain in the garden, ma'am. Now, let me fetch you a shawl, there's some nasty breezes, still, for all there's sunshine and flowers. And shall we take a book, ma'am? In case you'd like to sit and read outside?'

'A lovely idea. And it's there *are* some nasty breezes, not *there's* some. Am I annoying you yet?'

'Annoying me? Ma'am, I ain't had enough help in life that I can afford to get annoyed by it. I appreciate it.'

'Good. Because it's I *haven't*, not I *ain't*.' Mrs Finch threw her a sheepish smile as she wrapped the shawl around her shoulders. Mabs thought for the thousandth time that her mistress had as many facets as a gemstone pendant.

Outside it was cold and sharp, a diamond day. The sun

shone slantways and the garden, having enjoyed minimal attention since the family moved in, looked magical with its tangles
and shadows, green shoots showing through last year's dead
brown foliage. Mrs Finch picked her way cautiously among
the rose bushes which were black-branched and glistening in
the light. Being outside must feel so strange after so long,
thought Mabs.

'I've always preferred them untended,' said Mrs Finch.
'Gardens, I mean. When they're too cultivated they look like
young ladies, groomed and schooled to within an inch of their
lives. I'd rather loveliness than obedience. What about you,
Daley?'

'I've no opinion on gardens, ma'am. This is the first one
I've ever been in.'

'Really? Well, good heavens, how different our lives have
been. Look, daffodils. Do you not just love them?'

'I do. They're the most joyful of flowers, I always think.'

'Yes.' Mrs Finch kneeled in the grass, careless of the damp,
to smell the flowers then she resumed her rambling. 'Look,
Daley! A rose!' Sure enough, a solitary pale pink rose clung
to a branch. It was larger than a bud but not fully open.

'In March!' whispered Mabs. 'Fancy.'

'Is it very early, do you think? Though the weather's hardly
been clement. No, look.' She touched a fingertip to a pink
petal and the petal dropped away, showing a papery layer of
beige beneath. 'It's a pretty illusion but it's not really alive.'
Mrs Finch began to cry.

'Oh ma'am!' Mabs put her arms round her without thinking,
only to be shaken off at once. 'I'm sorry, ma'am, I didn't mean
to presume . . .'

'No,' said Mrs Finch through her tears. 'It's not that. You've
done nothing wrong, Daley. But the house. I don't want them

to see.' She turned her back on the house and covered her face with her hands, crying without restraint. Mabs kept her distance, but she could see the tears leaking from underneath her hands.

'I can't bear it, ma'am,' she said softly, 'that you should be so unhappy. Won't you tell me what's wrong? Can't I help?'

At last Mrs Finch rubbed the tears from her face and wiped her hands on her skirt. She lifted her head and took a deep breath. 'Excuse me, Daley,' she said. 'A stupid moment of mourning – or I'm overwhelmed, perhaps, by the feeling of fresh air. Look, a seat, albeit much rusted and leaf-strewn! Shall we risk our dresses and read a little?'

❅

Mabs didn't dare hope that the foray into the garden had been anything other than an isolated occasion, but the next morning, Mrs Finch surprised her again. 'Shall we go a-walking today?' she said when their breakfast had been cleared away.

'Walking?' echoed Mabs, dumbfounded. 'An actual walk?'

'Yes. And I promise to behave. No more silly outbursts like yesterday.'

'You wasn't silly. It was a big step.'

'Weren't silly. You weren't silly. I wasn't silly.'

'Thank you, ma'am. You weren't silly. I'll get me shawl.'

Mabs ran upstairs, wanting to seize the moment before her mistress changed her quicksilver mind. When she returned, she was subjected to a narrow scrutiny up and down her person.

'Have you no coat, no gloves?'

'No, ma'am.'

'*That's* how you've been going out all through the winter?'

'Yes, ma'am.'

'Good grief! I had no idea.'

She found a navy coat and a pair of woollen gloves which she insisted Mabs wear. 'Keep them,' she said briefly, then marched down the stairs, away from Mabs's protests and thanks. At the front door, she paused and cast a wry look over her shoulder. 'At last I am to see the promised land that is Hampstead. Let us sally forth, Daley. I expect to be dazzled.'

Mabs had to hand it to Hampstead, it *did* look dazzling for Mrs Finch's first expedition. Glossy red and pink camelias bloomed in the gardens of Willoughby Walk and the brown stone cottages looked soft and welcoming against their blaze. Blossom drifted through the air on a gentle breeze and a flurry of birds – blackbirds, magpies, swallows – rustled in the shrubs and flashed through the sky. It felt like the country village it had once been.

Mrs Finch maintained a blasé expression but Mabs could see the gleam of interest in her eyes as she looked about.

'Hampstead's said to have healing waters, like Bath,' said Mabs as they passed old Chalybeate Well. 'That's why people've always come here, to feel better about life.' Mrs Finch lifted her eyebrows into a perfect and sceptical arc.

When they reached the high street, Mabs hoped Mrs Finch would exclaim over it the way Mabs had when she first arrived but no exclamations were forthcoming. However, Mrs Finch was not the stranger to lovely things that Mabs had been and the woman was stubborn. *Just look at her face!* She seemed determined not to fall in love with the place, even when they passed the confectioner's, with its display of apple-green, rose-pink and lemon-yellow macaroons cascading off their stands like a candy-coloured waterfall.

Crossing the road, they passed the bakery, which boasted an extravagance of pies with pastry that looked as light as air and as golden as butter. They strolled by the bookshop, and the antique shop with its brass clocks, silver trinket boxes and jet beads. The cabbages, tomatoes and onions outside the grocer's were so simple and perfect that Mabs often thought theirs was the greatest beauty of all.

They crossed back across the street to walk along Downshire Hill. Mabs watched her mistress's dark eyes take in the large houses and the highly dressed ladies getting in and out of carriages. She would once have been just like them. *The exquisite Miss Farrah*, Elfrida had called her mother, bitterly. Mr Finch had been the unlikely suitor, never quite able to believe he had won her.

'Are you tired, ma'am?'

'Perhaps a little. But finish your tour. I shan't faint away.'

'I'm glad to hear it, ma'am. Well, all I wanted to show you was this.' They'd reached the far end of the street and ahead of them was the heath. The green and brown expanse stretched before them, a heath breeze blowing in and pinking their faces. 'Just so you can see how close it is, ma'am. Miles of walking it is. Now that you've seen a little something of the village, we might walk on the heath next time, if you'd like.'

'That sounds appealing, Daley. It's . . . rather pleasant. I can see now why you all drone on and on about the place.'

'Oh, I *am* happy. Otty will be beside 'erself that she missed this. You'll have to go out with *her* one afternoon. She's so proud of 'Ampstead, you'd think she'd built it herself.'

'Don't I know it,' said her mother. 'My daughter is given to great enthusiasms. You know, I *am* tired, Daley, but I don't feel like going back yet. Do you recall the very pretty tea shop we passed, with the bow windows? What do you say to going there first?'

'Astrid's, ma'am? That's the expensive one! Why, I should

like that better than anything! Now yer gettin' the 'ang of things!'

Mabs had often walked past Astrid's and peered longingly through the pretty window flanked by gold lamps. She'd never been inside because she couldn't justify the extravagance and because in her old shawl she felt that she'd mess the place up! In Mrs Finch's smart navy coat, she felt more as if she belonged there. The interior was, if anything, even prettier, with floral wallpapers and crystal bud vases on every table. Mrs Finch ordered Earl Grey tea for them both. Mabs wrinkled her nose at first, wary of the floral bouquet, but it grew on her as they progressed through the pot. Mrs Finch chose a buttered scone, while Mabs tried a cream puff as light as a cloud.

It struck Mabs that in another world, this was a pleasure that she and her mother might have enjoyed together. And one that Mrs Finch really should be sharing with her daughters. Mabs wondered again how things had gone so horribly wrong for beautiful, sought-after Abigail Farrah. 'Penny for 'em, ma'am,' she said after a long silence. 'Do you think you might come to be happy here after all?'

Mrs Finch tore her gaze from the window. 'I can see that you want me to be. But I have never pretended to you that my feelings were other than they were. I won't start now. You remember that rose we saw in the garden yesterday? It looked so perfect from the outside, but within, all was dry and withered? That is me, Daley. It's hard to take pleasure when the very core of your existence is poisoned. Blighted. And the rose garden itself, filled with the potential for life and beauty but sorely neglected and growing in disturbing directions? That is my life. And before you ask, no, I cannot explain.'

✿

That evening, Mabs knocked on Mr Finch's study door. He'd told her often that if she needed to discuss anything, she only had to search him out. Sure enough, there he was, the smell of the outside world still hovering around him and his coat in a heap over a chair back, as if he'd only just removed it. Workish-looking papers were strewn across his desk.

'I'm sorry, sir,' said Mabs. 'You're only just home. I'll come back another time.'

'No, please, it's fine, Miss Daley. What can I do for you?'

Mabs couldn't suppress her excitement. She hadn't mentioned the visit to the rose garden yesterday but it had seemed like so small a thing. But a walk around Hampstead – now, that was progress! 'I've got some very good news for you, sir.'

'Fire away!'

So Mabs told him that for the first time in months, his wife had gone outside. She couldn't help grinning with delight. It felt like such a milestone. She didn't mention the tears in the rose garden yesterday. Why mar the good news?

'Outside?' asked Mr Finch. 'Where?' His face was unexpectedly tense. For a fleeting second, Mabs remembered her conversation with his wife yesterday morning:

He'll be over the moon!

You're quite sure about that?

'Well, yesterday, just into the rose garden, sir. Mrs Finch didn't feel up to a walk but the fresh air must've done her some good because today we took a stroll about the village!'

'The *village*? Abigail? Well, goodness. Haven't you worked miracles?'

'I don't think it's me is the miracle worker, sir. I think it's spring coming round, if I'm honest. It lifts the spirits, don't it? It was just good to see her out of the house, with the sunshine on her face. I thought you'd want to know.'

'I do. Very much so. And was she . . . well after it?'

'Yes, sir, perfectly. Are you pleased, sir? I was sure you would be.'

'Well, of course I am! It's . . . excellent. Unexpected. Well done, Miss Daley. I should like to give you a small bonus.'

'What? Oh no, sir. That is, thank you, with all me heart, but I'm just doing me job is all. I don't need a bonus for that. Just seeing her out and about is reward enough.'

'Bless you, but just a small one. Here, three shillings. I feel it's important to celebrate these milestones. I well remember the state of my wife when you arrived, Miss Daley. The difference is marked. Please take it.'

'Very well, sir, thank you again.' Mabs pocketed the shiny shillings, thinking of her savings box, of Peg's birthday coming up, of Pa on the coal. But she didn't feel quite right.

'And where did you go today, exactly? Please, take a seat, tell me all about it.'

Mabs verbally retraced their route then hesitated. There was nothing wrong with mentioning the tea room, was there? Unless he thought it was a bit familiar, the two of them in a place like that together. But it would be a big thing to omit. 'Then we went to Astrid's, sir. Mrs Finch liked the look of it.'

'The tea room? So, you went there and . . . drank tea? Just the two of you?'

'Yes, sir. It were a proper treat for me and she needed a sit-down.'

'You met no one else?'

'No, sir. Well, I don't 'ardly know anyone around here and Mrs Finch no one at all.'

'And what did you talk about? Oh, pardon me, that sounds overcurious, dreadful of me! I only wondered because until recently she was so set against you – not you *personally*, you understand, but the idea of a companion. I just wondered what had changed.'

'I think she's just got used to me is all. And like I said, sir, spring makes everything better. We talked of Miss Otty's schooling and Miss Elfrida having a birthday coming up. My sister Peg's is on the same day, funny to say, sir. Thirteen she'll be, I can hardly believe it . . .'

It was a relief to change the subject. She wouldn't tell Mr Finch his wife's melancholy remarks over the pot of cooling tea.

It's hard to take pleasure when the very core of your existence is poisoned . . . blighted.

Within, all was dry and withered . . . that is my life.

Those remarks were personal, spoken in trust.

'Well,' said Mr Finch. 'I'm glad you had a pleasant morning. I'm sure Abigail will enjoy telling me about it when I see her later. I have some news for her. An invitation!'

'Oh?'

'From Captain Westallen! He invites us to lunch on Monday two weeks from now. I'll be able to arrange a half day without much difficulty. This is a tremendous opportunity for me.'

'I'm so glad, sir.'

'Yes, except . . .' He frowned and grew pensive. He turned and picked up a large card from his desk – the invitation, Mabs assumed.

'Except is it the done thing to ask the wife as well, when the husband has made an approach on a matter of business? Or does it strike you as odd? I can't decide.'

'Sir, I'm the last person as would know about that sort of thing. But this will give you longer with him, won't it?'

'I suppose you're right. The Westallens and the Finches, two fine families of Hampstead, on most cordial terms. That has a nice ring, doesn't it?' He turned the card over and over in his hands. 'It's just the way it's worded . . . well, it's very clear that he *expects* Abigail to attend . . . I mean, it's only this very week that she's gone out at all. They would understand, surely, if I explained that she's not yet strong enough for a luncheon.'

'I'm sure they would, sir, only why not ask Mrs Finch how she feels? It wouldn't surprise me if she felt able.'

Mr Finch kept staring at the invitation as though secret messages were written there in invisible ink.

'And was my wife in quite . . . *even* spirits today?'

It's hard to take pleasure when the core of your existence is poisoned . . .

'Yes, sir, perfectly even.'

'Then perhaps I will ask her, as you say. Thank you, Daley.'

Mabs let herself out of the study, slightly deflated; she had expected him to be overjoyed by her news. But then, change could be frightening, even when it was desired. She remembered what she had overheard him say that Wednesday night: *I would like nothing more than for you to have a normal, appropriate social life. But you know as well as I that you simply cannot be trusted. What you might say, what you might do.*

And Mabs could well understand. No one knew better than she did how volatile Mrs Finch could be. The more Mrs Finch did, the more she was in the company of strangers, the more chance there was that something embarrassing or shocking could happen, she had to admit. Only what was the alternative? Keep her shut up forever? No, that wasn't humane. She knew it and Mr Finch knew it, but he was right to be cautious.

Mabs

The days passed and Mabs slipped into contentment again. She and Mrs Finch now went out walking every day and the fresh air and variety created a more peaceful rapport between them. Mabs was certain that her mistress would be strong and even enough for the forthcoming lunch with the Westallens. They didn't talk a great deal as they strolled around the village or strode over the heath. The conversation they had usually concerned Otty's escapades and her progress in school. Personal enquiries and confidences were rare but Mrs Finch took an interest in Mabs's brothers and sisters.

'You mean to rescue them all with the wage you earn?' she marvelled. 'I know my husband pays well, but even so. It's a lot of responsibility.'

'Yes, ma'am, so people keep telling me. But the way I see it, you don't just help yerself, and not do anything for the people you love, do you?'

'No,' agreed Mrs Finch. 'No, you do not.'

When they were in the house, the reading lessons continued and Mabs was now learning to write as well. Her reading was coming on apace; Mrs Finch suggested she try reading a novel aloud and together they settled on *The Coral Island*.

'My only complaint is that Mr Ballantyne has, *of course*,

written about boys,' Mrs Finch sighed, 'but I always used to imagine *myself* having the adventures, you may be sure.' Mabs smiled and began the great adventure of reading her very first novel.

It hadn't escaped Mabs's notice that Mrs Finch was a similar age to her own beloved mother and that with Ma gone, hers was now the steady female presence throughout Mabs's days. No one would ever be Ma, and Mrs Finch was different from Maureen in every particular; even so, Mabs found herself leaning into their companionship as one might into a bank of cushions, aware that doing so was probably ill-advised.

They were sitting together on a day of spring showers when Betsy brought up a note for Mrs Finch on a tray. They exchanged a surprised glance. Mrs Finch never received correspondence. She thanked Betsy and tore it open.

'Well, this sounds rather promising! The note's addressed to me but it regards you. Read it yourself.' Mrs Finch held out the note.

'Really, ma'am? How strange!' Mabs jumped up, fearing the worst – word from the canal that Nicky was drowned, or from Jenny that Pa was missing – but Mrs Finch would hardly call that promising. She noticed the crisp, luxurious parchment, then the monogram printed in olive green at the bottom of the card: OW. Her heart leapt.

Dear Mrs Finch,

I hope this finds you well. I look forward to meeting you again at lunch next week. Meanwhile, might I beg leave to borrow your companion, Miss Daley, for a short conversation as soon as possible? I have some encouraging news regarding one of her siblings. I am

at home every afternoon/evening this week so she may
call when it suits you and herself.

With warm regards,
Olive Westallen

Mabs felt a flood of excitement and looked at Mrs Finch,
whose dark eyes were glowing as if she cared.

'What are you waiting for, Daley?'

'*Now*, ma'am? But it's working hours. I don't mind waiting,
honest I don't . . .'

Mrs Finch laughed. 'Yes you do! Go. I want to hear the
news just as much as you.'

So Mabs bundled herself into the smart coat Mrs Finch
had given her and raced up the steep rise to Polaris House.
She landed on the doorstep panting, hair awry.

Agatha opened the door and grinned when she saw the
state of Mabs. 'You didn't waste much time,' she said. 'She
was hoping it was you. Come through, please.'

She showed Mabs into the Westallens' pleasant drawing
room. Long, blue curtains printed with a yellow and green
floral design swept from ceiling to floor. Rich oils hung on the
walls: scenes of horses galloping across countryside, of galleons
on roiling seas, of a young Olive with an obstinate gaze. There
was no fire today; instead, a window was open and a soft breeze
stirred the drapes. Clover and Olive were sprawled on the
India rug, concentrating fiercely on a strange-looking game.

'Mabs!' Clover jumped up and hugged her legs, then flew
back to the rug.

Olive waved. 'Thank you for coming so soon. I want to greet
you with Clover's enthusiasm but I can't get up. My leg's gone
to sleep. I'm so sorry, I can't abandon Clover mid-game. It's

getting pretty desperate now. Take a seat and I'll struggle up as soon as we're finished here.'

'Mabs!' cried Clover. 'Come and play!'

Olive wrinkled her nose. 'Can you bear to? Please don't feel obliged. I can't claim this is the most comfortable spot in the room.'

'I'd love to,' said Mabs, happily lowering herself to the floor. 'Only I don't know what it is. What do I have to do?'

'Winks!' shrieked Clover, more excitable than Mabs had ever seen her.

'You don't know Tiddlywinks?' Olive was astonished. 'Why it's been quite the craze for several years now.'

'I've heard Mr Charlie mention it. But Mrs Finch isn't the game-playing sort. And before that . . .'

'Of course,' said Olive. 'Well, each player has a pile of winks, you see, and the aim is to flip your winks into this cup, using these squidgers. But you also try to block your opponents' winks by . . . yes, Clover, you're quite right, a demonstration is always best.' Aside, she added, 'Clover doesn't yet have the co-ordination to match her passion. We usually end up with winks flying everywhere like migrating butterflies.'

Sure enough, Clover began a frenzy of flipping, her little pink tongue poking out between her teeth. The coloured counters flew high into the air, into the fireplace and even, once or twice, into the pot.

'We're supposed to take turns, darling,' said Olive calmly. 'Let Mabs try. Now, Mabs, I simply can't wait to tell you my news. Can you concentrate while the winks are flying?'

'I'm sure I can,' laughed Mabs, taking her turn. Surprisingly tricky it was, and surprisingly fun. When one of her winks snapped into the pot, Olive clapped. 'A natural!'

Agatha brought lemonade and cake, then Olive got to the

point. 'Now, Mabs, you remember that I promised to keep an eye out for opportunities for your brothers and sisters?'

'Don't I ever?' said Mabs fervently. 'I've been praying something would come of it.' She flipped a wink onto a nearby footstool.

'It took me a while to get to it – Clover has needed me a great deal lately – and then I was disappointed because I tried several people with households, but none had any vacancies.' Olive took a sip of her lemonade. 'Delicious. Oh, there's a wink in there. Never mind.'

'Wink!' shrieked Clover.

'Oh yes, well done, darling. But I have a friend, Mabs, called Julia Morrow. Julia's a divorcee, and the virtuous of Hampstead make it perfectly clear what they think about *that*. But she's a lovely woman, Mabs. She's very proud, very independent, and it never occurred to me that she might be a solution, I merely mentioned my quest in passing. And she *astonished* me by saying she'd been considering taking on a boy.'

'A boy?' echoed Mabs, rapidly adjusting her mental picture from Jenny's delighted face to Jem's, or Matty's.

'Yes. She says she has no need for a maid, since she's more than capable of cooking, cleaning, sewing . . . I think she likes to keep busy. But she does get lonely – well, of course she does – and finds the maintenance of an old house hard. Window frames to be fixed, the garden to be tamed and so on. When I told her about the young Daleys, she positively transformed! She'd like nothing better than to take one of them to live with her, to be her odd-job man and errand boy. What do you think, Mabs?'

'It sounds like a wonderful job,' said Mabs immediately. 'Nicky could do those things, or Jem. Matty's maybe a little young yet. And either one would be grateful to live in a warm house and have plenty to eat.'

'Well, I'm glad you think so, because the more I think of it, the more perfect a solution it seems. Listen, Mabs. Julia said that she would teach the boy any lessons he might wish to learn. She's an educated woman. I know you want Nicky away from the canal but you did say that he doesn't have much enthusiasm for schooling whereas Jem's a thoughtful sort . . .'

'Jem,' breathed Mabs. It made perfect sense. Nicky did *have* a job, after all, and helpful, gentle Jem would be a great boon to a lonely, misunderstood lady. 'He'd be the boy for her,' said Mabs. 'Nicky would be bored on his own like that but this would mean the world to Jem.'

'Good!' Olive looked relieved and Mabs was touched by how much she cared. 'And Mabs, it wouldn't *just* be room and board. She'd pay a very small wage as well. It wouldn't be much but—'

'Room and board *and* a wage *and* lessons,' sighed Mabs. 'Oh Olive, I can't tell you how happy I'd be. What's next then? I suppose she'll want to meet him?'

'As a formality only. And for Jem to see what he thinks. He's very young after all and might not like to leave his home and family even though we, being older, can see the advantages.'

'Oh, he'll see 'em all right,' said Mabs. 'I'll make sure of it. Tomorrow's Wednesday, me half day. Will Mrs Morrow be at home, do you think? I could take him then if you give me the address.'

'Why, I'll come with you, of course! And yes, Julia never goes anywhere. I'll call on her in the morning to tell her to expect us in the afternoon.'

'*Wink!*' screamed Clover, throwing all the counters up in the air and laughing.

✻

The following day at half past two, Mabs set off on the familiar route home, enjoying the capricious sunshine which turned the streets into kaleidoscopic sequences of brightness and shade, warmth and cold. When she reached Mushroom Court she paused to look up at its grim contours and felt happy that she was taking one of her loved ones away.

'One down, five to go!' Mrs Finch had said when she left. 'Would you call in when you get back, just for five minutes, to tell me how it went? I'll be wondering all day.' Mabs had promised, touched.

She hurried up the stairs to their room and turned the door handle. It was locked. She tried again but it was rickety and she was worried it would come off in her hand. Strange.

'Jen!' she called through the door. 'Peg? Anyone home? It's me!'

She heard a low voice behind the door. 'Mabs? Is that you?'

'Yes, it's me! Let me in!'

She heard a key turning and the door was opened by Jenny, who pulled her in and wrapped her in a hug. 'Mabs, we wasn't expecting you! Is anything wrong?'

'The very opposite. But why's the door locked? I didn't even know we had a key.'

Jenny sighed. 'It's Pa,' she said. 'He's been drinking after work and the last few days he's been messing up the job 'cause he ain't fit.'

Not now! screamed Mabs inside her head. *Not when we're finally getting somewhere.* 'Has he lost his job?'

'No, but some of the men are angry. They say he ain't pullin' his weight, that he's putting them in danger.'

'So they come here to talk to him?'

'To teach him a lesson, more like,' said Peg. She was holding a baby Mabs didn't recognise. Girls around here could mind

a baby for frazzled parents for two pennies and a cup of tea.
'They pushed the table over, that sort of thing. It's the only
time I been glad we got nothin' nice here. They shoved Pa
around a bit and said he had to get himself sorted. Well, they
ain't wrong there. But it frightened the little'uns.'

'It frightened all of us,' admitted Jenny. 'They just came in.
I'm sure they was only trying to make him think. But we
thought we'd better lock the door, just in case.'

'Oh my Gawd.' Mabs sank down at the table and noticed
that it had a new wobble.

'One of the legs is loose now,' said Jem. 'I tried to fix it . . .'

'You did a grand job,' said Peg, ruffling his hair.

Mabs sighed. This stupid, stupid place, with its stupid
prevailing mentality. She understood the men's gripe with Pa,
of course she did. But why drag the children into it? Where
was their imagination? Couldn't they guess what a fright like
that could do to children? Little Angie was looking unusually
pale and anxious. Mabs drew her onto her lap and stroked her
hair. 'I need to talk some sense into Pa.'

'You can try,' said Jenny. 'But will it do any good? Anyway,
it's been quiet since. What's your news?'

'Well,' said Mabs, sitting up straighter and smiling. She was
determined not to let today be spoiled. One of the children
was getting out of here. 'Jem, you've got a chance, a wonderful
chance. There's a job for you, with a lady.'

Even as Jem's brow creased and his dark hair flopped into
his face, she could see his eyes sparking with hope. 'A job?
For me? But I'm only ten, Mabs. Does the lady know that?'

'She does and if you're willing, Jemmy, we'll go and see her
this afternoon for you to make certain you like her.' Jem
nodded.

Jenny hid her face behind her hands. 'Oh my Gawd,' she

said in a muffled voice. 'A chance for one of us at last. Oh my word, the relief. Where's the job, Mabs?'

'That's the best bit,' said Mabs. 'No, there's lots of best bits. But this is one of them. It's in Hampstead. We'll be able to come together to visit you on Sundays. I'll be able to keep an eye on you, Jem, and you'll have me close.'

'What's the job, Mabs? What does she want me to do?'

'Let me start at the beginning. I'm so excited, I'm not telling it very well. Her name is Julia Morrow and she's a friend of Miss Westallen, who I told you about.'

'She's rich?' gasped Peg, shifting the baby to her other shoulder.

'I don't think so. Not like Olive. But compared to us, well, most people are rich, ain't they?' Mabs explained the whole thing.

Jem frowned even deeper, his eyes shimmering with questions. 'So, I get to live in a big house, eat lots of food, learn whatever I want and she'll *pay* me?' he wondered, looking baffled. And no wonder; opportunities like that didn't fall into the laps of children like the Daleys every day.

Mabs nodded. 'Yes. And you'll get a day and a half off every week, just like me.'

Jem scratched his head. His dark hair stood up in a shock and Mabs's heart ached with love for him. Such a handsome, loving boy. Seeing him here in this drab room – seeing *all* of them here – made her head hurt. But it was changing. 'And all I gotta do is fix things and look after things for her and run errands?' he checked.

'That's it,' said Mabs. 'Easy for a boy like you, don't you think?'

'I do,' he said. 'Only Mabs . . .?'

'What?' *Please let him not be afraid to take it.*

'Is it all right for me to go? I'm the man of the house, now that Nicky's working. If I'm not here, the girls will be on their own all day with only Matty, and he's too little to protect them.'

Oh Lord, these children would just about finish her off, thought Mabs.

'Jem, love,' said Jenny. 'You're very good to think of it, and yer right, you are the man of the place now. But I'm the grown-up of the lot of us, with Mabs gone, and I'm tellin' you, you've got to do this for all of us. Look what gettin' out has done for Mabs! Look how it's helped us *all* – reading lessons and money and food and now *this*! This is what we need. You'll do it for us, won't you?'

Jem looked around, visibly struggling within himself. Mabs knew what he was feeling; she remembered all too well. He wanted to get out of here so badly that it made him feel it must be selfish to do it. Yet Jenny had argued persuasively and it was all churning round in his clever, ten-year-old brain.

'I'll do it,' he said, 'if you're sure you'll be all right. If you're sure it's the right thing.'

'It is,' said Jenny. 'Cross me heart and hope to die.'

Jem turned to look at Mabs. 'You think so too?'

'That's why I'm here, ain't it? I got plans for this family, Jemmy boy. I ain't said before, because I didn't want to get anyone's hopes up too soon, but I may as well say now. This place is a hellhole and you're too good for it, each and every one of you. Miss Olive is keeping her eyes out for positions for you. Folk ain't exactly queuing up to employ the likes of us, but look, already Jem's got something. It happens to be Jem first. But it'll be all of you, in time. And I don't want a single argument from any of you when it happens.'

'You won't get one from me!' vowed Peg. 'I'd give anything to get out of here.'

'That's why you gotta keep at your lessons,' said Mabs. 'You are practising yer reading, Peg?'

'Yes!' cried Peg indignantly.

'She is,' agreed Jenny. 'She's good like that. So, when are you going, Mabs? Now?'

'The sooner, the better. You ready, Jem?'

For a moment he looked fearful. 'Am I coming back?'

'Oh!' Mabs hadn't thought of that. 'I don't know. Assuming you like each other, I don't know if she'll ask you to start on Monday, or if you'll just stay, right away!'

'Well,' said Peg practically. 'It don't make much difference. It's not like he's got a lot to take.'

'True,' said Jenny thoughtfully. 'Only our love. We'll say proper goodbyes now, Jem, and if you do come back later, we'll say them all over again. If you stay, we'll see you on Sunday. That's only four days.'

Mabs stood aside while the children said their goodbyes. Emotion was a funny thing. There was no doubt in her mind that this was the best thing that could have happened. And yet, taking one of them away from the others, she felt cruel. She handed over the large bar of chocolate she had bought, trying not to feel that she was bribing them to part with their brother.

Then Jem was at her side, eyes damp, his face set with a certain heroism. 'I'm ready, Mabs,' he said.

'Good boy. Well, you others, I love you, don't ever forget it. Things are getting better for us, whatever Pa gets up to.'

✻

They walked in silence. Occasionally Mabs glanced down at her little brother, her heart wringing at the determination in his thin little face. When they reached the edge of Saffron

Hill, Jem stopped. 'It's the farthest I ever been, Mabsy,' he said.

'Are you scared?'

'A bit.'

'That's natural. Something new is always scary, even if a good thing. You're glad, though, Jem?'

'Yes, I'm glad. It's an adventure, ain't it? Not many adventures in Mushroom Court, or only the bad sort.'

'Ain't that the truth,' said Mabs with feeling. 'Well, I for one couldn't be happier for you, Jem. I've never met this lady, Mrs Morrow, but I trust Olive. She wouldn't send you somewhere you wouldn't like.'

When they reached Hampstead, the gardens were full of phlox, lavender and the extravagant sunshine of black-eyed Susans. Passers-by wore pastel dresses and carried parasols with ruffled edges.

Jem's eyes were wide, his face pale. 'It's like where the princes and princesses live in the stories. It don't seem real, Mabs.'

'I can't wait to show you everything. But we shouldn't be loitering, you got a job interview to get to!' They gave each other excited glances and Mabs took his hand.

Jem squeezed it, then let go. 'I'm a bit old for holding hands, Mabs,' he said apologetically.

'Course you are, love.'

They climbed Holly Hill and took a couple of zigzags to reach Polaris House. The gate was ajar and Mabs led Jem through it. 'This is where Miss Westallen lives.'

Jem stood stock-still. His pointed chin tipped up as he took in the grand door with its thick columns, the oriels glowing in the sunshine, the glittering windows and turret, the height of the red roofs. 'It's a castle,' he whispered.

'Very like,' agreed Mabs. 'The Westallens are the richest family for miles around. But they're the nicest, too, so you're not to be scared.'

'I won't,' said Jem in a small voice, but he reached out and took her hand. Mabs smiled. The front door flew open before they were halfway there. Clover came flying out, honeyed curls tumbling, in a blue summer dress.

'Mabs!' she shouted. 'Mama's coming!' She stared at Jem. 'Who's *this*?'

'This is my brother, Jeremiah Daley. Jem, we call him. Jem, this is Miss Clover Westallen.'

'Charmed,' said Jem, giving a little bow.

Charmed? Wherever did he learn that? wondered Mabs. She'd always assumed, in her infrequent romantic musings, that you couldn't pinpoint the exact moment someone fell in love. She learned now that that wasn't true. Clover held out her little hand for Jem to shake, and she saw her young brother fall in love, right there and then before her. She could see it as surely as if he'd been lit up in twinkly lights.

Olive came hurrying along the path. 'Hello, Daleys!' she called brightly. 'You must be Jem. I'm very pleased to meet you.'

'Very pleased to meet you, Miss Westallen.'

'What lovely manners. Are you excited about your new adventure?'

'Yes, ma'am. Thank you for thinking of me.'

'Well, bless you, I can see at a glance that it's *just* the right thing. Hello, Mabs. Clover, darling, run back inside. Mama won't be long.'

Clover pouted. 'Jem should come and play Winks.'

Olive laughed. 'No time for Tiddlywinks at present, my angel. Jem has a very important meeting to attend.'

Clover looked mournful, then brightened. 'Jem could make some biscuits?' she suggested.

'Why, bless me, child, that would take even longer. How about this? You bake biscuits with Mrs Brody while I'm out, and when I get back, we shall play Tiddlywinks. If Jem is willing to visit us one day, I'm sure he'll play with you then.'

'I want to come!' Clover threw her arms around her mother's leg, squashing her face into Olive's russet skirts.

Olive threw an anxious glance at Mabs. 'Now, darling, remember we talked about this? I'll come *straight* back, I promise. But it's a very important chance for Jem. You wouldn't want him to miss it, would you?'

'I want to come! Don't leave me, Mama,' grizzled Clover indistinctly from the tarlatan.

Olive crouched down and hugged and kissed her and whispered to her daughter. *Pleas, promises, bribery?* wondered Mabs, remembering her own experience of dealing with small, unhappy children. *Likely all three.*

Eventually, Clover sighed and gave a desolate little wave at the visitors, scuffing her pretty white shoe in the gravel.

'Excuse me, Miss Westallen, ma'am,' said Jem, going scarlet. 'Mabs told me you had a little girl and it ain't polite to go somewhere new empty-handed so I brought something for Miss Clover. Only it ain't very grand,' he sighed, looking up at the huge house again.

'Well, ain't you a good boy?' said Mabs. 'What did you bring?' She couldn't begin to imagine.

'Well, it's this,' muttered Jem. From his jacket pocket he brought out a small spinning top, purple with a yellow band around the middle, the bright paint scuffed and faded. Mabs wanted to cry. Pa had found it by the canal one day, when

Jem was as little as Clover was now. It had been Jem's favourite possession – indeed, his only possession.

Olive and Mabs watched as Clover's face lit up just as though she did not live in a house that was full of expensive toys.

'Good boy,' murmured Mabs, resting a hand on her brother's shoulder. 'How did you ever get to be so special and bright. I'm proud of you, Jemmy.'

He grinned. 'I ain't got the job yet!'

But he did, of course. Mrs Morrow was a lovely but sad-looking woman of around Olive's age. She welcomed Olive and the Daleys with lime sodas and chocolate cake and did her best to put Jem at ease. Then she showed them round the house.

Mabs wanted to laugh when she saw the room Mrs Morrow had prepared for Jem. It was ten times the size of her own at the Finches'. He'd get lost in there! He had a four-poster bed and handsome green curtains and a model stagecoach harnessed to which were four model horses carved from wood. Was she employing him or adopting him?

'Thank you, Mrs Morrow,' murmured Jem, looking a little bewildered.

'I'll wager you'll enjoy the view from your window,' suggested Olive. 'It looks out from the back of the house, does it not, Julia?'

Jem and Mabs went to the window. 'Mabs! Look!' he cried.

'Well, I never,' said Mabs. The Vale of Health was a small horseshoe of smart houses, with fronts facing inwards onto the street. At a greater or lesser angle, the backs overlooked the heath, which lay just at the end of the garden, and Julia Morrow's house looked directly over a great, shimmering pond. A cormorant on some submerged perch in the centre of the pond stretched out its ragged black wings to dry.

Olive and Julia were standing at the bedroom door. 'Thank you,' Mabs said to them quietly. 'This is more than I ever imagined for him. It means so much to know he's in a place like this.'

'He's a fine boy,' said Mrs Morrow, looking happy and sad at the same time. 'It will be a pleasure to help him a little and it will do me good to have some bright company about the place.'

When it was time to say goodbye, Mabs pulled Jem close for a long hug and kissed him furiously. 'Good luck, Jemmy, love. I'll call for you Sunday morning at ten, all right? And we'll go and see the others and you can tell them all about your new place.'

Olive

I really am feeling quite self-satisfied. My match for Jem could not have been more successful. Oh, happy conjunction. If I can only perform a similar magic for the remaining Daleys!

Mama has taken Clover out today, for the first time in several weeks. Their departure was devastating, with Clover screaming blue murder and tears streaming down her cheeks. I was all for giving in and letting her stay with me but Mama is stronger and insisted that Clover must learn to be happy with other people again. I must admit I was relieved to let her decide the matter. Solitude feels like a long-forgotten luxury now and I badly need some time to work on my new project: the Westallen Foundation. I wanted to call it the Hope Foundation but Mr Miles says it is a nebulous name that will not convince people to take it seriously. He says attaching our family name will attract attention, money and influence. So its formal name is the Westallen Foundation but in my own private thoughts I call it the Hope Project. I'm drawing up documents (remits, projected costs, possible venues, etc.) and a guest list for the ball, though I shan't complete that until Mama gets home. Social functions are her genius, not mine.

I'm chewing my pen when Agatha tells me I have a caller,

one Mr Lionel Harper. The name means nothing to me but apparently Mr Miles sent him.

He swipes off his hat when he enters and makes a bow. 'Miss Westallen, I apologise for calling so unexpectedly and without even the courtesy of a card. Not the done thing, I know, but I was in the area and decided to seize the moment. Mr Miles said I should not delay.'

'Mr Harper, welcome. Any friend of Mr Miles is a friend of mine. Please take a seat. What can I do for you?'

Mr Harper is around my own age, well dressed, with dark brown hair and a neat beard a shade or two darker. He has grey eyes and a sharp air about him. I detect a keen intelligence.

'I rather hope you will consider it to be a question of what I can do for you,' he suggests. 'Mr Miles has told me about the Westallen Foundation.'

Mr Harper explains that five years ago he began a small company importing gemstones and selling them on to bespoke jewellers. 'I have achieved a success I never dreamed would come so quickly,' he explains, not boastfully but with a great matter-of-factness. 'I invested in other schemes and made even more money . . . Now I am looking for a worthy project in which to invest in a different way, not for financial return but to do my part in society. Mr Miles assures me that your foundation is just that cause. Perhaps you have heard of my father, the financier William Harper?'

I regret that I have not.

'Philanthropy is a Harper family value, Miss Westallen. It's time for me to do as my father did and use part of my fortune to help others. Will you tell me about the foundation in your own words?'

I eagerly launch into an explanation of what I envision,

vastly grateful to Mr Miles for encouraging me to hone my ideas and package them in a short, effective speech. Mr Harper watches me closely as I speak. 'So, that is the plan in a nutshell,' I conclude. 'I can expand on any part of it if I have been unclear.'

'You have been most clear. Your undertaking is ambitious, but not overly so. Your intentions are of the very best and I can see your sincerity at a glance. I should very much like to make a donation, and help in other ways if I can.'

My first patron! 'Would you be willing to talk to youngsters about your business?' I ask at once. 'There is so much scope there. The art of jewellery, the mechanisms of import, inter-national trade, investment . . . Could we turn to you if we met young people with interest in any of those? The people I wish to help . . . they would never in a hundred years come within ten miles of a man like you. Exposure to other types of people, other ways of life, other sources of information than the ones they know is such an important part of my vision.'

He laughs a little. 'You are not hesitant, Miss Westallen! You know what you want and you're not shy to ask for it.'

'If I were, I could do little for the poor of London, Mr Harper.'

'I agree. Beating around the bush is a nonsensical pastime. To answer your question, yes, of course I'd be willing – in principle, of course. I would assess each enquiry on an indi-vidual basis; if I had reservations about the character of a young person, for example, I would demur. And at particularly busy times of the year I have not time to draw breath, let alone talk to would-be apprentices. But those caveats aside, you may count on me, Miss Westallen.'

'Thank you. I am more grateful and excited than I can say to secure your involvement. Money is important obviously, and Mr Miles has impressed on me how much this endeavour will need. However, money alone will not take my schemes forward. It is hope, Mr Harper, that these people need.'

'Hope?'

'Yes. And they will not get that from rows of figures on a page. They will get it when people take the time to educate them, encourage them, and prise off their blinkers.'

He raises his eyebrows. 'Quite! I must say, Miss Westallen, I admire you. That is, I admire what you are doing. No, indeed, I admire *you*. Mr Miles told me that you are good-hearted, uncommonly clever and rich. He had not mentioned that you were quite so . . . charming and lovely.' I must look incredulous because he hastens to undo his words. 'Forgive me! Inappropriate. This is a business meeting. I am not a flatterer, Miss Westallen, but I always speak my mind, as you do. Let us return to the matter at hand. How else might I aid the Westallen Foundation?'

'We need a meeting space,' I say without hesitation. 'A central office to which people can apply. At present I'm working from my study, as you see, but I cannot have a constant stream of people coming to the house.'

'I have an old warehouse in Euston. Not large, but it would serve. At the moment there are still old stocks and supplies occupying the ground floor but you could use the first floor right away. In time, if you expand and need the other floor, I could have it cleared.'

I shake my head. 'Mr Harper, you are quite miraculous. You have just solved my most immediate difficulty without a moment's thought. You are like the Saint Nicholas of charitable foundations.'

'My father would delight to hear it. I'm glad Mr Miles sent me to you. He said that my good intentions and yours might fit together nicely and so it seems. Now, I'll take my leave and I shall see about having the warehouse – your office – cleaned, and keys sent to you. Good day, Miss Westallen, and good luck!'

I rise and shake his hand. 'Thank you, Mr Harper, most sincerely, for coming here and for all you have promised. I'm grateful on behalf of all those I wish to help.'

'I hope we meet again soon.'

I show him out with my head spinning a little. It is rare that a man can match me in intelligence and decisiveness. He is successful and has a social conscience; he is just the right amount of outspoken to intrigue me. And he is not unattractive. I wonder if there is a *Mrs* Lionel Harper.

Charming and lovely? I slip into the dining room, where there is a mirror. My hair, hastily bundled prior to starting work this morning, has slipped, and I have a small smudge of blue at the side of my mouth from chewing the pen. I wear the locket that the servants gave me for my birthday over a neckline that does not suit a locket at all, but it has become something of a talisman for me and I wear it almost always now. I'm no Rowena Blythe! And yet, the slip-slide of my hair softens my face. I do blame Papa entirely for my jaw and, unlike him, I cannot dress it in a beard. I'm wearing an old dress, cream and pink. I rarely wear pink yet I believe the colour rather suits me. Or is it just a compliment from an attractive man that makes me think so?

Instead of returning to the study, I somehow find myself in my bedroom, absent-mindedly looking about, wondering what I came up for. A hairbrush? A change of dress? I realise I was propelled up the stairs like a sleepwalker by a vague impulse to consult my divination cards. Because of Mr Harper? Am I so deprived of male company that a single encounter sends me running to the altar to wait in hope? I tut. Certainly *not*. While I'm here, I would like to make a reading, though. Not on so feeble a subject as a *man*, but about the foundation. It's so important an undertaking, I can't believe I haven't done so before!

I withdraw the cards from their hiding place among my undergarments and settle myself on the bed. I think about my new endeavour, about everything that led up to it – Clover, my desire to make the world a better place for her, my trip to Harlowe Place. I shuffle and break and draw a card. And again. And again.

First is the Anchor. The illustration is a buoyant sea, with two ships atop. A huge anchor predominates over the fore-ground. The Anchor. In the Christian Church a symbol of hope. The Hope Project. My head spins a little. As often as I use these cards, and as much as I recognise their value, I can still be floored by a particularly pertinent card. There are more things in Heaven and Earth . . .

When I have marshalled my sense of wonder I read the motto, wondering not for the first time at the irregular use of capital letters. *A Person as honest as You in his dealings will never want a rich harvest of gain. Your wishes too are likely to be accomplished.* Well, that is promising.

The second card is the Sun. *You will make an unexpected fortune, use it so that nobody may Covet it.* Well, the Hope Project is a good cause if ever there was one. Surely no one would covet money intended to raise the wretched from the depths. The card shows a bright sun shining over a rural idyll of fields with a small church spire on the horizon. The fields, to me, suggest the teeming patchwork of London, and the spire represents Mr Miles, offering guidance and encourage-ment when I need him. A wholly encouraging reading so far! I turn over the third card.

The Tree. *Never regret labour or pains. A good work is its own reward, be this your Consolation.* Well, I don't need consolation, with or without a capital C. I decide to focus not on the rather pious message but on the picture of the spreading oak tree. Just now the Hope Project is naught but a tiny acorn. But Hope will be my anchor and the sun will shine on my endeavours and it will spread and grow and flourish.

I run back to the study, rubbing thoughtfully at the blue stain on my face with spit and my finger. I pick up the guest list for the ball and add Mr Harper's name. *Plus family?* I jot beside it.

I sigh, reaching the big sticking point in my scheme. If I am to court the rich and influential of the area, if I am to hold a ball inviting everyone who's anyone, then I must invite the Blythes. I wonder if Mama has thought of this. We shall have to put our personal feelings aside for the good of the foundation. For to hold an event of this nature and omit to invite just one family, and *such* a family, would look more than strange; it would be an insult. It would be tantamount to airing our personal grievances before society. No, indeed, we shall *have* to invite them . . . and hope they do not come.

Otty

When I hear Papa come home from the office, I barrel into his study and knock into a chair. Lord but I'm clumsy. I'm excited and I want to talk to him.

'Hello, Papa. Now, I wish to talk to you about my wonderful school. I've hardly seen you lately.'

He looks up distractedly. 'What? School? Well, I'm pleased you like it. I knew you would. Are they making a lady of you yet?' He looks me up and down, squinting. 'Why, yes, I fancy you look more refined already.'

I giggle. 'Well, I don't know about that, Papa, but I like the lessons very much. We had a test in mathematics today and I came top. We had one in French yesterday and I came second. My friend Edina got one more mark than me. Mr Ferris says I show a great facility.'

'Well, we know that, Otty. You've always been a conscientious student. I really don't see the need for tests in a ladies' academy, though, provided you're learning the basic accomplishments.'

'Mr Ferris wants to challenge us like boys, to fulfil our potential. You'll never guess, Papa – he said I'm bright enough to try for university one day and he only said that to *three* girls in my class. Me, Edina and Bea.' I can feel myself puffing up a little as I boast, but it really is the most exciting thing!

Since Olive planted the seed in my mind, the idea has grown; it fills me with excitement.

Papa looks nonplussed. 'University? Good grief, Otty, you're teasing! Surely no one at the academy said such a thing? I chose it because it's a respectable establishment. I hate to point out the obvious, darling, but you're a *girl*.'

His tone is gentle but I cannot describe the disappointment that crashes through me. It's cold and drenching. That's not at all what I wanted my father to say. 'I *know* I'm a girl, Papa. But that doesn't mean I'm not clever. It doesn't mean I wouldn't like to go to university.'

Papa runs a hand through his hair so that it sticks up in rather a sweet way. 'Otty, listen to you! Who has put these thoughts into your head? I've no doubt you *are* clever, but that's hardly the point!'

'What is then?' I really want to know. My voice is very small. Doesn't he think I'm capable of having my *own* thoughts?

'Darling, do you see your sisters troubling themselves about university? Of course not. That's why I'm working so hard, to be able to provide for you all sufficiently that you can marry *well*. By the time you're eighteen or so, we'll be rich indeed.'

'But Papa, marrying a rich man doesn't matter all that much to me. I'm not even sure I *want* to marry.'

'Well, of course not, darling, you're twelve! But that will change, trust me.' Suddenly Papa doesn't look so sweet to me. Does he think he knows me better than I know myself?

'But I *like* school. I like learning. I'd like to earn my own money one day. Then I wouldn't need a husband, or I could pick one I liked, not one that was rich.' Papa looks white. I almost feel sorry for him but I press on. 'Look at Mabs! She earns her own money and gives some to her family to help them out. Don't you think that's *splendid*?'

Papa ruffles his hair quite hard. He takes some time to answer. 'Is this what you talk about with Daley?' he asks, looking up sternly. 'I would never have allowed your walks with her had I known. If she's filling your head with nonsense of that kind, she'll be out of here faster than she can fathom and I don't care how many children she has to feed.' His voice has risen and I squeak with horror.

'I thought you *liked* Mabs!'

'I do. Of course I do.' He seems to calm down again. 'But she's from a different *class*, Otty! Her sort of people . . . well, they're different from us in every way. You're a *lady*! She is coarse and unrefined and has no other option than to work. And you shouldn't call her Mabs. It's a ridiculous name and completely inappropriate for you to be on such terms with a servant. I expect you to address her as Miss Daley.'

Tears are spilling now; I can feel their silvery coolness making tracks on my hot face. I'm afraid I may have got Mabs into trouble and that's the last thing I ever wanted to do. I take a deep breath. Sharing my excitement with Papa, telling him my good news, is all forgotten. All that matters is to make this right.

'I do call her Miss Daley, Papa, I only *think* of her as Mabs sometimes. And she's never filled my head with *anything*. We chat about our lives as we go around, that's all. She never said *I* should work. She's as respectful of me as you could ever wish, Papa, she treats me like a princess.'

Papa looks mollified. 'Well, I'm very glad to hear it. I must say, I was surprised . . . She's always seemed so deferent. I should be astonished and disappointed to learn that Miss Daley has lost sight of her place.'

'She hasn't, Papa, she hasn't. It's all come from my head – you know how I am!'

He rises, smiling fondly, and comes to stroke my hair. For the first time in my life it's all I can do not to pull away. 'I do indeed. My youngest daughter, the scamp! It's very endearing, Otty, this great spirit of yours, but it will not serve you when you're older. I indulge you because I want you to have a full and happy childhood, but when the time comes, I'll expect you to put away this whimsy of yours.'

'Are you saying . . . I'm not *allowed* to go to university?'

'Higher education for you will be . . . unnecessary! And problematical. Too much learning, for females, can cause a mild fever in the brain, you know. Your mother is delicate and you may follow in her suit. I should hate to see you curtailed as your mother is, dear; I couldn't bear that. Besides, an over-educated female is unappealing to gentlemen. University is expensive, and I couldn't agree to part with all that money for something that would certainly ruin your chances of a suitable marriage.'

I'm not even listening to him now. It's all too much to take in. 'But . . . but . . .' I say, unusually feebly. 'Olive is very clever. Olive has learned a great deal! About the stars and mathematics and . . . *she* isn't fevered! *She's* not delicate!'

'Yes, and *Olive* is not *married*, is she?' Papa's tone is scornful and I flinch. First Mabs, now Olive! The two people I love the most in the world, after him and Mama.

'Don't you like Olive?' I ask in a wavering tone.

'I like her well enough. But she's a very rich woman with only herself to please. She can afford to defy tradition. But Otty, surely you would not wish to grow up to be anything like *her*?'

I shake my head, even though really I'd like to be like Olive more than anything. It reminds me of telling the policeman that I wouldn't see Jill again, and not meaning it. I hate saying things because other people want to hear them. Why do I do it?

'Well, good. Now, let's be friends again and take our supper together. I remember what it's like to be young and high spirited. But when the time comes, you'll *want* to grow up the right way. You'll have changed naturally, and you won't want university or any other strange things. It's like growing out of dolls . . . or the nursery or . . . or chocolate pudding.'

I don't want to sup with him just now but I agree because I don't want to make things worse between us. I know that university is a very unusual choice for a girl – and Papa is an old-fashioned stick-in-the-mud, I have said it often – but I had not expected *this*. I need to think it all over later when I'm alone. But there are some things I do know, right away. Mabs is *not* coarse; she is the gentlest person I know. Olive is *wonderful*. And I will *never* grow out of chocolate pudding!

Mabs

On Monday, Mr Finch returned from the office in a great fluster, adjusting his tie, hastening his wife and altogether betraying his nerves at the impending luncheon with the Westallens. When they set off, he looked red-faced and uncomfortable, she coolly serene in a beige costume with a thin lilac stripe. She seemed amply ready for a social visit; she had continued her daily walks and her strength and spirits were much improved.

'Take the afternoon for yourself, Daley,' instructed Mrs Finch. 'I'll be tired when we return and you deserve it!'

It was a treat to have time off that was unplanned. Mabs began her bounty of time with a visit to the high street. Peg's birthday was coming up soon and the three-shilling bonus was still in her pocket. *I can't spend it all* . . . Mabs told herself as she wandered in search of the perfect present.

After a pleasant hour's browsing, she chose a silver chain with a horseshoe charm for Peg. Jewellery, she thought, was a suitable present for a girl turning thirteen. Peg would love having something special to wear and a necklace could easily be hidden beneath her dress when she went out in their less than lovely neighbourhood. For extra luxury she bought a length of butter-yellow ribbon for Peg's brown hair and a box of fruit jellies. The chance to spoil her sister was too delicious to be resisted; she'd never been able to do it before. Then she went home and placed the remaining coins in her box.

Otty was at school. Lou would be hard at work, so there was no point trekking over to Highgate. She didn't want to be presumptuous and call on Olive. Mabs read for a long time – *Little Women*, a story of sisters – then wandered down to the kitchen. Mrs Webb was sitting at the table, balancing the monthly household accounts. Betsy sat across from her, polishing silver. Mabs sat beside Betsy and took up a rag. 'May as well help,' she said.

Company and a steaming cup of tea made it a pleasant way to pass the time. After a long and peaceful interval they heard a knock at the front door. 'Get that, would you, Mabs?' asked Mrs Webb. 'I'm up to my eyes in these figures and I don't want to lose my place.'

Mabs laid down a dessert spoon, wiped her hands and ran to the door. It was a young man with a shock of tow-coloured hair. 'Delivery for Mr Finch from the office,' he said with a professional air.

'He's not here but I'll take them,' said Mabs, wondering why he looked familiar.

The messenger made a note of something on his sheet and held it out to Mabs. 'Sign here, please.'

Mabs hesitated, then realised, to her great joy, that she could write well enough to make a signature. She signed her name, beaming.

The young man grinned back as if he'd caught her good mood. 'Directly to Mr Finch now,' he warned, handing over a thick manila envelope. 'Important documents. Beg pardon, miss, but I feel like I've seen you somewhere before. Lord, that sounds smarmy. I'm not trying to be, I feel like I should know you.'

'I'll put them on his desk right away,' said Mabs, 'and I'll let you off because you look familiar too.'

He had bright blue eyes in a tanned face, and a shock of yellow hair with golden lights in it. He looked like someone who spent a lot of time outside. Mabs would assume he was a canal worker except that he wore a respectable shirt and trousers and looked very clean. Then the penny dropped.

'Oh my Gawd, it's *you*!'

All at once it was last September and every day was a struggle. She was locked in her old life with no promise of a way out. She was too weak to work properly and too dizzy to move out of the way when the ice fell. 'Oh my Gawd,' she said again, leaning against the wall. 'You saved my life!'

'I'm sorry, miss, you've got the wrong feller. I'd like to take credit, but I'd remember saving a pretty young lady like yerself.'

Charmer, thought Mabs. 'But do you remember saving a skinny boy in the shade last September?' she asked, recovering herself. 'Block of ice flyin' through the air, chap not movin', you leapin' on top to knock him out of the way?'

Understanding dawned. 'That was *you*? You was a boy?'

'Well, I pretended. Had to, to work on the wharf.'

'Blimey! I remember that! Gawd but I'm embarrassed I didn't know you was a girl. You don't look like no boy *I* ever seen.'

Mabs blushed. 'You just got straight back to work like it was nothing, wouldn't even let me thank you.'

He shrugged. 'You know how it is there. They don't exactly pay you to sit around drinking coffee. I'm happy to see you've come up in the world; that was no place for a lady. Housemaid?'

'Companion to the lady of the house.'

He whistled. 'And they treat you well?'

'Couldn't ask for better. I'm a lucky girl. You're not labouring either by the looks of it.'

'Office errand boy.' He plucked at his clean shirt with a cocky expression. 'Look what a gent I am! Seriously, though, I'm going places I am, miss, and the canal office is just the first step.'

'Really? What's next then?'

He hesitated and Mabs saw his tanned complexion grow warm. 'I want to be a writer, me. Write them stories in the periodicals that the ladies and gents read and get all excited about. A really good book, that's what I want to leave behind me when I die.'

'What a *wonderful* idea!' said Mabs, lighting up on the inside. Now that she was discovering the joys of reading, the thought of actually writing one of the stories she loved so much made her feel dizzy. She'd never heard such an ambition before, and definitely not from anyone of her own class.

'You do? You don't think it's stupid?'

'No! Someone's gotta write them. Sounds a sight more exciting than canal paperwork.'

He nodded thoughtfully. 'That's what I reckon. Only there's one problem, I can't write, or not very well anyway.'

Mabs grinned. 'But I bet you're learning.'

He grinned back. 'That I am, miss, that I am.' He held out a hand. 'Kip Miller, aspiring author, at yer service, miss.' Another rush of memory. Kipper. Of course.

Mabs shook his hand. 'Mabel Daley. Mabs.'

'Daley. That sounds familiar too.'

'Me father works on the wharf and me brother too now.'

'Ah, a canal family. You went by Mark back then, didn't you?'

'You've got a good memory! Well, Kip Miller, hadn't you

better be getting back? They don't pay you to sit around drinking coffee, you know!'

'Touché!' said Kip with a laugh. 'Well, it was good to see you again, Mabs.'

'Likewise, and good luck. Oh, and Kip? Thank you. Thank you from the bottom of me heart. The day that happened, it was one of the dark days. You know? When you just can't see how life's ever going to get any better. But it did, and I'd never have got the chance to see it if I'd died that day.'

Kip Miller tipped an imaginary hat and bowed. Then he set off along Willoughby Walk, looking back three times as he went. Mabs knew because she watched him go.

Otty

Two days after my difficult conversation with Papa I decide to try again. He *is* my papa, after all, and we've always been the greatest of friends. Perhaps I misunderstood him, or caught him at a bad moment. Today is the day he and Mama are having lunch with the Westallens, so I assume he'll be in a good mood. I wait for him in his study; it's a pleasant place to while away the time. I like the smell of his pipe and twirling the globe on his desk, planning adventures. I imagine myself a lady with a large travelling trunk and plumes of steam rising behind me from whichever train or boat I'm about to catch.

When he comes in, I get up and give him a hug. 'How was lunch at Polaris House, Papa? Do you think you'll do some business with the captain?'

His face and his words don't match. What he says is, 'It was most fruitful, my dear, an excellent prospect for me. The captain is a very cordial man,' which is exactly what he wanted. But his face is frowning as if he's very upset. I wonder if I should wait until another day, but I have my little speech prepared.

'That's good, Papa, I'm so pleased. I wanted to talk to you about my education, Papa, dear. I've been thinking a lot about what you said the other day and I understand exactly what you mean.'

'I knew you would, you're always such a good girl.'

'Women *do* always live a certain way, and many of them are perfectly *happy* with marriage and home. That's wonderful! But Papa, dear, we don't *all* want it! Just because things are the way they've always been, doesn't mean they always *have* to be that way. There's a women's movement, you know, and—'

'Stop!' Papa holds his hand up. 'Otty, darling, please don't tell me you're going to cite *those* women to me. Gracious, they barely *qualify* as women with their outrageous ideas. Of course, they'll never get anywhere but imagine if they did! Good heavens, society as we know it would not be able to continue.'

This is not going as well as I'd hoped. 'But Papa, *men* have changed things through the ages, haven't they? Like with the Factory Acts and abolition.'

Papa looks so shocked that I want to put my arms around him and protect him from the hurt I seem to be causing. I don't understand *that* at all.

'Ottilie Finch! Where do you get such notions? From that man, Ferris, I suppose. You're a girl of twelve. You shouldn't know anything about such things.'

'But they're *good* things, Papa. The Factory Acts stopped children like me being sent to work in horrible jobs! And abolition means people can't own slaves any more. You wouldn't like *me* working in a mine, would you?'

'No, darling, of course not. But—'

'And it's good that people can't own negroes any more, isn't it, Papa? People shouldn't own *people*. You wouldn't want someone to own *me*, would you?'

His face has gone white and still. 'Good God, Otty. What do you know about negroes? This is *not* a correct topic for my youngest daughter to discuss. They're no sort of people for *you* to think about.'

I feel myself grow still in response. I've never mentioned Jill to my parents, but I think about it, every week. It seems ridiculous to be able to talk and laugh so easily with someone, to have each other's very best interests at heart, yet never to see them. Now I have my answer, without ever asking the question. What he said is bad enough but the way he said it, the look on his face, is worse.

I bite my lip. I want to pursue it, tell him that I have been rescued by one of those people on whom he clearly looks down. I want to explode his ideas and make him see anew. But something tells me I won't succeed.

'Well, all I really wanted to say was that I love you, Papa, and I know you love me and want the best for me. And for me that means an education. So won't you try and understand, please, darling Papa? I don't *want* to marry at twenty, I want to go to university and learn something big. Please, Papa. *Please.*'

I'm so proud of myself for biting back my angry feelings. I shall fight the Jill battle another day. I look hopefully into his face. This is the man who taught me to ice skate. This is the man who took me to the river to feed ducks.

But those memories feel a long time ago now. He's looking at me incredulously. 'Otty! When you said you'd been reflecting on our conversation, I certainly didn't expect you to *challenge* it. This is not *your* decision to make. My answer is a categorical and final no. Good God! It seems you have more of your mother in you than I had thought. While you're here, I should tell you that after our last little talk, I've decided to move you to a different school. I've found a far more suitable alternative and they can take you at the start of next term.'

'Move *again*?' I squeak. 'No, Papa! Not so soon after Durham, it's too much. And I love the academy.'

'Another move is regrettable, but I can't have your head being filled with this sort of thing! It's . . . well, it's *disgusting*!' He gives a sort of a . . . *sob* and buries his face in his forearms, which he rests on his desk.

I stare at him for a long time. I can feel that my mouth is wide open and my forehead is creased in a frown. No doubt it is very unladylike and unbecoming. But I can't seem to move and there is not a single thought in my head, only an impression that, perhaps, this is not quite right. 'But don't you care if I'm *happy*?' I plead after I don't know how long.

He looks up and he's all blotchy, like Averil when she's upset. 'Darling, of *course*. But if you follow my guidance, happiness will ensue. I promise.'

I don't believe him, not for a second. But I have the feeling of having reached a brick wall with no footholds and no gate. So I wish him goodnight and leave the study. I stand in the hall for a moment, frighteningly confused. I suppose since there is an expense involved and Papa refuses to pay, then I cannot go to university. The disappointment engulfs me like seawater. And why should it be a bad thing to have Mama in me? What *exactly* is wrong with her? And is the same thing wrong with me? *I* don't think there's anything wrong with me, so . . . maybe Mama is fine too. But if *that's* true, why does she live in her room? Why is Mabs here? But I'm not sure I can ask anyone these questions – they're far too big.

Mabs

The following day, Mabs woke with a sense of pleasant anticipation. Yesterday had been a lovely day and today she was looking forward to hearing how lunch with the Westallens had gone. She relished the warmer weather as she dressed, then hurried downstairs, tummy rumbling.

'Good morning!' she sang out as she went into her mistress's room, then stopped. The room was dark, the drapes drawn. It was eerily silent and for a moment she thought it was empty. Something had happened, and could still be felt, hanging on the air.

Mabs stepped carefully, in case of broken glass or china, but there was no tell-tale crunch beneath her feet. She drew back one drape gingerly; somehow it seemed disrespectful to flood this brooding room with sunshine. Mrs Finch was in bed, covers drawn up to her chin. Mabs felt a thin curl of fear in her stomach; her mistress was as still as a stone.

'Mrs Finch?' said Mabs in a fearful voice. 'Ma'am?' She laid a hand on her shoulder. To her relief, she felt the rise and fall of breathing. Perhaps she should just leave her in peace but somehow that felt wrong. She shook her. She shook harder, but her mistress slept on.

Mabs looked around the room for clues. Nothing broken,

everything in its place. She opened the wardrobe, an odd thing to do perhaps, but she wanted to reassure herself of normality. All Mrs Finch's lovely dresses were hanging as usual.

'What's happened?' whispered Mabs to the beige dress Mrs Finch had worn yesterday. The dress had no answers for her. She returned to the bedside.

'Mrs Finch,' she said loudly and shook her again. 'It's me, Daley. Time you were up. Time for your breakfast.' Mabs's own appetite had vanished. She opened the drapes fully, hoping the light might creep into Mrs Finch's awareness and rouse her. In the rose garden four new buds were showing. 'The roses are coming lovely,' she said. 'Shall we go into the garden today?'

Silence. Mabs sighed. Biting her lip, she ran down to Mr Finch's study. But when she knocked, there was no answer.

'Hello there, Daley!' Charlie Finch was in the hall, on his way out. 'Pa's at work. Nothing wrong, is there?'

'No, sir. I just had a quick question. I don't know why I thought he'd be in.'

'Always worth a try,' said Charlie cheerfully. 'Well, I'm off. These spring days are a treat, aren't they?'

'They are, sir. Have a lovely day.'

Mabs went to the kitchen and ordered strong coffee and toast, hoping the aromas might stir Mrs Finch. She took the tray up herself and placed it on a little table next to the bed.

'Lovely coffee!' she all but shouted. 'And toast! Come on now, rise and shine!'

Mrs Finch slept on. Mabs stood and paced, then sat and drummed her fingers. In the end, when the coffee and toast were cold, she ate and drank them herself. They were disgusting, but somehow helped Mabs to order her thoughts.

Firstly, it seemed safe to assume that this was no natural sleep. It seemed highly probable that Mr Finch had given his wife a sedative again – there must have been some incident during or after the lunch. But he'd gone to work as usual, and left no message for Mabs, so he must not be *very* concerned. Or perhaps he didn't know how heavily she was sleeping.

How long could she sit like this and watch her sleep? Should she call a doctor? If only she could have seen Mr Finch, even for a moment, to ask for guidance. She could walk down to the canal and find him there but she didn't want to leave Mrs Finch for that length of time. She felt herself back in those early, confusing days when she'd had no idea how to handle the situations in which she found herself.

She's breathing, she told herself sternly. *She's alive. She'll wake up when it's worn off and you can get to the bottom of things then.* So she resigned herself to a strange day, watching and waiting.

Around two o'clock she grew hungry and fetched some lunch, just for herself.

'Mistress off her food again?' asked Mrs Webb.

'Having a nap,' said Mabs. 'Tired out after yesterday, I think.'

'Eat down here with us then,' suggested Lydia.

But Mabs made her excuses. She couldn't bear to leave Mrs Finch alone.

It wasn't until four o'clock that Mabs, staring out of the window, heard a rustle behind her. She whipped round. Mrs Finch was turning over, her eyes still closed. Mabs flew to her side, crouching down beside the bed.

'Wake up now,' she murmured. 'Please wake up at last. It's all right, I'm here, it's Daley.' Her mistress's eyes fluttered open and regarded her blearily. 'It's all right,' said Mabs again, smoothing her hair back off her face, 'it's all right.'

Mrs Finch frowned and swallowed. Mabs leapt up and brought her a glass of water. Mrs Finch struggled to sit up.

'Oh, thank goodness! Oh, thank the heavens,' muttered Mabs, sliding her arms under her shoulders to help. 'Let me move the pillows. There, is that comfortable? Oh merciful God, you're up. Ma'am, what the 'ell happened?'

Mrs Finch was too disoriented still for conversation and reached for the glass. She swallowed it down in one. 'What do you need, ma'am? Food? A chamber pot? Sherry? How can I make you comfortable?'

But the other woman merely reached out and took her hand, holding it firmly in her own as if to reassure Mabs and silence her. Her mother used to do the same thing when Mabs grew too fussy. The afternoon wore on around them. At last Mrs Finch cleared her throat and asked hoarsely, 'What time is it?'

'Half past four, ma'am.'

She frowned. 'What *day* is it?'

'Tuesday, ma'am. The day after your lunch at the Westallens'. You've been dead to the world all day.'

She closed her eyes and drew a deep breath. Then she looked at Mabs. 'What am I to do, Mabel, dear? What on earth am I to do?'

Mabs said nothing about the use of her first name, or the endearment, and considered. 'Well, ma'am, much as I know it ain't my business, it's time for me to ask you some questions. And for you to answer them. Otherwise, how can I possibly help?'

The bursting silence was interrupted by the sound of the front door opening and blowing shut. Mabs saw her mistress's face blanch, a flare of terror in her eyes. 'It's all right, ma'am. It'll just be Otty home from school.'

But Mrs Finch shook her head. 'Lucius!' she hissed.

Mabs cocked her head. Sure enough she heard his voice

talking to Mrs Webb. Then they heard footsteps on the stairs.

'Tell him I'm asleep,' said Mrs Finch, diving under the covers. 'Tell him I've been awake, but I've gone to sleep again. And Mabel, *please*, don't leave me!'

Mabs only had time to pull the covers straight and return to her chair when the door opened. Mr Finch's face appeared around the door frame. 'Ah, Daley,' he whispered. 'How is my wife today?'

'She's been sleeping a great deal, sir. I've been worried.'

'She hasn't been asleep *all* this time, surely?' He looked alarmed and came into the room in a little rush.

'No, sir, she woke a while back, to my relief. But she's just gone back to sleep.'

'I see. And how was she when she woke? Agitated? Delusional? Hysterical?'

'No, sir, nothing like that. She was just very tired, very quiet. I weren't surprised when she lay down again.'

'And did she tell you . . . anything?'

'Not a thing, sir.'

'We should leave her to sleep. Come with me, Miss Daley. We'll talk.'

'Oh, I don't like to leave her, sir, while she's like this. Can't we talk here?'

'How very commendable. But Abigail obviously needs the sleep and you must have questions. Come along.'

Mabel, please, don't leave me! Mabs wracked her brains for some clever reason to stay but none was forthcoming. She rose reluctantly. 'Very good, sir, but I'll come straight back here then. Straight back, the *moment* you've finished with me.' She said it loud and clear, for Mrs Finch's benefit.

As they walked down the stairs, Mabs's heart hammered in

her chest from the strain of her divided loyalties. She was lying to him, at his wife's request, and not for the first time. Mabs *knew* Mrs Finch had difficulties of the mind; that was why she was here! And yet, that flare of terror in her eyes . . . *Don't leave me*.

Mr Finch opened his study door and stood back to let Mabs go first. For once she felt irritated with his lovely manners. This felt like one earnest conversation too many in this room.

'Sir, what *happened*?' she asked at once. 'I couldn't wake her for trying. I was so worried.'

'I'm sorry, Miss Daley. You must have had quite the shock. I wanted to warn you but I left very early this morning, before six, and there was no opportunity to hurry home at lunchtime. Regrettably, yesterday, she was . . . difficult. When we came home, she became quite, quite unmanageable and I had to use Dr Broome's drops. I never like to do it, as you know, but . . . it was imperative.'

'Was the luncheon not a success, sir? I'm sorry, I know you had high hopes for it. But she was right as rain when I waved you off yesterday. I felt sure it would go well.'

'The lunch itself was rather good. I have some hope that the captain will, after all, invest a little money in my scheme. The Westallens are congenial people, though the daughter is . . . unusual. She is charming despite, but I do not think she's a suitable friend for my wife. Too headstrong by far – Abigail needs no encouragement *that* way. The two of them, over lunch . . . well, let's just say some rather inappropriate remarks were spoken and I was displeased.'

Mabs frowned. Knowing what she did of Olive, it was hard to imagine her exerting a bad influence on a luncheon guest of her parents.

'I raised the matter when we arrived home and it became

rather a *discussion*. Abigail grew wild. Hence the need for the measures I took. I can't pretend I'm not deeply upset, but my feelings on the matter are well known to you, Miss Daley. I daresay we shall all regain our equilibrium. Perhaps a social occasion was too much, too soon, but oh, the temptation to attend a luncheon with my wife on my arm, like any married couple . . . was so great.'

He sank his head into his hands then immediately looked up. 'But there, I won't be self-pitying. I shall think of this as an isolated, regrettable setback. But I have this fear, Miss Daley, this dreadful *fear*, that it will happen again, perhaps often.'

'Oh sir,' whispered Mabs, devastated. 'Surely not.'

'And so, I have decided to summon Dr Broome of Durham. I found him very wise when Abigail was in his care. If he could visit even briefly, and give me some guidance . . . I miss my wife, Miss Daley. I should not speak of such things to you, of course I should not, and I beg your pardon. But I am at my wits' end; it's so very long since we had a normal life. And the worst of it is that she simply cannot be reasoned with. Delusional – she thinks the world is against her. She's capable of believing all kinds of things that are quite untrue. And where can one even begin, in a situation like that?'

❋

Where indeed? Mabs climbed the stairs slowly, grateful for the moments when she was with neither Mr nor Mrs Finch, moments when she could try to make sense of things.

She heard Mr Finch's words again: *delusional – she thinks the world is against her. She's capable of believing all kinds of things that are quite untrue.*

Then Mrs Finch's: *Lucius! Tell him I'm asleep! Mabel, please, don't leave me*.

Mabs shook her head to clear it of both of them. At Mrs Finch's door, Mabs hesitated. It was all too much. She had some savings to keep her going. She could get another job. She could just *leave* . . . Except, of course, she couldn't.

'I'm back, ma'am,' she said, closing the door behind her. 'I'm alone.'

The figure in the bed stirred and sat up. 'Daley,' said Mrs Finch.

'I'm sorry I had to go after you asked me not to, but how could I explain saying no?'

'You couldn't. I know. And my husband, what has he told you?'

Mabs drew a chair to the side of the bed and sat down. 'In short, ma'am, that you and he had words yesterday after the luncheon and you became very wild so he used a sedative. He says you think things that aren't true, ma'am, and that he can't reason with you because of it. He says he misses you.'

She gave a sad, twisted smile. 'Do you believe him?'

'I've no reason to doubt him. And I've seen you raging, remember. Sometimes I don't know what to expect from you from one day to the next.'

'But? There is a *but*, isn't there, Mabel? I have to believe there's at least a crumb of doubt in your mind.'

'There's more than a crumb, ma'am. To be honest, there's half a cake, but I can't say why. He's kind and clever and . . . steady and I owe him everything. But you . . . you act mad, sometimes, you do. And yet you're clever and strong and caring. When he talks of this fragile, excitable woman who doesn't know what's real, it's not *you*, ma'am.' Mabs watched

Mrs Finch's face carefully as she spoke, and saw an expression like a drowning man being thrown a rope. 'There's only one problem, ma'am.'

'Only one?' They both gave a shaky giggle.

'There's plenty, but only one you can help me with. I know Mr Finch's side of it. Oh, don't get me wrong, he's never told me anything private, nothing I'd find it uncomfortable to hear. But I know the facts, according to him. But you've never said a single word.'

'I know. I have to tell you now. And it's the one thing I have feared above all else because I dread you disbelieving me. I dread losing you. You've made this life bearable, Mabel, slightly.'

'What happened yesterday? What did you say at luncheon that was so terrible?'

Mrs Finch looked down at her hands and sighed. 'The subject of Otty's education came up. He's moving her to a new school, you know.'

'What? *Why*? She *loves* that school!'

'I know. But Lucius is . . . *conservative* on matters of women's education. She's probably told you about her teacher, the debates, the tests. Lucius is appalled. I said that he should leave her there, since she's thriving and has already gone through so much change in a short time. Olive agreed. Olive is . . . *not* conservative! Lucius was very uncomfortable, I could see, and would not change his mind. He never does. Well, I have paid for it now.'

'I see . . .' Mabs murmured. *Is that why I wasn't to let him know about the reading lessons?* she wondered.

'Mabel,' said Mrs Finch. 'It's asking a lot of you to think differently about a man who's given you employment, a living and every courtesy. I'm sorry to have to do it. But I promise,

I am not delusional and I am not lying. Do you still wish me to tell you everything?'

Mabs swallowed. 'Yes, ma'am.'

'Then I think I should start at the very beginning.'

Abigail

I come from a wealthy family. I was one of two sisters and two brothers. I was the youngest. Spoiled, no doubt. Certainly vain. Everyone told me I was beautiful; I had suitors from a young age. Of course, my parents chaperoned me to within an inch of my life; my courtships were all very sweet and innocent. Life was . . . gilded. I was full of joy.

I met Lucius Finch when I was only sixteen. He was far below me in the social order, but I cared nothing about that. I had many faults but snobbery was not among them. He was nine years older than I, and not handsome. He was overeager to know me and I found that a little off-putting. But *all* the young men were keen to know me, so I thought little of it. He was just *there*, on the periphery of my social circle, often overlooked, nudging his way in when he could.

My favoured suitor in those early years was Emmanuel Hillier. He was handsome in the way that sets every young girl dreaming: dark hair, flashing eyes, all that. He was rich and sought after. But there was another man, Jonathan Ingram, who was *not* rich. He was twenty years old and in the process of making his way. An opportunity had arisen for him in India and he was to go for two or three years to make his fortune. A fortune fit to woo a young lady of means. Fit to woo *me*.

I was aggravated! In my silly, adolescent appraisal of things, Emmanuel was the dashing romantic hero; Jonathan was my *friend*. We talked about things, we laughed . . . I didn't want him to go. Two or three years seemed like an eternity to me back then. I said I didn't care if he was rich or not and I was too young to think of marrying anyway. He insisted he *would* go, that when he returned, I would be older and he would have sufficient fortune to offer me.

I admitted to no one how much I missed him. My life continued with balls and parties and men falling in love with me wherever I went. Emmanuel remained attentive and I was flattered. I turned eighteen. I edged towards nineteen. I heard from Jonathan in only occasional letters. I was still too young to imagine what life with a man like him could be like, but I sensed it as a sort of glorious light at the edge of my awareness. Too far away to be trusted.

Lucius Finch still floated across my path occasionally. I felt supremely ambivalent about his big blue eyes, straining after me across every room, his over-effusive manner, his little misplaced attentions. I was always nice to him when our paths crossed, however; he received slights enough.

Emmanuel proposed to someone else, a newcomer called Francesca something-or-other. My pride was wounded; my heart was not. But the very next day my elder brother and sister, James and Charlotte, were killed. A road accident. The horses bolted, the carriage overturned and neither survived their injuries. *That* destroyed me.

My parents were devastated. My remaining brother, Hedley, and I clung together, but suddenly I was one of two, instead of four. It was not enough. Our noisy, busy home was silent. The point, salient to my tale, is that Emmanuel's inconsequential desertion became all bound up in my mind with the tragedy of James and Charlotte. I felt broken in so many ways that my public embarrassment became one of many painful fragments. Emmanuel didn't matter, but it *felt* as if he did. *Jonathan* mattered, but he was not there.

While other suitors stood back in respect, Lucius Finch came a-calling, all sympathy and condolences. My parents were nonplussed as to why this fish-eyed, russet-haired *nobody* was presuming to proffer comfort at such a delicate time, but they were too wrapped in grief to notice very clearly. He became something of a fixture in our home.

Not two months later, he begged me to marry him. He apologised for his timing but could not live a moment longer without me, he swore. He had merely wanted to offer solace at first. But the more time he spent with me, the deeper in love he fell; he wanted nothing more than to marry me, and look after me.

I said no at first, you may be sure. But Mabel, our home was so very *sad*. I couldn't bear to be in it. I believe I would have accepted *anyone* who proposed to me then, purely for the escape it represented.

My parents were surprised, but still too confused by grief to understand the full unlikeliness of my choice. Hedley knew I would never have made it in ordinary circumstances. 'Don't rush into anything,' he pleaded. 'The pain will ease in time. Don't take a step that you'll regret down the years.' I wish to *God* I had listened to him.

As soon as we were married, Lucius asked me how I felt about children. If it was too soon, he would understand, he said; he would not even push for marital relations if I was still too raw. I thought him very kind. Well, the thought of physical intimacy with *anyone* could not have appealed to me then, but the thought of children . . . With two of my siblings dead,

I was desperate to make a new family, to make me happy again. I became pregnant with Charlie very quickly. Lucius was ecstatic to have a son and heir. He set to making money with zeal. *There*, I told myself, *he is a good father, a good provider*.

As for Jonathan, a few weeks after the death of James and Charlotte, he heard the news and sent me a letter but I would not read it, or not closely. What use was a *letter*? I threw it in the flames. And so I didn't absorb that he had immediately set about making arrangements to take a leave of absence to sail to England to be with me. No, in my pride and pique, I had no idea. By the time he arrived, I was married.

Jonathan called once or twice on the newly married Finches but received a cool welcome from my husband – I did not blame Lucius for that. Realising that the reason he had come back was not *his* reason any more, Jonathan returned to India after just three weeks.

They say it can take any amount of time to recover from grief. In my case I started to feel a little like myself again three years later. It was like waking up from a deep sleep to find yourself in someone else's life. I had gone to sleep Miss Farrah and woken as Mrs Finch. I was a mother of two with a husband I could not quite believe I had lain beside.

I saw clearly then that grief had made me vulnerable and I had, as Hedley had suggested, taken a step I would never have taken otherwise. One wrong choice in an uncharacteristic moment can change the course of a life forever. The awful truth was that I wished I'd never married him. But none of this, I told myself, was Lucius's fault. There was no going back and besides, there were the babies. So I buried all my feelings of regret and distaste, determined to make the best of it.

I had hardly left the house since I married. I was too sunk

in grief and busy with babies. I decided I would visit my family much more. I began to arrange picnics for myself and my husband; I had always excelled at the art of a picnic. I wanted to show Lucius that I appreciated his patience with the lacklustre, vacant version of me that he had married.

This is the part of my tale that grows hard to believe. I struggle to believe it myself, and I was there! I came to learn that the lacklustre, vacant version of myself was exactly the version he wanted. I cannot possibly recount two decades of marriage to you in one evening but let me give you an illustration or two.

I arranged a dinner for his parents and mine. We had not held such a normal family occasion since we wed. I sent invitations. I spoke to the cook about the menu. I searched out our wedding gifts, long unused. People had been generous; we had some beautiful things. I arranged the table days beforehand, wanting it to be just right; I had always been commended for my artistic flair. Lucius was strangely disapproving.

He told me off like a . . . child. He said I should not have invited them without his permission – that was the word he used. He lectured me about the cost of the meal I had ordered. He called the table settings fripperies. He cancelled the invitations and told them I was unwell.

I was mystified; I had done nothing that any normal wife would not. But what followed was even stranger. When I asked him about it, he snapped shut his book and looked at me as though I were a house with a leaking roof, a loose window and many other deficiencies. And he said – I will never forget it – 'I was just reading about the delicate mental condition of women, due to their interior feminine parts and the delicate humours they exert on the female brain.'

Yes, that look on your face, that's exactly how I looked at

him. 'But I merely invited our parents to dinner,' I said, incredulously.

The look on his face, Mabel, I can only describe as smug! He said, 'And there, my dear, you prove my point.'

You may well imagine that I grew frustrated. 'But *how*?' I cried. 'Please explain it clearly.' He told me I was growing wild and needed to rest. I was not wild, I was exasperated. And I did not want to rest. But he insisted and bundled me off to bed. I capitulated out of sheer confusion and lay there all night, fuming.

The next morning, I asked again what I had done that was so indicative of wrong-thinking. He never did explain, and that niggling question stayed with me for years afterwards. *Had* I inadvertently committed some dreadful faux-pas of married life? I could not be completely certain, not for a long time.

My brother Hedley was married by then. Two weeks later I told Lucius over breakfast that I would call on Hedley's wife that afternoon; she had begged me more than once. I left at three and I was home by four. The front door was locked. I rattled the handle, annoyed with the servants. I was rather keen to use a bathroom so I hastened round to the servants' entrance. They were astonished to see me. I told them the front door was locked and they were amazed. A little later I saw my husband, who calmly explained that *he* had locked the door.

'Why?' I asked.

'To teach you a lesson,' he said.

'Why?' I asked again.

'If it isn't apparent, I don't think I can possibly make you understand,' he said.

Mabel, I cannot conceivably recount the toing and froing of that desperately baffling conversation. I had called on a relative for half an hour. I had drunk tea. I had even told him beforehand of my plans. And for this, he felt the need to teach me a lesson. I would demand answers this time.

Eventually he snapped. He was not angry, he was not violent, but he *wailed*, Mabel, that is the best word I can use. He wailed that he missed the wife he had married and wanted her back. He wailed that I had become quite impossible and no man should have to put up with my 'deviant compulsion to pursue hedonism and company of all kinds'. Then he sent me to my room again, because he couldn't bear to look at me. In truth, I was no keener to look at *him*.

Soon after that, I discovered that I was pregnant again.

Mabs

M rs Finch fell quiet. The narrative must have been exhausting for her; Mabs had a headache just listening.

'I can't imagine, ma'am,' said Mabs softly, taking her hand. 'I've never been to parties and balls. I've never even had a feller.'

'Never, Mabel?'

'No. Although . . . there is this one chap who's caught me eye. Well, that's another story, ma'am, and we're still in the middle of yours.'

'I haven't bored you to tears or lost your sympathy so far?'

'Neither, ma'am, though it's a lot to take in. I can understand if you're tired tellin' it. Would you like a drink of something while we carry on?'

'An excellent idea, Mabel. For the next part I shall certainly need one. Ring for something stiff, if you please, and for yourself too.'

Mabs was not a drinker but when Betsy brought up the brandy, she poured a decent measure for them both. She tried it, wrinkled her nose and set it aside. Mrs Finch threw hers down in one draft and motioned for another, which she cradled in her hands. She did not resume right away.

Mabs thought again of her own parents, of the way they

were a support and comfort to one another, taking delight in each other's company and often chuckling at private jokes. The fond glances they exchanged over the heads of the little ones when their youngest did something funny. That was marriage, so far as Mabs knew.

Abigail

Over the months of my pregnancy, there were countless incidents. He poked me if I dozed off in front of the parlour fire, calling me indolent. He criticised me if I ate too little, or too much, or foods that *he* did not like to eat. When he received a caller, I always spoke too little, or too much. You may be sure I never spoke in a way that pleased him.

'Perhaps you will be better after the baby is born,' he used to say.

Averil arrived and enchanted us both, as Charlie and Elfrida had done before her. We had, perhaps, a month of tranquillity. For the first weeks after giving birth, I was not motivated to do anything but dote on her anyway. Then it began again. When my parents came to visit the newborn, I realised how little they saw of their grandchildren in general. I asked them if it was painful seeing the babies, if it reminded them of James and Charlotte.

'No, dear,' they reproved me gently. 'You never ask us, and we don't like to intrude.'

I frowned. 'Never ask you? I've sent countless invitations.' They had never received them.

Now, what do you suppose had happened to my notes, Mabel, between the hall table and my parents' home? I took to asking my maid to deliver the notes by hand, and . . . can you guess? They all reached their destination. For a while I was blessed with a flurry of visits from my parents, then they eased off. I asked my maid if she still delivered the notes and she said yes.

I chanced to see my father in the street one day and he declared his delight at seeing me out and about. Was I better? he wanted to know. 'I have not been ill,' I declared. Apparently, Lucius had called one day to ask them to desist with their calls. Lucius said their visits upset me and made me ill. My parents asked why I kept inviting them in that case. Out of a sense of duty only, Lucius told them regretfully.

He explained that I'd been very delicately balanced indeed for over a year. He told them that he'd consulted an excellent doctor who said that my condition was quite common among highly strung women and that the best remedy was complete rest and a total lack of stimulation, including company. Mabel, I could not believe what I was hearing.

I did not want to tell my father that my husband was either delusional or a liar on such a scale. Looking back, I should have told him everything then and there and gone home with him while I had the chance. But then, what of my three children waiting in my husband's house?

And I was *still* confused. Oh, believe me, looking back, I feel impatient with myself for having been confused for quite so long! In hindsight it's all so clear. But hindsight, as they say, is a blessed thing and it was so *strange*, Mabel. I kept saying to myself, *There must be some mistake*. I didn't want to admit to a fictional derangement so I merely told Papa that Lucius had greatly exaggerated the matter, and that I would always be delighted to receive them.

I hurried home and tackled my husband. We had another

row, which is to say he wailed some more, begging me to stop
torturing him, pleading with me to see that no man should have
to tolerate the slights I had subjected him to. And that was the
first time I understood. My husband, not I, was the one with
whom there was something very wrong, and there would be no
reasoning with him, not ever. I left and returned to my room
where I sat, cradling Averil, my heart beating very fast.

I saw clearly for the first time how he had taken advantage
of my grief and vulnerability to coax me into a marriage I
would never, as Hedley had pointed out, have made otherwise.
I was rich and beautiful and Lucius was wildly ambitious.
Marrying me was a shortcut, in social discourse, to proclaiming
his own worth. It opened avenues for him that he could never
have walked otherwise. Thanks to me, he rose through the
ranks, becoming known and respected in the world of men,
where all is finance and progress. As for me *personally*, it was
easiest for him if I just faded into the background.

I was not born to keep to the shadows, Mabel. Some stormy
years followed. I insisted on joining him at social events – I
don't know why because I cringed every time. He was doing
well in business, yes, but his manners were still too blatant,
his desire to rub up against his superiors like a cat was embarrassing. I rebelled against him in any way I was able. I sent
notes to relatives whenever I could get past him and the
petulant girl in me smirked when they arrived and he could
not send them away. Our nonsensical rows drove me to the
point where I would scream and break things. It was war,
Mabel, of a very peculiar sort.

But then, he brought in an ally. Dr Broome. To this day, I
don't know whether my husband promised him advancement
in fine circles in exchange for his compliance, or whether
they're simply kindred spirits – a match made in hell. They

both believe that there is a direct link between a woman's reproductive organs and her brain, that the female nature is fundamentally wild and weak. They hold that in the majority of cases, appropriate training can keep us in check, allowing us to become, despite our shortcomings, useful members of society. The part we may be permitted to play is subservient, naturally, yet valuable enough in the world as it is structured. Dr Broome was well into his fifties then and had treated many women. I was not going to change his mind.

He became an almost daily visitor to the house. He conducted regular inspections of the two problematical areas of a woman, the brain and . . . well, you know where. To have his bony old fingers probing around the contours of my skull, reaching up underneath my skirts was . . .

I'm sorry. Yes, water. Thank you. Remembering it makes me feel terrified all over again. My life was a living hell. Oh, I objected, you may be sure. I objected most strenuously. And my husband and the doctor took this as proof of their position. Can you imagine – *please*, try to imagine – what it is like to state your will, and to be told that, oh dear, you are simply *wrong*. But don't worry, here comes this *man* to fix it, to make you the way you should be.

And when you shout – you *scream* – that you do *not* want this old goat touching you, that you do *not* grant permission for him to grope your private areas, you are told regretfully that that is simply part of the syndrome.

I *did* go a little mad for a while. How could I stay sane in such a situation? I couldn't run, because of the children. I don't know whether their speedy arrival was planned by my husband as the master stroke in a long-term strategy or whether, by then, they were just a lucky ace for him. But because of them, I could not escape.

Do you know that in our enlightened day and age, if a woman divorces, there's no guarantee she may be allowed to see her children? It used to be completely forbidden. Then a few decades ago, a bill was introduced allowing a woman to *petition* for access. But the outcome is by no means guaranteed. And the mother has to prove that she is stable and worthy. Lucius had spent years by then establishing that I was mentally unsound. He had doctors' reports galore proving it. At that time, Charlie was eight, Elfrida seven, Averil five. If I had left, I would never have seen them again. Oh, I was well and truly stuck.

His other trump card was Dr Broome's magic drops. At first they started me on a very low dose and, if you can believe this, I welcomed them. They dulled everything and put me in a sort of a haze that was actually preferable to sharp awareness. But then they were used as weapon and punishment, in stronger dosage. I would lose half a day to sleep, sometimes a whole day.

I truly thought I would die in that house in Durham. I didn't want to leave my children without a mother. I learned that the more compliant I was, the less Dr Broome visited. The only behaviours that did *not* provoke a doctor's call were sitting in my room, playing with the children, and looking out of the window. So that is what I did. Every single day. Occasionally I was taken out and brushed off, like an old coat, when there was a social occasion that he couldn't attend without me. I would be given strict instructions about what to say and what not to say.

Do you know, Mabel, that it only takes two men to commit a woman to an asylum? A husband and his doctor is the perfect pairing. My husband let me know that he had such papers in his keeping. Dr Broome signed them without hesitation. There was talk of a place for delicate and depraved women in Yorkshire. I don't know if you've heard about such places, Mabel, but most are not humane. Many are run by people like my husband and Dr Broome, for whom every natural reaction is nothing more than proof of woman's instability. I had to be very careful.

I started counting. My husband accused me of having a number of compulsions but this was my only one. I prayed that my children would grow up to make happy marriages at the usual sort of age – twenty, one-and-twenty. If Averil married at twenty, I had fifteen years yet to endure . . . I concentrated on my children, I read whatever books I could smuggle to my room. I counted off the days. My life was slipping away and I was missing it all.

Mabs

Mabs remembered her brandy and felt glad of it. She took a large swallow and didn't notice the burn of it after all she had heard. She started to cry quietly. She didn't mean to but the story was too horrible to absorb with equanimity.

'I distress you,' said Mrs Finch, laying a hand on her shoulder. 'I'm sorry. Should I stop?'

Mabs shook her head, wiping her nose with the back of her hand. 'It ain't for you to comfort *me* now. You were the one who went through it. I just can't bear it for you is all.' She took another swallow of brandy and realised her glass was empty.

'Another?' asked her mistress before pouring. Mabs set the glass down again. It was comforting to have it there but really, drinking couldn't help.

'I'm ready now. Oh ma'am. I can't think how you could keep all this from me for so long.'

Abigail

I've told this story only twice before, Mabel. The first time was to my former best friend. When things were at their worst, we saw each other for the first time in years at a dinner that Lucius needed me to attend. I thought it a rare chance. I bundled her into the pantry and poured out the highlights of my tale, dizzy with the chance to confide in a friend. Poor Ella, I suppose I must have seemed rather frantic.

She did not believe me. Or professed not to. Later that night my husband mentioned to me that he had recently given her husband a significant position in his latest company. It was another blow to my spirits at a time when they were already lower than low. Ella and I had once been so close. If *she* could abandon me to my fate like that, I could have no faith that anyone else would ever believe me.

I went back to playing the game and waiting for time to pass. Occasionally I had to submit to my husband's physical desires. I loathed every minute but he was never rough, at least, and it never lasted very long. He always took care that I should not fall pregnant – I shall not embarrass you with *those* details – yet despite this, ten years after Charlie almost to the day, Otty was born. I had to start counting from zero all over again. I loved her instantly, but she had just extended my sentence considerably.

A decade later, Jonathan returned to Durham. I heard rumours that he was fabulously wealthy, still unmarried and standing for Parliament. I never imagined I'd see him. But he called unexpectedly one afternoon. My husband was at work. I was unwelcoming, terrified of all the incorrect behaviours Lucius would attribute to me if he knew we'd met. Besides, I didn't *want* to see my old and dear friend, who embodied, as no one else could, all that I had lost. I didn't want the deluge of emotions that he could unleash. We had a short, stiff conversation and he left.

But a week later he returned, and every week thereafter. I took a shocking risk. It needed only one of the staff to mention it to Lucius . . . but they never did. Perhaps they did not like him much either. We re-established a friendship – nothing more – and the old cordiality reasserted itself, that feeling of warmth in his presence, the sense that here was someone I could trust.

So I told my story a second time. He believed me, Mabel, believed me without question. I told him that I could never leave my children but that if he could think of any way out of this insoluble conundrum, I would be grateful forever and for an eternity after that. He immediately set to work, questioning solicitors on points of marital law, enquiring into Lucius's business affairs in the hope of finding something shady with which to blackmail him. He sought him out at social and business functions with a view to ferreting out any weakness. But he got nowhere.

By then, Charlie was smitten with Felicia Browne and I expected to see him engaged any day. Elfrida always plays her cards very close to her chest, but I had a strong suspicion that she had someone too. But Averil was unattached and Otty, of course, too young. My conscious decision was still the same – to be dull and bide my time until Otty grew up. But I was being tested beyond endurance and I began an affair with Jonathan. Are you shocked?

At that time my husband was involved in a venture that took him often to London; he would stay away for three or four days at a time. Looking back, I'm astonished that he didn't arrange for Dr Broome to check on me daily, or employ a companion. But I think he was complacent at that time. He knew how I felt about the children and Otty was still so young. I think he thought I had given up the fight. I *had*!

Until I saw how tirelessly Jonathan was prepared to work on my behalf. Until I saw how he cared. Until I admitted to myself that he was the man I should always have married. I was a broken woman by then, but he saw me as whole; he saw a potential for my life that I had all but forgotten.

Of the twelve months that Jonathan was back in my life, we were lovers for only six. He was my rock in a desolate sea. He made me feel that I had somehow claimed the life that should have been mine, even if only in a strange, fragmented way. But I was living two lives at once – and no one can do that.

Lucius's absences had become a welcome fact of life. When he was at home he talked about the canals, their possibilities for advancement for a clever man. I paid little attention. Suddenly, the London trips stopped. He was at home all the time and then one day, he confronted me. He said he'd known about the affair for two months; I have no idea how. At first, his London visits had been linked to the job he held in Durham. But since learning of my aberration, he'd gone there to secure himself a new job. We would leave for London the following week.

He broke the news to the children that night. They were

devastated. They were so close to stepping into their independent adult lives; everyone they knew and loved was in Durham. All to take me away from Jonathan. Lucius told them it was because my health was declining and I would benefit from a change of scenery *and* because he had a wonderful opportunity that would make us all very rich. These were, of course, nonsensical reasons to uproot the whole family at that all-important time. When I pleaded with him, he said the alternative was to tell them we were fleeing from a scandal of my own making. He said that my licentious nature had brought our world crashing down around our children's ears.

Once again, I was caught in doubt, for I had, after all, had an affair. For those fleeting hours, I *had* put myself before my family. If anyone knew about it, I would be censured, of course. That was always Lucius's art, to find the cracks in my soul and exploit them, to make me wonder, just that little bit. But the fact was, there *was* no scandal! No one *knew* about the affair – except for Lucius. We could have stayed. He could have banished Jonathan, locked me in my room, and still the children might have continued their lives. But no. He removed us with an efficiency that was dazzling. Within the week our household was packed and dismantled, our servants dismissed. I was locked in my room throughout; I could send no word to Jonathan.

It was clear that the children resented me, though it was a complicated resentment for they could not blame me for ill health. Only Otty was delighted at the prospect of a new adventure, bless her innocent soul. Just like that, our life was ended. My children's prospects are set back by months or years. And he has ripped me from Jonathan. Hidden me, effectively, hundreds of miles away.

When we arrived in Hampstead, I was presented with this

house, fully equipped and decorated, bedrooms allocated and staff in place. All but one. I was told I would be furnished with a companion, someone to sit with me through the hours. A keeper, in essence. I reverted to my behaviour of all those years before, crying, screaming, throwing and breaking things. I wanted to break my husband, break myself, break my stupid life that I had brought about with that one ill-advised decision when I was a grief-stricken girl of nineteen. But I couldn't maintain such rage, especially when it affected you so adversely and influenced my fate not at all. I have resigned myself anew to this life until Otty comes of age and then I will leave him, or I will try, and I will succeed or fail.

Lucius has played out a master plan. He made only one miscalculation – perhaps. When he chose a companion for me, he made the most unlikely choice. She was scruffy and starved, had no relevant experience and could not even read. Her speech was appalling. Well, I'm sorry, but we are working on that. Lucius didn't *want* a companion for me, he wanted a spy, so he chose the most utterly dependent person he could find, someone who would owe him everything. Someone who *needed* to stay in this household. She would be very little use to me, more of an irritant! But she would be supremely useful to Lucius. He thought he had chosen perfectly. So did I.

You, Mabel, were inexperienced, naive and had no idea how to handle me. But once you got over your befuddlement, you started to make sense of things for yourself. You seemed genuinely to care for me; it wasn't just your job, or so I have hoped. My opinion of you started to change very early on; in fact, it was that first time you found me sedated. My husband gave you permission to go out and explore, but you wouldn't leave me. Yes, I heard that. It was the start of a great change for me.

I know, my dear, that there is nothing you can do. You cannot make Otty advance ten years overnight, you cannot challenge my husband and set me free. You're an eighteen-year-old girl with enough problems of your own to sink a rowboat. I ask nothing of you, Mabel, but to stay at my side. I cannot even ask you to believe me, for you either will, or will not. But even if you find you do not, I *beg* you not to tell my husband I have told you.

Mabs

Mabs couldn't sleep that night and spent the following morning in a daze. What Mrs Finch had told her was impossible to believe, yet she thought perhaps she believed it. It was her half day, but she didn't feel right about leaving her mistress alone. Mrs Finch insisted.

'Above all things, he mustn't guess I've confided in you,' she pleaded. 'Even if you're still trying to make up your mind what to think, it's your afternoon off, your sister's birthday. If you suddenly refuse to leave me, Lucius will suspect something, and if that happens, you will lose your position here, Mabel, with a haste that will make your head spin. Until you decide that I am lying and he is in the right, act as you always have, I beg you.'

'Very well, ma'am, but then you'd better stop calling me Mabel. Don't get me wrong, I like it very much, only it shows something's changed between us. You only started doing it when you came round from the sedative.'

'Good heavens, I'd hardly noticed I was doing it. It's how I've come to think of you, you see. Daley sounds far too formal, dismissive almost. I know you go by Mabs but Mabel is so pretty.'

Mabs smiled. 'It's what me ma used to call me. She gave

the others murder for callin' me Mabs. I'll see you in the morning then, ma'am.'

'See you tomorrow, Daley.'

Peg loved her presents and her ragged little party and her delight soothed Mabs's nerves. But as the afternoon wore on, questions circled like carousels inside her head, repetitive and dizzying. How Mabs longed to confide in someone. But, as ever, this was what she *couldn't* do, and now the prohibition was twofold.

On her walk home Mabs was glad to be alone. The longer, early summer evening meant there was light and a little warmth. When she got back to Hampstead she went to sit on the heath. She couldn't face going back to Willoughby Walk yet; what if she saw Mr Finch? Their terrible, tightrope conversations would be harder than ever now. She found a patch of dry grass to sit on and stared into the gathering dusk. It *couldn't, couldn't* possibly be true. Could it?

Mrs Finch was a troubled woman; that's *why* Mabs had a job. Mrs Finch was unpredictable, a troublemaker, petulant and selfish. She had betrayed her husband with another man. Her own daughter was furious with her. But that story. How could anyone make it up? The ring of truth in her voice was undeniable. Or was she, to use Mr Finch's word, delusional?

If it was true, it was almost too much for Mabs to comprehend. Mr Finch . . . *not* a saviour, but narrow, manipulative, cold. Mrs Finch a virtual prisoner, sacrificing her own well-being to stay close to her children. And the future . . . impossible to contemplate with any equanimity. What good way out of this could there be?

And Mabs – what was her role now? Was she nothing but a pawn, and if so, whose pawn was she? Was it wrong to keep working for a man who treated his wife thus? Was it duplicitous to keep smiling at Mr Finch and pretending nothing was wrong? Was it self-serving? Was it wrong not to spit in his face? She certainly couldn't abandon Mrs Finch – but what if none of it was true?

She couldn't come to terms with any of it, let alone decide a course of action, while there was this shadow of doubt in her heart. Either way, something was very wrong in this household, wrong enough to make Mabs sick at heart.

For three days, Mabs went about her business as though wedged firmly inside a thick, dark cloud. Everything was muffled, grim and hopeless. When she was with Mrs Finch, she believed her with all her heart. When she saw Mr Finch, she thought, *He* can't *be that other man, he just can't!* She grew listless, her throat scratchy and her head foggy. A dull pain bloomed through her skull.

'Miss Daley,' said Mr Finch one evening. 'You don't seem yourself. Might you be coming down with something? If so, you're most welcome to take a day or two to rest and recover.' Mabs's eyes pricked with tears. He was still as dear and lovely as ever – but she couldn't take pleasure in it.

'I will, sir, thank you,' said Mabs in a thick voice. When she told her mistress she was going to bed, Mrs Finch said nothing, but looked at her with shrewd eyes. Mabs went to her room and stayed there all that afternoon, all through the night and well into the following day. Lydia came up at intervals to offer soup but Mabs had no appetite. She tossed and turned, the questions wheeling like stars.

Stars! Suddenly Mabs's head cleared and she sat bolt upright. She knew what she must do: talk to Olive Westallen. Yes, it would constitute a grievous lack of discretion. Yes, it would mean telling the secret of the woman who had begged her to tell no one. But Mabs, for the first time since coming to Willoughby Walk, didn't care. This tangled family secret was heavier than any load of timber or ice. She was eighteen, she had no mother and the truth was, this was simply too much for her to handle alone. She didn't know who to trust in Willoughby Walk, but she knew she could trust Olive.

It was four o'clock. Not a bad time to pay a call. Of course, Olive may be out, but Mabs could not wait. This was the first moment of clarity she'd experienced in days. She tidied herself in minutes and ran down the stairs. She paused on the landing, wondering whether to tell her mistress that she was going out. She didn't want anyone to think she was gallivanting when she was supposed to be ill. But what if Mrs Finch guessed Mabs's guilty purpose? No, she couldn't face her just now.

In the hall, she came across Averil standing before the mirror, touching her hair and gazing at her reflection with an expression of wonder. She wore a periwinkle-blue dress and there was a becoming flush in her freckled cheeks. When Mabs hurried into the hall they both jumped.

'Oh! Miss Daley! Gracious, you startled me. I was just . . . fixing my hair!'

'You look beautiful today, miss, if you don't mind me saying so.'

'Oh Daley,' Averil suddenly sat down on the stairs. 'I *feel* it! I just had luncheon with Toby Elias and—'

'Oh, you're in love, miss!' An image of Kip Miller's tanned face and bright smile flashed across her mind.

'I am! I hope that very soon now he may . . . but I should not count my chickens. Oh Miss Daley, promise you'll say nothing to Mama or Papa? I shouldn't have spoken, only you caught me in a moment of wonder!'

Another blessed secret for another blasted Finch! 'Of course, miss. I think they'd be very happy to hear, though.'

'Oh, they would, I know. It's just that it's so . . . miraculous! I can't speak of it for fear it will just go up in a puff of smoke. I'd rather wait until he has actually *said* . . .'

'I understand, miss. Well, I'll leave you to it. My head's very sore and I thought some fresh air might help.'

'I'd heard you were off colour. I beg your pardon for not enquiring. Are you any better?'

'I think so. Leastways, my legs feel stronger. If I can just shift this headache, I think I'll be right as rain.'

Mabs hurried out before another Finch could come along and confide in her. Goodness, Averil hoping for a proposal! That would be one less daughter for Mrs Finch to worry about. *If* her story were true. Oh, how unbearable it was to second-guess every single thought!

Mabs was in luck. Olive was at home and Mabs was welcomed by Olive and her parents. Clover sat on the floor at her mother's feet, playing with Jem's old spinning top. The captain wanted to talk to Mabs about the ice cargoes; he had several times commanded a ship to sail the six hundred nautical miles from London to Norway.

'Oslo has consistently cold, dry winters, you know, and a blessed lack of pollution, which is why their ice is such good quality. Crystal ice, they call it. Do they use that term on the wharf, Miss Daley?'

Mabs was grateful for the way he spoke to her as an equal. Another day she would have loved to talk with him for hours and hear his stories of life on the sea – but the last thing on her mind now was blasted ice! Olive soon observed her agitated manner and suggested a stroll in the gardens. Clover immediately scrambled up to follow them.

'What's wrong?' Olive asked in her direct way, once they were alone under the pale blue sky and surrounded by the fantastical shapes of magnolia branches.

'Oh miss!' cried Mabs, overwhelmed at last. She sank onto an ornamental bench facing a bed of lavender bushes. A stone sundial stood amongst them and bees floated and hummed. It was so peaceful that Mabs wanted to crawl into the very heart of the bushes and sleep there for a month. She covered her face with her hands. 'It's too awful. It's the worst thing I ever heard in me life. And that's sayin' something.' She burst out crying. She hadn't cried since her mother died and now this was the second time in days.

'Clover, darling, why don't you look for fairies?' suggested Olive. 'It's such a perfect day, they must be out, don't you think? Stay very close now, so I can see you.' Clover moved off just a little way to explore the flower beds, far enough for Mabs to feel more comfortable relaying her grim adult tale. Olive sat beside her and rested an arm about her shoulders. 'Is it one of the children, or your father?' she asked in a quiet voice.

'None of them. It's the Finches. Only it's . . . peculiar and I can't even . . .' The tears made it impossible to speak.

'There there, dear,' said Olive. 'Have a good cry first, then we shall get to the bottom of it, you and I.'

When the tears ceased, Mabs felt as if she were coming out of the far side of a tunnel. Olive was there, patiently waiting. Mabs had somehow slumped into a heap at her side; she sat up now and wiped her face. Olive passed her a hand-kerchief. She removed her arm from Mabs's shoulders and took her hand instead. 'Tell me,' she said.

Mabs took a huge, noisy breath. 'I hardly even know where to start, miss. Olive. Well, the first thing is, I shouldn't be talking to you. *Mr* Finch wouldn't like it, and *Mrs* Finch wouldn't like it. I want you to know that I've always been good and loyal to them. I've never told one thing to anyone that they've said not to. I've been . . . discreet and confidential and all them things he said I had to be if I wanted the job. And I only ever wanted the best for them all. I want you to know that.'

'I do know that, Mabs. It's immediately apparent.'

'Yes, but you see how bad it must be, if I'm discreet and all and I'm still telling you their most shocking, private things.'

'Bad indeed.'

'Yes. I'm afraid someone may be in danger, only not the sort that falls on your head or drops on your foot at the canal. I don't know what to think or what to do and I'm only one person, Olive. It's too much.'

'Then you've done right to come to a trusted friend. If someone is in danger, they will need help. And if you are unable to help, someone else must enter the picture. Tell me now, dear, for frankly, I've never seen you look so hunted.'

So Mabs told her Mrs Finch's story exactly as she had heard it, except shorter in Mabs's version. 'Even Mrs Finch don't hardly expect me to believe her,' she finished. 'She said either I will or I won't. And I think I do. Only believing her makes . . . makes . . .'

'It makes your benefactor, the man on whom you depend for your livelihood, a monster. It makes the likelihood of you remaining long in that apparently idyllic position you were so happy to acquire extremely slim. It means that your mistress, whose well-being you have been charged with, is living in a nightmare. And it means your happy time at Willoughby Walk is over. No wonder your brain resists it. And if you disbelieve her?'

Mabs felt tears fill her eyes again. 'I don't think that's even something to consider any more. But oh, I don't want it to be true.'

'Of course not.'

'I have to ask, Olive. What do *you* think? Do *you* believe it?'

'Oh yes,' said Olive evenly, at once.

'Just like that, miss?'

She smiled. 'I've always had a feeling about Mr Finch, Mabs.'

'You *have*?'

'Yes. Even before I met him. It was you, in fact, who alerted me that something was amiss in that household. The first time I met you, you were so tense, so careful when you spoke of your job, which sounded, yes, quite perfect on the face of things. I wondered if you were shy with *me*, because of my social position and all that guff. But you had already told me about your family and then you were relaxed and warm. When you spoke of your employers, it was a different story. No one should have to look quite that scared of saying the wrong thing.

'Then there was the matter of his wanting to meet my father. Oh, dozens of men share his avarice, it doesn't mean they are all wicked to their wives. But it's always an undesirable facet to a character. And I've *met* them, Mabs. If that woman's an invalid, then I am married to ten men. She's not highly strung, she is clever. She's not delusional, she sees truths that he does not *wish* her to see. And she is not weak, far from it. Whereas he . . . well, there was nothing very special to observe about *him* – the disparity between them alone sent a warning shot across *my* bows.

'When they came to lunch a few days ago, all my impressions were validated. There was a tension between them, my dear, that you could have cut with a knife; it went beyond ordinary marital discord, though I never could have guessed at something of this magnitude. I'm not siding with her out of a biased sense of sisterhood, Mabs. I trust my instincts.'

'Oh!' Mabs's shoulders dropped three inches and she suddenly felt starving hungry, where she hadn't wanted to eat for days. 'Oh Olive. I hadn't realised how much I needed to hear you say that. If you'd said you thought it was impossible, or unlikely, I would have felt so . . . alone.'

'Because deep down, underneath your fear and confusion and the great, great strangeness of the case, you know it to be true.'

'Yes.'

'Well, my dear, one must never be alone. We all need someone with whom to share life's joys and we all need someone on whom to call in times of need. The question is, what are we to do?'

Mabs

It was not a problem easily solved, even for Olive Westallen. Olive was all for Mrs Finch abandoning her children at once.

'I'm a mother myself now so I understand!' she exclaimed. 'But for heaven's sake, they are older than *you*, dear! And rather selfish and indulged from what I hear. They can get along just fine without a mother. Of course, there's Otty. A different kettle of fish . . . Oh, very well, I realise it's not that simple.'

'It really isn't,' sighed Mabs. 'Even if Mrs Finch did scarper, she'd still *miss* her children. If she told them the truth, would they believe her? If they did . . . Mr F wouldn't accept that, he'd fight; he'd turn them against her if he could.'

'Yes, I expect he would. And Otty would be stuck with her father, alone, for years to come.'

'But he adores Otty. He's a good father at least.'

Olive raised her eyebrows. 'Apart from abusing their mother. Apart from ripping them from their Durham life to punish her. And now moving Otty to a different school so she can be turned into a different girl. I tell you, Mabs, I would not want to see Otty living alone with that man. Well, we shan't solve it today. You must go home and speak to Abigail. Let her know she is not alone and that she can trust you. It will be a great balm to her. I shall deliberate further.'

They rose, and Mabs internally said a mournful farewell to the lavender bed, an oasis of tranquillity in a complicated life. 'Thank you, Olive, with all my heart. I couldn't deal with this alone, I couldn't. I don't much fancy going back there, if I'm honest.'

Olive looked grave. 'I know. Don't think I like the thought of you living in that house. But if you were to leave now . . .'

'Oh, I can't. I know that. To keep her safe, I 'ave to carry on just as if nothing's happened. I'll be all right, as long as he doesn't guess.'

'So, you will have to act, my dear. You must make your daily life a performance worthy of Ruth Herbert.'

'Who?'

'A famous actress, dear. You won't be able to let your guard down for a second. Call upon me whenever you need comfort and let us hope you won't have to manage like this for very long.'

'Can I come and sit here sometimes? Just ten minutes by the lavender?'

Olive seemed to understand perfectly. 'Of course, Mabs. Consider my lavender your lavender.'

'Thank you. And Olive, don't worry about Clover. Angie was just like it with me after Ma died. She'll come out of it.' Despite all her fears, Mabs couldn't help noticing how clingy Clover had become and how worn and weary Olive was starting to look. It wasn't easy; Mabs knew that.

'Thank you,' sighed Olive. 'It's all starting to feel a little . . . too much, if I'm honest. I hardly feel myself any more and I'm so tired all the time. But there, I have made my bed and all that. And I love her so.'

A periwinkle dusk was falling; Mabs hadn't realised she'd been out so long. But she felt unburdened. If anyone could do the impossible and find a solution for Mrs Finch, it was Olive. As she walked down the hill, she planned how she would handle things over the coming hours and days.

Arriving at Willoughby Walk, she squared her shoulders and went inside. The hallway gleamed a welcome as ever. Mabs couldn't look at the portrait of Mrs Finch in her lilac gown. She made her way to Mr Finch's study and knocked. If she didn't approach him now, she never would. When she heard his voice, her stomach turned, but in she went.

'Evenin', sir,' she said brightly. 'I hope I ain't disturbing you.'

'Not at all, Miss Daley. Are you feeling better?'

'Yes, sir, that's why I'm callin' in. I'll be working again tomorrow. I went out for some fresh air this afternoon and the headache's cleared quite well. I reckon an early night and it'll be done for.'

'Excellent! Abigail will be pleased.'

'I thought I might call in on me way up, sir, to let her know.' Mabs had already decided to be as compliant and open with Mr Finch as she possibly could. Let him give permission or withhold it and think he was still pulling the strings.

'You're most considerate, Miss Daley. Goodnight.'

Mabs pulled the door behind her with a huge sigh of relief. *Bravo, Mabs, girl*, she told herself. *Ruth Whatsername 'erself couldn't have done better*. But goodness, she was glad to be away from him. Her skin was crawling all over.

Then she heard his voice. 'Oh, Miss Daley?'

She peered back in. 'Yes, sir?'

'Just to let you know I've had some good news. Dr Broome has cleared his patients for a few days to pay us a visit. He'll be here in four days' time.'

Mabs's stomach churned but she mustered the brightest smile she could manage. 'Goodness! That's good news. Will he be staying nearby?'

'Oh, he'll stay with us. He's a family friend as much as a physician. I'll have Mrs Webb ready the spare room.'

Mabs stumbled upstairs, dizzy, her headache returned with full force. Things were changing fast. She found Mrs Finch seated at the window, wearing a long blue robe. She smiled when she saw it was Mabs.

'I wasn't expecting to see you tonight.'

'I just wanted to let you know I'm feeling better, ma'am, and I'll be in with you in the morning.'

'Thank you, Daley. Have the last two days been . . . restorative?'

Mabs closed the door behind her and went in. 'They've helped me see things clearly and I want you to know I believe every word you said, ma'am. I'll stay by your side and help if ever I can.'

She almost flinched from the intensity of the relief that washed across Mrs Finch's face. Mabs perched on the windowsill and grabbed her hand. 'Ma'am, I've got two things to tell you. Do you want the bad news first or the news that will sound bad for a minute but really it's good?'

Mrs Finch gave a delicate laugh. 'I'm not sure I like the sound of either very much!'

'The bad news first then. Dr Broome is coming in four days.'

'Oh God.' She closed her eyes and Mabs could only imagine the memories and fears flashing through her mind.

'I didn't know if I should tell you . . .'

'Thank you for warning me. I'm glad you did.'

'But I'll be here, ma'am. I know what's what now and I

won't let anything happen to you. I don't know exactly how we'll fix it, but fix it we will.'

'Thank you. And the other news?'

'Ah, well, I done something today, ma'am. Did something. You'll be livid at me for a minute but please consider it carefully because then you'll see it's a good thing.'

'What did you do, Daley?'

'I went to see Olive Westallen and I told her everything.' The look of horror on the other woman's face would almost have been comical if it were not so real and heartfelt.

'Wait, ma'am, don't say all those things you're thinking. *Listen* to me. You're stuck. You can't think of a way out. Your Jonathan couldn't either. I sure as eggs can't fathom it. I can be a comfort to you, but frankly, that ain't much use. I can't *help* you, not really. But Miss Westallen can, maybe. I *trust* her, Mrs Finch, as you and I have got to trust each other now. We can't be alone with this; we need a friend outside this house. So I ain't taking no nonsense on the matter. Either you want things to get better or you don't.'

She waited, heart fluttering, while her mistress, breathing heavily, bit her lip. 'What did she say?' she asked finally, in a voice full of grit.

'She believes you too, ma'am. I didn't even have to persuade her. Said she always knew there was something fishy about Mr F. See, she's smarter than me. She agreed it's a tangle, but if I were you, I'd feel a lot happier havin' her brain on it than mine. So please tell me you think it's good news.'

'Dear child,' said Mrs Finch. 'I thank God for sending you to me. I had long given up trusting in Him, you know. But for salvation to arrive *at the behest of my husband*, half starved, illiterate and blown in from the wharf . . . well, that's a degree of poetry that surely has to hint at divine order.'

Mabs wrinkled her nose. 'I'm not sure I'd call me salvation, ma'am. That's a bit of a tall order.'

'Indeed, and I would not put any more weight on your young shoulders. We shall stick together, you and I, and put our trust in God and Olive Westallen.'

Olive

No wonder I have been so reluctant to meet the Finches. Some small, prescient part of me must have foreseen that I would become hopelessly entangled in that family's affairs and that they would not be joyous. The next morning, I don sturdy boots and go out walking, early, while Clover is asleep and Mama willing to watch over her slumbers. At this hour I have the heath mostly to myself; I do not feel equal to chit-chat.

In the main, the law is a very good thing, I reflect, but sometimes it traps good people in its net. No system can be perfect. But still, there should be provision for women in a situation such as this. The law should view women differently altogether! That a woman of Abigail Finch's qualities should have endured *so* long, knowing that no one could really help her because of the weight and deference the law gives to a man's word first and foremost . . . it makes my blood boil. When I have got the foundation onto a firm . . . well, foundation (who is not fond of a pun?) my next cause shall be the 'woman question'.

Abigail's story makes me shiver to my core. Like me, she had intelligence, fortune and, no doubt, a loving family. Yet these things are not the absolute protection I have always thought them. Her fate turned on a sixpence when she made a bad decision in the wake of tragedy. Once she made that choice to marry Lucius Finch, her family couldn't protect her. Her fortune became his property. *She* became his property. The very same thing might have happened to me, had circumstances led me to marry an unworthy man. I thank the heavens and the stars and every power there is that I have not done so, that my life is still my own.

The morning is big and bright. This early summer sunshine is the very best sort; a dreamlike warmth that has not yet bloomed. The air is clear and the trees are bursting with the calls of blackbirds, thrushes, wrens, chaffinches . . . a cornucopia of winged songsters. Before long I am flushed and panting. The heath is starting to restore me. I stride up Parliament Hill and look all about. London is spread at my feet.

Over there is Highgate, where the Blythes are doing whatever Blythes do – looking in a mirror in Rowena's case, probably. Over there is Belsize Park where widowed Mrs Lake waits out her lonely existence with her one remaining servant. And there is dear Hampstead, where Julia Morrow is not so lonely, now that she has Jem. I suppose *that* direction is where Mabs hails from, Clover too. Poor Mabs. Imagine living in that house, knowing what she knows, having to put on a bright face before that man. It cannot go on much longer. In fact, all over London, at this very moment, there are women and girls, rich and poor, clever and not so, who are suffering in their domestic situations, and the law is perfectly content to leave them to it, believing as it does in the rectitude and superiority of men. It is so far from being right that it makes me breathless.

'Good morning! Miss Westallen, if my eyes don't deceive me!'

I whirl around to see Mr Lionel Harper toiling up the western slope of Parliament Hill. 'Gracious! Mr Harper! What a great surprise. How do you do?'

'I do very well, thank you. What a glorious morning.'

'It is. And you are abroad early in it.'

'I start work at nine. If I am to open my lungs and see nature, I must do it very early or very late.' He comes to stand beside me and survey the views.

'Do you often take in the heath before work?'

'The heath or Regent's Park. I'm surprised I haven't happened across you before – though I suppose I wouldn't have recognised you before a week ago.'

'I'm rarely abroad so early. Generally I prefer a more leisurely start to the day, some tea and reading. But this morning was too lovely to be resisted.'

'Well, I'm glad to see you now.' He smiles at me and does indeed look *very* glad. I might be blushing a little; I hope it may be mistaken for the flush of exercise. 'My clerk sent you the keys, I trust?'

'He did. Thank you again, Mr Harper. I've inspected the premises and they are most satisfactory.'

'I'm glad. How are your plans coming along?'

I tell him the latest good news, a donation of five hundred pounds from a rich lady who specified it should be used for the professional training of young women. Mr Harper nods approvingly, which I'm glad to see. So many men like to keep women in the traditional sphere, and will only allow certain professions as suitable for the feminine worker if work she must. Governess, nurse, companion . . . Look how well *that* has served Mabs!

Filled with a surge of good spirits, brought on, I think, by a conversation that is not about the Finches, I become confiding.

'You know, Mr Harper, I consider myself a rational woman and I don't know if what I'm about to tell you will strike you as odd, but occasionally, at turning points in my life, I use divination cards.' I brace myself to be derided or patronised.

'How very *interesting*,' Mr Harper says, looking at me keenly. 'Do you refer to the tarot, Miss Westallen?'

'No, they are a deck of oracle cards, similar to Lenormand but an earlier, English deck.'

'Fascinating. I imagine the artwork alone must provoke creative thought. And do you use the *I Ching* at all, the ancient Chinese divination text?'

'Ah, the *Book of Changes*! No, though I *have* used it. I have a cousin who swears by it. Do you?'

'I found it invaluable when I started my business, and whenever I take a new direction. I realise it is rather scorned these days but it's been influential for more than two millennia. People say we are more rational now but I question that. I think we have much to learn from the ancient civilisations, the Egyptians, the Chinese – but we're too conceited to admit that anyone can teach us anything.'

The wind plasters a swatch of hair across my face. I pull it from my mouth and tuck it behind my ear. 'So true! Such arrogance to suppose that science and divination are incompatible, to be unable to accommodate two diverging truths and so insist there is only one!'

'We have much in common, Miss Westallen. But I interrupted you. You were telling me about your cards.'

'Yes. It was just that I conducted a reading regarding the foundation. And the outcome was uncanny; all extremely auspicious cards. You are investing wisely!' I laugh.

'I have no doubt of it. Miss Westallen, I've so enjoyed meeting you again. I must go now or I'll be late – not a good precedent if I'm to act as mentor for your foundation. Would you allow me to call on you one day, so that we may talk longer? I regret, I'm rarely finished at work before six, which is not the most socially acceptable time for a visit.'

'Why, certainly! I'd like to hear more about how the *I Ching* affected your business decisions. It's rare to meet someone who uses such tools in an intelligent way. We're not an overly formal household, Mr Harper, so please call when it is convenient for you. My parents are very supportive of the Westallen Foundation and would be pleased to know one of its patrons. My mother is much involved with planning a ball to launch the project in society. Perhaps you and your wife would be pleased to attend?'

'I cannot avow for my wife, since I have none. But I should be delighted.'

I am a little astonished that so admirable a man has no wife but pleased also, despite all the reasons why I should not care. Of course, I cannot think of marriage, not now that I know what happened to Abigail, and not now that I have Clover! I must protect her future as well as my own and, if Papa is to be believed, she will be an impediment to any such prospects anyway. Even so, I march back to Polaris House in much improved spirits, a smile playing at the corners of my mouth. The dance of attraction is timeless and irresistible. Providing I take no irrevocable steps, I don't see why I shouldn't enjoy myself a little.

Mabs

M abs went before breakfast to see Olive, only to learn
that she had gone walking on the heath. It was too big
to go searching; Mabs left a note explaining that Dr Broome
was imminent.

Then the days crawled. Mabs and Mrs Finch found themselves jumping at every little sound. They hardly had the spirit
to venture out but they continued their daily walks, to keep
up a semblance of normality and to relieve the pressure of
waiting. The weather was glorious, unclouded. The stretches
of heath were preferable to streets and houses.

On the second day they bumped into Olive and walked
with her for a while. She embraced Abigail tightly, then
distracted them with chat about the Westallen Foundation;
her plans were coming on apace. There was no denying that
her company was uplifting. Its only sorry effect was the contrast
with their own shadowy secrecy and stifling constraints.

'I shall say nothing of your predicament until I have something solid to report,' said Olive when the time came for
farewells. 'I see no benefit for you in hearing my every thought
along the way. I'll tell you when I have something positive to
impart and that is all. The thing meanwhile is to keep your
spirits up in any way possible.'

'I understand,' said Mrs Finch, her face ghostly pale as she shook hands with Olive. 'You are very good.' They went home with a gloomy step.

On the fourth day they couldn't help but discuss, compulsively, when Dr Broome might arrive and flinch with every knock at the door. But he didn't come. On the fifth day it was worse. When they heard Mr Finch come home at seven, Mabs couldn't stand it any more. 'I'm off to talk to me employer, ma'am,' she announced. 'I'm only doin' me job.'

She hurried down to the study before he could get engaged in supper or paperwork.

'Ah, Miss Daley,' he said when she appeared. 'It's been a few days. How have things been?'

'That's what I was thinkin', sir, that it's been a few days,' said Mabs, hovering on the threshold, trying to look casual. 'I won't keep you a minute, sir. I only wanted to let you know that it's all been very peaceful and quiet. We've had a couple of nice walks on the heath. Nothin' exciting to report, sir, but I expect that's just what you was hoping for.'

'Indeed it is, Miss Daley, very heartening. Thank you.'

'You're welcome, sir. Did you need anything else from me, whilst I'm here?'

'Nothing springs to mind. You are well, and your family?'

'Yes, sir, thank you.' Mabs turned as if to leave. 'Oh sir, when's the doctor coming? That one from Durham you mentioned.'

'Oh yes, I should have said. Well, it's the damndest thing, Daley. Oh, pardon my language. The oddest thing, I should say. Come in a minute and shut the door, won't you?'

Mabs did as she was bid, her tummy boiling with the many possibilities that this 'oddest thing' might be.

'I expected him yesterday,' said Mr Finch, rubbing his

forehead and leaving a red blush. 'But then this morning I
received this letter' – he waved a piece of creamy letter paper
at Mabs – 'in which he tells me he's retired! Of course, the
man must be seventy now. But we've corresponded regularly
of late and he's never mentioned any such plans. And just the
other day he promised to visit. How can he have changed his
mind so suddenly? But there, he talks of buying a small property at the seaside in Scarborough.'

Mabs wanted to laugh and cry at the same time. She had
to screw up all her emotions very tight like a fist to keep them
hidden. 'That's a shame, sir. Very nice for the doctor, though,
I'm sure. Well, at least Mrs Finch is doing well again, nice
and even.'

'Yes. I'd like to find another like-minded fellow, in case of
further relapse, but it's tricky. There are doctors aplenty but
to find the right sort . . . Anyway, the thing for now is to keep
Abigail on an even keel. Let us keep her protected from further
social interactions.'

'Very good, sir.'

❋

With the immediate danger of Dr Broome removed, a lull fell
over the house. Mr Finch put in long hours at the office once
again. Mabs and Mrs Finch passed the time reading and
walking on the heath, as well as with an occasional outing
further afield: London Zoo; a theatre to watch a Gilbert and
Sullivan matinee; a stroll along the Embankment. London was
all new to Mrs Finch and Mabs had certainly never seen it
like this before. They did not mention these adventures to Mr
Finch.

Mrs Finch continued to work on Mabs's speech, picking
her up on every little thing with no qualms about interrupting

her. Sometimes, despite Mabs's immense gratitude, it did become annoying. Sometimes a girl just wanted to finish her sentence. Yet under such vigilant tutelage, Mabs couldn't deny that her speech was changing more quickly than she could ever have imagined.

Otty was looking pale and pensive these days. Her mother and Mabs repeatedly asked what was wrong, but Otty insisted she was well. Sometimes she joined them for outings after school and a little of the sparkle came back into her eyes. Mabs kept a close eye on her but stopped asking questions; experience told her that Otty would tell her when she was ready and not before.

They paid no calls, but several times bumped into Olive on the heath, where she was able to explain the unexpected retirement of Dr Broome.

Knowing time was of the essence, Olive had spoken to her father. 'I know, and so the secret spreads,' she said, noticing Mrs Finch's fearful face, 'but you may be sure that my father is a man not like any other. His sense of what is right is unparalleled. And he would never, ever, betray you, my dear. He travelled to Durham at once and looked up Dr Broome, intercepting the filthy beast as he was packing for his trip to the south.'

The urgency of the matter had given Captain Westallen no time to gather evidence against the doctor. However, Dr Broome did not know that. The captain wore no mark of his rank and gave a made-up name, claiming to be carrying out an investigation for the medical board following several complaints by former female patients of his and even one or two of their husbands. He carried a thick file, which he hoped the doctor did not demand to see. But he was able to give sufficient accurate details of his malpractice, and the doctor's conscience was so guilty that he didn't question the matter, only begged and repented and made excuses.

The captain was unsympathetic. 'My father is the best of men, but he is also the most authoritative,' added Olive. 'When needs must, he can be as ruthless as steel.'

The doctor would be hauled before the courts, he explained. His name would be blackened along the length and breadth of the country. He would be convicted and would spend his retirement years in a dank, filthy prison cell. 'A man who has abused his professional standing so thoroughly will not fare well among the criminals and villains,' the captain observed. 'For a man of your age it will bring on a swift, unhappy end.'

The doctor begged and pleaded some more. He had been encouraged and threatened by unscrupulous husbands, he swore. He had long ago stopped any work of this kind. He had seen the error of his ways. He was sorry, so very sorry. His watery blue eyes wept and his elderly frame shook. The captain displayed not one shred of compassion. 'Think of the women you have claimed to treat,' he exhorted. 'Think of what you have done.'

'I regret! I regret everything! Is there any way I can be pardoned? Is there any way to avoid this dreadful end?' he sobbed. The captain remained impassive a long time, continuing to remind the doctor of his terrible deeds. At last he appeared to relent. There was *one* way that the doctor might be allowed to escape justice.

What was it? Dr Broome demanded to know. Anything, he would do anything.

If, and only if, he retired immediately and did not visit the Finches of Hampstead. No questions should be asked, nor enquiries made.

If the Finches heard anything about the matter, the investigation would be taken to the justice. If he ever 'treated' another woman, the investigation would be taken to the justice. If he ever again advised a colleague or a husband, the investigation would be taken to the justice. The doctor agreed. His career was finished.

'Your father is very good,' said Mrs Finch in a husky voice, belying tears. 'That he would go to such trouble for me when he does not even know me, not really. Olive, how can I ever repay him?'

'You do not need to. Papa is a great philanthropist. I suppose he may help a friend and neighbour just as well as the anonymous masses. He's removed the immediate danger but you are still in a great predicament. Thank us when we have solved *that*!'

'I wish all those things your father said were true, Olive,' said Mabs. 'After what he did, I wish he *had* been investigated and humiliated and took to the courts and all that.'

'Taken to the courts,' Mrs Finch corrected her absentmindedly.

'Mabs, my dear,' said Olive. 'There will be time enough for all that.'

Otty

On Sunday it is a curious breakfast around the Finch family table. Papa is tetchy, I am miserable and Mama is present. She always joins us for lunch on Sundays, but rarely manages breakfast. Charlie, on the other hand, is nowhere to be seen. Elfrida broods, which appears to be her only mood nowadays, unless she has company and then she is as charming as a daisy. Averil is flushed. Her hands keep fluttering over the table like white butterflies, then she changes her mind and lays them in her lap. Is she on a diet again?

'Averil, dear, whatever's wrong?' asks Mama when Averil knocks over the salt and jumps out of her freckled skin. 'You seem restless.'

My sister turns bright eyes on her. 'I am, Mama, but nothing's wrong. In fact, I have some news, but I should wait till Charlie joins us and tell you all at once.'

'How intriguing. I wish he'd hurry,' says Mama. 'Have you seen Charlie this morning, Lucius?'

Papa grunts a no. I look at him unhappily. I haven't spoken to him properly since our great disagreement. Of course, we've exchanged goodnights and good mornings and please pass the peppers. The end of term is fast approaching. Edina and I both dread the day that I have to leave the academy.

I've always loved Papa so. I've always thought him amiable
and kind and everything a father should be. But our last two
talks have called my entire family into question! Why is Elfrida
always so cross? Why are we *here*? And why cannot Papa be
more gentle with Mama? Take this morning. Down she came
in a pretty dress the colour of a morning sky. She's trying to
converse and make a pleasant breakfast. Wouldn't you think,
if she's so very ill and he's so worried about her, that mornings
like this would lift his spirits?

Mabs and Mama have both noticed that I'm unhappy but
how can I confide in them? Papa is always so good to them
both. How can I complain about him without seeming spoiled?
What if they agree with him about my education? In a house
crammed with people, I feel all alone.

Mama addresses a couple of remarks to Elfrida and she's
so short in her answers as to be positively rude! 'For goodness'
sake, Freds!' I cry. 'What's the matter with you? You never
used to be like this!'

Elfrida has the grace to colour up and apologise. Averil
reaches for the water jug then realises her glass is already full.

'And where is Charlie?' I continue, wanting them all to
behave as a proper family should. 'He's never so late, and I
want to hear Averil's news. Shall I fetch him?'

Mama glances at Papa and he shrugs. I wish Papa and
Elfrida would just go away sometimes.

'Why not?' says Mama. 'Run up, Otty, and bid him hurry.'

I scamper up to Charlie's room where I knock, but receive
no answer. I go in, expecting to find the curtains closed and
Charlie still asleep. But to my surprise, the curtains are drawn
back; the window stands ajar, letting in the fresh air. I frown.
Perhaps he's gone for a walk. It's only the breeze stirring a
folded sheet of paper on the bed that makes me notice the

letter. On the outside is scrawled: *Family*. That includes me, so I read it. And I cannot believe my eyes.

'Mama!' I bellow, belting back downstairs. 'Papa! He's gone!' I fly into the dining room and four startled faces look up at me.

'Otty? What's all this shouting?' asks Papa. 'It's quite unladylike!'

'Never mind *ladylike*! Charlie's gone!' I thrust the letter before him. He begins to read, the others fidgeting with curiosity. Papa finishes reading – it's a short letter – and hands it to Mama.

'Read it aloud!' begs Elfrida. So Mama does.

'Dear Parents, Freds, Averil and Otts,

I've left at dawn. Felicia and I can no longer stand to be apart. Her family remains opposed, thinking us too young, and me not sufficiently grand. They were pleased, I think, when we left Durham. But the months apart have only made us surer of our feelings. Please know the elopement is no reflection on you. You're all splendid fellows and we wanted you to see us marry. It's her lot that's hard to manage. So off we trot and when I next see you, I shall bring Mrs Charles Finch to call. Don't worry! It's all arranged.

Love, C'

'Well, good grief!' says Elfrida, looking lost. 'Good *grief*!'

Suddenly I feel sorry for her. She and Charlie have always been the closest pair. I'm surprised he didn't even tell *her* his plans. I can see quite the tussle going on inside Freds. Obviously she wants him to be happy, but she must be hurt as well. Who would have thought him capable of such decisive action? I feel quite proud of my brother.

'Good grief!' echoes Averil in a whisper, her face flooded with red. 'Good grief!' she says again, as if there is no other phrase available to us this morning. Then she adds, 'The timing!'

As for Mama, if I had to guess her feelings from the look on her face, I should have to make at least forty guesses, so I give it up and look at Papa.

'Badly handled, Charlie,' he says, standing up and throwing his napkin onto the table. 'The Brownes will give him nothing but trouble and he won't see a penny from that quarter. As if there aren't plenty of eligible girls in Hampstead.'

'Yes, but . . . Charlie *loves* Felicia,' says Freds softly. 'She was always the only one for him.'

'I'm going to my study,' says Papa. 'I'm not to be disturbed before lunch, if you please.' He leaves us very rapidly.

'Oh, but Papa . . .' says Averil. 'Oh, he's gone.' She looks so disappointed, I get up and give her a hug, then do likewise for Freds, even though she can be a nuisance sometimes, and then I give one to Mama. I can feel her heart beating very hard through her bodice.

'What do *you* think, Mama?' I ask. 'Do you think it's a good thing?'

'I do,' she says at once. 'They were always a lovely pair and they'll be happy together. Don't worry, Elfrida, you'll see them soon, you may be sure. Charlie wouldn't settle too far from you.' Freds nods gratefully. 'And Averil,' Mama continues. 'Poor dear. You had news and now Charlie is gone and Papa is locked away for the morning. Shall you wait till luncheon, or will you tell us now?'

'Tell us now, Avs!' I beg.

'Shall I?' She looks around and Mama nods encouragingly. Even Elfrida manages to look tolerant.

'Well, it's this.' Averil takes a deep breath, her eyes shining, her face all blotchy, and smiles. 'I'm engaged.'

'*What?*' All three of us shriek at the same time. Elfrida snatches her left hand and inspects it: no ring.

Averil reaches into her collar and pulls a golden chain from inside her pretty peach bodice. From it dangles a gold band bearing the most enormous diamond I have ever seen! Elfrida, not wanting to break the chain, leans so close her nose is practically in Averil's bosom. '*Who?*' she demands. I can tell that even she is impressed by that ring.

Averil unclasps the chain and passes the ring to Mama. 'It's Toby Elias,' she says. 'He asked me last night. I've been hoping for days. He's going to call on Papa later to ask his permission – he wants to do it all properly – but I couldn't wait. So perhaps it's as well that Papa's not here.'

She's breathing very hard and Mama has tears in her eyes. I think I know why. I am the baby now, but Averil was for a long time before me. Because Charlie has always been in love, and Elfrida is *such* a lady, it's easy to think of Averil as young and freckly and a bit daft, really. But here she is, dignified and proud and so very happy that I feel a bit teary myself. We all give her hugs and say kind, solemn things, even Freds.

Olive

I'm wandering in the grounds with Clover, enjoying the sunlit morning, when Mama comes to find me. 'Olive!' she calls across the tennis court. 'Some news, my dear!'

I wave and make my way towards her. 'Pom-pom!' cheeps Clover as we go, pointing. By this she means a bumble bee, one of those so fat and fluffy they seem to float rather than fly. I meet Mama at the stone fountain. Amidst the waters, a statue of Diana draws her bow.

'What news, Mama?' I ask, giving her a kiss.

'Thank you, dear. Well, it's this. Agatha has just told me that she's engaged. She's given her month's notice!'

'Agatha? Don't you mean Anne?'

'No, though I understand why you would check. It's Anne who's had one beau after another since we've known her.'

'And now the erstwhile Colin,' I muse. 'And yet . . . *Agatha*? But who?'

'A Mr Dean, apparently. A draper from Primrose Hill. He's been courting her these last six months and she's kept very quiet about it. But she looks happy and her mind is made up so we shall have to adjust, my dear. We must buy them a suitable engagement gift and look for a new maid.'

'Mama!' I gasp. 'A maid of the Daley variety?'

'I thought it might have to be,' she smiles. 'At any rate it will save us the trouble of advertising. Which of Miss Daley's sisters do you have in mind, Olive?'

'Jenny, the eldest. The eldest after Mabs, that is. By all accounts she's sweet-natured, intelligent and mature for her age, which is fifteen. She has trouble with her eyes, on account of the very poor light in their home. We might furnish her with some spectacles.'

'Very good. I'll leave it to you to make the necessary arrangements.'

'Leave it *all* to me, Mama! Oh, how nice it will be to give Mabs some good news again. And Mama, before I speak to her, there is *one* more scheme I wished to discuss with you . . .'

'It surprises me not at all.' Mama can be very wry. 'What is it?'

I tell her my idea as we stroll back to the house and she sighs, then gives me her blessing. She offers to take Clover for a bath as my daughter is hot and sticky and her hands are brimming with rose petals. 'Since she's decimated my Queen Louise, she can scatter them in the bathwater,' says Mama. Mama does have such pleasing ideas.

'Won't that be lovely, darling?' I bend to kiss Clover's head. 'Won't you be the princess?' To my relief, Clover concedes that she will and consents.

I find Agatha and give her my heartiest congratulations, then gain my study, intending to look over the foundation accounts. But I'm distracted by the conundrum of Abigail Finch. Much as I am loathe to trouble him further, I shall have to turn to my father for help again very soon. He does not share my love of meddling in the affairs of others, but I have found no elegant solution. I've come up with wild schemes aplenty: Abigail removing herself to a sanatorium but in truth living a life of rustic simplicity in the Swiss mountains, the sanatorium merely a helpful address via which she can correspond with her children; Abigail and Otty fleeing in the night, changing their names and living incognito in the south of France; my good self contacting Jonathan so that he and Abigail can run away and live bigamously while Otty completes her education in the attic of Polaris House. They all need quite some refining, I realise.

Thankfully I'm saved from my thoughts by Anne coming to tell me I have a visitor. It's Mabs, which is uncanny timing after all.

'What news, Mabs?' I ask when she comes in.

'Ever so many things!' And she goes on to tell me that Averil Finch is engaged and Charlie Finch has eloped. There's an astonishing amount of matrimony in the air. It must be the summer breezes.

'So that's two young Finches the fewer to keep her in her marriage,' I observe.

'It's the first thing *I* thought,' agrees Mabs. 'Only two left, and only one that counts, which is Otty, of course.'

'Well, Otty isn't likely to marry any time soon. I still have no solution, Mabs, I hate to admit. I have good news on another score, though.'

'What's that?'

'Let's walk in the garden,' I suggest. 'This is news best delivered in sunshine, not in a stuffy old office.'

Once we're outside I tell her that Agatha is leaving, and we wish Jenny to have the position. Mabs's face is a picture. She bursts into tears, but it's clear they're happy tears.

'I'm sorry,' she gasps, wiping her face. 'Every time I come here I cry! It's just, *Jenny . . . here!* Of all the houses! If there was one place on earth where I know I'd never need to worry about her ever again, it's here. Thank you, Olive, thank you. Only, I hope you don't feel obliged, because you know me. If you needed to take someone else, I wouldn't think bad of you. Badly.'

'Nonsense. I'm rather hoping she can start as soon as possible so that Agatha can train her while she's working her notice. We'll provide her with spectacles so she needn't worry about her sight getting worse and, of course, the terms will be very good. I'll speak to Papa before I give you all the details but you know she'll be well off here. And there's something else besides. I want Angeline to come with her.'

'Angeline? You mean, our Angie?'

'Yes. As a companion to Clover.'

'Olive, you can't! It's too kind! You're just doing this for me now, aren't you?'

'I'm not, I promise you. Listen.' We've reached the ornamental bench by the lavender where we sat the other day. 'Come, sit, and let us have a happier conversation than our last in this spot. It's not for you, I swear. The fact that it relieves you is simply a bonus. Clover's too solitary. She's always in the company of adults, and mostly just me of late. The youngest person she knows is Otty! I know one or two ladies with small girls, but they've made it clear that they disapprove of unmarried mothers and of little girls from Clover's background.'

'Oh Olive! How could they? I'm so sorry.'

'Oh, I care not a whit, thanks, Mabs. Though it does leave me in a jam regarding Clover. I truly think that a friend of her own age will do her so much good! I thought that Angeline would make a fine companion for Clover the moment you told me about your family, but I hesitated to suggest it because she's very young to come alone to a large new house. But if Jenny's coming, Angie could come too, couldn't she? She'd have her big sister under the same roof. You may be sure, dear, I would treat her just as I treat Clover. I shan't call her daughter for she has a father and the memory of a mother who loved her dearly. She doesn't need a parent. But she does need schooling, care and opportunity, and those I can happily provide . . . Clover Westallen and her companion, Angeline Daley,' I muse. 'It has a nice ring to it, don't you think?'

Mabs throws her arms around me and sobs some more on my shoulder. The poor girl will be as wrinkled as a raisin by the time I'm done with her.

Mabs

On Wednesday, Mabs went home and bore her sisters off to their new life. It was Peg who worried her now: two sisters taken care of in one fell swoop and Peg the only girl left in Mushroom Court, effectively playing mother to Matty while her father and brother were out at work. But it had to be: this was the only suitable place they were ever likely to find for four-year-old Angie. Better one of the older girls be left behind with the boys than Angie. But still, with Peg loving elegance and feminine things more than any of them, it did seem cruel.

'Your chance will come, Peg, love,' vowed Mabs, gripping her arms and staring into her eyes when they left. 'I promise. And it'll be perfect.'

Peg nodded but Mabs could see the tears behind her bright smile as she waved them off. *I need to do something to lift her spirits*, Mabs told herself. *Fast!*

She didn't worry about Jen or even Angie despite the sudden and entire change this would be for them. She took them to Polaris House in a cab because Angie's legs were too little for the walk and saw Olive's home anew through their eyes when they arrived. Softened by the late afternoon sun, its oriels and tower and pointed roofs looked more magical than ever. Angie's thumb crept into her mouth.

'We're to live *here*?' whispered Jenny. 'Oh my.'

Mabs took them in and introduced them to Olive, who was beaming in a plum silk dress that whispered and shone. The opulent furnishings threw Jen's and Angie's threadbare state into harsh relief. *They look like scarecrows*, thought Mabs as she looked at them tenderly. Then Mrs Westallen appeared with Anne to bear the girls off for hot baths and a change of clothes while Mabs hurried back to Mrs Finch.

She didn't see them again until Sunday, which was Whitsun. There was to be a huge fair on the heath and so the Mushroom Court Daleys came to Hampstead at last, all except Pa. Mabs was up bright and early to walk halfway and meet them. As she tiptoed through the house she noticed that Otty's bedroom door was ajar.

Mabs tapped quietly on the door. Through the gap Mabs could see Otty in her white nightgown sitting on her bed, very still. She tapped again and went in.

'Otty? You all right, love?'

Otty turned to her with a vacant look and nodded.

'Are you ill? Can I do anything for you?'

Otty gave a small smile and shook her head. 'I'm all right. I didn't sleep well last night.'

'Nothin's worse than a bad night. Why don't you come to the fair later, meet me and the kids? Olive says the heath fairs are fine fun. "'Appy 'Ampstead," she says people call it. It's from a song.'

'Yes, maybe. Thanks, Mabs.'

'How about if I say we'll be at the Spaniard's Road gate at noon? That'll give you plenty of time to come to. I bet some fresh air and fun will set you right in no time.'

'All right. Say hello to everyone for me.'

When Mabs saw Jenny and Angie, she could hardly believe

her eyes. Jenny had a uniform, of course, but today she was wearing a costume that Olive had procured based on Mabs's description of her colouring and figure. It was a dusty blueish-grey in colour, bringing out the blue of Jenny's eyes, in layers of cotton and muslin to suit the weather. She wore little round spectacles that took the strain from her face. Angie wore a red-and-black check tarlatan dress with little black shoes that she kept waving in front of her, pointing her toes, as if she couldn't believe her own elegance. Peg was now the only sister still wearing a stained and raggedy old frock. Mabs was deeply grateful for her own foresight when Jenny handed her a paper parcel.

'This is for you, love,' said Mabs, handing it in turn to Peg.

'What is it?' asked Peg. When she opened it, a green and white sprigged muslin dress slithered out.

'Come on, scram behind those bushes and let's get you changed,' grinned Mabs. 'I had it made in one piece so it'd be easy. We don't want half of Hampstead seein' yer undies!'

'But, but . . . *how*?' asked poor Peg, clutching the dress as if it would be taken away from her at any moment.

'I asked Olive to order you a dress while she was sorting out Jen's. I paid for it, though she didn't want me to. Couldn't have you being the only one without something pretty to wear on a special day.'

'Oh my Gawd, Mabs. You are the *best* sister!' shrieked Peg, diving behind the bushes and disrobing with surprising speed. When she was dressed in her new finery, Mabs fluffed her hair and pulled her silver chain and horseshoe out so that it could be seen.

'Yer the belle of the ball, Peg,' she told her with a kiss.

The fair was as much fun as Olive had promised. The heath was absolutely smothered with folk from all over London wanting to escape the press of the city. Couples danced to music provided by Italian organ grinders who flashed wicked smiles at the passing girls. There were donkey rides, the prospect of which set Matty bouncing up and down with such euphoria that Mabs forced herself to overlook how reluctant and ill-fed the donkeys looked so that her brother could have a treat. She forced herself to look at his delighted smile rather than the prominent ribs of the poor beast beneath its dirty white saddle cloth.

There were coconut shies and skipping ropes and stalls selling penny licks and sweets. Grubby children hollered, 'Penny licks! Hokey pokey!' at the ice-cream stands. Olive had told Mabs that 'hokey pokey' came from the Italian *O che poco* – oh so little – because the licks were only a penny. Mabs had taken out some of her precious savings last night so she could spoil the children. It was a delicate art, balancing her big plans for the future against the knowledge that today's pleasures were also important and, after all, the only ones that could truly be counted upon.

But Jem had brought his own money, bless him. Jenny had wages from her first three days of work (clearly a result of Olive's thoughtfulness rather than a usual arrangement) and Angie carried a tiny purse containing a shilling: 'a present from Clover'. So between them the Daleys, for once in their lives, were well furnished for a splendid day out.

At noon they repaired to the gate to wait for Otty but she didn't come. Perhaps Mr Finch had insisted Otty have lunch with the family; on reflection, Mabs should have suggested a later time. Or she might be coming down with something. Either way, Mabs knew it wasn't fair on the children to keep them hanging around. After three quarters of an hour they gave up.

By the time Jem had won a coconut, Matty had ridden two donkeys, Nicky and Peg had danced themselves silly and they'd all bought sweets to take home, it was five o'clock. The heath wasn't even nearly clearing out but Matty and Angie could hardly stand and Mabs was tired too; this enjoying yourself business was hard work!

'That was the best day ever,' said Matty through great lion-like yawns. It was obvious that he couldn't walk the five miles to Saffron Hill but they'd spent all their money in a glory of indulgence so Mabs would need to dip into her savings again. After saying goodbye to Jenny, Angie and Jem, the others shambled off to Willoughby Walk, tired feet scuffing the pavements. Peg and the boys oohed and aahed when they saw Mabs's pretty place of work.

They waited for Mabs on the street while she hurried upstairs to the attic. The house seemed oddly quiet, she thought as she knelt down and reached her arm beneath her bed. She couldn't feel her savings box; it must be out of reach. She stuck her head underneath to see where it was and the spinning carousel of her world jerked to a halt. The box was gone.

For a moment, Mabs crouched on the floor, observing a spider's web and a large dust ball. But no box. In an ice-cold panic, Mabs searched everywhere, even the most unlikely corners, all the while knowing it was gone. It *couldn't* be gone. In that box reposed all her dreams for her family.

Mabs remembered that they were waiting for her outside. Feeling sick, she trudged downstairs. She knocked on her mistress's door, wondering if she could shed any light. There was no answer, but she went in anyway. Mrs Finch wasn't there. Not only that but her bed was made more tidily than Mabs had ever seen it. Mabs frowned; something wasn't right.

It was too still, too . . . empty, somehow, even though all the furniture and ornaments remained in their places. She saw a space on the bookshelf, as if two or three volumes had been removed. In the wardrobe, too, there was a space, the width of about three gowns. Had Mrs Finch been having a clear-out? If so, it was a remarkably modest one.

Confused on two counts, she trailed down to the ground floor where she saw Mrs Webb.

'Oh Mrs Webb, could I borrow a shilling, please?' she begged. 'I hate to ask but I promised the children cab fare and my money is . . . well, it's gone! I'll pay you back.'

The housekeeper looked sober. 'I'm sorry to hear it, I know how hard you worked for it. It doesn't surprise me, though.'

'What do you mean? You don't think Lydia or Betsy took it, surely?'

'Lydia or . . . oh *no*, Mabs. You haven't heard, then?'

'Heard what?'

'Here, let me give you that shilling . . . then you'd best go into the study. They're all in there.'

Feeling increasingly as if she was having a bad dream, Mabs gave the shilling to the children, bidding them a very absent farewell. They were too tired and hazy with delight to notice. Then Mabs went straight to the study.

Mrs Webb was right: they were all there except Mrs Finch. Otty was sitting on the floor in the corner, as still as a statue. Averil was slumped on the window seat and Elfrida was a graceful column of fury, smouldering near the door. Their father paced up and down, hands clasped behind his back.

'What's happened?' asked Mabs. She went at once to Otty's side and crouched down to take her frozen hands.

'She's run off with her *lover*,' spat Elfrida. 'The one I told you about. He's found her, somehow, and enticed her away.'

'*The one you told her about?*' echoed Mr Finch, looking startled. 'Good heavens, Daley, you never mentioned it.'

'I begged her not to,' said Elfrida. 'I shouldn't have said anything but I was upset at Christmas and Daley was so kind, it just . . . came out.'

'Miss Daley is a true friend to the whole family,' said Mr Finch. 'But how embarrassing. How irregular.'

'And *I* can't believe you never told the rest of us, Elfrida!' said Averil. 'To know Mama had an . . . an *affair*, and not tell us? Otty, well, she's too young, but not to tell me or Charlie?'

'Where was the point?' wondered Elfrida. 'It was a ghastly business, we had to run away to London because of it, it wouldn't have made happy conversation.'

'But . . . but . . .' said Mabs, standing up because her legs were cramping but still holding Otty's hand. 'How? What . . .?'

'Last night,' sighed Mr Finch. 'I went to see her this morning and found her gone. She took just a small bag, and left a note saying that she found life with me intolerable; that she had left with . . . *him*.'

'*Jonathan*,' sneered Elfrida.

'I find it so hard to believe,' said Averil softly. 'I know Mama had her troubles, but she was always so kind and I *know* she loves us. Yet there was no mention of us, Papa says. He's burned the note now, of course.'

'I couldn't bear to read it a second time,' he shuddered. 'Couldn't bear to look at the piece of paper bearing a message I'd been dreading for years, if I'm honest.'

Mabs didn't know what to make of any of this. She had spent *yesterday* with Mrs Finch. Mabs could have *sworn* there was no secret in the air. How could Jonathan have appeared and snatched her away overnight? And, of course, Mrs Finch wouldn't have left her children without a word. And yet . . .

what other solution had she been offered? Even Olive hadn't thought of one.

She looked at Mr Finch. Either he was telling the truth, or he was the best damn actor in England. As always, in this strange family, there was a question mark. If all was *not* as it seemed, Mrs Finch might be in danger, and only Mabs knew enough to know it was a possibility. She felt numb, and Otty, at her side, seemed very much the same. She hadn't spoken at all.

'I've no idea where they might have gone,' said Mr Finch. 'No idea where to start searching.'

'Why would you want to?' demanded Elfrida.

'*Freds!*' exclaimed Averil. 'She's our *mother*!'

'And then what? She's shown how much she cares about *us*!' Elfrida's unforgiveness was glacial . . . until it began to melt. Then tears ran down her face and her whole frame started to shake. 'She's our mother and she *left* us!'

Mabs looked on, horrified. To see Elfrida lose her composure so completely was harrowing. Averil stared, open-mouthed. Otty didn't react at all, still gazing into space like a lost soul. Mr Finch patted Elfrida absently on the shoulder and muttered, 'Poor child. Oh dear, dear.'

When Elfrida had calmed, Mabs cleared her throat. 'Um, sir? I don't suppose you know anything about this, sir, but my box is missing.'

'Your box?'

'Yes, sir, I keep my wages in it. All my savings since I started here. I kept it under my bed.'

'I know nothing of a box. You're telling me . . . she has stolen all your money?'

'Oh no, sir! But . . . it is gone. I hoped there'd be some decent explanation.'

'Oh Abigail, Abigail.' He shook his head and collapsed at his desk. 'I'm so sorry, Miss Daley. I really do believe she thought highly of you.'

'You think Mrs Finch has taken my money, sir?'

'What other explanation can there be? She would have wanted a purse for her escape, I suppose. Even so, to steal from her faithful companion, when you, Miss Daley, have exercised the patience of a *saint* . . .'

Mabs swallowed. Mrs Finch knew better than anyone that Mabs had had a substantial little sum of money amassing in her attic room. But she also knew better than anyone what it was for. She'd always taken such an interest in Jenny and the others. She'd been so happy when first Jem and then the girls were placed in excellent positions. She wouldn't do this. Besides, Jonathan was a wealthy, successful man; why would she need a servant's savings?

Otty started to tremble. 'If I can't do anything to help, sir,' said Mabs, 'I might take a walk to clear me head. And shall I take care of Miss Ottilie? Do you want to come for a walk, Otty?'

Otty shook her head.

'Gracious heavens! Ottilie, forgive me, darling. I'd quite forgotten that you're still here. You're too young for this; it must be very shocking for you. Miss Daley, would you see Otty to her room? And I need not remind you that confidentiality is of the utmost importance?'

'Of course, sir. Come on then, Otty, you can't sit here all night.'

She tugged an unresisting Otty to her feet and led her from the study. The atmosphere there, Elfrida's maelstrom of emotions and their father's comments could be doing her no good.

'Oh, and Miss Daley?'

'Yes, sir?'

'I'm . . . I'm very much afraid this means you will have to leave us. I have no hope that my wife will return. So naturally I don't need a companion for her any more. I'm so sorry, Miss Daley, you've been an invaluable part of our household. But my finances aren't such that I can continue . . .'

'I understand, sir. When should I go?'

'I'll pay you for another month, of course. You must have time to make other arrangements. And you will leave with a glowing reference. I deeply regret that my wife has put you in this position when we all value you so much.'

Mabs

Mabs towed Otty up the stairs and settled her in her room. She drew the curtains against the intensifying dusk and got her into her nightgown.

'Into bed, love, that's it, nice and comfy. What are you thinking, Otty? Do you want to talk about this?'

Otty shook her head. She seemed completely blank. Mabs was surprised. That Otty was in shock was natural, but she was such a passionate, lively creature. Mabs would have expected tears, questions, fury.

'It'll be all right, darling. I know it feels 'orrible now but humans are the most amazing creatures. We can get through anything. And I'll look after you, I promise.'

'But you won't be here.' They were the first words Otty had said all evening and they reminded Mabs of her own impending departure from Willoughby Walk. Her dismissal, in fact. She couldn't think about that now.

'I will for a while. By the time I go, you'll be adjusting, I promise. And we'll still be friends, I'll still see you, we can still talk.' She meant it, of course, with all her heart, but what freedoms would a new position afford her? Where would she actually *be*? Oh, how she would miss Hampstead and Olive and Otty, the good-natured staff and the sweet house. She would miss Mrs Finch! She couldn't think about that now.

'I'm going to get you something for the shock, Otty. You stay here, warm and safe. I'll be back in a jiff.'

Mabs darted down to the kitchen where Mrs Webb, Mrs Derring, Lydia and Betsy were all sitting around the large, scrubbed table, doing nothing at all.

'Well,' said Lydia when Mabs walked in. 'There's a turn-up.'

'Always knew she was a funny one,' said Betsy.

'Come and join us, Mabs,' said Mrs Webb. 'We don't know what to make of it, to be honest. Can't settle to anything.'

'I've got a nice game pie if you're hungry,' added Mrs Derring.

'I'll come in a bit, I'd like that. But I'm looking after Otty at the moment. The poor girl's not said two words in all this time. I'm worried about her. Can I have some brandy, Mrs Derring, and some cocoa? And some buttered toast, if it's not too much trouble? She needs something comforting to bring her back to earth.'

'Selfish bitch,' muttered Mrs Derring, setting to. 'Leaving a lovely little girl like that. *Twelve!* The things parents put their kids through sometimes.'

Mabs leaned against the range while she waited; it was comfortingly warm. It had always felt so *normal* down here. She'd sometimes envied the others their straightforward role. She'd been an in-between creature, not one of the family but all too caught up with them nonetheless. Perhaps it really *was* time for a new job.

'Did any of you ever think . . . ever wonder . . .?' she began then stopped.

'What?' asked Betsy.

It was hard to break the habit of discretion but she was

leaving now anyway. 'Did any of you ever wonder if it might be *him*?'

'If what was him?' asked Mrs Derring, pausing in the stirring of the cocoa to look at Mabs.

'What was wrong between them. Or . . . what was wrong with her, even. Do you all really think it's her who's . . . the bad one?'

'Well, good Lord,' murmured Lydia. 'Bets and I always thought you and Mr F were thick as thieves, didn't we, Bets? Are you saying he's been up to no good?'

'I don't know, Lydia. I just . . . wonder sometimes.'

'Marriages are difficult things,' said Mrs Webb, with a concerned expression. 'No doubt there's always fault on both sides and I do feel sorry for the poor woman, if I'm honest, even now. But Mr Finch . . . well, he's always been an exemplary employer, that's all I know.'

'Yes,' sighed Mabs. 'Yes, he has. So, you don't think there's anything more to this than he's told us?'

Mrs Derring arranged a tray with brandy, cocoa and toast. 'Like what? If she hasn't run off with a lover, where do you think she is?'

'Do you think Mr F's done away with her or something?' asked Betsy. 'Surely you can't think that?'

'No, of course not. I'm just having trouble believing it, that's all. Thanks, Mrs Derring. I'll take this to Otty and come back, all right?'

'My old grandma did have a saying,' said Mrs Derring suddenly. 'Street angel, house devil. Means someone who's as charming as can be when he's out and about has the whole world thinking well of him, but behind closed doors it's a different story.'

'Yes,' said Mabs, taking the tray. 'My mother used to say it too.'

'Go on, Mabs, and hurry back,' said Mrs Webb. 'You need something for the shock too.'

Otty was as unresponsive as ever. As unresponsive as her mother had been once upon a time. Mabs insisted she drink the brandy, then made her eat one slice of toast, relenting over the second, before leaving her sipping cocoa.

'I need some fresh air, love,' she said. 'Then I'm going down to the kitchen for something to eat. I'll be back after. If you're still awake, we can talk, and if you're asleep, I'll sleep here with you. You won't be alone tonight.'

She hurried downstairs again, starting to feel like a bouncing ball with all the ups and downs of the evening. Outside, the sky was navy; huge, round spots of rain were splatting on the pavement and on her skin. The brightness of the Whitsun fair was giving way to a summer deluge. She was just regretting the late hour, thinking how much she longed to talk to Olive, when she collided with a hurrying figure: her sister Jenny.

'Mabs! Where are you off to at this time? I was just coming to see you – there's been such terrible news.'

How does she know? wondered Mabs mutely.

'It's Miss Clover,' Jenny went on. 'She ran off and Miss Olive lost her in the crowd at the fair. She's beside herself, and she wanted me to let you know.'

'Oh Lord.' Mabs stood rooted in the street. She was alone with this; Olive mustn't be worried about Mrs Finch tonight. And then it sunk in: Clover was gone. In danger. Would they ever see her again? 'Oh God, Jenny! No!'

'I know. It breaks me heart. Such a sweet little girl. And Miss Olive loves her so much . . .'

'Don't I know it. Can I do anything to help?'

'No, the whole family's out looking for her, the servants too, and the constable. Miss Olive just wanted you to know. I'd best get back, Mabs. We'll send word as soon as there's any news.'

Jenny hurried off into what was now a steady rain and Mabs went back to the house. It was all too much. Mrs Finch vanished. Clover lost. Her money gone . . . Mabs could feel her head growing lighter and lighter and her heartbeat speeding up. She forced herself to take deep breaths. She could do nothing for Olive tonight. And Olive could do nothing for her. If there was anything more to Mrs Finch's appearance than met the eye, there was no one but Mabs to solve it. She couldn't see a way through any of this. But that didn't mean there wasn't one, she reminded herself sternly.

First things first. She had to eat, take care of herself. Then she would sit with Otty as she had promised. And sleep, if she could. Those were the next steps and they were the only ones she had.

Olive

I'll never forget this day, never as long as I live. The worst of days. Coming home without Clover went against every wish I ever had. But I had to tell my parents what happened, enlist help. I had to recount the dreadful story and its impossible result . . . If Clover is not found, I want to die.

I love that girl with every fibre of my being. Despite that, she has slipped through my fingers. My parents insist that I'm not to blame; it's true that I cannot see one particular in which a lack of foresight on my part was responsible for what happened. That does not alter the fact that two lives are, perhaps, destroyed.

Perhaps I was never intended to be a mother. Perhaps it was only my own determined will that took me down that road, when I should have left it to fate. I heard from Mrs Jacey only last week that Gert has run away. Imagine! A child of eleven, as she is by now, out in the city alone. I felt desolate when I heard the news, and so grateful that Clover was safe with me. Now both girls are at large and in danger.

Papa lost no time in assembling a search party for Clover. He recruited all the servants but Jenny, who is to stay and look after her little sister, and be here in case – oh, hope of hopes – Clover is brought home while we are out. It's possible,

I suppose, that some kind soul might spot a small child wandering alone and try and help. Clover is not the biggest talker and very shy with strangers, but I know she knows our address.

So they have all gone and I shall follow once I've rested and taken some sustenance, though my stomach is a whirlpool of boiling acid. Still, it's true that I've been running round the heath on an empty stomach for hours and I feel very weak from the horror of it all. I shan't help Clover if I collapse in a ditch somewhere so I force myself to wait, as instructed, until I'm fortified before issuing forth again into the pelting rain.

How different the weather is now from when Clover and I set off in such high spirits. We went out at lunchtime after a late breakfast, with a picnic hamper full of Clover's favourite things. That I have abandoned on the heath; no doubt some starving Londoner had a fine feast and I wish him joy of it. We spent an hour or so enjoying ourselves, watching the dancing, taking a little jig ourselves, perusing the brightly coloured stalls. There was a silhouette artist at work under a spreading chestnut tree and I promised Clover that we would commission a paper-and-scissors portrait of her. But there was a queue of people before us and we were hungry, so we spread our picnic blanket nearby and decided to tuck into our lunch first.

We sat, as always, side by side, not an inch between us. Never for a minute did I take my eyes off her. She was not the victim of pickpockets or child-snatchers or any evil of the world, except perhaps her past. It's the only explanation I can imagine. We had just unwrapped our first packet of sandwiches when an organ grinder struck up a merry tune. Clover, bubbling over with high spirits, shot to her feet and started dancing prettily. Even then I was vigilant. 'Stay on the rug, darling,' I said and I stood up too.

A boy of around twelve passed by and paused, looking at her. He was dressed as shabbily as could be; he was filthy and as thin as a blade. He seemed to be shaking, perhaps from hunger, perhaps from some kind of disorder. He did not look sinister, merely pathetic; he didn't watch Clover with ill intent, merely with great interest. Even so, I called her to me and she came at once. I took her hand while I spoke to the boy. 'Hello there,' I said. 'Can I help you?' I was prepared to give him my sandwiches.

Then Clover turned and saw him, and that was the moment! Her face changed in an instant and my quiet, docile daughter, who rarely cries, rarely speaks and rarely goes without a smile on her face, screamed. It was high-pitched and piercing and *terrified*. And then she bolted!

She tore her hand from mine and fled in less than an instant, darting into the crowd, which was so dense, so vast, that she was at once lost from sight. I have never moved so fast. I was propelled through the throng by a force greater than I. But she was gone. I called her name and shouted, 'Find my daughter! Find my daughter!'

I stopped and stared all about me, narrowing my eyes to seek a flash of sunshine-yellow organdie between all the staring revellers. But I couldn't see her. I ran some more, not knowing if it was the right direction. Then I ran back, thinking that she might calm down and come back and look for me. But she didn't, so I summoned the constable and described her minutely and impressed on him the infinite preciousness of her.

He told me it was hopeless to search in such a crowd as this and to go home and leave it to the professionals. I could

do no such thing! He was right, though: that crowd numbered
in the thousands. As easy to find Clover in it as to find a
particular pebble in a swirling ocean. Even so, I ran and I ran,
calling her name until my voice could produce no more than
a raspy croak. Every few yards I stopped and asked the revellers if they had seen a little girl of four with honey-coloured
hair and a bright yellow dress. No one had. It was hours before
I admitted defeat and trailed home with my dreadful admission
to make and the possibility heavy upon me that I might never
see my daughter again. I have found the last weeks, Clover's
increased dependency upon me, so hard. I bitterly regret every
sigh, every reluctant thought. I should not have minded, not
for an instant. Am I being punished?

Papa was most comforting, laying out any number of
scenarios in which Clover is returned to us safe and sound.
And he's right, they're all possible. It's just that there are also
so many in which she isn't. And now, to add to my fears, it
seems that God has decided to send the second flood. The
torrents are inconceivable. Clover is wearing nothing but a
summer dress! When the food has found its way to my legs
and brandy has numbed my horror just slightly, I wrap myself
in an outdoor coat, then step out into the dark and the rain
to look for my daughter.

Mabs

Otty was asleep when Mabs crept into her room. It was a blessing, Mabs decided. It would do the poor child more good than anything. There was a chaise longue in her room so Mabs helped herself to blankets and a pillow and curled up there. Her mind felt like a blocked drain.

Astonishingly, she slept. Then, nature having woven its magic, she woke, and realised the blockage had shifted. The rain had burgeoned into a summer storm and was crashing against the window like an ocean over a ship's prow. Thunder rolled and there was an eerie flash of lightning . . . Mabs glanced at Otty but she slept on.

The clock showed five o'clock in the morning. Mabs had slept for a good six hours – a miracle under the circumstances. And although there was still much that she *didn't* know, she had woken with the certainty that Mrs Finch had not absconded with Jonathan. And she had not taken Mabs's money. Mabs sat cross-legged on the chaise, blankets wrapped around her, and stared into the darkness.

Really, she thought, this whole thing boiled down to the same old question. Was Mr Finch to be trusted, or was Mrs? And the answer was the same. Yes, Mrs Finch had every reason to run away after so many years of self-sacrifice. But she wouldn't leave Otty. And, Mabs felt with sudden certainty, she wouldn't leave *Mabs*, and *definitely* not without a word. Averil would be married in just a few weeks. Having come this far, loving her children as she did, she wouldn't miss that. If she *were* going to run away with Jonathan – and who could blame her? – it wouldn't be now. She would have waited until after the wedding. She would have told Mabs, made provision for Otty.

Mabs tapped her fingernails on her teeth as she thought, not with the tired, clogged struggle of last night, but a clear, sharp appraisal. Betsy's words came back to her.

Do you think Mr F's done away with her or something?

Mabs had to hope that, whatever he was, he wasn't a murderer. But there were holes in his story. According to him, Mrs Finch had left a note – but there was no note to be seen because he had burned it. According to him, she had stolen Mabs's money for her flight, but she'd disappeared during Saturday night or in the small hours of Sunday morning. But Mabs had taken her money out and counted it on Saturday evening, just before she went to bed. She'd taken out the money for the fair, put it in her pocket and put the box away. So if Mrs Finch *had* taken it, she would have had to creep in while Mabs was sleeping. She wasn't so heavy a sleeper. Likelier that someone had taken it during the day while she was out at the fair – but Mrs Finch was gone by then.

She thought back to everything she knew. Mr Finch liked to be in control of his wife. He liked her to be constrained and live small, despite his show of care. But lately, Mrs Finch had been expanding. Mabs had succeeded with her in a way that he never thought she would. And he didn't like it. He'd called his old friend the doctor to increase the measures that kept her suppressed. But he'd been thwarted and the doctor hadn't come. Well, if he couldn't medicate and torture her into submission, what else could he do?

Do you think Mr F's done away with her or something?

And then she remembered something Mrs Finch had said: *Do you know, Mabel, that it only takes two men to commit a woman to an asylum? A husband and his doctor is the perfect pairing. My husband let me know that he had such papers in his keeping. Dr Broome signed them without hesitation . . .*

Mabs's blood stilled. Was *that* it? It would get her out of his hair once and for all, wouldn't it? It would ensure she never said anything controversial in company again. And he could pin all the blame on her.

I don't know if you've heard about such places, Mabel, but most are not humane.

Mabs swallowed.

There was talk of a place for delicate and depraved women in Yorkshire.

Had he taken her there? But Mrs Webb had said that he was around all day Sunday. Mabs had seen him on Saturday evening. She wasn't sure quite how far Yorkshire was but she didn't think he could have got there and back in just a few hours. Were committal papers specific to one institution? Or were they general, ensuring she would be taken in anywhere? Mabs had no idea. She was out of her depth and needed Olive more than ever but she couldn't talk to her yet – maybe not for a long time if Clover wasn't found.

Mabs stood up, glad that she was still dressed from last night; the household would be stirring in forty-five minutes. Quietly, she slipped downstairs. The house was still and silent within, whilst the rain hammered at the windows and walls. There was no sound from inside Mr Finch's study, no light around the door. She opened the door and paused, then went inside and lit a candle. As quickly and methodically as she could, she went through the papers on his desk, not really expecting to see anything damning there in plain sight. Then she went through the desk drawers. The last one was locked. She couldn't find a key. Mabs glanced at the clock. Half past five. She was cutting it fine. It only needed for someone to be up early, restless after the events of last night . . .

She went to the door and opened it a crack. The hall still slept. She continued her search, getting more and more frantic, knocking things over and forcing herself to replace them carefully. He mustn't guess that someone had been here. Mabs needed to stay at Willoughby Walk as long as possible for Otty.

She was about to give up for the time being when her eye fell on a small crystal bud vase on the windowsill across the room. She hurried over and picked it up, hearing a faint rattle. Inside was a tiny key. Mabs tipped it into her hand and glanced at the clock. Twenty before six. She ran to the desk and opened the last drawer. A sheaf of files lay balanced on top of a box. She pulled them out and hastily looked through them – nothing about asylums. Time to go. She was about to stuff them back in the drawer when she noticed that the box looked awfully familiar. It was *her* box. And it was full of money.

She hesitated. If he realised the money was gone, he'd know someone had been here. Would it be safer to leave it under his very nose? But who knew how long it would stay there? No, it was hers, she'd earned every penny of it. Mabs stuffed it all into her pockets, returned the empty box and files to the drawer, and locked it. She dropped the little key into the vase and hurried out. Then she went to the kitchen – strange to see it all in darkness – and made herself a pot of tea. Lord knew she needed it!

So far she'd discovered nothing to help Mrs Finch. But she had her money back. And she had proof that Mr Finch was lying. Mabs carried her tea up to Otty's room, settled back on the chaise and blew out the candle.

Mabs

Later that morning, Mabs went to Polaris House, leaving Otty in bed, awake but still not speaking. She'd eaten breakfast, so that was something. There was no question of her going to school.

Mr Finch was at home, pacing the hall, brooding in his study, acting the part of the deserted husband to perfection. Mabs told him where she was going and he looked at her so sharply that for a moment she thought he'd discovered her theft – if it can be theft to take something that is your own. But he merely said, 'Not a word of this to the Westallens, Miss Daley. This is private – a disgrace.'

'Of course, sir. I only want to see if Miss Clover's been found.' She hurried out before he could change his mind.

The first thing she did at Polaris House was beg to see her sister. She gave Jenny all her money. 'Keep it safe for me, love. I can't explain now.'

The Westallens were in the parlour and Olive looked shocking, ashen-faced and stricken. 'Mabs, you came!' She enfolded Mabs in a tight embrace and started to cry.

'Oh Olive. You haven't found her then?'

Olive shook her head.

'Not yet, no,' said Captain Westallen. 'But it's only a matter of time. I'll be going out again in a minute. Thank you for coming, Miss Daley, we appreciate it.'

'Of course I came. I'm just so *sorry*. Is there anything I can do? Anything at all?'

Olive shook her head again. 'No. There are still plenty of us out searching. We're taking it in turns now, three or four at a time, as we're all feeling the strain. But how can we rest?'

'I don't know. I know I couldn't. Oh, that darling child. How did she . . . or don't you want to tell it all over again?'

Olive sighed. 'I never want to *think* of it again, but I want you to know, Mabs.'

'I'll set off again,' said the captain, looking out of the window. 'At least the rain's stopped. All's hopeful with a fair wind.'

'I should come too, Papa.'

'Stay and tell Mabs, then follow on. We'll cover more ground if we're not together.'

'I'm coming with you, James,' said Mrs Westallen, looking very grey-faced, thought Mabs. They couldn't have had ten minutes' sleep between them.

'No, Margaret, you were out all night in that rain! You got drenched. You haven't even been to bed!'

'*Bed!* Please, James, one last turn for my own satisfaction. I'll rest this afternoon. Goodbye, Mabs, dear.' She left the room and a moment later they heard the front door.

'She wasn't asking,' sighed her husband, following.

'They're so good,' groaned Olive. 'I feel *terrible* putting everyone to this trouble. Most terrible of all about Clover, of course.' And she told Mabs how it had come to pass that she and Clover had been separated. 'Thank goodness Angie went to the fair with you and not with us,' concluded Olive, 'or I might have lost her too!'

'Well, you didn't and it's not your fault. Look, Olive, I don't know where Clover is. But it'll be all right. I just know it.'

'Do you? I don't. I mean, I always thought I had a great faith. But bad things do happen in the world, that's just a fact. There's no reason to suppose none of them will happen to me. You know, Mabs, I see lack and I try to compensate for it, I see need and I try to meet it. I try to fix everything for everyone and I feel so proud and powerful, but when it's my own little girl . . . I'm useless. No amount of money and no amount of cleverness will bring Clover home.'

'Don't be afraid, Olive. Just . . . keep looking and you'll find her. I *feel* it, though I can't explain it.'

'But . . . after a whole night outside alone? In that deluge? You really think she might have survived it?'

'I do.' Mabs nodded firmly. She meant it. She was filled with a conviction that surprised her and she wanted Olive to feel it too. 'Don't give up. I *know* she'll come home. And besides, you don't know that she was outside all night. Some kind stranger might have given her shelter and they might be on their way here this very minute!'

'I thought of that. One imagines all the awful sorts of people that might have found her so I have to remind myself that there are good people too. But if they found her last night, why didn't they bring her back then?'

'Maybe it was too late. Or maybe Clover was too upset to tell them where she lives. I've seen it, you know, at the canal, when there were accidents, or deaths . . . Sometimes when people have a terrible fright, they scream and babble and say the most awful things. But sometimes they go all still and silent and it takes time for them to come out of it.' *Like Otty, now.*

'Oh Mabs, what a tower of strength you are. You're right,

of course. I'll gain nothing by imagining the worst. Will you come with me? Could Abigail spare you, do you think? You'll lift my spirits when they start to flag.'

'Oh Olive.' Mabs was desperately torn. 'I want to help you, more than anything, but I can't leave Otty alone for long.'

'Why? What's wrong with Otty?'

'She's . . . unwell. Tummy upset. Poor little thing. I promised I'd be back very soon.'

'Why is she alone? What's happened, Mabs? Is there something you're not telling me?'

'No.'

Olive narrowed her eyes. 'I know I haven't slept and my brain isn't as agile as usual, but you're a terrible liar, Mabs. We both know it.'

'It's nothing for you to worry about, Olive!' cried Mabs rather desperately. 'You've enough to handle. I'll tell you all the latest when Clover's safely home. Only Otty's poorly and I have to stay with her today.'

To her relief, Olive was too distraught to be dogged. 'Of course you must stay with Otty. The poor child.'

'Go on now, Olive. Go and look for Clover. As soon as Otty's well enough, we'll come up together and help you look.'

As they talked, Mabs and Olive went into the hall and found their coats. 'Right,' said Olive on the doorstep with desperate determination. 'A-searching I will go.' The look in her eyes was so plaintive that it wrung Mabs's heart.

As Mabs walked down the hill, something niggled at her. Something about Otty being so still and silent. What was it? Then she realised. With all of yesterday's upsets, Sunday morning, when she'd gone joyfully to meet her family, had faded from her mind. But now she remembered it. She had seen Otty on the way out, sitting in bed, staring into space.

Mabs had invited her to the fair. And Otty had been very strange *then*. The state she was in hadn't come over her since she heard the news about her mother. She'd been in it before that.

'Oh my Gawd!' said Mabs, stopping dead in her tracks, earning a scowl from a passing gent. 'Otty knows something.'

Mabs

Mabs had seen enough people damaged by life's cruelties to know how to coax people out of a state like Otty's. Best was if they came out of it themselves, but if Otty knew something that could help her mother, Mabs couldn't wait any longer to find it out. After what that woman had suffered for the past twenty years, Mabs didn't know if she could stand one more horror.

At Willoughby Walk, the first person she saw was the last person she wanted to: Mr Finch. 'Have they found the little girl?' he asked.

'No, sir, but they're all out searching.'

He nodded and wandered off, to Mabs's relief. She ran up to Otty's room and found her just as she had left her.

'All right, Otty, love,' she said gently. 'You and me have to start talking again 'cause there's important things to say.'

She sat on the bed and pulled back the coverings to take Otty's feet in her hands. They were freezing, which didn't surprise Mabs, so she rubbed them as she talked. 'You have to start telling me what's on your mind now. I know you know something, and I need you to tell me so I can help her. I know you must be very angry with her just now but there's more to this than meets the eye.'

Otty sat up abruptly, her feet sliding from Mabs's hands, her dark hair tumbling forwards. 'I *know* that, Mabs,' she whispered. 'I'm not angry with *Mama*!'

'Then what? Otty, you know you can trust me.'

'Only it's so bad, Mabs, you might not believe me!'

'I will. Trust me, the things I've had to believe since coming here . . . It's been hard keeping them from you, to be honest, only your ma thought it best.'

'You promise you'll believe me?'

'Yes.'

'Mama would never run off like that. It's Papa, Mabs. He's . . . he's *lying*!' And Otty burst into tears.

'There, there,' murmured Mabs, holding her and glad that the storm had finally broken. 'I know. It'll be all right.'

Eventually Otty sat back, wiping her face on a sheet and pushing her cloud of hair out of her eyes. Her colour had come back and her eyes looked sad and frightened, which was better, Mabs thought, than looking blank.

'Mabs,' she said. 'I've wanted to talk to you for *weeks* now but I couldn't . . . Mabs, is it wrong if you . . . dislike your papa? Does it mean you're a bad, wicked person?'

'No, love. It's not wrong. We want to love our parents more than anyone because they're our parents and that's how we start out. But sometimes things change. Sometimes we see things that we know aren't right. It can be very confusing but it doesn't make you bad.'

'It *is* confusing! That's exactly what it is. Mabs, I've always *adored* Papa!'

'I know, love.'

'But lately . . . well, we haven't been seeing eye to eye. He's going to move me to a different school.'

'Yes, your ma told me all about that.'

'And he won't let me go to university! He says it's bad for women to be educated, but I don't think that's right, Mabs, I really don't. Look at Olive! I've been trying to understand him, Mabs. I told myself he's my papa after all, and he's just trying to do what's best for me. But now I know that he's . . .' Otty's eyes filled with tears again and she took a great shuddering breath. So, the shock hadn't been about her mother's disappearance at all. It was the realisation that her father was in no way the person she'd thought he was. 'That he's a bad man,' Otty finished softly.

Well, thought Mabs, *her ma wanted to protect her from knowing, but she's worked it out all by herself.* 'I know, love.'

Otty gave a great sigh of relief. 'Then I can tell you. I woke up in the middle of the night. Saturday night. It was one o'clock. I don't know what woke me, but it felt funny. I went to the door and opened it just a crack and there was a light in the hall. I could hear Mama and Papa talking. I don't know why I didn't just go out and ask what was happening. They were in travelling clothes and Mama had a bag; they were saying something about Charlie and Felicia. Papa said they needed Mama. I didn't want Mama to go but she looked so serious, and they were in such a hurry they were gone before I knew it. I went to the window and saw them getting in a cab.

'They just *went*! I couldn't sleep after that. I knew I'd miss Mama, especially with the new school ahead of me. And I kept thinking how strange it was that they would go in the middle of the night like that but if Charlie had sent for them . . . I thought he or Felicia must be ill and I was frightened.

'The next morning when you asked me to the fair, I hadn't slept and I was just waiting for Papa to come and explain

everything. But I waited all morning, Mabs. I saw Averil and
Freds at lunchtime and it was obvious *they* didn't know
anything. Papa eventually called us into his study in the afternoon. He looked so grave I thought for sure he was going to
tell us that Charlie or Felicia was dead. And then he told us
that Mama had run away with a . . . a lover!'

Otty's brow creased into a mystified frown. 'But I saw them
leave together, with my own eyes. If Mama did have a . . . a
gentleman, I don't think Papa would take her to him, would
he? But why would he lie? Why would he say such a horrible
untrue thing about Mama? *Why*, Mabs?'

'Oh, God love you.' Mabs wrapped Otty in her arms and
rocked her for a while, wondering what on earth Mrs Finch
would want her to tell her daughter.

'*And*,' added Otty indignantly, 'he said she stole your money,
which she *wouldn't*. *And* he's given you notice and said it was
her fault. And most important of all: where's Mama?'

'I don't know,' said Mabs. 'Golly, Otty, there's so much I
want to explain to you – it'll be an awful lot to take in! And I
think that when your ma comes home, she'll want to talk to
you about it all herself. I'll tell you what I can, I promise, but
first I need to do whatever I can to find her. I'm . . . a little
worried about her.'

'What do you think has happened, Mabs?'

'It goes back to what your pa said about women and education, I think. A lot of men believe it, you know, that if we
overuse our brains it makes us funny in the head. You know
he's been saying that yer ma is ill? Well, she's not. She's as
smart as can be and there's nothing wrong with her at all
except what he's made her be. I think, Otty, he might have
sent her to an asylum. But I don't *know*, and it would be like
looking for a needle in a haystack.'

'How *dare* he? Why, I'm going to tell him that I know he's lying. I'll tell him I saw them last night. I'll *make* him tell us where she is!'

'No, Otty, you mustn't! He'll never admit it and he'll never let her be found unless it suits *him*. He's a very clever man, your pa. Honestly, if you want to help your ma, and if you want me to stay here as long as he said I could, you have to pretend you don't know anything. I know it's horrible and hard; I've been pretending for a while now and it's the worst thing I've ever done – and that's saying something. But don't let on, Otty, or Lord knows what he'll do.'

'All right, Mabs. We're not speaking very much lately anyway. I can keep out of his way. Maybe I'll go to school or visit Olive a lot.'

'Otty, love, do you remember me telling you about Clover?'

'No, what about her?'

'I thought you hadn't taken it in. She's gone missing too, love. She got lost at the fair yesterday. Olive's beside herself and they're all out searching. We can't trouble Olive.'

'Oh, poor Clover! She's so little! Oh Mabs, you must have thought me so selfish. We should go and look for her too. Can we? I don't want to stay in this house any more anyway.'

Mabs nodded. 'Well, I can't say as fresh air will do you any harm. And I'm desperate to help Olive, if I'm honest. When yer pa goes back to work, I'm raiding that study from top to bottom in case there's any papers I missed that'll tell us where yer mother might be.'

Otty jumped out of bed. 'I'll help.'

Olive

It is now more than a full day's span that Clover and I have been parted. Oh, the things that can happen to a four-year-old girl in four-and-twenty hours! Despite Mabs's fortifying optimism, I cannot help but lapse into dark imaginings.

Mabs reappeared with Otty early this afternoon. The dear child was pale but determined-looking; it did me good to see her. Mabs still hasn't told me the latest instalment in the Tale of the Finches and I can't confess I'm sorry; I can think of nothing but Clover for now. The search was fruitless. Papa and Mama retired first, Mama looking very tired and Papa insistent she rest. Then Otty became exhausted – no wonder after an illness – so Mabs bore her off too. Then the servants, one by one, returned home.

So now I, too, am walking home, weary, footsore and utterly forlorn. I keep seeing flashes of yellow everywhere. I had always thought it an uncommon colour but today it is positively ubiquitous. I see Clover from the corner of my eye every other minute, but when I look, it's a dandelion, or a child's ball. It's the sign over a seamstress's window, or the curtain in some-body's breakfast room. I arrive at Polaris House without my usual sense of pleasure; it is not home if Clover's not here. I leave the gate open in case Clover comes home.

I toil up the path and Jenny greets me at the door. 'Can I get you anything, Miss Olive? A warm drink? Something to eat?'

'A bath, Jenny, if you please. I want nothing but a hot bath.'

'Yer mother said the same when she came home. She's in bed now, thank goodness. I hope you'll do the same, miss.'

'Yes,' I say hopelessly. 'I suppose I'll have to.'

I greet Papa then I sink into the tub and feel the water scorch the iced insides of my bones. Luxury is so empty when so great a sorrow resides in the heart. No pleasure can be taken in anything when a loved one is lost.

I go to kiss Mama goodnight but she is asleep in bed. At last I climb into my own. The sight of Clover's little bed on the chaise crushes me to tears. I've long ago bought her a proper bed but she likes this one. With all the disturbed nights she suffered, I had started to despair that she would ever sleep in her own room. Cuddling her while she slept was a privilege at first, then it felt tiresome; I longed to stretch out and roll over with ease, to sleep according to my own rhythms. Now I would give anything I own to have her curled up in my arms again. I sob long and hard, in agonies of fear. I remember the night, only eight months ago, that she first slept in my room. It was all so strange then, and now she is my whole world. I wanted a child in part to protect me when I lost my parents. But there is no protection from loss, I know that now. We can none of us escape our portion of heartbreak.

For a moment I think of my cards but I cannot bring myself to use them. They are a plaything for a rich woman contemplating this or that new path for her own diversion. This is a matter of life or death and I will not give them ordinance over that.

Thanks to soaking in the hot water, I have found a brief pause, some relative peace. Let me sink into it now and rest if I can, let me not stir my mind anew. I pull the covers over my head and close my eyes, praying for peace, and praying for Clover.

I sleep.

And suddenly, I wake. It's dark, the middle of the night. I sit up. What has woken me? Is Clover home? Will Mama come knocking at my door any moment, holding my little one by the hand? But there is no disturbance within, though the rain is back, beating mercilessly on the window. Perhaps that is what disturbed me. I go to the window and look over the garden, the protected expanse of loveliness it has been my privilege to grow up within. I lean my forehead on the cold glass and groan. If this is the end of motherhood, will the pain ever, ever lessen?

I close my eyes and it all washes over me again. The day on the heath, Clover screaming, vanishing in the crowd. *Who was that boy?* He must have been someone from her past; he *must* have been, for her to react like that. And yet he meant her no harm, I feel sure. Perhaps he simply reminded her of a place, a time. He was just opening his mouth to speak when she bolted.

How certain she had been that day at Mrs Jacey's. There was Gert, all fury and illogical sabotage of her own best chance, but Clover, less than half her age, had been calm and determined. I see again her little fist clutching my green skirt, her face earnest. *I wish you would be my mama.* God help me, I have failed her.

I lift my head and stare bleakly into the streaming rains. I'm about to get back into bed when something in the garden catches my eye. A glimmering; a soft, small light that is barely there. Through the sheets of rain and the density of darkness, I can sometimes see it, and sometimes not. Oh, dear God! Is it Clover's soul? Is she dead? Has she come back to the one place on earth where she was happy?

I peer through the darkness. Gone. It was my imagination, nothing more. I turn away but as I do so . . . there it is again! Tiny! Barely visible. It looks as if it's coming from the greenhouse. Why would Clover's soul haunt the greenhouse? How could there be a light in the garden, if it is not supernatural?

I light a storm lamp and make my way downstairs. In the hall I pull on an overcoat of Papa's, big and heavy to cover my nightgown. I don my own good, sturdy boots and step out into the rain. Strange to walk in our grounds at this time and in such weather. They do not feel familiar at all. They feel not like the stamping ground of humans but of animals and beings from other worlds: fairies, dryads. Ghosts, perhaps.

The otherness of it is disorienting. I rely on the storm lamp which gives only a wavering light, and jogs in my hand as the wind buffets me. Eventually I reach the greenhouse where I can see clearly the light which beckoned me from the house. Now, it dips and dances but shines without disappearing. I do not think it is a soul. I think it is a candle.

I frown. If there's a candle in the greenhouse, I suppose there is someone with it. Why would anyone want to sit in our greenhouse by candlelight? Perhaps a passing tramp found the gate unlocked and wanted shelter from the rain. Do tramps *carry* candles as a matter of course? If it *is* a tramp, I suppose I should not beard him alone. I should fetch Papa. Yet suppose, when we return, the candle and its bearer are gone? Then I would never know . . . I *must* know. I open the door and step inside.

The rush of cold air blows the candle out at once, but my lamp still burns and by its gentle light I see a sleeping woman wearing a midnight-blue dress. She is slender, with long dark hair which lies in ribbons across her face. She's lying on her side on the stone path. Her arm curls protectively around another small sleeper, who . . . *Dear God!* I step closer. My hand flies to my mouth. She has a tumble of honey-coloured curls and, beneath the coat that covers her, I see a flash of yellow.

'*Clover?*' My voice, disbelieving and desperate, shatters the fragile peace of the tableau and the little girl sits up at once. It is indeed my Clover.

'Mama!' she cries, her eyes all joy and tears. She jumps to her feet but then hesitates, which breaks my heart. 'Are you cross?'

'No, of *course* not!' I cry, holding out my arms. 'Darling, I *love* you. Oh, thank God you're home.' And she runs to me at last.

I hold her small body as tightly as the need not to suffocate or crush her allows. I feel her arms grip me just as tightly and my heart tumbles and flutters until it finds its normal rhythm again. 'Oh Clover,' I murmur. 'You're home, you're home.'

After a great deal of hugging and crying, my attention returns to the woman sleeping on the ground. I'm amazed she still sleeps after the scene we have made.

'Who *is* that?' I say.

'A nice lady,' says Clover.

'Well, I'm glad to hear it, but I'm sure she'd be much more comfortable in a bed.' I step closer, avoiding her strewn skirts and hair, to shake her gently by the shoulder. 'Excuse me,' I say clearly. 'Won't you come inside?'

She rouses slowly and groans. 'Oh Miss Westallen,' she says. 'I do beg your pardon.' She eases herself stiffly to a sitting position and I gasp. It is Abigail Finch.

❄

Stories can wait. I don't know where Clover has been, or why Abigail is here. I don't know how their paths crossed, or why, having come to Polaris House, they decided to spend the night in the greenhouse. My curiosity can be satisfied in the morning. The one thing that I desperately needed has been given to me: Clover's return.

We hasten to the house. Abigail holds the lamp and I carry Clover in my arms, her legs wrapped around my waist, her muddy little shoes bouncing on my posterior. Both Clover and Abigail are damp and trembling. I decide to let Mama and Papa sleep. I'm worried about them after their exertions of the past two days; they are not the youngest chickens in the coop. If it was just Clover, I would see to her myself. As we have an unexpected guest, I enlist help, waking Agatha because she's leaving us soon, whereas poor Anne and Jenny must endure us indefinitely longer.

Between us, we draw two hot baths in the kitchen, to save the time and effort of carrying the water upstairs. The room is always pleasant anyway, with the residual warmth of the day's activities. I run to fetch towels, nightgowns, robes and slippers, so they can step out of the water into decency and comfort.

'Gracious, what a novelty,' murmurs Abigail, looking from her tub at the range and the copper pans hanging about it. 'I'm so grateful, Miss Westallen, you can never, ever know.'

'Please, call me Olive. Surely we are beyond formality now. I ask you no questions save one. Are you hungry or thirsty?'

'Both.'

'And you, little missy?' asks Agatha.

Clover nods emphatically, her hair wet and dangling in her eyes.

'Bless you, little cherub,' says Agatha, kissing the top of her wet head. 'I couldn't have gone away happy if she wasn't back, miss,' she says to me as she sets to preparing a midnight feast. Or a two-o'clock-in-the-morning feast as it is by then.

When the bathers are dried and warmly wrapped, we sit around the table, all four. This is not the time for revealing conversations, it is a time to relish safety and togetherness. We tuck into chicken pie with cold water to wash it down, and treacle sponge with cream for pure celebration. I don't know about the others but I've only eaten one meal since Clover disappeared. Suddenly I'm famished.

'Oh, me wedding dress,' sighs Agatha, tucking into the pudding.

When we have feasted, I ask Agatha to show Abigail to a guest bedroom. Abigail begs us not to mention her presence here to anyone outside the house. She has run away then. We both reassure her.

'Thank you,' says Abigail as she bids me goodnight. 'I'll explain everything in the morning, I promise.'

Then I tow my daughter away to our room, where her bed will remain unoccupied for another night because I simply cannot bear to let her go. We both climb into my bed and she wraps her arms around me, resting her head in the crook of my neck. With Clover restored to me, all my senses come back and I'm able to feel the comfort of it again, the warmth and softness, the wonderful pillows. It is warm and dreamy and any moment now we shall both be sound asleep. If Papa wakes before us in the morning, he will wonder why there are small footprints on his overcoat.

Otty

Since Mabs coaxed me out of my stupor yesterday, I've almost wished she'd left me in it! My innocent childhood is quite gone. My father is not the man I thought he was – so far from it, in fact, that I quite detest him. That is a hard thing. And who knows if I will ever see my mama again? What if Mabs has to leave and Mama is still lost? I never thought my life could so quickly become intolerable.

Yesterday we went to the heath to hunt for Clover but there was no trace of her. The world is suddenly a terrible, unsafe place from which people I love keep vanishing. Tomorrow it may be Mabs, the next day Averil, for all that I know.

We prayed that Papa would go to work today so that we could hunt for clues in his study but Papa has not so much as taken a walk. He stays in his study like a dragon in a cave, coming out at intervals to pace the hall and breathe fire. Well, there are no flames, but he does keep staring out of the window as if checking for something or someone and he sighs a great deal. He looks terrible, eyes bloodshot and hair standing on end; I wouldn't doubt his story for a minute if I didn't know for a fact he's lying.

Around noon I receive a note from Olive. I know it at once by the stationery and handwriting.

Dearest Otty,

Clover has come home to us safe and well, God be thanked. I must see you and Mabs <u>as soon as possible</u>. I cannot emphasise enough that you must come as soon as you possibly can. <u>It is the best news you could possibly wish for.</u>

    Awaiting your arrival impatiently,

OW
PS Wear something <u>pretty</u>!

Of course, the best news I could possibly wish for would be Mama's return, but Olive doesn't know that she's missing. Still, the second-best possible news is a wonderful boon. Mabs is in the kitchen so I go to show her the note. We hug and laugh and cry and Mrs Derring says she's 'very glad the little girl's been found'. She wraps up half a batch of lemon biscuits in greaseproof paper as a welcome home gift for Clover, which is very nice of her, *I* think, then we race off to get changed.

Mabs runs to her attic, taking the stairs two at a time. I reach for my usual walking costume then remember that I am to wear something pretty. That's odd. Clover and Olive have seen me a hundred times in my walking costume, sensible, grey and dull as it is. And worse, in my Ladies' Academy uniform! What does it matter how I dress? I consider instead my pale blue dress with cream lace. It's Mama's favourite and the sight of it makes me sad. But I decide to wear it anyway as a link with her. I brush my hair and tie it back with a blue ribbon. I'm still very pale.

Mabs thunders back. 'Oh, you look pretty,' she says. 'Are you ready? Are we off?'

'Yes, and yes. Mabs? Do you think there's something a bit odd about Olive's note?'

Mabs reads it again and shrugs. 'Not really. I mean, it's a bit bossy, but she's excited, ain't she? Isn't she?'

'Yes. But . . . all those bits underlined. And the *rush* – I mean, Clover's not going anywhere, is she? Olive will never let her out of her sight after this. And why do I have to wear something pretty?'

'I suppose she wants us all to feel festive. Bless you, Otty, you're seeing hidden meanings everywhere. But if there is something, we won't find it standing here.'

She's right, of course, so we hurry on our way and arrive at Polaris House panting. Mabs rings the bell and reaches out to tidy my hair, which has immediately become a mess. The tender gesture makes me want to cry.

'Thank you for being my friend, Mabs,' I say in a muffled voice. 'I don't know what I'll do when you're gone.'

'Well now, we're not worrying about that because we'll sort it out and you'll never lose me. And I'm *honoured* to be your friend. In fact, you're like another sister to me, that's how much I love you.'

I don't know when anyone ever said something I wanted to hear so much. 'I love you too, Mabs.' I throw my arms around her, untidying my hair again.

Olive herself opens the door, with the brightest, widest smile on her face. Then Clover comes flying down the hall and throws herself at me. I bend down to hug her then take a good look at her. She looks none the worse for her adventures; in fact, they both look radiant.

'Now, where exactly have you been, young miss?' Mabs asks Clover. 'You've had us all frightened to death!'

'Plenty of time for questions,' says Olive, her eyes sparkling like sunlight on a pond. 'But first we must go into the parlour. Come now, don't waste any time. Otty, you should go first.'

Mabs and I exchange a quizzical look. I set off towards the parlour. And I stop so suddenly that the others bump into me. For there, just inside the doorway, in an unfamiliar bronze-coloured dress, is the best possible thing: my mother.

'Mama?' My voice is wavering and childlike. I sound about six years old.

'Otty, my darling!' Mama steps forward. I run to her and she holds me tight. I sink into her arms. She smells of lavender, a lovely, fresh, hopeful scent; I can hardly bear to let her go.

Behind me, I hear Mabs exclaim, 'Oh my *Gawd*! How on earth?' We're blocking the door so the others cannot get in. I hold on tightly to Mama as we shuffle into the room.

'Oh ma'am,' says Mabs, in a low, trembling voice. Mama kisses the top of my head, extricates her arms and embraces Mabs.

'No more of that. Call me Abigail now for you're my companion no longer and the truest friend I could have had. Mabel, my dear, were you *very* worried?'

'Horribly, ma'am. Sorry, it'll take a while. Abigail. I can't explain how scared I was. We were trying to find out where you'd gone. And here you are at Olive's . . .'

Mama laughs and I realise it's a beautiful sound that I haven't heard in a very long time. 'At last I'm free. Not in the eyes of the law, but in my heart, and everything else will flow from there. Come, let us sit. I'm still tired.'

She sits on a long sofa but despite the plentiful space for sitting, I climb onto her lap. Then Clover scrambles into *my* lap and the fact of three people sitting on top of each other in a pile is so ridiculous that everybody laughs. Olive rings for champagne and cake and everything is perfect. For the first time in ever so long, everything is absolutely perfect.

✿

'Perhaps champagne wasn't the best idea, so early in the proceedings,' laughs Olive after a while, looking ruefully at her glass which is empty for the *second* time. *I* was only allowed one glass – a small one. 'I don't know how Abigail can be expected to produce a cohesive narrative, but my dear, we all need to know. *Everything!* Can you tell us at last?'

'Yes,' says Mama, sitting up a little straighter and removing me from her lap. 'Sorry, dear, my legs are now completely numb.'

Clover has by now left us to go and play with Angie. I sit beside Mama on the sofa and snuggle into her side. She looks anxiously at me, then at Mabs.

'It's all right, ma'am. Abigail,' says Mabs. It will take time for her to get used to that – it took her long enough to remember to call Olive Olive! 'Otty knows most of it. Not the details – I thought that was for you to tell – but she knows her father was behind you disappearin'. And she knows he . . . ain't right. She'd worked an awful lot of it out for herself.'

'Oh darling.' Mama puts her arm around me and pulls me to her. 'I'm so sorry. I know how close you and your father have always been. And I'm sorry, too, that I haven't been much of a mother to you since we came to Hampstead, but that's all going to change now, I promise.'

Abigail

Your father woke me on – when was it? Saturday night? He told me he'd received a letter from Charlie earlier that day, but forgotten to open it until just then. Apparently, it said that they were married, back in London, and that Felicia was gravely ill. Charlie was begging me to go to them. 'Shall we go at once?' said Lucius. 'We'd never forgive ourselves if anything happened to her.'

I don't know why it never occurred to me that he was lying. Perhaps because I was half asleep, or because it was very plausible. Felicia has never been the most robust of girls and the strain of a long journey and elopement would tax her. I imagined the worst as I sprang from bed and threw a few things into an overnight bag. At the same time, I was excited to see them both – my son, my new daughter-in-law – I longed to be of help to them.

For the first part of the journey all I could think about was Felicia, praying that Charlie wouldn't be left a widower at the age of one-and-twenty. After a while I realised, from the one or two landmarks I could distinguish through the darkness, that we were travelling south, through London. I was certain that Lucius had said Charlie and Felicia were staying some-where in the north of the city. No, no, he assured me, I had misheard; they were in Kent. That was when I started to wonder.

I asked to see the letter Charlie had sent; Lucius said he'd left it on his desk. 'You can remember their address?' I asked. He said yes. What was the nature of Felicia's illness? I asked. 'A fever,' he said. And then I knew.

'Lucius, you're taking me to an asylum, aren't you?' I asked, and he said, 'Yes, my dear, I'm afraid I am. A reputable place in Dartford. I regret the step, but now that you're out and about in our neighbourhood, speaking to people like the Westallens with an unguarded tongue, you pose a threat to all I'm trying to achieve. I wish to rid myself of the burden now, while I still have *some* semblance of control over my family. Charlie has gone, in a most ill-advised way. Averil's engaged to a man she hardly knows and Otty becomes more ungovernable by the day.'

There was no point raging in the old way. I fell very quiet and used the time to think. I wasn't entirely sure where Dartford *was*. I thought perhaps Surrey or Kent – one of those places not too far from London. I knew I'd only get one chance to escape and this certainly wasn't it; the carriage was travelling apace. I thought about what I had packed: only clothes and books. I slid my hand into my skirt pocket. There was a coin there, just one, and a half-used candle and matchbook, there for a long time, since my disturbed nights in Durham.

I couldn't think about the asylum. It would have paralysed me with fear. I only thought about whom I might turn to if I escaped. Not to you, Mabel, since you live in my husband's house. That left only you, Olive. I was loath to draw upon such a scant acquaintance but I knew you would shelter me.

I tried to gauge how far we had travelled; when the carriage started to slow, I thought I'd been right about the distance of

Dartford from London. I waited for my moment; I had to exercise the tightest control. I saw a large, dark building looming up at the end of a street. It had an air of tragedy about it and I was determined not to be part of its story.

The cab stopped. Lucius got out. 'Allow me, my dear,' he said, for the driver's benefit, I suppose. Or perhaps he was trying to convince himself, even now, that he was a solicitous husband acting in my best interests. When he was three-quarters of the way round to my side of the carriage, I threw myself out of the door by which he had exited and ran. I left my bag; I didn't look back.

I heard him shout after me and call to the driver for help. The area was not especially salubrious, which is to say that I found myself in a maze of narrow streets, all the better to disappear in. I turned right, then left, then right again, twisting myself into the town with no logic beyond keeping out of sight of my pursuers. Lucius has grown portly with his role of successful businessman, whereas fear made *me* as fleet as a deer. As for the driver, perhaps he had little enthusiasm for chasing a runaway wife that was not his own. Soon I found myself alone, and all I could hear was my heart drumming in my ears. The houses around me were terraced but they had small gardens and I let myself into one of those. The night was dry, thank goodness, so I hid myself behind some currant bushes and waited for hours.

When first light came, I crawled out and dusted myself off, terrified that I would be discovered. I walked and walked with no sense of direction until I came to a river. It was broad and fast and dirty and I dared to hope it was the Thames, knowing that if it was, it would make my job much easier.

I walked all day, dogged by doubt that I was going the most direct way, or even the right way. I didn't dare ask – I knew

I was getting very dishevelled, even though I was finely dressed, and that is a combination that attracts attention. Yes, Olive, I know what you're thinking. Why didn't I hail a cab and let you pay the fare when I arrived? I should have, of course. But I am not used to thinking of others as a resource, nor to having friends. The fact that I was coming to you at all was a big departure for me.

In the afternoon I had to stop and buy some bread and jam or I should have collapsed. I drank a little water whenever I passed a public fountain, and when I really couldn't go on without food any longer, I climbed down some steps to one of those little pebbled shores that punctuate the Thames so I might be out of sight of the passers-by. I ate half the bread and jam, then continued on my way. When night came, I found another garden in which to hide.

Then the rains came. Those torrential rains you had here too. I crawled underneath my leafy cover as far as possible but there was no holding them off. By morning I was soaked and cold. I couldn't afford to fall ill; I had to get back to Hampstead. I looked even stranger the following morning: stiff, footsore and bedraggled, still clutching my bread and jam. When I realised I was in London again, the relief was immense. I stood out less there; the city shelters folk of every description of strangeness, does it not? I felt safe enough to ask for directions twice. I saw Lucius on every street corner but each time it was a stranger.

It wasn't until I got to the heath that I truly knew where I was. It was evening by then and the place was emptying of crowds. I remembered Mabel mentioning a Whitsun fair. I wasn't, in fact, sure of the way to Polaris House, having been here only the once. It had been so strange being out with my husband after so long that I took nothing in. I knew it was uphill at least, so I set off along the edge of the heath. I was growing weak from fatigue and hunger and fear, and decided to stop and rest before deciding what my next steps should be.

I took myself into a little copse of trees – the rain had stopped by then, though I could feel it would not stay off for long. I rested and tried to quieten my spinning head so that I could be strong enough to go on; I had no desire to spend a third night outside. And then I heard a child crying. I got up and followed the sound, and found a very small person in a yellow dress hidden as deep in the bushes as I had been the previous night.

I lifted the branches and begged to help her. She looked exhausted, filthy and terrified. I know now that she had passed a full four-and-twenty hours alone on the heath. Dreadful! She didn't run – and thank goodness, for I had no strength to give chase. I coaxed her out and we sat together and established that we were both lost. I promised to help and asked her name and she said – this was rather strange, Olive – 'I'm not Nellie, I'm Clover.' *Time enough to puzzle that out*, I thought. The point was, of course, that Clover was a familiar name to me. She was terribly subdued – it was hard to get her to say much at all – but when I said, 'Not Clover Westallen?' she brightened instantly! She said, 'Yes, my mama is Olive Westallen and I live in Polaris House.' Well, you can imagine my astonishment. Hers too, when I explained that my destination was also Polaris House!

I gave her the last of my bread and jam, and we set off hand in hand, hope renewed. Of course, we still didn't know our way. Clover got very frustrated. 'Mama brings me!' she cried. There was no one to ask – by then the rain had started again and it was heavy. The storm disoriented us further. We found our way into the streets of Hampstead but recognised nothing!

And then, Clover recognised a neighbour's house by a garland of summer flowers on its door, sadly battered now. From there she knew the way. To my great relief, the gate was open. I have never in all my life been so happy to arrive anywhere. The only fly in the ointment was Clover. She started crying, howling actually, and flatly refused to go to the house. She was beside herself, distraught, and couldn't say why. I couldn't pick her up and carry her – she wouldn't let me near her. But I daren't leave her to go to the door. Suppose she ran off? I couldn't understand her distress so I didn't know what she might do.

We were at an impasse, standing there in the lashing rain, both exhausted and overwrought. I saw the greenhouse, and she consented to go in there. It was dry, it was tolerably warm; as a place to rest, it could have been worse. I remembered the candle in my pocket, praying the matchbook wasn't empty, or damp. It wasn't. I lit the candle, took her in my arms and eventually we fell asleep. We were woken, sometime later, by Olive.

Mabs

When Abigail finished her story, there was a great silence. The celebration, the hugging and the laughter, had all gone before. Now, Olive looked pensive and Abigail exhausted – no wonder she'd waited until they were all together; you wouldn't want to tell *that* story twice. Otty was leaning against her mother, a million thoughts clustering in her dark eyes.

'We should have known it, ma'am,' said Mabs, her head reeling. 'The doctor not coming, Charlie and Averil gone or going . . . it was all bound to make him want to take back some control. Oh, I should have thought.'

'Mabel, dear. *I* didn't think. And I have lived with the man for longer than I care to remember.'

They lapsed into silence again, but as the clock struck four, Mabs began to gather her scattered thoughts. It occurred to her that they couldn't simply sit there enjoying each other's company until bedtime. The prospect of returning to Willoughby Walk caused her spirits, which were as bright and buoyant as a balloon here in Polaris House, to plummet. But they had to burst their happy bubble sometime. One way or another, life as she had come to know it was over. And she had no idea what the next chapter might be.

'What happens now?' Mabs asked. 'What about Otty? I won't leave her if she's got to go back there.'

'You must both stay here,' pronounced Olive at once.

'No,' said Mabs. 'As long as I know Otty's with you, I'll go home. To Saffron Hill.'

The others protested mightily but Mabs held up her hand to stop them. 'Listen,' she said. 'It's not what you think, I'm not giving up or anything close. You two don't have anywhere else to go. I do. It's not luxury, but I'll be with family. It's straightforward, at least. I can read and write now, thanks to you, ma'am . . . Abigail. I know what I'm capable of – I'm not going back for good.'

In fact, Mabs wanted nothing less than to leave Hampstead, but it was the right thing to do. She could see that Olive was already itching to find her a new life but that wasn't Olive's job; it was hers. At least her home was full of love, which was more than could be said for Willoughby Walk.

It took some time to convince Olive but Mabs persisted and eventually, reluctantly, they readied themselves to go to Willoughby Walk. *For the last time*, marvelled Mabs, a little sad despite everything.

They called on Mr Finch, the three of them together, to tell him the good news of Clover's return. Mabs was heartily glad of Olive's presence; she wasn't sure she could have faced him otherwise. Olive enquired after his wife as if she knew nothing about anything and he told her that Abigail was sleeping. Mabs could practically feel Otty gnashing her teeth behind her. Olive asked him to convey her regards then asked if Otty might stay at Polaris House for a few days. 'Only if her mother can spare her, of course,' she added. 'But I'd be eternally grateful. Clover has specially requested it and I can deny her nothing after the fright I've had.'

To Mabs's relief, he agreed, distractedly. His normally ruddy complexion was pale; perhaps he was worried that his errant wife might turn up at any minute and explode the myths he'd perpetuated about her. Otty went to pack her bag and Olive waited on the street, purportedly to enjoy the sunshine, but really to allow Mabs to speak to Mr Finch without having to keep up the pretence that Mrs Finch was at home. With the two of them gone, Mabs felt unaccountably afraid.

'Excuse me, sir,' she said. 'I was just thinkin', I know you was so kind as to say I could stay a month but with Mrs Finch gone and Otty not needing me, it don't seem right to stay. I was thinking I might pack up and go home today, sir, if you don't need me for anything.'

He thanked her in the same preoccupied manner. 'That makes perfect sense; you are most considerate as always. I'm sorry it's ended like this. Let me pay you what I owe you for this last week.' He fumbled in his pocket for some coins.

'Thank you, sir. I hope everything works out all right. I wish all of you the very best.'

Then she shot out of the study and belted upstairs as if he might appear and stop her from going. After enduring for so long, she couldn't wait to be out of that house. She had so few possessions that it took her only two minutes to pack, but each was a memory. The beaded bag that Otty had given her for Christmas. Averil's cream dress that she had worn to the party on the day that Elfrida divulged her furious secret. The coat and gloves that Mrs Finch gave her when they had started taking walks together.

It had been an unmixed relief to escape from the study, Mr Finch's lair, but Mabs looked around the attic room with more complicated feelings. Impossible to forget how she had felt when she first arrived: her wonderment at luxuries like towels and a nightgown. In the hall, too, she paused, looking for the last time at the portrait of a young and dazzling Abigail, the damsel Lucius Finch had ensnared with manipulation and her own vulnerability. She remembered setting foot inside this house for the first time, only eight months ago; how impossibly grand it had seemed to her. She shook her head in astonishment at how it had all turned out, then went outside. Olive and Otty were waiting at the end of the street.

'How was it?' Olive asked.

'All right,' Mabs shrugged. With a sigh she took a last look back at the house with the pretty blue door, once her house of dreams, now something very different.

Olive

We walk to the high street, where I hail a cab to take Mabs home; Abigail Finch has done enough walking for all of us lately.

'Mabs,' I plead as the cab draws up. 'Please reconsider. Stay with us, just for a few days. There's still so much to discuss and I shall *miss* you.' Separation feels cruel having only just recovered Clover. I would like to collect my loved ones together in one place and nurture them all, I realise. But Mabs is independent.

'I'll miss you too.' There is a tremble in her voice; she takes my hand and holds it tightly. 'All of you. But this is the right thing. I need to decide what's next. And I'll come and see you very soon.'

'Very well,' I sigh, recognising a mind made up when I see one. 'I shall set my mind to finding an opportunity worthy of you.'

Mabs hugs Otty, then me. We are neither of us inclined to release her and the driver grows impatient. Then she is gone.

Back at Polaris House, things feel a little strange. Mama is in bed, still suffering with a bad cold and mild fever. Dr Stickland has been, and promised that it will pass and leave no ill effects. I feel Mabs's absence; although she was not here every day, knowing there is no possibility that she will call, or that I will bump into her in the street, feels unsettling. How I hope she doesn't settle for some meagre post that does not require or deserve her strength of character and compassion. I wonder if she has any idea of her own qualities.

Abigail is relieved to have her daughter safely at her side again – how well I know *that* feeling! I'm filled with a deep, deep gratitude for her service to Clover – and many questions. What on earth is Clover's side of the story? Given her age and her paucity with words, I wonder if I'll ever know.

While Otty and Abigail walk in the garden, engaged in a serious heart-to-heart, I go to prise Clover away from the fierce and chaotic game of Tiddlywinks that she's playing with Angeline and curl up with her in her favourite window seat in the drawing room.

'Darling, why did you run away?' I ask gently, removing a lock of hair from the centre of her face with a fingertip. Immediately she stiffens; I hate that there's anything in her life to make her feel that way. 'Please don't be afraid, my sweet girl. I'm not cross with you. But I'm your mother and I need to know. I was so very scared, you see, when I thought I'd lost you. Why did you run away from that boy at the fair? Tell me, Clover. I promise you're safe.'

Her huge, dark eyes slide away from my face and stare into the middle distance. I've never seen her look so detached. She doesn't speak. I don't want to push her, risk making her stop speaking altogether. Perhaps I should wait a few years to try talking to her about this, but by then these events may have been pushed so deep into her memory that I will never know. I'll try just once more, I tell myself.

'Did you know him? Had you seen him before?'

Clover shrugs, but at least it is a response.

'When you got home, with Abigail, why didn't you want to come into the house? Did you think I'd be angry?' At this she gives one of her emphatic nods. 'Why, darling?'

'Because I'm not allowed to run away.'

'No, that's true. But only because it's not safe and you're so precious, my darling. Had you run away before? Did you get into trouble?'

Clover nods sorrowfully. 'Smacks,' she whispers, looking up at me with tears in her eyes.

I cuddle her close. 'Oh, I see. Well, that's terrible, darling. I would never smack you. Whatever you do, even if you're naughty, I want you to know you can come to me, all right? I promise never to smack you. Do you understand?' Clover nods. 'Good girl. And darling, Abigail said that when she asked you your name, that night out on the heath, you said you were Clover, *not Nellie*. Is Nellie what your name used to be, before we found each other?'

Now her eyes are fixed on my face and I can hardly breathe for fear of saying the wrong thing. It's like sitting very still in the hopes that a wild bird will come close. She frowns, as if she's trying to puzzle out what to say.

'Nothing you can tell me will change anything,' I tell her. 'Nothing will ever change how much I love you. You will never be taken away from me. This is your home and you are Clover. You are my daughter. Whatever happened to you before is finished.'

At that, she slumps, her forehead against my chest, and I kiss her head and stroke her back. It's a yes without words, I can feel it. Her name used to be Nellie. I think of my visit to Harlowe Place. I remember the thin, shaking boy on the heath. I imagine a life so bad that any reminder of it causes her to bolt, a mother who would beat her for wandering off.

'Was that boy nasty to you, back when you were Nellie?' I whisper. Without looking up, she shakes her head, side to side. 'But he reminded you of the old days, is that right, darling?' She nods. 'Who was he?'

Clover looks up at me. There is a knock on the door and Anne announces Mr Harper. Good heavens! I had almost forgotten about Mr Harper. It feels as though he belongs in another lifetime. What timing! Well, never mind. Clover has had enough, I realise. Her small bright self is wilting beneath the weight of memory. How hard it must be for such a little person to reconcile two such wildly different lives.

'Promise me you'll never run off again,' I murmur, kissing her curls again.

'Promise,' she whispers. That is the only word I need from her, really. All the same, I make a concerted effort to fix the boy's face in my memory – just in case I can ever help him.

'Good girl. Then why don't you go back to Angeline and finish your game?' At once Clover brightens and hops down. I think this is all that I will ever learn about it, but at least I understand her a little better now. I go to my study, where Mr Harper is waiting, making a mental note to postpone the ball. I want Mama to be fully fit and able to enjoy it. Just as well I hadn't sent the invitations to the printer's.

In my heightened emotional state, I see and feel everything more vividly than usual. Colours seem brighter these last days, priorities clearer, my feelings shine. I'm pleased to see Mr Harper and I'm in a mood to embrace life. I'm across the room and shaking his hand before he has a chance to address me. He looks pleasantly surprised.

'Miss Westallen. So very good to see you again. Work has kept me very busy this last week, I regret, or I should have called sooner. But I foresee a calmer month ahead, thank goodness. I hope I don't interrupt you.'

'Not at all. Shall we go into the parlour and take some refreshment? Had you come a few days sooner you would have received a poor welcome for it's been a tempestuous time in the Westallen household. We are just returning to normal.'

'I'm sorry to hear it. What has happened, Miss Westallen? And yes, refreshment would be most welcome, thank you.'

'Oh Mr Harper. On Sunday, my daughter went missing. She's only four. We were out most of the night and all the next day looking for her and you *know* the terrible rains that have plagued us. She's back now, safe and sound, thank goodness, but poor Mama got thoroughly soaked and has been unwell ever since . . .'

I pause, noticing that Mr Harper wears an odd expression. He looks as if he has a lozenge stuck in his throat. 'Mr Harper, are you well?'

He coughs. 'Perfectly, thank you, Miss Westallen. I . . . hem . . . I'm sorry to hear about her mother and wish her a swift recovery. But, ah . . . did I hear you right? Did you say your *daughter* went missing?'

'Oh gracious! Have I never mentioned Clover to you before? That's quite extraordinary, Mr Harper, and fortunate for you, since I usually bore people senseless about her. I am the most besotted of mothers, you see!'

'Ah! Then have I been in error? Should I have been calling you *Mrs* Westallen? No, wait, you're the captain's daughter . . .'

I laugh cheerfully and put him out of his misery. 'Miss Westallen is perfectly right, Mr Harper. Clover is adopted. I did not think myself likely to marry, you see, but I wanted to be a mother. I chose Clover from the girls' home in Belsize

Park. Or perhaps it would be truer to say that Clover chose me, but either way, we are a match made in heaven.'

'You didn't think you would marry . . . so you adopted a child,' he repeats.

'That's right. Not that I'm averse to marriage in the future, should the right opportunity arise,' I add encouragingly. *Oh flirtatious Olive!*

'Well, I should think that highly unlikely now, don't you?'

And then I realise that he is shocked. Despite his overt admiration of me, his praise of intellectual women, his interest in esoteric matters . . . he is convention-bound and there are things he cannot tolerate. Well, everyone has their limits. Mr Finch cannot tolerate a woman having a single thought in her head that he has not approved, so Mr Harper is doing quite well, really.

'Indeed, Mr Harper? And why is that?' My tone is bland.

'Well, for goodness' sake! It's a very . . . unusual step you have taken. I doubt any man would be comfortable marrying a single woman with a child. And *such* a child, of uncertain background, I mean.'

I feel, quite literally, hackles rising on my neck and suppress a snarl. He is talking about *my child*!

'Oh, there's no uncertainty about Clover's background. I looked into it. She was born in a slum to a very disadvantaged family indeed. Lemonade?'

'Oh, I cannot stay for drinks, er . . . I came only to enquire as to the progress of the charity.'

'It does very well.'

'Excellent! Then I must be off, a pressing matter. Good day to you and, er, good health to your mother.'

He shoots from the room like a startled dog. I stand, smiling gently, until I hear the front door close behind him. Then I sink into my chair. So be it. I had entertained some hopes of Mr Harper. It had felt . . . *illuminating* to experience that flicker of excitement that can exist between a man and a woman, a flicker that has been all too rare in my life.

I remember Papa, all those months ago, asking me, *What man would want a woman who has encumbered herself thus? It's too unconventional.* Perhaps he is right. But Clover does not feel to me like an encumbrance; I see her as a delightful shield, diverting men of weak convictions and nonsensical thinking away from me so that they may flow in a different direction.

'Farewell, Mr Harper,' I murmur, standing again.

Mabs

Despite her determination to be independent, Mabs's heart sank as the cab travelled into the heart of Saffron Hill. She stopped it some way from Mushroom Court – you couldn't take a cab very close – and sensed the driver's relief when she did. She'd been so desperate to leave Willoughby Walk but was she going from the frying pan into the fire? Mabs put her head down and hurried home.

Peg and Matty were astonished and overjoyed to see her, especially when they learned she was staying for a while. They were full of questions but Mabs made them wait till Pa and Nicky were home. She didn't want to explain everything twice.

Peg was horrified and fascinated by the story of the Finches. Pa's main concern was the loss of her salary. 'Just when we was doing so well,' he moaned. Mabs would have found it annoying at any other time but compared with Mr Finch, he was looking rather wonderful as a father, so she just hugged him and told him everything would be all right.

'Will you go back to the wharf while you're here?' he asked. Mabs almost laughed at his lack of imagination. True enough, the weather was good, and money had been such a preoccupation for so long that there was a compulsion to keep earning at all costs. But Mabs knew that if she went back to the canals, she'd be too exhausted to think about anything and that life would swallow her up. Then it would all have been for nothing. Just as she had resisted the temptation to stay with Olive, so she resisted the pressure of her father's worries.

It was odd being back in Mushroom Court: the cramped quarters; the unsettling odours; the shouts that startled you awake in the middle of the night. Not having a proper bed, suspicious neighbours who wouldn't pass the time of day. Feeling unsafe in her new dress, refusing to wear the old one, and not having a uniform any more, Mabs didn't even know how to dress in this world. She took to wearing the old trousers and shirt of Pa's that she'd worn for labouring. It was harder to keep clean here, but she tried, carrying water from the pump a couple of streets away, glad of the fine weather that made it a tolerable thing to do. It was lovely to be with her family, to talk and help out and laugh with them again. It was also strange, with half of them gone.

From the very first she longed to visit Olive; she missed everyone, and couldn't stop wondering how they were getting on. But she couldn't let Olive fix everything for her. Probably she would turn to her for help at some point. But before she did, Mabs needed to know her own mind.

It was hard to think here, it always had been; this place *compressed* Mabs and stopped ideas from sprouting. So, she went for long walks, often meandering along the canal, part of her hoping to catch sight of Kip Miller. She thought hard about her situation as she trod the towpath every day, sometimes passing through the clamour of a wharf, sometimes walking for long peaceful stretches where the only interruption was the clop and ripple of an occasional passing barge.

It would be easy enough to look for a position as a companion or maid. Mrs Finch would give her a glowing reference and so would Olive; any reference with the Westallen name on it would be sure to get her the job. But was that what she *wanted*? Mabs had never had the luxury of being able to consider that question before. Properly speaking, she didn't have it now, and yet . . . she had some savings, some experience and good friends who valued her . . . It occurred to her that she'd made a decent fist of things these last eight months and would no doubt do it again wherever she went next. It gave her confidence. It made her dream about what might be possible.

One afternoon, she found herself at the wharf where she used to work. Careful not to get in anyone's way, she took a quick historical tour of her time there: the ice wells, the coal carts, the timber stacks. She watched the dredgers wearily dragging buckets through the water to remove the silt that built up so quickly and stopped the heaviest barges travelling. There was something affirming about revisiting the place where she had felt so unhappy, so helpless, and considering how enormously everything had changed. Recognising the distinctive stamp of Rose's lime cordial on a stack of crates, Mabs kept a weather eye out for Nicky. Soon enough she saw him, one foot on the wharf, the other on the side of a barge, loading crates. 'Oh Nicky,' she groaned, covering her eyes.

She was about to shout out and tell him to get onto the barge, when she remembered that here, he wasn't her little brother, he was a worker. Just as she wanted to find her own way, so did he. Mabs forced herself to look again, to see things through an outsider's eyes. It was a fair evening and the wharf looked as attractive as it could, with the water shining in the mellowing sunlight and that atmosphere of early summer that always made spirits lighter. Laughter and banter floated on the air; it was almost the end of the working day. Nicky was laughing too, bending and lifting with such ease that even Mabs was forced to consider that perhaps it suited him here.

When all the crates were loaded, and both Nicky's feet were planted firmly on solid ground, Mabs called out.

'Mabs!' he cried, loping over. 'What a grand surprise! What's up?'

'Just walking and thinking again,' said Mabs. 'Thought I might say hello to Pa and all.'

'Don't bother. I've heard he ain't around again. Sloped off early, no prizes for guessing why.'

'He won't have a job much longer if he keeps this up,' sighed Mabs. 'I'll have to speak to him again.'

'Actually, Mabs, I've sorted it. 'Ad a word with Ducky, his foreman. He's just about had it with Pa, so I said we'd swap. I'll work on the coal, starting tomorrow. I know the pay's less but at least I'm not going to drink the beer, am I? And the money I do get will come home with me. Pa can go on the lime, where he gets paid in full and there's no free beer. Ducky spoke to my foreman. *He* don't care who shifts the cordial, just so long as it's done.'

Mabs stared at her little brother. 'You're so clever,' she said. 'Didn't I always say you were? How did you think of that?'

Nicky shrugged. 'Makes sense.'

'It really does! Yer a good boy, Nicky. And I know you've heard it all before, but you do deserve better than this.'

Instead of rolling his eyes, Nicky looked serious. 'You know what, Mabs, I know that. Home's less crowded now with the others gone, but it still ain't no nicer than what it was. I'm not happy that I'll be breakin' me back hauling that coal and not takin' home a full wage. It's just the lesser of two evils with Pa like he is. I'm all right for now. The weather's good, I like bein' outdoors. But I promise you this, Mabsy, when winter comes, I'll have thought of something else.'

He's grown up, thought Mabs. *Still so young, but all grown-up.* 'All right, love,' she said, feeling a weight lift from her shoulders. 'I'll leave it to you.'

Mabs wandered along the towpath, away from the hustle and bustle. The slanting late sunlight was quite beautiful now. She shaded her eyes to look into the falling light and saw men unloading sacks of coal from carts and hauling them into the yard of the Black Pony. A barge laden with timber toiled up the river, bright roses and castles painted on its sides, the giant brown horse bending its head to the harness.

Mabs realised she was in the very spot where Lou had accosted her about the job in Hampstead last autumn. There was the boundary marker on which Lou had perched. Mabs sat down and wrinkled her nose. Lou had been right: it wasn't comfortable.

The dreams that were taking root in Mabs, she realised, were enormous. She had thought a lot, over the past days, about what had made her Hampstead life so special to her. She wanted to continue her education, she wanted to live in a beautiful place and she wanted to be close to her friends. She wouldn't *mind* being a companion again, or a maid, or anything like that, but not forever. Ultimately, she didn't want to be dependent on someone else for her home, her way of life. And she wanted to do something she could feel proud of, like Olive and the Westallen Foundation. All that was a very long way off, she knew. But it was good to have a vision, wasn't it?

'Nice throne!' said a voice behind her. Mabs turned to see Kip Miller. He tipped his hat and smiled. 'Well, well, Miss Daley, fancy seeing you here.'

Mabs felt herself colour. 'Hello, Mr Miller. How are you?'

'Fine and dandy. Gone up in the world again. I'm a clerk now. You're dressed like a boy again. You're not back labouring, are you?'

'No, never,' said Mabs, standing up and resisting the urge to rub her painful backside. 'There's no stopping you, Kip Miller, I'm impressed! From labourer to clerk in just a few months. I've gone the other way, I'm afraid. The job came to an end so I'm home for a while. But I'll sort something soon.'

'I've no doubt you will,' he said. 'I've no doubt you could do anything at all when you set your mind to it. And what are you doing here? Hoping to see me, I suppose?'

Mabs pulled a face. 'Don't flatter yerself! I'm building some grand schemes, and for some reason this seems to be the place to do it. I've been thinking and walking for days now. How's your writing coming on?'

'It's good! I've found a class for working men, one night a week. I still couldn't tell you the difference between a semi-colon and a comma but my spelling's getting better.'

'I'm glad. I miss learning. My mistress was teaching me to read and write at the old job. I want to carry on.'

'You should. You're too good to end up back here. And I'm too good to stay, even as a clerk. We're going places, Miss Daley, you and I. How about the first place we go is the tea room in Clerkenwell one day? I'll be curious to know how you're getting on and you owe me a favour, seeing as I saved yer life.'

Mabs grinned. 'No thanks needed, *you* said!'

'I did. Yer right. Well then, how about it, not because you owe me, but just because you'd like to?'

Mabs looked at him consideringly. 'Perhaps I might like to an' all,' she said and strolled away.

Mabs

TWO MONTHS LATER . . .

Mabs hurried home, clutching a package wrapped in brown paper. It was a scorching blue and gold day in August, the very weather that Olive had prayed for. Tonight was the Westallen Foundation ball. Mabs's stomach made little skips whenever she thought of it. Her very first ball! The only thing that marred her pleasure was that Lou wouldn't be there. Mabs had asked Olive if she might be invited and, of course, Olive had said yes but the Blythes wouldn't give any of their servants an unplanned evening off. It was desperately unfair.

Hampstead seemed rather stunned by the bright afternoon light. The sun was so high that shopkeepers kept their blinds half closed and the glare from the pavements was blinding. Mabs was perspiring. She'd have to dive into a tub of cold water when she got back, otherwise she'd look a right state tonight.

It was a relief to turn into the shade of Covenant Row and even more so to step into the cool hallway. She hurried to her room, eager to unpack the dress and shake it out before anyone saw it. She hung it from the wardrobe door before peeling off her damp garments and climbing into the bath of cool water that was waiting for her.

She submerged herself, then wiped the water from her face

so she could look out. Her room was on the ground floor and looked into the garden. The gauzy curtains were closed, but there was a gap just wide enough for her to see a listless frond of willow and a cluster of bright yellow roses. She closed her eyes and smiled. Last August she had been working on the canals. Never in her wildest dreams could she have imagined such a life as this.

Mabs had gone to see Olive very soon after that last walk at the canal. Finally Mabs knew what she wanted; she just didn't know how to make any of it happen. Kip's words had buoyed her and helped her keep her sights high: *I've no doubt you could do anything at all when you set your mind to it.*

It had been so wonderful to see Olive again. They sat together on the bench by the lavender beds and, first things first, Mabs demanded to know all the news of Abigail, who was hastily summoned and took Mabs in her arms in a heartfelt and silent thank you.

The same week that Mabs was in Saffron Hill, deliberating over her hopes and dreams, Abigail took refuge at Polaris House. She rested after her ordeal, spent time with Otty and thought hard about what her life had been and what, perhaps, it could be now. That Otty knew the truth about her father changed everything. Abigail could no longer stay married to Lucius Finch.

When she announced her decision to the Westallens, it was universally applauded. The captain immediately called upon his lawyer and his doctor, both fine men of integrity. It was clear that, left to his own devices, Mr Finch would fight his wife on every point. He would refuse the divorce, poison the children against her, delay, obfuscate and do everything possible to keep her tied to him. The only strategy could be to pre-empt it all.

Dr Stickland provided a letter pronouncing Abigail entirely sane and the lawyer, Mr Popplethwaite, produced a paper stating that she had a strong case for divorce and custody on the grounds of cruelty. From the asylum in Dartford, Captain Westallen procured paperwork regarding Mrs Finch's expected admittance, which proved that Mr Finch's tale of his wife running off with a lover was nothing but slander. Armed with these testimonies, the captain and Abigail marched off to Willoughby Walk.

'You can imagine how I longed to be a fly on *that* wall!' Olive remarked. Mabs shivered at the thought of it.

Lucius Finch was beginning to suppose, or hope, that his wife had met an untimely end on the streets of Dartford. Imagine his horror when he saw her walk into their house, accompanied by none other than the man he most revered in the world! He immediately began to tell Captain Westallen about his wife's mental difficulties.

The captain did not let him get very far. Mabs could imagine that he'd been magnificent! 'Mrs Finch's true story is well known to us at Polaris House,' he said. 'She is under my protection and will remain so until appropriate arrangements can be made. That's where you come in, my dear fellow.'

Abigail left them to thrash out the details and went to the kitchen. Just before she entered, she heard Betsy say, 'I'm telling you, Lyds, it's Captain Westallen! That's who she run off with! I *saw* them!'

Unable to suppress a laugh entirely, Abigail went in and sat at the table. All the servants were there, looking confused and embarrassed. She gave them the barest facts, sufficient to stem ridiculous rumours. She thanked them for their excellent service and apologised for having been such a remote mistress. Mrs Derring poured her a cup of weak India tea, just the way she liked it. Half an hour later, she and the captain left Willoughby Walk, everything arranged to the captain's satisfaction, and walked back up the hill.

Lucius Finch had agreed to grant his wife a divorce. In truth, he did not really have much choice. The papers Captain Westallen had procured were damning. If the matter went public, there would be no future for Mr Finch and his survival instinct trumped his need for control. His time at the canal was over; Captain Westallen had seen to that. And he would never work in London again. In fact, there was only one avenue open to him: Captain Westallen had conceded to recommend him for a junior position at a small shipyard in South Africa. Mr Finch's ruddy face grew pale at the mention of such a remote and difficult country and begged for the chance to try Ireland, or Wales. But it was South Africa or disgrace in the courts.

Furthermore, whilst the law demanded no financial provision for divorced wives, the captain convinced Mr Finch that in view of all the 'misunderstandings' between Lucius and Abigail over the years, a single generous settlement would set them both free. Without it, there could be no guarantee of even the South Africa position. It would leave Mr Finch with just means enough to pay for his passage abroad and to live modestly until his first salary was paid. His position and lifestyle would be humble indeed compared with what he was used to but South Africa was a place of opportunity for a man of resilience and character, the captain assured him, somewhat ironically.

The final condition was that of custody. Charlie was by now a married man. By the time the divorce was finalised, Averil would also be married and Elfrida would be one-and-twenty. That only left Otty. Mr Finch could, of course, take her with him to South Africa. But was that fair to the girl? Was that country a suitable place for a child like Otty? She was sure to run wild. And would not the care of a twelve-year-old daughter greatly inhibit Mr Finch, preventing him from doing justice to his new position? A divorced woman was, even now, rarely granted custody of an older child, there was no way around that. But if the father agreed to it as a condition of the divorce, the way would be smooth. He would, of course, be granted visitation rights, should he ever find himself in the country. Mr Finch agreed, with his teeth positively grinding.

'Captain Westallen, you're a miracle worker,' said Abigail as they neared Polaris House. 'I can scarcely credit all that you've achieved for me.'

'A little bribery, a little coercion and a thorough approach,' he laughed. 'They go a long way.'

Averil's wedding was two weeks later. Her father attended, then departed the country the following day. It was the last time that Abigail and Lucius ever appeared in public as a pair and there was no cloud over the wedding day. Charlie and Felicia were there and all the young Finches wished their sister well for her married life, and her father for his new adventure. Averil and Elfrida were disabused of the notion that their mother had left them for a lover, and they were all rather confused by the turn their parents' lives had taken. But their own lives were moving on, and they were content for their mother and father to fade into the background.

Elfrida moved back to Durham; she had been invited to stay with the family of a dear schoolfriend. Abigail and Otty decided to stay in Hampstead, Abigail persuaded at last that it was a pleasant place for a new beginning. Otty was ecstatic to keep her place in the academy.

They rented a house, smaller than the one in Willoughby Walk and further from the heath, but not by much. Of financial necessity, theirs was a much-reduced household. In order to preserve their capital and make provision for Otty's education, they took the further step of taking a lodger. That lodger was Mabs. And for such a modest household of three ladies, they really needed only one maid, and that maid was Peg, though it was a nominal position when they all chipped in with whatever needed to be done. The only other member of the household was a garden boy, to tend the roses. And that was Matty. For Mrs Finch now had a rose garden that was full and lovely and vibrant, everything that the old one was not. Sometimes Mabs thought, fancifully, that Hampstead itself was like a rose garden, and all the wonderful women she had met here – Olive and Julia Morrow, not to mention Abigail and Otty – were the roses, stubbornly blooming no matter what life threw at them. Herself too, come to that.

Nothing gave Mabs greater pleasure than the neat way it had all worked out. Pa and Nicky now lived in a much better appointed room in a far more appealing area. Pa had a lady friend. He was still drinking too much, every now and then, but it was up to Daphne to handle it now. Nicky still swore he would have stopped labouring before winter came. Mabs had no doubt of it.

A knock on her door made her start. She wasn't red and sweaty any more, but she was as wrinkled as a currant. 'I'm in the bath,' she called.

'It's me, Peg! Have you got my dress?'

'Yes! I'll be there in a jiff, love!'

Mabs climbed out, careful not to slosh water over the edges, and wrapped herself in a robe that Abigail had given her for her nineteenth birthday last month. It was pale blue satin with pink trim and Mabs loved it more than any other possession. Then she hurried to Peg's room.

'Here it is, love!'

Already, after just a month in her new life, Peg's face had lost its pinched appearance and her brown hair was starting to shine. Her gap-toothed smile was as bright as ever but it was more often genuine, rather than forced and brave. Since stepping into a life with more loveliness to it, she had been able to indulge her sweet vanity, curling her hair and wearing the silver locket Mabs had given her every single day. She also made sure that her room always had a small vase of fresh roses.

'Thank you, Mabs,' she breathed. 'You're the best sister in the world! It's just lovely.'

It really was, thought Mabs, as Peg held it up against herself. The colour was reminiscent of the lavender beds in Olive's garden. For Mabs, it would always be the most hopeful of colours. It had short sleeves and a scooped neckline and a sash of satin ribbons that fell in streamers from the waist. The hem was embroidered with a border of yellow celandines.

'Try it on, then!' Mabs couldn't stop grinning as her sister stripped to her undergarments and carefully wriggled into her new dress. Of course, she had taken Peg to the dressmaker to have her measurements taken, but she'd said nothing to Peg of the design, or fabric or colour. Even Mabs could never have imagined how wonderful it would look on Peg, feminine and colourful, the perfect outward expression of Peg's true nature.

'I love it,' said Peg, swaying her hips and swishing her skirt before the glass. 'Completely, entirely love it. It's perfect, Mabsy, thank you.'

Mabs smiled and left her to it. No point offering to do Peg's hair, Mabs was terrible at things like that. Peg, before they left, would arrange hair for everyone. Since coming to Hampstead she had discovered magazines, and now she was copying the latest styles with ease. Mabs went back to her own room and dressed in the cream dress that Averil had given her. There had seemed little point spending money on a new dress when Mabs still loved it. She'd treated herself to new shoes, though, low-heeled cream pumps with a little bow on the front.

Shortly, Mabs, Otty and Abigail were lined up before the large mirror in Mrs Finch's room, with Peg pacing backwards and forwards like a school teacher, brandishing a collection of roses like a cane.

'Oh Mabs!' cried Otty. 'You look *beautiful*!'

'You do,' agreed Peg, sighing. 'I'll never be the beauty of the family, but I'll make the best with what I've got.'

'Peg, dear,' reproved Abigail, 'you're a very pretty girl, and you have time yet to grow into your looks. And they're right, Mabel, you do look quite beautiful. Mr Miller will be bowled over.'

Mabs blushed. There had only been one person she wanted to accompany her to the ball, though she'd wondered if a modest man like Kip, still working as a clerk, would own a dinner jacket. It transpired that he did.

'Got to be ready for anything,' he said. 'When good things show up in life, they have to find you ready.' And that summed up a great deal of what she liked about Kip Miller, thought Mabs.

'Now,' said Peg. '*Lady's Vanity* says that fresh flowers are the perfect adornment for summer occasions. I thought we should all wear roses – to show that we're a . . .' She paused. It was hard to define the relationship between the Daley girls and the Finches. Peg was the maid and Mabs was the lodger, but these were merely formalities and didn't nearly describe their life together on Covenant Row.

'A family,' Abigail finished for her. 'What a lovely thought, Peg.'

'Now, because roses are quite *big*,' Peg went on, 'there's a limit to the styles I can do.' She looked quite aggravated, as if they were at fault for not having larger heads. 'And we can't all have the same one. But I've got some ideas, so don't you worry. Now, obviously we got no lilac roses, so I'm wearing yellow to match me embroidery. Otty, yellow for you too, to match your lovely dress. Mabs, cream for you. And Mrs Finch, you was tricky. Green dress . . . well, there's no green roses! So I'm using a green ribbon, and I'll tuck one red rose into it, so you're the same as the rest of us.'

'You've thought of everything, Peg. You're quite extraordinarily clever. You could earn a lot more in some fine household, you know?'

'Now, why on earth would I go and do that?'

Soon they were arriving at the ball, their carriage slowing on the gravelled approach to The Picardy Room, a place that Olive's mother had assured them was *the* venue of north London. They rattled through the gate into a vast parkland bordered by railings and fringed by willows. Otty was leaning out of the window and suddenly gave a huge start. Mabs clutched her involuntarily.

'What's wrong, darling?' asked her mother.

'Oh, nothing,' said Otty. 'I thought I saw a wolf. But it wasn't, of course.'

'A *wolf*,' scoffed Peg. 'In London. Very likely.'

'My stars!' cried Mabs when they stepped out. 'That's not a *room*!' In fact, the Picardy was a huge hall, with wide white steps stretching up to the entrance, which was grand and vaulted. *Bet Lou wouldn't like to donkey-stone those!* thought Mabs. It had a broad terrace on two sides and already guests were scattered there, drinking champagne and enjoying the evening sun.

Peg was round-eyed and silent. Otty was jittering up and down like a little girl. Only Abigail took it in her stride, returning to the Abigail of old, before her marriage, before all of it, sweeping them in with great assurance.

They climbed the steps slowly, holding up their hems. Liveried footmen greeted them, checking their names off a list many pages long. In the vast marble foyer, a maid offered them champagne from a silver tray and Olive came rushing over to greet them.

'Oh, you look *marvellous*,' Mabs cried. It was so rare that Olive wore anything other than brown or dark green, or bothered much with her hair. Tonight she wore a dress of rich indigo; the deep inky-purple taffeta glowed. A magnificent necklace of diamonds glittered upon her collarbones; her hair had been swept and curled by an expert hand and studded with glittering stones like stars. 'Like stars against the night sky!' Mabs added, suddenly realising how appropriate that was. 'Olive, you should wear that every day!'

Olive laughed and laid a hand over her stomach. 'Darling Mabs, I would die! I've never been so uncomfortable in all my life. But you know, I *am* rather pleased with the effect . . . But look at all of *you*! All looking so lovely.'

While they mingled, Olive welcomed more guests; they were pouring in like grain from a sack. Within the half hour Mabs could barely move and fought her way to the terrace to gulp down the air. The light was softening now. It still wasn't dark but the heat was more tolerable.

Mabs leaned against a balustrade, looking out over the grounds. It was nice to have a moment to herself. Every time Olive introduced her as 'Mabel Daley, assistant manager of the Westallen Foundation,' she wanted to look around to see who that important, lucky person might be.

When she'd seen Olive for the first time since departing to Saffron Hill, she told her the fruits of her deliberations. 'I need to earn money again as soon as I can, I know that. But I don't want to jump into any old thing. I want to keep learning, Olive, even it's just reading in my room after work. I want to become properly independent, the way a schoolteacher is, or a shopkeeper, or . . . or a *man*! I want to do something that makes a difference in the world, the way you do. I know it won't happen overnight, but whatever I do next has to let me work towards that.'

'Well, my dear,' Olive had said, 'those are fine and noble aspirations. You're only wrong about one thing. It *can* happen overnight.'

Mabs frowned. 'I don't think so, Olive. It would take ever such a long time to train for the sort of job I'm thinking of.'

'Indeed it would, but you see, I want to offer you a job myself.'

'Olive! You *can't*! Your house doesn't *need* any more staff!'

'It doesn't, but I don't want to employ you in a domestic capacity, I want to employ you at the foundation. Mabs, dear, you look as if I've lost my wits. Listen to me. When I began the Westallen Foundation, Mr Miles told me that I would hate to manage every aspect of running it every day. He said that my genius – well, genius was not his word, it is mine – lay elsewhere. He was right. Yet events must be planned, paperwork kept in order, money counted, so I decided to employ a manager.'

'You *have* lost your wits!' Mabs cut in. 'I can't be your manager, I wouldn't know where to start!'

'Of course not, dear, you'd be quite useless to me at present,' said Olive patiently. 'I've secured a manager, a gentleman by the name of Alexander Gladstone. The miraculous Mr Miles recommended him to me. He knows how to do things, from the most mundane to the most ambitious in scope. I'm vastly impressed. There is one problem, however.'

'What?' asked Mabs.

'He's five-and-sixty and was just about to retire. He had not looked to begin a new challenge at this stage of his life and I had to be *most* persuasive. Finally he relented, but warned me that he would be able to give me only a year, two years at the most. You know how time flies, dear – all too soon I would have to seek a replacement. Then he suggested that I should recruit his successor *now*, so that he can teach them, ensuring all his expertise will not be lost when he goes.

'The foundation cannot pay two full-time managers. Therefore, the position is for only three days each week, at a modest salary. The sort of job a clerk might do, perhaps, but with a view to stepping into Mr Gladstone's shoes in a year or two. The solution is perfect, Mabs, elegant. You would learn the job whilst doing the job, from the person best qualified to teach it. You are insufficiently educated at present but you will have the other days in your week to remedy that. My dear, you cannot say no!'

Mabs had been so dazed that all she could think of to say was, '*Can* a woman be a clerk? Or a manager?' Olive had snorted and refused to grace the question with an answer.

Mabs was now attending classes for adults offered by a local tutor. She was the only woman there. She'd been working alongside Mr Gladstone for a month now and every night she went to bed tired and happy, her head ripening with new knowledge. She had never before been part of something that was evolving every day, where everyone's ideas were welcome. She knew it was an entirely unique chance.

A light touch on her shoulder brought her back to the ball. She turned to face Kip Miller. The late sunlight glowed on his tawny blond head, reminding Mabs of Rumpelstiltskin's straw turning to gold. He looked distinguished in a midnight-blue dinner jacket, a flute of champagne in hand, almost a different Kip entirely, except that his smile was exactly the same.

'You came!' exclaimed Mabs. 'Isn't it something?'

'A once in a lifetime experience, I shouldn't wonder,' said Kip. 'Thank you for inviting me. You look beautiful, Mabs,' he said seriously. Mabs was suddenly very aware of her sparkling dress and the cream roses in her blonde hair; her breath caught as he looked at her.

'Thank you. Shall I introduce you to some people?'

'Lead on!' Kip grinned and they were back to their usual easy cordiality.

Mabs led him inside. Through the crowds, she could see Olive's parents and Peg and Jenny. There was Abigail, talking to people Mabs didn't know. Otty was nowhere to be seen; Mabs wondered where she was. She introduced Kip to her sisters then excused herself to go and check on Olive. Hosting an occasion like this must be exhausting!

She made her way to the foyer, where the guests were still pouring in. She joined her friend. 'Are you all right, Olive? Can I help you with anything?'

Olive smiled at her, eyes sparkling. 'Hello, Mabs. It's going rather well, don't you think?'

'*Rather well!*' exclaimed Mabs, viewing the throng. 'Olive, we'll raise enough money for *all* our ideas. Our difficulty will be deciding where to start! I think your mother must have invited the whole of Hampstead!'

Olive laughed. 'Oh no, dear. She's invited the whole of *London*!'

Otty

I nearly fell out of the carriage when I saw Jill standing by the gate. I explained my surprise with some ridiculous fluster about a wolf (*A wolf! Really, Otty!*) and although the ball is *wonderful*, all I've wanted to do since I got here is escape the milling crowds and see if I can find her. At last I have my chance to slip away and I run across the grassy expanse towards the gate.

It's not as though I haven't seen Jill in all these months. I haven't told Mama about her yet but I will. It's only that after all Mama's been through and with the divorce to deal with, I don't want her to worry about me just yet. But Mabs is living with us again as our lodger and it's quite the most perfect arrangement; she takes me to see Jill sometimes, at the canal. We chat for an hour or so by the water after she finishes work and Kip or Nicky are always around, keeping an eye on us. It's wonderful that our friendship can actually take place in real life again, instead of just in our hearts. We've told each other everything that's happened to us this spring and summer and feel closer than ever. I told Jill about the ball, of course, but I never imagined she'd appear like this.

'Pssst! Otty Finch!'

I whip round. The voice comes from a nearby willow tree

drooping beside a narrow stream that's only a trickle in this August heat. I push through its trailing fronds and find Jill, in her usual clothes, sitting on the grass.

'Jill! What are you doing here? Is anything wrong?'

'No, I'm fine, Otty, just fine. Sorry if I startled you. I don't want to spoil your night. I just wanted . . . to *see*.'

Her voice drops as she admits this and she looks wistful; it makes her appear younger than usual. She's always the wise one of the two of us, the one who knows how things are and seems to be able to accept them. Tonight I've seen the depth of her longing for the first time.

'My mother loved fine fabrics,' she says. 'Our house was full o' them, like a rainbow.'

'Was she a dressmaker?'

'No, m'deah. She was a beauty.'

I digest this. Perhaps where she comes from, her mother was the lady who commissioned the dressmakers. Jill's never talked much about her family. I still don't really know why she's here at all.

The last time I went to see her, we were on our way home when I saw a familiar face on the street. Dark skin, a scraped-up topknot, an evil expression. I couldn't help myself: 'Maggie!' I called.

She stopped and glared. 'Oh, it's you, is it?'

'How are you, Maggie? I haven't seen you for a long time.'

'Let's keep it that way. And it's not Maggie, it's Marguerite. I only go by Maggie because you white people can't accept that someone like me might have a lady's name.'

I had no opinion whatsoever about what name she should or shouldn't have and I told her that I thought Marguerite was a beautiful name, that I would call her that from now on. Then she said something that surprised me.

'And by the way, Jill ain't *her* real name either.' Then she flounced off.

Mabs looked at me with an arched eyebrow. 'Friendly!' she remarked. Such is the effect that Marguerite has on people.

But I've been wondering about Jill ever since. If Jim is what she goes by at work because people mustn't know she's a girl, and Jill is a name she uses because people mustn't think she's too fine, then what's her real name? Who *is* she? One look at the sadness in her eyes tells me tonight is not the night to ask.

'Oh Jill. I hate the world sometimes. I'm so sorry I couldn't invite you.'

'It's not for you to apologise, Otty Finch. You didn't create this world and it's not your party. Do you see any brown faces here? No.'

'I should have told Olive about you. The richest folk in London are here, Jill, but there are servants too. All sorts of people. I'm certain she would have said you could come.'

'And wouldn't I have made a fine sight,' says Jill, ruefully holding up the fabric of her grey dress between a thumb and a forefinger. 'I couldn't have said yes anyway. But Otty, I must ask . . . *why* didn't you tell her about me? Are you embarrassed?'

'No, Jill, I'm proud that you're my friend. I was afraid that she'd say that we *shouldn't* be friends.'

'I expect she would, m'deah.'

'Well, I don't think so. I admire Olive very much. I *love* her. When Papa said . . . unpleasant things about your people . . . well, it *shocked* me, of course, but . . . it didn't really surprise me. He's like a lot of people. Olive isn't. If *she* said there wasn't a place for you here, or that negroes are different in their hearts or minds . . . I couldn't bear it, Jill. I'd never feel the same about her again and I can't bear to feel differently about another person I love.'

'I understand. You want to keep your illusions.'

'I don't think they *are* illusions. I just don't have the courage to test them yet.' It's true. Since I came to Hampstead I have lost my papa. Worse, I've learned that the man I loved never really existed. Olive can do *anything*. I still want to be just like her when I grow up. If she's not that person either, I would feel like a compass without a magnet, and I'm not strong enough for that.

Jill takes my hand. 'It really matters to you, that the people you love should feel the same way you do about me. That the world should be fairer.'

'Oh, so much!'

'Otty, you're just a little girl now. But one day you'll grow up and be smart and important like your Miss Westallen. Maybe then you'll change the world.'

'Do you really think so? I'd like that, Jill, I really would.'

'I do. Otty, there's another reason I came. I have news. I have a new job, in Plymouth. I'm leaving the day after tomorrow. I wanted to tell you. It's in a fine house and the money is good, the lady sounds nice. She knows where I'm from. It will be safer and more refined than my life on the canal. It's a good thing for me.'

'Well then, I'm very happy for you, Jill. She'll be lucky to have you and I'll be glad not to think of you working at the wharf any more. Oh, *Plymouth*! Do you think you'll ever come back?'

Jill frowns. 'One day. Perhaps.'

'Only, I shall *miss* you, Jill! We've only just started being able to meet again, and now I shan't see you again. I know you can't stay because of me. I wouldn't want you to. But you'll be far away.'

'But you know the good thing, Otty? We can write to each

other. Here's my new address.' She slips a piece of paper into my hand and I study it, then tuck it inside my purse. 'We can't see each other very often now. But we can write as often as we want. I call *that* an improvement too.'

I smile, feeling better that I won't be losing her altogether. 'I suppose it is. Thanks, Jill. I'll write tomorrow so you'll get a letter right away.'

'I'd like that. We'll always be friends in our hearts, Otty, remember?'

'I remember.'

'But for now, you should go and enjoy your party so you have something to tell me in your letter. I'll leave London feeling happier for seeing my friend in a pretty dress with yellow roses in her hair.'

I reach up to feel where Peg has pinned the roses. I work one free, holding my breath. If I ruin this hairstyle, Peg will kill me. It comes loose and I give it to Jill, who tucks it behind her ear and grins.

'Peg said we all had to wear roses tonight. Me, her, Mama and Mabs. Because we're all a family. Now you have one too.'

Jill gets to her feet and gives a last glance at the silvery hall, at the ladies in beautiful dresses on the terrace and lawns.

'Thank you, Otty Finch. I wear it proud.' She squeezes my hand and slips away.

Olive

I greet guest after guest, though there are several I'm yet to see. One is Mr Harper. I have not set eyes on him since the day he learned about Clover. I hope he will come because he is a trustee; I want to know that Mr Gladstone and Mabs can continue to call on him. I want him still to care about the foundation, even if he cannot approve of the irregular woman who began it.

Another person I keep searching for – pointlessly, since I have no idea what he looks like – is Jonathan Ingram, Abigail Finch's true love. Yes, I continue to meddle. I looked him up a month ago and wrote, explaining all that had happened. I enclosed a second letter for her parents, asking if Mr Ingram would kindly ensure it reach them.

The final party I am on tenterhooks to see is the Blythe family. It's a strange scenario. I *want* to see them because if they *don't* come, it will be the most almighty snub. I don't care if they insult my family (we are used to it after all) but I do not want them to disregard the foundation. At the same time, I *don't* want to see them because . . . well, they're dreadful!

These are the reasons why I haunt the hallway like Banquo at the feast. I realise I cannot stand here all night and welcome every single person myself, but I do not want to miss the arrival of these few. Once they're all here, I shall join my friends and drink buckets of champagne.

Then I see someone I invited but did not expect to attend: Mrs Zenobia Lake, the lonely widow of Belsize Park. I also invited her sole remaining servant, Bertha, but Mrs Lake has come alone.

'Good heavens, Mrs Lake!' I hurry and take both her hands. 'How very, very good of you to come.'

My old friend, the tumbled queen of Hampstead, regards me morosely. 'Olive, I wouldn't have dusted myself off for anyone else. I have not attended a ball for more than twenty years. We both know that my fortune is gone and I'm as useful to you for raising money as a chiffon umbrella. But if my presence gives the event any prestige at all, then I am willing to suffer.'

She is *still* a queen. Look at her! She wears a rich blue gown decorated with cream bows, in a style some thirty or forty years old. Her hair, which is still plentiful and snowy white, is piled up on her head and though she leans on a cane, her expression is determined. I want to drop a curtsey before her long, hard history and enormous presence.

'I'm more honoured than I can say to have you here.' I look around, grateful that Mabs is still nearby. I introduce them, keeping an eye on the door at all times. Mabs will take Mrs Lake to my parents and make sure she has a chair.

Almost at once, Mr Harper arrives. The look on his face, when he sees me in my indigo and diamonds, is perfect! 'Why, Miss Westallen!' he says as I shake his hand. 'You look . . . My goodness, what a very handsome woman you are.'

'Thank you, Mr Harper,' I say lightly, as though I receive such compliments twenty times a day. In fact, I *have* received rather a lot tonight. 'I'm very glad you came.'

'Oh, I wouldn't miss it. It's the event of the decade, in all probability. And for such a worthy cause.'

'I'm glad you still think so. We're very honoured by your involvement, which I hope will continue.'

There is a look on his face. Not sheepishness – he is too assured for that – but it's an awareness, I think, of what has passed between us.

'I can promise that it will. I believe, very much, in what you're trying to do.' Then his expression intensifies. His admiration is clear to see. 'In fact, Miss Westallen, I regret that I had to depart so hastily on my last visit. Would you permit me to call again and avail myself of the promised lemonade?'

'I understand perfectly, Mr Harper,' I assure him, for I do. The world is as it is and it shapes us. It can only change so quickly. But I hesitate. I like Mr Harper, I always did. And there is something admirable about a man who can reconsider his stance on something, concede that he might be wrong. But could I seriously consider someone who reacted as he did to the fact of Clover?

'And the visit?' he presses.

'Miss Westallen, good evening to you!' A booming voice interrupts us. I jump a little and turn. The Blythes are here at last. The entire clan!

There is Malvern Blythe, my father's old friend-turned-enemy and his brightly coloured wife. Both of them tower with their own self-importance and fix me with cold eyes. There are the sons, all three: Felix, Crispin and Ignatius. They are good-looking young fellows with expressions ranging from mild to amiable. They greet me cordially with handshakes while their parents stand back, erect, as though physical contact with a Westallen might melt them. And here is Rowena Blythe, gazing about her with sparkling eyes, and my heart sinks. I cannot help it. I had thought myself so handsome tonight. But now, my dress feels drab, my diamonds an empty attempt to bestow loveliness. I feel too tall, too deep-voiced, too everything.

She is a rose. She wears a pink gown the colour of spun sugar. Her skin is satin-shiny. Her endless golden hair swirls about her head like sea foam and is decorated with pearls. Her eyes are bright blue, her face as dainty as a cat's. She is femininity personified. We shake hands, and she favours me with a smile.

'It's good to see you again, Miss Westallen,' she says. 'Twice in less than a year! We are doing well, I think.'

'A pleasure, Miss Blythe,' I say, trying to match her smile. 'You are all welcome.'

'We are so impressed by what the foundation sets out to achieve,' she says. 'My father wishes to make a substantial donation.'

I am not too astonished; it would be terrible form if he didn't. 'I should be vastly grateful, sir,' I say, forcing myself to smile at him, though clouds of hostility radiate from him. I have to look away. Who is standing beside me? Of course, it is the mercurial Mr Harper.

He is gazing at Rowena with a look I have seen before. Not as he looked at me, with admiration and interested pleasure. No, Mr Harper is lost. He's a man delirious with sunstroke. He is Icarus. I resist the urge to take his arm and hang on to him, to save him from being drawn into Rowena's gravitational tide.

'Allow me to introduce Mr Lionel Harper,' I say quickly. 'He is a patron of the Westallen Foundation – our very first patron, in fact – and has already done so much for us.' I name all the Blythes and edge away from the little group as they begin to make polite conversation.

My friend Julia Morrow appears, escorted by a very smart, besuited Jeremiah Daley. I feel Maude Blythe's glare of disapproval at the sight of the divorcee. We chat for a moment then I risk a glance over my shoulder. The Blythes are moving off, but Rowena is caught up behind them while Lionel Harper makes earnest conversation with her. Her face looks blank and I honestly cannot imagine what a spoiled society beauty might have in common with a sharply intelligent man of business like Mr Harper. But then, Rowena Blythe would make Helen of Troy wish to hide in a darkened room. I don't think I need to deliberate over whether or not Mr Harper may call on me.

The flood of arrivals has slowed to a trickle. I've seen no sign of Jonathan Ingram but I don't wish to stand here all night and miss my own party. I feel a sudden overwhelming urge to hug my parents.

I pass a happy half hour with Mama and Papa, Mabs and Kip, Abigail and Otty, Mr and Mrs Miles, Julia and Mrs Lake . . . goodness! Everybody! Then I take a turn about the room. I see Rowena Blythe, now talking to another young eligible with a lovestruck expression. I pause. She wears the same blank look that she did with Mr Harper. I assumed that his conversation was flying over her head but perhaps I did her a disservice. The blankness, it strikes me now, might be boredom. I've never before bothered to imagine what it's like to have that many men instantly and ardently smitten with you – it's a problem I am never likely to have – but I imagine it now and I think it must be slightly annoying. One earnest swain after another cornering you . . . Perhaps all Rowena wants is to gossip and laugh with her friends.

On an impulse, I test the waters by stopping to greet them. She introduces me with great enthusiasm as though I am a lifeline. 'How is your charming daughter, Miss Westallen?' she asks. 'Such a sweet child. Is she here tonight?'

The gentleman excuses himself and she wilts with relief. 'Thank you,' she says to me.

'You're welcome,' I say, wondering if all she wants now is to fly to the other pretty birds. If so, neither of us quite knows how to take our leave so I answer her. 'Clover is very well, thank you, Miss Blythe. Yes, she is here, with her little companion. They were last seen looking for fairies on the terrace, I believe.'

'How dear. Might I see her? I doubt she'll remember me, but I adore children.'

Well, you have your choice of potential fathers, I think. The inside of my head can be a churlish place! 'Certainly. Shall we try the terrace first?'

She nods and follows me – strange turn of events! Sure enough the girls are weaving garlands of jasmine, Otty watching over them. All evening they have been minded by someone I love. If not my parents, then Jenny; if not Jenny, then Mabs; if not Mabs, then Otty. For a moment my heart catches at their innocence, at how very protected they are. And I think, for the thousandth time, of Gert, still vanished and living who knows what sort of a life who knows where. She was not meant to be mine, that much is clear, but still, I pray for her. I shall always pray for Gert.

'Miss Blythe, this is Miss Ottilie Finch, a young friend of mine. You remember my daughter, Clover, of course. And this is her companion, Miss Angeline Daley.'

'Why, how adorable!' Rowena exclaims, crouching down to the girls' level. Her magical pink skirts sweep the dust of the terrace – I would have imagined her to care about things like that. Then she looks up at Otty and apologises. 'So rude of me! I'm delighted to meet you, Miss Finch.' Otty gives a beautiful curtsey. Rowena chats to the girls for a minute while I talk to Otty. She asks me a strange question out of nowhere.

'What do you think about coloured people, Olive?' she asks.

For a moment I'm confused and think perhaps she means people wearing rouge, or people who've coloured their hair artificially – there are a fair number of both here this evening. Quickly I realise that she means people from overseas, with dark skin.

'What do I *think* of them?' I puzzle. 'Why, the same as I do of everyone else. Some are ghastly, some are wonderful and the rest are everywhere in between.'

The look on her face seems very much like relief. 'And do you know any?' she asks.

I consider it. For some reason, I can tell, this matters to her. 'I can't say I do. I've *met* two or three, and had brief conversations. But that's not the same as *knowing* someone, is it?' Even as I speak, my head starts turning. It's the way society's arranged, isn't it, that people *like me* – whatever that means – should never cross paths with that group of folk? It's like the separation between rich and poor, the laws regarding men and women, the formality between servants and masters. Strange.

'And do you think they're just like us? On the inside, I mean?'

'Well, *yes*, darling. I know a lot of people don't, but honestly, how could they not be? Why do you ask?'

Otty beams and throws her arms around me. 'I knew it!' she exults into my shoulder. 'I knew it. Oh Olive, you *are* wonderful.'

'Yes, darling, I am,' I tease as she detaches herself. I think I can guess what this is about. She must have witnessed some unkindness or disrespect towards a negro. As if the poor child hasn't had her innocence shattered enough lately. 'Otty, the world is a very strange place. People are often . . . not very nice. You know that better than anyone, I think. But we must strive to be the best we can be, and do whatever we can to make the world a better place when the chance comes to us. We have to accept that it's not a perfect affair, without letting that knowledge pull us under.'

Rowena stands up. The girls have tucked sprigs of jasmine into her hair. 'Thank you, Miss Westallen. They are both wonderful little girls. You are very lucky.'

This is not the Rowena I thought I knew. My prickle towards her vanishes. 'I am. Thank you.' The children have torn off an inordinate amount of jasmine for their 'fairy house' but I glance at Otty, her eyes ten years older than when I first met her, and I cannot find it in me to reprove them. How many other nights will they sit and look for fairies and cover themselves with the scent of flowers without a care in the world? How many other little children would give anything to be in their shoes?

Someone calls Rowena's name. 'It's Verity,' she says, looking reluctant. 'I should go and talk to her. Good evening, Miss Westallen, and good luck.' At this moment, I almost feel I could like her. Silliness.

Otty says she's happy with the children, so I go inside again. The orchestra has struck up a waltz. Dancers swirl around the floor in a kaleidoscopic turn and turnabout of colours. Around the edges, clusters of people talk, laugh and quaff champagne. I notice a tall man, a stranger to me, standing on the threshold between the hall and the ballroom. He has dark sideburns and a face made more than good-looking by a wry expression and a vivid warmth. He has the deep tan of one who has lived abroad. As I observe one characteristic after another, I realise that he is Jonathan Ingram.

I make my way towards him, not letting him out of my sight and bumping into several people as a result. As I beg-your-pardon my way around the room I see his gaze settle with a peculiar intensity. I follow its direction and, of course, he has spotted Abigail, who is talking to Julia. I'm spellbound as he strides towards her, threading his way through the throng with grace. Abigail and Julia start to laugh and Abigail turns and sees him. The laugh dies on her lips, her cheeks colour and her eyes drink him in. The look on her face . . . I will never forget it. He reaches her side and takes her hands.

I make my way towards them but they walk away, not to the terrace, where most of the lovers have congregated, but to the hallway. When they get there, Mr Ingram points. I see an older couple, hovering anxiously, standing with another couple of around Abigail's age.

Abigail spots me and reaches out a hand to me. She looks white and stunned. 'Olive,' she says and her voice is not quite connected to her body. 'This is Jonathan Ingram. And over there . . . my parents. My brother Hedley. And his wife Lavinia.' Her voice breaks and she rushes into her mother's arms.

'Miss Olive Westallen, I presume,' says Mr Ingram in a pleasing, deep voice. 'I owe you enormous thanks.'

'Mr Ingram,' I beam. 'You owe me nothing. But if you feel so moved, you could always make a donation.' He laughs. I like him. We will be seeing a lot more of him; I don't need my divination cards to tell me that.

And somehow, it is almost the end of the night. People have started to leave, though many yet remain. The ball is a glittering success. I made my speech and it was very well received; a great many pledges have been made for the aid of the needy and the distribution of hope. I have danced a hundred dances and caught sight of myself in a dozen mirrors. I am not too tall and my gown is not too dark and my diamonds are not too gaudy. It was not Rowena's beauty that briefly eclipsed me, it was my own envy. But there are many ways to be handsome, just as there are many to be good, or wicked, or humorous. There is room for us all in this big, beautiful world.

Acknowledgements

I wrote much of *The Rose Garden* during lockdown, and I'm immensely grateful to the Power that sends me stories for this one. It provided me with the perfect mental escape from the pandemic, and I hope it will offer readers delight and escapism too. Life changed completely last year, and I could not have got through it without my core people, albeit at a distance: my brilliant parents, and my wonderful partner. Mum and Dad, you are the best. And Phil, what would I have done without you? I love you all so much.

    The Rose Garden is largely a story about female friendship, about the ways in which we surprise and celebrate each other, and support each other too, since no individual can keep all of the bases covered all of the time. This is certainly true in my life so a huge and heartfelt thank you to all my friends, both near and far. You know who you are and how much you mean to me. Special people. Thanks are also due to the women and men of the past who thought outside the box, expanding their hearts and minds to make our society a fairer place for women.

A BIG thank you to my early readers, who battled through an initial, unwieldy draft, loved my characters and story and cheered me on as I wrote and polished . . . Jane Rees, Marjorie Hawthorne, Beverley Rodgers and Gill Paul. There's no way to describe how much your encouragement at those early stages buoys me through. (Also thank you Gill for a Hampstead plotwalk!)

Another particular thank you to my author friends. I do believe that our community is a magical one and it's wonderful to have people with whom to share the joys and trials of the writing life, who understand what I'm doing and wish me well on the journey. Your messages and company mean the world. And thank you to those who've provided lovely quotes for *The Rose Garden* – so appreciated.

Extra-special mention to the Historical Fiction gang with whom I've shared a cocktail via Zoom on many a Friday evening throughout lockdown: Gill Paul, Jenny Ashcroft, Dinah Jefferies, Liz Trenow, Eve Chase, Hazel Gaynor and Heather Webb. There IS a luxurious afternoon tea in our future . . .

I want to say an enormous thank you to the whole team at Pan Macmillan and especially to my divine editor, Caroline Hogg, for her enormous belief in my writing and my story, and for being a truly lovely person. From that first croissant I knew it!! The whole team at Pan Mac has been tremendous including: Gillian Green, Rosie Wilson, Rebecca Needes, Anna Shora, Mairead Loftus, Lucy Hale and Kinza Azira. Also thank you to Neil Lang for the sumptuous cover design, to Lorraine Green for copy-edits and Natalie Young for proofreading. And thank you to stable-mate Lucinda Riley.

Thank you to all the bloggers, reviewers and the book Twitter community who share the love of books that drives us all. What you all do means the world to us authors and interacting with you is a real joy.

Finally, thank you to all my readers. You are what it's all for and you're brilliant.

Bibliography

I dipped into many sources to pull together the world of *The Rose Garden*. Particularly informative and/or inspiring were:

Robert Bard: *Hampstead and Highgate Through Time*, Amberley Publishing, Stroud (2015)

Benson Bobrick: *The Fated Sky: Astrology in History*, Simon and Schuster, New York (2005)

Judith Flanders: *The Victorian City*, Atlantic Books, London (2012)

Malcolm J. Holmes: *Hampstead to Primrose Hill*, The History Press, Stroud (2009)

Lucy Lethbridge: *Servants*, Bloomsbury, London (2013)

Joyce Marlow (Ed): *Suffragettes: The Fight for Votes for Women*, Virago Press, London (2000)

Michael Patterson: *Life in Victorian Britain*, Robinson, London (2008)